MW00353330

SHELKAGARI

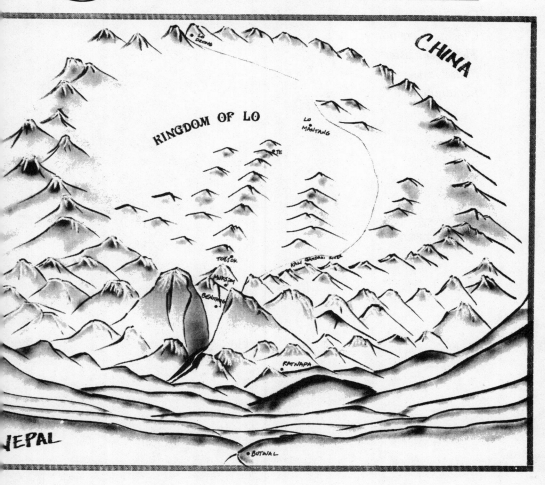

ALSO BY HAROLD KING

SHELKAGARI

Harold King

DONALD I. FINE, INC.
NEW YORK

Library of Congress Cataloging-in-Publication Data

King, Harold, 1945 Feb. 27–
  Shelkagari.

  I. Title.
PS3561.I476S5 1987   813'.54   84–81328
ISBN: 0-917657-09-8 (alk. paper)
Manufactured in the United States of America
10 9 8 7 6 5 4 3 2 1

THIS BOOK IS FOR MA,
A TRULY RARE GEM

Hear ye all, mighty potentates, covet not Shelkagari. For he who embraces the Mountain of Light, shall he inherit the Island of Jewels, yea also suffer the violence of the divine faces. Until heir of the third princely son loosen the hounds of azure, shall only the Divine One possess the Miraculous Gift.

◆ALEXANDER

◆ PROLOGUE

JHELUM RIVER
326 B.C.

ALEXANDER, SON OF PHILIP, King of Macedonia, Pharaoh of Egypt, Lord of Asia, returned drunk to his tent.

The king made his way to his private quarters and changed tunics, tossing the gray wine-splattered robe to his eunuch and slipping a fresh white one over his head. He held the tent mast for support then slumped into the royal chair. Beside him, on a rug of red velvet, lay his armor. It was the breastplate, shield and winged helmet that he'd taken from the temple of Zeus in Athens, rightfully his as the acknowledged son of Zeus. The armor gleamed in the light of the lamps, all polished. Nothing of the grime and blood remained as reminder of this day's work. For several minutes he held himself still, waiting out the nausea that brought perspiration on his forehead. He stared at the jeweled box before him. The gift from his vanquished opponent.

The battle that had ended only hours ago might have been lost. It might have been Poros, the Hindi, sitting here, staring at a Macedonian treasure box. He had finally faced an opponent worthy of his challenge, and it had taken all of his genius to defeat him.

Alexander stared at the jeweled box, remembering.

The Hindi king was no coward. Not like Darius. The king of Persia, at the head of his overwhelming army, had fled from the plains of Gaugamela at the first hint of defeat. But not Poros. Here was a master tactician who equaled even Philip's capacity for strategy. He was also a giant, this Hindi. Easily a full head taller than the tallest Macedonian,

Poros was broad-shouldered, muscular and, mounted on his great bull elephant, he looked like a god.

And he fought like a tiger, even to the end when his mount collapsed from under him and his own wounds all but prevented him from raising his weapon, he fought until his battle-weary legs would no longer support him. It was the elephants that nearly won the day for him, of course— and the rain.

Darkness had prevailed even after dawn as the whole sky had been crowded with black rain clouds. Resounding thunder kept the horses in a nervous state, and lightning illuminated stretches of the battlefield like glimpses of a nightmare. Poros had known that his adversary had never faced elephants in battle. It was his greatest advantage. Arranged at the front of the battle line were two hundred war elephants—enormous beasts that lumbered forward, their bamboo *hawdahs* swaying on their broad backs to the cadence of the war gongs. Mahouts, perched silently behind the beasts' heads, maintained the animals' alignment, prodding with their hooked goads, sometimes bending to whisper into a great flap of ear. Behind the mahouts, in the *hawdahs*, the javelin throwers waited, unblinking against the rain.

Alexander could still see the battle in his mind's eye. The two armies engaged each other like the surf attacks a reef. At the sound of the war horns, the elephants waded into the first wave of Macedonian infantry, trampling soldiers, crushing their armor and bones like fragile crockery, into the mud. The sounds of the enraged beasts were like screams of maddened demons as they trumpeted their death shrill, raising their trunks like clubs and bashing men and shields aside to give the javelin throwers clear targets.

The tide of battle turned only after Alexander commanded the horse archers to aim their arrows at the mahouts. The brain of the beast was the slave on his back. "Kill the mahout, and the elephant will lose its purpose." A thousand missiles arced across the black sky. The mahouts fell.

The slaughter that followed was fought in a quagmire. Without their guides and the target now of Thracian arrows, the elephants milled about, circling in pain and confusion in the sucking mud. The vengeful phalanx fell on them then, using their deadly *sarissas* to poke at their eyes, chopping with axes at the enormous legs and slashing through trunks with Persian scimitars. Butchered and bleeding, the elephants turned in panic, trampling and flailing their own troops to get away.

And over it all the rain poured down. War horns and gongs and crashing thunder rose above cries of the dying as the horde of men and beasts wallowed in the slimy bog of human blood and elephant dung.

Tears welled in Alexander's eyes. Against a superior number, against the trumpeting beasts, against even the swollen Jhelum and all the natural elements with which this strange land could oppose him, he'd won. The final obstacle in his quest for Ocean was removed; he'd defeated the last king who would stand up to him and now all of Indi was his. He was truly *the* king of kings. His victories would for all time be remembered, from Illyria to Kashmir. From the Aegean to the Persian Gulf and across the great belt of desert to the Sea of Aral, Alexander ruled. And now, after Jhelum, Indi.

The king stared at the jeweled box. The Hindi king had yielded. He had called Alexander the Revered One—Chakravartin—Universal Emperor, true ruler of the Four Quarters. And with it he offered his most sacred prize, the Stone of Miracles, symbol of the Chakravartin. Contained in its great jeweled box, the Stone of Miracles was a magic stone. The Hindi who bore it to Alexander's tent testified that it was truly the greatest treasure in all Indi, this stone that light shone through, for it was the body of a Hindi prince turned crystalline by the gods and so hard that no blade on earth could scratch a mark upon its surface.

Alexander stared at the jeweled box. Shelkagari was their name for it. Mountain of clear crystal. It was to be preserved and honored by the Chakravartin. It was his strength. Demons inside demons would be loosened by Ushas, heavenly goddess of dawn, should harm come to it. There would be no end to the rage of the Ancients.

The king rose unsteadily from his chair and made his way to the treasure box. He had dealt with legends before. Did not Alexander— Alexander alone—put to rest the challenge of the Gordian knot? An indestructible gem was only so to other mortals. He was Alexander, the son of Zeus, Lord of Asia. By right of conquest it belonged to the Chakravartin. To the Universal Emperor. To Alexander.

He removed the stone from its place, setting it on the flat lid of the box. It was larger than he remembered it from the light of day, the size of a calf's head, wider than tall. The flickering candlelight did not produce the sparkling fascination he'd seen in it before. It was a rock, only that. A large stone, surely, and translucent, but where was its magic? The heathen Indis were barbarians to believe supernatural power emanated from such an object.

Alexander moved back to his royal chair, holding it for support as he bent to retrieve his sword. If this cold stone belonged to the Chakravartin, then to him it would yield.

The king sliced the air with a measured swing and approached the jeweled treasure box. He raised the sword with one hand and chopped down upon the stone. The weapon clanged as if striking iron. The fingers of Alexander's hand stung. The stone was unscratched. Again, he struck the stone, and again it remained uncleaved. Angry now, the king planted his feet. He gripped the handle with both hands and, raising the sword over his head, called out, "By the god Zeus almighty . . . *yield to me.*" Alexander swung and the blade sang in an arc through the air, done with all the velocity and strength he'd ever put into a death blow.

Sword bit stone.

The force of it severed the steel blade cleanly at the point of impact and the broken shaft flew end over end across the tent. The sudden physical exertion caused Alexander to reel, stepping back to catch his balance. The wine was still with him, blurring his senses momentarily. Lightheaded, he grasped the tent mast for support, dropping the fractured sword. When he had control of himself, he felt the sting in his fingers from the shock of the blow. It was like striking a solid block of iron. He opened his eyes wider to better see the damage he'd done.

Instead of shattering the massive diamond, the blade had cleaved its jutting end, the cut as clean and smooth as glass. Several thumbnail-sized stones glittered among the chips. Alexander picked up the piece he'd hacked from the larger stone. It was heavier than it looked and cold in his hands. When he set it back down again, it immediately came apart —three equal stones, each one the size of a woman's fist.

"By the god Zeus . . . three little sisters . . ." Alexander reached for them, and, touching the first, felt the light flash as much as saw it. The stones, all of them at once, emitted a sudden brilliance—spectacular hues of the rainbow—reds, blues, greens, yellows . . . Dazzling, magnificent brightnesses that lit every corner of the tent; revolving, spinning colors bounced and reflected from every surface, climaxing with a nearly blinding white luminance that died like a flame in the heart of the mother Shelkagari.

It was over in an instant. Alexander blinked back his astonishment. Had he witnessed a miracle, an omen, or were the wine and his exhaustion playing tricks with his mind? A breeze cooled the perspiration on his face as he inspected one of the stones against the candlelight. The only fire he saw was that reflected by the dull flame of the lamp.

From outside came a sound of wind. The top of the tent mast swayed, causing a rippling down to the wall poles. The tent fabric undulated in great rolls against the abrupt gust, then a force of wind loosened a panel from its support. A light stanchion blew over. Another panel tore, ragged edges flapping violently inward as the wind became a gale. Alexander braced himself against the sudden fury, protecting his eyes from the sand and debris swirling around him. A wall pole bent and snapped from the strain, ripping the tent to the crown as the flapping tether caught the mast and wrapped itself around it. Through the tear, the light of dawn touched Shelkagari.

The defiled diamond refracted the sun's rays with furious brilliance. Its intensity blinded Alexander. He dropped the stone he'd been examining, trying to feel his way away from the light. In the confusion for escape he heard the woman's voice.

Om mani padme hum.

"What?" Alexander spun around. "Who's there?"

Om mani padme hum.

The king tripped and fell into the sand. "Who is it?"

Rivet thine heart to the violence and tenderness of the divine faces.

"Who speaks? Show yourself."

On hands and knees, Alexander found his broken sword and blindly cut the swirling sand with violent slashes.

"*Show* yourself."

Oh, heart of man, communion to the invisible, achieve deliverance to the six realms . . . hail the jewel of the lotus.

Om mani padme hum.

Om mani padme hum . . .

As suddenly as the wind had come, it died away. Alexander lay in the sand, panting, his tunic wet with sweat. His sight returned. The air was calm.

A dozen guards answered their king's summons. Dazed and shaken, his tent in tattered flaps around him, Alexander ordered them to find the woman whose voice he heard. But there was no woman. No one had heard a voice. He sent the guards away and stumbled to his bed. He had drunk too much wine. It was the wine that made him irrational. He lay back into the duck down of his pillows. He'd had a dream, an hallucination. He closed his eyes. It would end.

Om mani padme hum.

Alexander felt a tear of sweat roll past his ear. It was an imagining. He did not hear . . .

Rivet thine heart to the violence and tenderness of the divine faces.

He opened his eyes. The scent of incense was in the room. A tiny line of smoke wafted from the smudge pot. Nothing else. He closed his eyes tightly.

It was a vision. A sign? It meant . . . nothing.

Om mani padme . . .

The victor of Jhelum buried his head in the pillows. Enough. By the gods, *enough*. The little brown Hindi had warned him. The Stone of Miracles must never be defiled. There would be no end to the rage of the Ancients. Shelkagari was to be preserved and honored by the Chakravartin. Demons inside demons would be loosened by Ushas should harm come to it.

Rivet thine heart . . .

The Chakravartin and Universal Emperor stifled his tears in duck down. Unafraid of man or beast, the self-proclaimed son of Zeus trembled. Demons he'd let loose from the stone were with him now. They used the voice of a woman, and he could not make it leave him.

Rivet . . . thine . . . heart . . . to the violence . . .

Alexander was filled with the same sort of mad terror he had seen in the eyes of a thousand of his victims. The ruler of all the world—of the Four Corners, of Illyria to Kashmir, of all that surrounded the great belt of desert from the Persian Gulf to the Sea of Aral—now screamed out his fear because he knew. The demons were not just with him. The demons were *in* him, settled in his brain. And they would never leave.

Hail the jewel of the lotus.

♦ ROMANOVNA

◆ ONE

BENARES, INDIA
November 1929

A SINGLE FUNERAL PYRE burned at Pari Jalsain Ghat, before the terraced steps that led down to the holy river. A lame *dom,* an untouchable one, fed crooked limbs of sandalwood into the blaze. Only *doms* were permitted this duty as if the celebration of death was best attended by the one caste without social standing. It was an enigmatic virtue of this land that only an unperson, wholly unacknowledged, presided at this final ritual, preparing the charred remains of life as gritty scrappings to deliver to Mother Ganges in a tiny brass pot. If life were a joke, Mother Ganges had no comment. Silver gray and smooth, she reflected the orange glow of fire like a shimmering mirage, flowing silently eastward over the dark, muddy residuum of a billion souls.

Romanovna crouched beside the wall below the pyre, shielded in shadow from eyes that might find him. His legs ached. All night he'd been here, half-sitting, half-kneeling, ignoring sleep to watch the darkness and listen. High above, dawn's first light touched the *chhatra* of Shiva's temple spire, while across the water the far bank remained shrouded in mist. With the rising sun, the decayed grandeur of The City of Light would soon emerge, illuminating winding, dilapidated streets, faded paint and crumbling plaster walls, and over it, like layered fog, would hang the thin pall of smoke from a hundred other fires carrying the scents of burnt sandalwood and incense. Like yesterday, this day would be indistinguishable from any other. The life wheel crept ahead another notch, and since its last movement, the local faithful believed, another man's soul was tormented by the *churels*—malignant ghostwomen, dead in childbirth, who haunted lonely roads on feet turned backward at the ankles. They invaded men's minds in the hours of darkness. They infected sleep, death's sister, with the promise of hell.

Romanovna tucked the ragged hem of his garment under his haunches against the morning chill, the mist from the river saturating his robe with itchy humidity. It wasn't a *churel* that tormented him. He was beyond that. He was after a man. A man he was going to kill.

The women would be coming soon, the bathers and the old ones with their brass pots for tea. At dawn they always came, a multitude of them, streaming out from their hovels in a continuous tramp of bare, shuffling feet, invading the steps of the ghat like locusts. He'd been right to disguise himself as a Hindu. The walnut juice he had applied to his face and limbs hid his pale skin. Barbaree would not expect that. Somewhere tonight, Barbaree was asleep. Possibly somewhere near. Romanovna hoped he slept contentedly. He felt the slender length of the knife in his belt. Tomorrow —today—he would find Barbaree. He could end his own nightmare by giving it to Barbaree. He wanted to see Barbaree's eyes, that moment of dread recognition, before he plunged the knife into him.

He raised his head to see over the wall. Two Brahmin priests, each under his own bamboo umbrella, sat cross-legged at the river's edge, silently watching the *dom*'s patient work. Still as paintings, the little brown men stared in meditation at the blaze, occasionally interrupting their poses to scratch at a flea or shoo a fly from their bony shoulders.

Benares was the most sacred of the seven sacred cities to Hindus, a city of nearly a million souls squashed together by the attraction of the holy river and the railway. It was a place where two thousand temples rose like grand empty towers above dark and forbidding alleyways, and where untended cattle roamed sun-baked streets for favors and left their dung as reward. Romanovna remembered when he thought it was a beautiful city, a place to start again, to live. But the Hindus came here by the millions, brought by the trainloads and on the backs of camels and other beasts, to die; most believing, at least praying, that this life might end the suffering, that it might be the last incarnation. So in a way it was a city of hope. That it was also filthy and ripe for disease was a blessing their gods had given them, for in despair there was redemption and in the pain of quiet affliction, nirvana. It was a monument, this city was, Romanovna thought, and it existed to suffer death and breed flies. And deliver dreams into nightmares.

His dream began nearly three years before. The nightmare came later.

* * *

"You're French, are you?"

It had been a blazingly hot morning in Bombay when he first set foot on Indian soil. The pilot of the launch from the *Marigold* had suggested that his first purchase in India be a hat, and Romanovna agreed. It was his new straw hat that he held at his side as he stood before a finely polished desk in the harbor master's office. The British customs official, actually a British army officer, was a thin man with an obligatory trim mustache and creased uniform. He studied the gray passport without glancing up. Overhead, an electric fan with large leaf-shaped bamboo blades revolved slowly in the heavy air. It was a counter productive effort, as it simply forced warmer air from the ceiling toward the desk, rippling the odd paper but cooling nothing. It seemed, to Romanovna, indicative of what the British had come to represent in India.

"A French citizen, yes," Romanovna said. "As you can see."

"Yurev Alexander Romanovna?" The British officer looked up. The pips on his shoulder identified him as a major. "Born in Petrograd?"

"It was St. Petersburg then," Romanovna said. The curtness in his voice surprised him a little. He didn't actually hate the British. It wasn't the British who killed his parents. It was Russians who did that, but they used British bullets. "I went to Paris after the war when I was a child. Naturalized French."

"You're not a Bolshevik, are you? We're not keen on Bolshevism in India just now."

"I'm a French citizen."

The major waited. When it was obvious Romanovna had nothing more to say, he sighed, making a show of it. "Right. Another froggie, that's what we need in India." The major glanced at the other officer in the room, who was sitting in a cane chair polishing one of his brown leather boots. The officer shook his head and rolled his eyes. The major copied the passport number into a ledger, scratching it in with a sleek black fountain pen that spit dried ink. "Have you ever been to India before?" He did not look up.

"No."

"Know anyone here?"

"Not at the present."

"I assume that you speak French. Are you fluent in any other language besides English? Urdu, for instance?"

"I also speak German," Romanovna said. "And Russian, of course. I'm presently studying Hindustani."

"What is your business in Bombay?" The major was staring at the passport again, thumbing through the thin pages. He'd already inspected the heavy envelope with the letters of introduction and the bank draft. It lay in front of him on the worn desk blotter, still open.

"My business in India is to investigate the gem market."

"Investigate the what?" The major glanced up with a look of surprise.

"The gem market," Romanovna repeated. "Precious stones. I cut—"

"You mean rubies, emeralds, sapphires . . . that lot?"

"Yes . . . and diamonds, of course."

"Diamonds? In India?" The major nodded. "Oh, right." He looked at his companion. "Hear that, Reg . . . diamonds. And all the time we were thinking the beggars were stone poor."

Romanovna had always known the British to be arrogant, but he'd never understood why. He shifted his hat to his other hand. "Is there some problem with my papers?"

The major produced a stamp from a drawer and imprinted it twice on separate pages, then handed the passport over. "No, no problem." He lifted the envelope as if testing its weight. "It's just that we don't often meet Russian merchant seamen with French passports bearing fifty-thousand-pound bank drafts."

"Is it illegal?"

The major frowned. "Of course not."

"Then . . . is there something else?"

The major made a jerking movement with his head. "No." He pushed the envelope across the desk. "I will give you some advice, though." The major stood up. "Don't trust anyone in India who doesn't speak English. King's English, I'm saying. You've a temporary visa here. Get your business done and leave."

"Is that the official British greeting?" Romanovna said.

"Advice is what it is. Good advice. You don't know what is happening in this bloody place."

Romanovna raised his eyebrows. "And that is?"

"They think they want independence," the major said. "They think they can run this country themselves. It makes them hard to deal with, that kind of thinking. No telling what they may make of you. A man with more money than judgment could find himself asking for trouble. They can't add two columns, but they can pick a dead elephant to the bone before tea, if you know what I mean. A word to the wise is what I'm saying."

Romanovna slipped the envelope into his breast pocket. In all her history, India had been a place where other men ruled. Greeks, Persians, Mongols, Arabs, they all had conquered this land, stolen its treasures, but always India healed herself, adapted and survived. Now it was the turn of the British, the benevolent British, to try and make their mark here. For two hundred years they'd given orders and called it help, and still India survived.

"Thank you," Romanovna said. He put on his straw hat. "I'll try to stay away from elephants."

"A Russian exile, a Frenchman by default and a stonecutter with a vision." Fa Shing touched the linen napkin to his lips. "It is an odd mixture in one so young, I think."

The Chinaman, as he was known, wore a white suit and white shoes and held an umbrella against the sun when he met Romanovna in the courtyard of the hotel. Fa Shing spoke perfect English, and when he bowed, a long elegant gesture, Romanovna was embarrassed. The Chinaman, he guessed, was in his mid-fifties but it was difficult to judge, never having known an Asian; his body was lean and frail, his eyes clear and his mind alert. Romanovna was awed when he learned that the man was nearly eighty. A private car took them to Fa Shing's residence, an estate on Malabar Hill east of the bay, where they ate lunch in the shade of a gazebo on the lawn, British tea and lamb, and talked mostly about Romanovna's sea voyage. Below, the *Marigold* was a small gray hulk surrounded by specks that were Indian fishing boats, like ants around the carcass of a dying beetle.

Fa Shing raised his water glass toward Romanovna before sipping from it. His fingernails were easily an inch long and polished.

"Yes, well I know the existence of an exile. I came to India in the aftermath of the Boxer uprising. With not a penny." The Chinaman smiled, opening his delicate hand in a gesture to indicate his home. "But not everlastingly penniless. India has become my home, and I am respectful of her grace and beauty. It is, I suppose, the secret to my success in business if a secret is what it might be called. My European friends do not understand my devotion, either religiously or ideologically. I am, like India herself, something of an enigma to them, I'm afraid."

Fa Shing's voice had the fragile sound of a breeze through silk. His manner was effeminate but it did not leave an impression of weakness. His strength was in his eyes. They were intelligent and, somehow, omniscient, as if infinite awareness were stored behind them. Enigma was indeed the Chinaman. He was a Roman Catholic in a city of a million

Hindus. He dealt in gemstones in the poorest country on earth. And he was the greatest diamond cutter in the world.

"I want to learn from you," Romanovna said. He sat forward in the cane chair, under Fa Shing's thoughtful gaze. "I came here because I want you to teach me how to cut."

The Chinaman nodded. His eyelids almost closed, covering for a moment his steel-gray eyes and their look of purpose.

"I am honored that you have come so far to flatter an old man. But I have seen your work, what you sent me. It is very good already."

"No." Romanovna tried not to sound impatient. "I only know how to cut a diamond. In Antwerp a hundred men know how to cut stones. But it isn't enough. I've seen your work. It is"—he searched for the right word—"magnificent. Your stones are cleaner, clearer, more perfect than anything I've ever seen."

"I think it is the stone that makes the difference," Fa Shing said gently, "not the cutter."

"I don't believe that. You can find the soul of a diamond. I've *seen* your work. I've seen the best that stonecutters in Europe can do. There isn't any comparison. *You* are the best. I want to learn from *you.*"

Fa Shing's gaze moved to his glass. He stared at it several moments, rolling the stem slowly between his fingers.

"It is gratifying to hear these things, young friend. There is a saying here. Do not permit the goat with one eye to lead your sheep, as it will only go backward." The Chinaman glanced up. "I am like that goat. I have not cut a stone in more than ten years. I explained that to you in my correspondence. I cannot see the fire anymore."

"It isn't what you see with your eyes," Romanovna said. "You feel something in every stone you've cut, something no one else feels. I want to learn what that is. I want to know what is in your head and your heart when you study a stone. I want to know how you think. The rest of it I already know."

Fa Shing smiled. "I see that humility is not an inspiration to you."

"I did not travel six thousand miles uninvited to impress you with my humility, Mr. Shing."

"Ah." The old man agreed with a nod. "Plainly so. And you think this feeling is something one can teach another?"

Romanovna glanced toward the bay. "I don't know, I truly don't." He looked back into the Chinaman's eyes. "I've come here to find out. It is a risk I am willing to take. I will do whatever you ask. I have brought money enough to buy my own stock of roughs. I will pay you for your time. Anything, if you will allow me to work with you."

"And if you do not find what you seek?"

"I'll find it, I have to."

"But if you do not?" He held up a slender finger before Romanovna could respond. "You are not, I think, a patient man. What you seek, if it is possible to know, or worthy of knowing, is a judgment you cannot make. It is only a judgment that I may make, I think. If I agree to this tutoring, you will accept my conditions?"

"Of course, I—"

"Do not answer too quickly. I may, perhaps, know tomorrow. Or perhaps never. This request is a thing I have never been asked to do. If I decide I cannot, then you must accept my decision. It must be the first condition. You can accept this?"

Romanovna could feel his heart beating in his chest. "Yes," he said.

"Then we shall see."

"I know I can—"

"Please. You know too much already, young friend. Be more aware of those things that you do not know. There is a saying that a man who knows too much is a man too smart to learn. It is a vice of pride, knowledge, and the enemy of humility. Let it be our second condition."

"To be humble?"

"To respect patience," Fa Shing said. "India is a great teacher of patience. If you are to learn how we think here, you must first learn our ways. I think the third and final condition should be an understanding of this culture. Two years is not too short a time, I think."

"Two years!"

"For what you seek, is it not worth your time?"

"But I hadn't thought—"

"There will be time." Fa Shing gave a short bow and smiled. "Every stonecutter must temper ambition with patience, young friend. Since I was with my first stone, I dreamed one day that I would have before me the Stone of Miracles, greatest of the great. That dream is not to be, but perhaps, if it is destined, through you . . ." With a shrug, he opened his small hands in a gesture of hope. "Perhaps there is time."

Romanovna didn't understand. "Stone of Miracles? I never heard—"

"I will tell you," the Chinaman said. "It will be part of your education. India is a riddle, bound up in mystic superstitions. You will learn that. You will learn that the great stones of history came from India and that they are all gone from here . . . stolen by conquerors across the span of ages. But one remains, hidden from the thieves. It is Shelkagari. 'Beloved prince of ancient dawn.'"

◆ TWO

A FLOCK OF PIGEONS took sudden flight with a great flap of wings as the *dom* made his way to the river's edge. Only cinders remained of the funeral pyre now. The ghat was a deluge of people, and Romanovna watched as the caretaker of the fired Hindu hobbled patiently through the crowd and down the steps to the river. He carried a brass pot filled with human ashes and scattered them over Mother Ganges with a practiced flick of his wrists. Purified by fire, the soul was set free. There was nothing morbid or noteworthy in the final ritual, just inevitability.

Romanovna took it as his signal to leave. Barbaree was not far away, he was sure of that. He'd find him in the bazaar. He moved among the press of races from Upper India. Near the temple an old woman, bent double, laid out pats of cow dung on the steps to dry in the sun. She glanced up as he passed, his shadow falling over her work, and, after a moment, smiled—one dark eye staring past him but the other fixed on his face. The look she gave him was at once pitiful and knowing, as if she could see into his soul. She knew, Romanovna thought. She knew. He stumbled on, moving as quickly as he could, finally finding the street. He fell behind a caravan of slow-plodding llamas, loaded with sandalwood logs like misshapen limbs for funeral pyres. Tea stalls with their open kettles released the sweet aroma of thick *chai* to mingle with the smell of animals and sweat and smoke in the street. The stench of life was no more or less objectionable to the street beggars than to the merchants. Oxen and ponies and monkeys and humans shouldered indifferently past one another in the narrow alleyways like a stream of purposeful termites. No one paid attention to the haggle between the woman and the street vendor or to the cursing a camel driver gave to his obstinate charge; the rule of the street was to move or get out of the way.

Romanovna knew the rule. He threaded through the street, dodging beggars, slapping the rump of an ass aside, occasionally cuffing a surly caravan dog, moving on, eyes alert for the next obstacle. He prayed the dye on his face and neck would stand up to the sun; beneath the cotton garb his skin was as pale as Moscow in winter.

At the fountain in the center of a square he stopped momentarily to get his bearings. This section of the bazaar was not familiar, and he looked for the landmark of the blue-and-green top of the high gateway.

He saw Barbaree. The Englishman stood barely forty feet away. It was a shock, seeing him again. He was dressed in the same khaki shirt, the same dirty trousers he wore on the footbridge. He was arguing with a Hindu, waving a British note in the air and shouting orders in English. It was as if the months since their first meeting had not happened. Barbaree was unshaved, and his boots were still caked with Himalayan mud, but otherwise he was unchanged.

The sight of him made something snap inside Romanovna. He had played this scene a thousand times in his head—finding Barbaree and killing him. It was to be very simply done. A light hand on the shoulder from behind like an old friend, then, as the Englishman turned with that curious half smile on his lips, Romanovna would use the knife. He wanted to see the look in Barbaree's eyes when he recognized him. He wanted to see the surprise and, when the knife sliced into his belly, the shock. This is for Abby, he was going to say. And this, as he ripped the blade up to the sternum, is for the rest. But now that the moment was finally here, the rage was too powerful to contain. He grabbed his knife like an assassin and crashed through the crowd toward his victim.

The Englishman did not recognize him. He only saw a madman with a knife, felt the blade slash across his arm as he raised his hands in defense against the crazed Hindu. Romanovna drew back to strike again and, too late, saw the boot. The Englishman kicked in desperation and caught Romanovna below the kneecap. He kicked again, and Romanovna went down, rolling beneath the legs of a camel to avoid Barbaree's crashing heel and scrambling back to his feet. The crowd had moved back, clearing an open area in the street. As Romanovna slapped the camel aside he saw the Englishman running. There was blood on his sleeve, and he ran with one hand over the knife wound. He ran without looking back, stumbling into street people, yelling for help. Romanovna ran, too, as best he could, ignoring the fire in his shin from Barbaree's boot. Ahead, Barbaree turned into another street, but lost his balance and fell over a cart of melons.

Yurev had him.

He held the knife at his side, pushing past a beggar, knocking his brown bowl in the dirt. Barbaree couldn't get away. He lay on his side, panting, screaming for help, clutching his bleeding arm. Then he turned on his back in the dusty street, eyes pleading, and Romanovna saw his face plainly. It wasn't Barbaree.

"Please, don't . . ." The Englishman crawled backwards, using his feet and elbows. "Please . . ."

Romanovna could only stare at the man on the ground. It wasn't Barbaree.

When the blow came from behind, he threw his arms out, the knife spinning out of his hand. In front of him was an urchin in a dirty turban and Isabella-colored clothes. The expression on the boy's face registered surprise, not fear, but he was gone before Romanovna could grab him for support. He had the foresight to twist his body so that he would land on his shoulder, not his face. In the moment before pain turned to darkness he remembered the snow, the cold bitter sting of it on his face. It was a lifetime ago.

"Yurev!"

He heard his name called, turned and saw his mother across the snow. She was carrying Tamara, his three-year-old sister, a bundle of flapping blanket whipped by bitter cold wind. A gust caught his face, and he squinted, fighting to catch his breath. They'd been running. He was with his father, trying to keep up, trying to step into the same holes in the crusty snow. It was only another hundred meters to the boat, across a plain of swirling snow to the wooden dock. It was not a large boat but he could make out the figures on it, urgently waving them on. They'd been running for weeks, hiding in barns and cellars, sometimes traveling by motorcar or train, moving from St. Petersburg (he wasn't yet used to calling it Petrograd) to Rybinsk and Moscow and back. His father's magnificent black boots, a present from the empress, had been reduced to grimy footwear, thick with mud and stained in white creases by dried watermarks from the melted snow. Murmansk was only a spot on paper from his history lessons, between the White Sea and Norway, but now it was a place to reach, a place they had to find to survive. And when they'd found it there was more running ahead. They were to reach a deserted fishing village and find a certain boat dock—this dock—where the boat would be waiting and their running would be over. He understood none of it except that the czar was dead—the Czarina Alexandra, too, with the children, all of them shot like geese in a Yekaterinburg cellar—and that his father, a cousin of Nicholas II, was a hunted man. Already, many of his friends had disappeared, and he'd heard the mention of Litovsky Prison in hushed tones from his mother, and there were tears in her eyes.

He heard his name again, a cry this time, and when he stopped to look he saw his mother's face, suddenly surprised. She cried out, the air from her mouth a visible cloud of vapor in the bone-white cold. She fell to her knees with Tamara, and he saw the men in the distance behind her, several of them, silhouetted against the dawn, their coattails whipping as they ran down an embankment. They were mere flecks on the landscape, two of them standing quite still as if they were measuring something. When he realized what they were about, it was already too late. He called out, raising his arms against the wind.

The report of the rifle reached him like a knife in his heart. His mother was crawling, snow over her face and shawl, holding Tamara with one arm as she tried to regain her feet. When she fell again, knocked forward by the impact of the bullet, her shawl blown up by the wind, one end held secure under her body as the other end, its frayed tip fluttering like fingers, flapped across the snow as if motioning for help.

He started for her but his father's voice stopped him. Go, the voice commanded. His father pointed toward the boat. Go now. Quickly. Run. And he ran. Tears froze on his face. The surrounding whiteness echoed more reports—sharp, deadly sounds that cracked across the cold. He ran and did not look back. The boat was already moving, untied from the dock. There were bits of ice in its wake and the smell of oil and exhaust flooded his senses. His boots sounded hard against the wood of the dock as he ran over frozen planks. Men from the boat yelled for him to hurry, to jump. The gap seemed too far. He leaped from the wrong foot, his hat came off, but he snagged an outreached hand. As he dangled below the gunwale, a strong back hauled him up. Only then did he realize that the boat motor was gunning, moving away, leaving his family behind. A dozen strong hands and arms kept him from jumping into the gray sea. As the boat gained speed, he called out for his father but there was no sign. He saw only dark lumps in the snow, far away, and men in great heavy coats running along the shore, waving their fists.

* * *

Yurev Romanovna came to on the dirt floor of one of the merchant stalls. The pain at the back of his head made his eyes water. He tried to get up but slipped against the brick wall and ended up in a sitting position. He crossed his legs and hugged his knees and tried not to vomit. The place smelled of overripe vegetables, rank tobacco and cow urine.

"Sahib?"

Yurev saw the dirty, unclad feet first. The legs attached to them were like tree trunks. The pounding in his skull would not allow him to lift his head. He leaned back. The wall was warm, at least not hot. The nausea settled below his chest. Flies buzzed around him. He hadn't the strength to brush them away. Outside in the street a stray dog relieved itself beside a lame camel.

"Sahib?"

The voice drifted back to him. The word was pronounced *saab*, the Indian way, not sa-heb, which like most other things interpreted by the British in this country was bastardized. The barefoot figure squatted beside him.

"Are you all righty, sahib?"

Yurev forced himself to glance up.

He was a large, dusty man with a huge head and a beard dyed scarlet by lime. He wore a faded red turban, sign of a Mohammedan, and a white robe that had been beaten gray against rocks in the Ganges. His wide brown face was dominated by an Arab nose and fierce black eyes. His neck and shoulders belonged to a bull. He held out a wooden cup with water. It was then that Yurev realized that he was being addressed in English. He hadn't spoken English in weeks.

"Drink please, sahib."

Yurev drank, gulping and sloshing the water over his chin, ignoring the smell.

"So fast is not so good, sahib," the Mohammedan said, tilting the cup away.

Yurev leaned back against the wall. Even from the inside the bricks were warm. Nothing in this country was cool during the day. "*Isha ma—*" He licked his lips as if to force his mouth to work against the dulling pain in his head. Think English, he told himself. "What . . . hap . . ."

"A low caste bashed you with a stick, sahib. On the head. I was not so close to kill him myself when I saw that you were a sahib."

"How did—?" he couldn't finish the thought.

"You do not walk like a Hindi, sahib. When I saw your true skin."

Yurev nodded and felt immediately dizzy. His turban was gone, surely exposing the line on his forehead of walnut juice that he'd dabbed over his face and neck. He closed his eyes until he felt the lip of the cup against his mouth.

"Slowly, sahib . . . please."

Yurev sipped the water. The ache inside his head had lessened and now he felt the sting of the bruise on his scalp. He found the lump behind his ear. His hair was matted and sticky. When he touched the split of the cut it sent a bolt of pain through his brain that made his eyes tear. He brought his hand back and saw the crusted dark red flakes that had stuck to his finger. Even blood baked hard in this heat.

"Nasty, but not large, praise Allah. Your brain, it stings with the ring of twenty bells?"

"Who . . . are—" Yurev winced. Talking did not help the pain.

The Mohammedan bent closer and spoke in a hoarse breath flavored with garlic and jessamine oil. "I am called Mahbub Ali, sahib. A trader of horses. I am also Afghan." This last was delivered proudly, as if it were a distinction worth noting.

An old woman reached over the Mohammedan and took the wooden cup. She barked something in a Muslim dialect that Yurev hadn't mastered, then disappeared out of his view. He noticed that the stall was full of vegetables and flies.

"Ah, an invitement to leave," Mahbub Ali said without surprise. "Sahibs are not so welcomed in these hereabouts. You will permit me, sahib. I have a quarters for living not far from these places." He looked quickly over his shoulder. "Can you manage it?"

"What . . ." Yurev felt a wave from his stomach at the back of his throat. There was a sound that he couldn't quite place. A noise like a shrill whistle. "I can't—"

"The police," Mahbub Ali said with quiet urgency. "They are coming. Can you walk?"

Yurev gave a weak nod, and the Mohammedan immediately stood up, offering his hand. Yurev's knees were like jelly. He could stand only with help. He made himself shuffle into the alleyway, supported by Mahbub Ali's massive shoulder. The sun was intolerably brilliant, its stifling heat in the crowded thoroughfare making him gasp for air. The nausea rose from his stomach. His feet moved only because Mahbub Ali moved, the Afghan cursing and jabbing with a stick everything in their path. Sweat stung Yurev's eyes. The sound of the whistle was closer. "Can't . . . make . . ."

"Hold, sahib."

The darkness started at the edges of his vision. He was moving without knowing why. Around him were only blurred images of fading color. "Can't . . . see . . ."

Through the slowly graying mist of consciousness came the same insistent demand above the clamor of disjointed sounds . . . "*Hold*, sahib." But something else had a grip on him. Something dark and soothing that had no depth, like the yawning blackness of an approaching tunnel, and when it engulfed him, there was relief, and solitude, and no pain.

"Yurev, my sweet, beautiful Yurev."

Celeste's voice was like the call of an angel. Blonde, she had the look of a dancer; taller than most French girls at twenty and slimmer, too, she had small pointed breasts and smooth, almost muscular thighs. Her eyes were so blue as to give the impression that she was Scandinavian but her lips proved she was French. Only French girls had lips as full and soft as hers. He felt her presence now, close by, like the faithful feel their god.

He had met her in 1927 when Bombay was in springtime, eight months after his tutoring with Fa Shing had begun. He'd met her at a market, of all places, counting tomatoes. She was a student then, an artist, and unimpressed with politics. She hadn't known of his daring escape at thirteen from the Octoberists, or that he'd carried a fortune in gemstones sewn into the lining of his coat. Nor did she know he was a diamond cutter, at least not at first. She was simply Celeste, a vision of absolute beauty who somehow found in him, he said, not a hero but something quiet and vulnerable.

Her father was a textile merchant in French Surat, but she lived with her aunt and uncle in Mora, across Bombay Harbor. Every day he'd meet her in a cafe on the Alexandra dock where they'd drink Coca-Cola while she waited for the harbor ferry. He was impressed with her dedication to art (she talked about almost nothing else), and she was awed at his facility with languages (he was speaking Marathi and Rajasthani and reading Hindi after only three months) and hungry to learn about Paris, a place she'd never seen. Though she was French, she spoke mostly English because in British India it was the language of commerce and academia. Still, they often spoke French so she could practice. It took some time for Yurev Romanovna to get over the idea that he was a Russian correcting the pronunciation and grammar of a French girl who had never seen her homeland.

He would tell her stories about Paris and his Uncle Nikolayev. Baron Fyodor Nikolayev was a wonderfully gruff old Russian, without patience or a wife, who was forever angry at the world but protective of his nephew. He had been a minor official in the czar's treasury, an assistant curator of the royal gems. When the revolution came, Nikolayev was already in Paris, ironically working out a deal to buy more gems for the czar. It was Nikolayev who arranged the escape for his brother's family. When only Yurev survived the escape, Nikolayev became his guardian and sponsor in Paris.

Paris had been a grand city to grow up in for a boy of aristocratic heritage. Yurev attended gala balls in the Russian tradition and spent holidays at country homes of wealthy Parisian families who were attracted to the idea of a Russian count in the family. But Nikolayev was always there to chaperone his nephew, and if the holiday turned some business for him, that was all right, too. Nikolayev had always insisted that Yurev's education not neglect the important matter of life, which was, of course, a solid schooling in gemology. By the time Yurev was eighteen, he'd taken particular interest in the uncut diamond trade and made trips to the cutting marketplaces of Antwerp and Amsterdam, taking two years in Antwerp as an apprentice cutter to learn the business. He'd been admitted to the Diamond Trading Bourse and regularly attended sights at the DeBeers headquarters in London. He had a "clean eye" for picking raw diamonds for cutting. But Uncle Nikolayev was against his new interest. Diamond cutting was a pursuit of tradesmen, his uncle had said, not for one of aristocratic lineage. "We *buy* cut stones," Nikolayev had raged at him a hundred times, "we don't dirty ourselves grinding them down."

Celeste loved Yurev's stories, especially those about Uncle Nikolayev. It was a great sadness to her when she learned that he had died six months before Yurev left Paris. For all of his gruffness there was a side that even Yurev had not known . . . Uncle Nikolayev had a mistress, a woman who baked pastries in a shop near his office. They had been seeing each other for nearly twenty years, the Russian baron and the French baker. He died on a cool summer night, in her home, in her bed.

It was shortly afterward that Yurev made up his mind to approach Fa Shing. Yurev's life had been devoted to gemstones, and diamonds were his first love. It had been true all his life. It only changed when he met Celeste.

She introduced him to her friends (including a surprising number of Indians, which was normally against the accepted protocol for Europeans in British India), who regarded him at first as an outsider, then, gradually, because he was handsome and charming and an exile with outrageous, fascinating stories about Russia and because they were the most shameful romantics, he became one of the group.

He knew he was in love with Celeste from the first moment he met her, but then, everyone was in love with Celeste. His most challenging rival was a sculpting instructor named Migel, a moody, vulgar Goan with a Roman profile who was ten years her senior, twice divorced, and, obvious to Yurev, biding his time for the opportunity to be the first man she would open herself to. Yurev had terrible visions of the grimy sculptor's studio flat and the uncovered mattress he slept on (he'd seen it once when the group was there to witness the unveiling of his most recent creation—a bust of Napoleon without ears) and imagined him lying over her, touching her, demanding more. It was silent agony he endured to hear her talk about Migel as if he were Michelangelo reincarnate, dismissing his swings of mood as the temperament of genius.

With a plan to save Celeste (he made himself believe she needed rescuing), he had ten bottles of wine anonymously delivered to the studio, knowing chief among Migel's several weaknesses was his love of vino, and hired a woman more in need of money than passion to satisfy the sculptor's second favorite recreation. When Michelangelo failed to show up that evening at a student watercolor showcase, among which were many of Celeste's works, Yurev convinced his broken-hearted love that the stone artist was exercising one of his temperaments of genius—he was certainly working and simply lost track of time. Yurev dried her tears and, with the rest of the group, tramped off to the studio.

The place was no more a mess than usual, but empty wine bottles littered the floor. They found Migel lying on his back, his legs wide apart and dangling off the narrow bed. The woman was arranged similarly, facing him, though one leg rested on Migel's hairless chest. They were both naked and thoroughly drunk, the sculptor sucking one of her toes.

Thereafter, sculpting and older sculptors were less an attraction for Celeste and, except for a brief flurry of dramatics, Migel was not heard from again.

In the months of their courtship Yurev was not once her lover, though he was her love. Consummating his affection was his greatest ambition, but her shyness and his lack of experience combined against it. He spent every spare moment with her, and when she unexpectedly invited him for a weekend to visit her family in Yanam, an occasion he recognized as special, he bought a car to take her there. It was a yellow two-door Citroën coup, and they learned to drive it together, to the consternation and sometimes terror of pedestrians in the crowded Bombay streets. At her parents' house—actually a farm with the minimum of electrical services— he also met her grandmother and an aging, mongrel shepard dog called Toulouse, who found a new home in the boot of the Citroën. The family gathering went well enough, though he drank too much and announced to her father earlier than he'd planned that his intention was to marry Celeste if she would have him. Celeste accepted him with a smile and a kiss. Her mother cried more openly, and Yurev was treated to a drinking celebration with his father-in-law-to-be, past remembering.

The drive back was marred by a driving rainstorm and a defective fuel hose. In Ulhasnagar he found a mechanic who agreed to look at the car but charged him outrageously because the roof of his garage leaked. Even so, the repair required a part that could not be installed before morning, and Yurev, soaking wet and frustrated, explained to Celeste that they would have to stay overnight. She nodded without comment and rather bashfully asked where they could find rooms.

The Ashram was not a large hotel, but it had been a popular stopping place for tourists in its good years. Since the Noncooperative Movement there had been few tourists, and the long-term effect had devastating impact on upkeep of its twenty-four rooms. Even so, this night the hotel was nearly full; a traveling circus from Karachi was also stopped by the storm.

The single window in Yurev's room held only a dreary view of the rain. He cursed his luck and the weather that the place hadn't any adjoining rooms left (he was fortunate enough, he'd been told, that there were two rooms at all). While changing for dinner, lightning lit his room, then plunged it into darkness. The electrical power was interrupted, obviously, but he heard the details of it from the middle-aged woman (a relation of the mechanic's) who rattled on about her travails in the hotel business when she came to fetch him for dinner, holding a large candle out in front of her as she walked as if it were some great torch. The crashing thunder and lightning flashes did little to make the candlelit dinner the romantic setting it might have been (nor did the antics of a group of acrobats who tossed plates across the room to one another). Celeste jumped at every roll of thunder, hardly touching her food. Yurev was anxious and nervous, unable to read Celeste's quiet mood. Here he was in a strange hotel with his true love, and he didn't know how to press it to his advantage. Afterward, the manager, a corpulent little man with an enormous mustache, escorted them to their rooms carrying a lantern and apologizing every step of the way for the inconvenience, blaming everything except

God for his troubles. If Yurev had had a chance to be alone with Celeste, this little man quashed it. They said awkward good nights in the passageway and, with a supply of candles furnished by the management, went off to their separate rooms.

Yurev debated long precious minutes whether to go to her, helping himself to the complimentary bottle of wine that came with the room. But a gentleman doesn't invite himself to a woman's room, he told himself. It just wasn't done, at least not without some indication from the woman. But he was Russian. Russians didn't need a pretense. . . . Besides, Celeste was his fiancée. He had another glass of wine, trying to imagine how Celeste would receive him, then, his courage shored up by the drink, he decided now was the time to find out. He went to the door, unlatched it and quietly pulled it open to the darkness.

Thunder crashed outside—from the sound of it, directly over the building—and lightning illuminated the passageway, also illuminating Celeste, who stood in front of his door, her hand raised as if to knock.

She was in his arms at the boom of the next thunder, trembling against his chest. "Please, Yurev . . . let me stay. I'm so frightened of the storm."

They waited it out, huddled together on an ancient settee with uneven legs. She wore the patchwork quilt from the bed over her shoulders like a shawl and lay curled against him. It was well after midnight when the last of the thunder died away. Yurev ached from sitting too long in the same position but didn't dare complain. Celeste was asleep, her head in his lap. He managed to slide out from under her and stretch a bit. He opened the window and discovered the storm had left in its wake a beautifully fresh clean scent in the air. The moon was visible among scattered clouds, big and clear, reflected in hues of gold from the pools of rain in the cobblestone street.

"Yurev?"

He turned, startled, to find Celeste standing beside the settee. The quilt had slipped from her shoulders. She wore a sheer pink nightgown with ruffles around the neck. The slight breeze from the window pressed the gossamer garment against her. Her breasts were all but visible, bud-tipped mounds like tiny peaks beneath the gown.

Yurev went to her.

"I want . . . I want to be with you, Yurev," she whispered. "I don't want to wait. Do you think—"

He kissed her, and she moved against him. "I love you very much," he said. He held her face between his hands and kissed her again, then led her into the shadows beyond the footboard.

They were married as Catholics, though Yurev had no belief. The ceremony was small by czarist standards, in the parlor of the farmhouse with her family and friends. It was a crisp autumn afternoon with full sunshine. Leaves of a hundred hues of crimson and copper and lemon hung from the trees, colorful decorations for the event. Fa Shing attended, a strange sight, this old Chinaman wearing his white suit adorned with black rosary beads around his neck. Though they had never met, he was charmed by Celeste, and by the end of the evening Fa Shing, slightly high on homemade wine (Yurev had never seen him drink anything stronger than tea), was calling her Czarina Celeste and explaining that she must aspire to have no less than ten children. It was the proper Catholic attitude, he said, with perhaps a bit of Chinese bias.

Jean Ivanovich was born in summer, under the sign of Leo, and Louise Eleanore, in the late spring of 1928, was a month early. They lived in Bombay, but often traveled to Surat and the farm. Grandmamma always cried when they left, as if each time were the last. Toulouse, after a bad start, came to accept the children and grew more and more protective of them until even the old dog seemed afflicted with severe despondency whenever they prepared for the return to Bombay. If Yurev could have been happier, it wasn't apparent how. The god or gods had been good to him.

Christmas 1928 was spent on the farm. Yurev had left Fa Shing a stone, cut and polished as perfectly as any the master had finished, and gone on a mysterious errand for Father Christmas. The mystery was revealed on Christmas Eve when Celeste and the children arrived to find the house completely wired for electricity. The tree, a white pine specially ordered from Kathmandu, was ablaze with glittering lights. Grandmamma cried all through the present-opening, dabbing her eyes with her apron and switching the light in the kitchen off and on. After the children were finally bedded down, Yurev and Celeste toasted her parents with wine. Her father, his pipe fixed in the corner of his mouth, could only nod his appreciation. In bed, Yurev made love to Celeste, and afterward, when she coughed, lying snuggled against his chest, she said it was nothing, only a cold.

But it was not a cold. The influenza that swept Bombay that winter took twelve hundred lives. Two hundred more people, mostly children, died in the spring due to complications. Thousands were sick with fever and respiratory ailments, and the hospitals were choked with the epidemic's victims from December to March. Louise and Celeste were admitted to Victoria Hospital three days after Christmas. Jean joined them the next day. The doctors were concerned but not worried. People had not yet started dying. Yurev spent every day at Celeste's side. She was getting better, she told him. All this concern was silly.

The baby died first, on January 8. Jean was next, on the tenth, and Celeste three days later. Pneumonia was the actual cause of death, according to the certificate. Celeste never knew about the children. Whenever she asked, Yurev simply kissed her burning cheek and told her they were safe. Before she died, she touched Yurev's hand, next to hers on the bed. It was very late or early in the morning, Yurev was never sure. He'd been in a hardbacked chair all day, just sitting, praying. Her breathing was ragged and noisy but her eyes were clear when she spoke. It was as if she'd never been sick, to hear her voice.

"Yurev, my sweet, beautiful Yurev." The voice of an angel. She closed her eyes then, and left him.

The god he didn't believe in was the god he blamed. For weeks he went nowhere, saw no one. He spent hours in the cemetery, just standing in the cold, staring at the stone markers. *Louise Eleanore. Jean Ivanovich. Celeste.*

Names cut in granite.

His mind passed beyond the loss, into a netherworld of guilt. In the days and nights of his vigil with Celeste, exposed to the fever and the contagious virus, he never once got so much as a chill. He never coughed. He never suffered. The disease that had marked his family would not touch him. A thousand years of Russian blood was his insulation, and his punishment.

The world rumbled in rhythmic bumps and creaks, vibrating like a train building steam. Yurev came awake slowly, aware of the commotion but not sure of it, sensing the tremor of an earthquake. His eyelids seemed glued shut, such was the trouble to open them. He found himself lying on the wide thick mat of a pallet raised several inches above the floor. The room was lit by arched windows high on the opposite wall. Chipped plaster at the crowns revealed agelessly dull reddish bricks, which were also wet. It took a moment to realize that it was raining. An enormous peacock-blue drapery hung below the windows from wall to wall, held on an iron pipe by woven rings. In a corner, carpets in dusty bales were stacked precariously atop one another behind elaborate geometric screens. In the other corner, piled like crockery, were Persian water jugs, dulled copper incense burners with friezes of running devils and tarnished silver belts knotted like rawhide, and all of the pieces jiggling together with the tingling sound of brass beads in motion from the tremor that also shook his bed.

Yurev raised himself on an elbow, not sure where to run. He'd heard stories of quakes in India and remembered seeing the rubbled remains of an ancient shrine in Calcutta, toppled by a quake that had crushed fifty people.

"Ai! Ai! Ai—"

The woman's sudden cry startled the wits out of him. Sitting now, ready to bolt for the door, Yurev jerked his head around toward the frightening sound, and caught his breath.

The rear wall was a mass of faces; Tibetan devil-dance masks, a hundred easily, horned masks, scowling masks, masks of idiotic terror, all hung like bobbed heads from tethered leather thongs, and all agitated, in motion to the frantic vibrations. Below, on a table of heavy timber anchored to the wall and covered with embroidered rugs and thick pillows, reclined a huge, shapeless woman clad in a greenish, almost transparent, silklike garment that was pulled above her blubberish hips and lay in folds above her navel. Obese legs raised and bent outward like ponderous limbs from a sandalwood tree, she cried out, head flung back, beefy fingers clinging to the edges of the table as the bulk of Mahbub Ali, clothed and standing on his toes, thrust himself at her again and again and again.

With every crashing together, the woman's entire body, an unimaginable corpulence of flesh, rolled and shook like waves of almond-colored pudding lapping against themselves. Her breasts hung like quivering one-eyed sandbags over the mass, sadly enduring, while bracelets that had worked down to her wrists tinkled dully against each other in established rhythm. The wooden floor and Yurev's pallet echoed the final shuddering violence of copulation. Veins strained at the back of the Afghan's bull neck as he pushed himself up on his toes, hands pulling the woman's shoulders with such power Yurev felt sure her arms would rip away.

"Aii-aiiiii-*aiiiiiii* . . ."

The after-quiet was brief. Mahbub Ali disengaged with a not quite jarring thud as he let himself down on his heels, and Yurev turned his head away at the sound of the sluggish sucking noise. Yurev's movement produced a creak from the pallet.

"Ah, sahib, you are awake. Good . . . *good.*"

Yurev saw him from the corner of his eye. The huge Afghan wiped himself with the hem of his gown. He walked to a water basin and dabbed his fingers, shaking them dry. When he stood over Yurev there was patient concern in his face.

"It was a worriment to me, sahib. You slept a full day and another without food." He touched Yurev's forehead with the back of his hand. A ruby ring was cool to Yurev's skin. "You were fevered, sahib. But that is gone. I think your head was not so hard as I was thinking. It is better, the pain?"

The woman, Yurev noticed, was gone. He heard her somewhere, her bracelets chattering. He was both angry and embarrassed at what he'd just witnessed.

"Sahib?"

Yurev acknowledged the giant Afghan with a hurried nod. "Yes, fine."

"It is not a troublesome to you?" Mahbub Ali touched his own head in the same general area where Yurev had been hit, his fingers gently tapping a spot on his turban. "In these whereabouts?"

"No, I'm all right. It's only a little sore. It's all right."

Mahbub Ali's eyes grew round with apparent joy. "Only? Ah, praise Allah."

"How long have I been here?"

"It was two days last since I brought you to my apartments, sahib. You slept the sleep of restless demons. All matter of hell exhaled from your lips. It was a great concernment to my mind that the low caste had done extreme injurement to the cradle of your brain."

"I talked?"

"Oh, doubtlessly, yes, sahib." Mahbub Ali seated himself on the woven carpet beside Yurev's pallet. He sat straight down, Hindu style. It was a graceful move, without the awkwardness one might expect in a man of his size. "Cries of anguish and terror. There was one you called for again and forever. A personage of great affectionment to your soul. Someone, I think, who has taken the path to higher enlightenment. You talked with great pain and great anger."

Yurev kept silent.

"These things,"—Mahbub Ali's wide forehead frowned with compassion—"these things from the weave-web of your past, they are a troublesome to you still?"

"What *things* did I say?"

"You spoke of the snow hills. The back of the great beyond. Something most terrible that happened. A search of earnest importance, but"—

Mahbub Ali's large shoulders rose, then sagged—"you spoke in riddles. I could not follow it."

"I was delirious. I—" Yurev shook it off.

"Were you in the land of winds, truly? The high hills?"

"It isn't important." Yurev stared past him at the carpet bales stacked in the corner. He remembered walking, rather shuffling, through the street, half-carried by this enormous man. It was the last thing he remembered, except the heat. "What is this place?"

"Sahib?"

He looked directly into Mahbub Ali's large almond eyes. "Where *am* I?"

"You are in a place of no danger, sahib." The Afghan's face broke into a wide smile. "It is the teachings of the great and wonderful Allah, blessing and peace upon his name, to show compassion to strangers."

"What do you want?"

"Only to serve you, sahib. To make you well again." Mahbub Ali held up his large hand in a gesture of peace. "First, we eat, I think. Then talking comes. Talking is always best after food, yes?" He clapped his hands twice. "The old woman, it is her most happiness to serve us."

Yurev smelled the rice then. From another room it wafted across his senses, saffron-tinted rice and strong-scented cardamoms. Suddenly his mouth watered, and he realized how desperately hungry he was. An image flashed through his mind of mutton stewed with butter and cabbages, onions and garlic, greasy sweetmeats . . .

Mahbub Ali clapped again, louder. He looked at Yurev with almost a frown, then called out in his bull voice. In a moment the woman Yurev had seen before entered with a large tray. Steam trailed after her. She said something that Yurev didn't catch, and the Mohammedan frowned, then gave her an acknowledging nod. It was a brief communication meant to be private, Yurev thought. If it had anything to do with him, it wasn't apparent in the big Afghan's face because he was smiling again, gesturing to Yurev to eat. When the woman was gone, Mahbub Ali said, "The old woman, she is a good wife. I beat her a little—not much—just a little, when she was young." Looking toward the beaded door she had passed through, he added, "Maybe I treat her with too much goodness. Perhaps I should beat her again." He nodded to himself, scratching with one beefy finger at his red beard. When he looked at Yurev, both hands moving now, his gestures became emphatic. "Eat, eat, sahib. You are a sight of patheticness. Your bones stick out as from a sick cat. You must eat, or the friends of Mahbub Ali will think I am not a proper-worthy host. Eat and praise Allah. Today is to rejoicing friendship."

The food was a feast—hot rice piled in a mound over which steaming vegetable curry was poured, hot cardamoms, fried cake and a lump of sour tamarind conserve at the side. Yurev ate it all as if it were his last supper, only half-listening as Mahbub Ali practiced his English. The Mohammedan had eleven sons and four wives and three residences. Benares was a good place for business, rather it had been until Gandhi started stirring up the population with his talk about self-rule. Everybody knew that only the British could rule India. But now there was turmoil; economic and political disturbances with riots and strikes every week. The Hindus were going to ruin India.

The place to be, if one had to be in India, was Lucknow, not Benares, Mahbub Ali was saying. Everyone was going to Lucknow. Only Hindus lived in Benares, and these days that meant they were sick or dying or begging. They were not the clientele Mahbub Ali was keen to cultivate. On the other hand, Lucknow was a cleaner city—Mother Ganges didn't go there—and there were plenty of British sahibs who had money to buy his trinkets.

"It is a sad thing to be a merchant in these times," Mahbub Ali said. The teacup he held was tiny in his hand. He had eaten twice as much as Yurev but it could not divert him from talking. It had gotten dark, and the old woman had come in once with more bowls of food and lighted several lamps. Outside was the heavy sound of the rain. Yurev had taken a blanket from the pallet and draped it over his shoulders while he ate. He felt an eerie sensation sitting here, listening to the rain and watching the shadows flicker across the silent devil masks on the wall. It reminded him of the nights on the high passes, sitting beside a fire in the thin air and not being warm.

"Always there are problems. Not so much when I was trading horses. It was meant that Afghans should be in the hills. Do you know, sahib, that my family for ten generations came down from the markets of the Back of the Beyond? Caravans of a hundred horses." Mahbub Ali shook his large head. "But the times of my father have passed. Horses are not so popular." He motioned over his shoulder at the heap of trinkets. "Now it is the little things."

"You've been into the hills?"

"Yes . . . yes, as a boy, with my father and his nine brothers, in the passes of the north. Very far places. Where the Ancients live."

Yurev almost smiled. There were so many gods in this land that some didn't even have names. The "Ancients" covered a multitude of divinities that only time had not forgotten, hidden away from the disease and misery that infected everything below them. "There are no gods there," Yurev said. "There is only wind . . . and some goats."

Mahbub Ali swallowed the last of his tea, studying Yurev across the empty bowls. "Perhaps you were called *Rashi Gorah.*"

Yurev glanced up. Rashi Gorah was a name the hill people had for foreigners, especially the British, on the few occasions they ever met. Translated from Tibetan it meant, roughly, white man of wisdom. The hill people, many of them nomadic Bhots whose tribes had traveled the high hills since the time of the Great Khan, were well known for their sense of humor. They thought the British with all their regulations and official etiquette to be an interesting race, well-meaning and harmless, but fools all the same. Rashi Gorah was not a term intended as a compliment. The hill people had called him that, too, but not because they thought he was harmless.

"I'm not British," Yurev said irritably. "I'm not like them." He pulled the blanket close around him, searching the room for something else to look at. The air was strong with the rancid scent of the butter lamps.

"Ah, yes, surely not. Still, it is a great puzzlement."

"Don't worry yourself."

"It is a great puzzlement to my mind," Mahbub Ali persisted, "why a sahib would get on the rags of a low-life Hindu and wear the stain of the walnut." He paused a moment, Yurev could hear him scratching, then in a quieter voice: "Was it so important to you, in the dust of the bazaar . . . to kill the Englishman John Barbaree?"

Yurev turned abruptly to the Afghan. *"What?"*

But Mahbub Ali was already standing up. These last startling words had been spoken by a man standing in the beaded doorway beside the old woman. He looked frail and weak beside her, his white suit wet and flattened against his thin body.

Fa Shing. His sad, wrinkled face glistened with rain in the flickering light. He seemed older by decades, though it had only been two months since Yurev had last seen him. "I am happy to find you alive, young friend," the Chinaman said, though there was not joy in his voice. "There is much, I think, you have to tell me."

"Mahbub Ali is a friend, I should tell you that first," Fa Shing said. They were seated on pillows around a small table. It was another room with better light and away from the sound of the rain. Fa Shing had removed his suit coat. The old woman had taken it, and he now wore a shawl over his bony shoulders against the night air. The Afghan sat on Yurev's right. He'd said almost nothing since Fa Shing arrived. They each of them had tea but only Fa Shing seemed interested in it.

"Since the day after you left Bombay," Fa Shing continued, "I've had friends all across India to keep an eye out for you. When you turned up in Lucknow several weeks ago I tried to contact you." A brief shrug. "Unfortunately, you were already gone when I arrived." He was slightly hoarse. Yurev worried that he'd been out in the rain. Fa Shing was too old to be in good health.

"I'm sorry, I—"

"Not to worry. Lucknow is a beautiful city. I have not been uncomfortable there."

"You've been in Lucknow since then?"

"Yes. When they said you were going into the hills, I knew why. I expected you would return there, too." He sipped his tea, set it down gently, his eyes never off Yurev. "I was told that the American woman was quite handsome."

Yurev wasn't ready for this. He had wanted to explain why he had left Bombay so suddenly. He had wanted to tell this wrinkled old man why he couldn't face seeing the same people who had known Celeste and the children. He had wanted to do that, but he couldn't. Bombay had become like a tomb to him. The streets and shops and merchants that he'd known with Celeste had haunted him with the memory of her. A woman's perfume, a particular phrase, a view of the bay from Malabar Hill, they came to him in pieces of time, prying his mind open to what had been. He felt her touch then, heard her voice. When he'd learned about the Abbaye inquiries—that someone was looking for an expert in gemstones who would go into the mountains—he saw it as a chance to get out from under the memories, a chance to escape, a chance to give his life a new purpose. Even now, he didn't know if he could make anyone understand.

"My friend?"

Yurev nodded apologetically, returning to the present. "I'm sorry. Yes, she was a handsome woman." He tried to remember her face, Celeste's face. But all he could see was the American, Abby. "I want to tell you what happened. I don't know where to start."

"There is time."

"How much do you know?"

"Only that three whites left Lucknow six weeks ago, two men and a woman. They were to go to a village beyond the foothills to find an old one who lived among the Bhots. An archeological expedition, according to the consul. There was some trouble in the mountains. A man died. The police are looking for you in connection with it. There is an official investigation concerning the death, though the details are not altogether clear to me. This man who died, he was from the mountains?"

"An Old One," Yurev said. "Barbaree caused his death."

"John Barbaree, the Englishman?"

"Yes. Look, it was more than an archeological expedition. We were searching for a Tibetan monk. What we were after was a necklace . . . a special necklace, with six stones." He had been staring at the edge of the table. He looked up at Fa Shing. "You know the one."

The Chinaman's glance touched Mahbub Ali, then returned to Yurev. "Yes."

"It exists," Yurev said. "Shelkagari exists. I've seen the proof."

"The six Pearls of Light."

Yurev opened his palms. "I held them in my hands. The size of walnuts. Still their original cuts. They hadn't been marked for a thousand years."

Fa Shing touched his hands together, resting them on the table. For several moments there was only silence. When he spoke, he spoke to his hands. "And these stones you found in the central hills, among the Bhots?"

"No. We were further in. Up the Kali Gandaki gorge. Past Annapurna."

The old man glanced up, startled. Even Mahbub Ali seemed to catch his breath.

"The forbidden country?"

"It's where the Old One was, the *bairagi* . . . and the stones."

"And for the sake of these stones you have returned to kill your companion—the man in the bazaar—John Barbaree?"

"Yes. I would have killed him, but not because of the diamonds. If I find him, I *will* kill him."

"But a man is already dead, what—"

"More than one man was killed," Yurev said quickly. He remembered the caravan of goats and the Arab who led them. He remembered the blood on Abby and the broken body of the figure on the rocks below the walls of the lamasery, and Barbaree at the rope bridge, sawing the thick hemp with his knife. He was very good at remembering just now.

Yurev took the tea in front of him on the table and drank half of it down before he faced Fa Shing again. The Chinaman's eyes were patient, waiting. "Let me tell you how it was," Yurev said. "From the beginning, I mean."

Fa Shing nodded. "It is why I am here, to listen."

"We met in the Avadh Hotel," Yurev Romanovna began. It came back to him now, every detail: the tablecloth and the crystal wineglass that flanked the faded photograph and Abby's voice that gave substance to the illusion. He looked into Fa Shing's old eyes. "It was very warm . . ."

◆ THREE

LUCKNOW

Avadh Hotel

THE MASSIVE LATTICE ARCHES were gold with sunlight in the late September afternoon. Their pattern of swastikas, elongated from the slanting light, filled the dining room with hundreds of bent crosses, the ancient Hindu good-luck sign. Like so much in India, the Indian motif had been absorbed or, rather, subjugated into the Islamic arabesque of the hotel's decor.

They sat at a small table in the balcony, beside a polished brass rail that afforded a view of the entire main floor. They'd been drinking an excellent white wine from long-stemmed crystal glasses. Yurev was on his third glass as he listened to the American across the table. Her name was Abagail Abbaye, pronounced Ab-bay, and she was from Chicago. She wanted to go into the Himalayas, and she was looking for a gemstone expert (she kept referring to him as a "stone man") to accompany her party. They'd been here at this table nearly an hour and a quarter, and she'd explained everything about the expedition except why she wanted a gem expert. Yurev had been attentive for the most part, but also fascinated by the Indian boy who straddled a bicycle contraption on the level below, peddling with rhythmic grace and powering an overhead fan through a series of belts and pulleys. The boy appeared unaffected by the heat as he worked the pedals, an effortless motion, but his blank expression indicated that his thoughts were elsewhere, as if mind and body were separate entities unto themselves. It was one of the traits he most admired about the Indian consciousness—the ability to become totally detached from surrounding reality.

"The bureaucracy is as bad in India as it is at home," she was saying. "Worse, if that's possible." She ground out her cigarette in the porcelain dishtray, her sixth by Yurev's count. Abagail Abbaye smoked Lucky Strikes, a brand he'd seldom seen, and as quickly as one was extinguished, an Indian waiter retrieved the dish that contained its smoldering remains to replace it with a clean one. She held a thin gold lighter in her hand, absently rolling it end over end between her fingers. The inscription was a single word, "Abby," with the y ending in a swirl of loops. She wore trousers and a khaki bush jacket with wide deep pockets. She wasn't at all what Yurev had expected, despite what Simpson had said. He'd only said that she was American, as if that was explanation enough.

"First they told me I couldn't go because I didn't have the proper papers to enter the Kingdom of Nepal. When I got the papers they said I could go but only if I had a proper guide. They told me I'd never find a guide because it was considered unmanly somehow for Hindus or Moslems to hire out to a woman, especially a Westerner. Well, I have a guide. Now they're telling me I have to have a certified gemologist along. It isn't enough that I *know* what I'm looking for. I'm required to have 'an experienced expert, approved by the office of the British consul.' " This last was said with her head up and chin out, imitating some British assistant consul with nasal congestion. She shook her head and lit yet another Lucky Strike. "Christ, save me from friggin' *bureaucrats.*"

Yurev nodded. He'd never met an American before. Even so, he didn't believe Abagail Abbaye was the typical American female. No woman who came to India alone to sponsor an expedition into the Himalayas could be a typical anything. She was a tall woman, in her late twenties, he guessed, and she had red hair like he'd never seen before, long and silky. In parts of India red hair was thought to be a sign of evil, in others it was a mark of insanity. In either case, even without makeup, she was extraordinarily beautiful, at least to his Western eyes. She was also impatient. He'd heard that Americans were famous for that, too.

"So, what do you think, Mr. Romanovna?" She rested her chin on the palms of her hands, elbows on the table. Her cigarette trailed blue smoke in the porcelain dish. "Are you interested or not?" Her eyes, he noticed, were green like dark emeralds.

"Yes, well, you haven't told me what you need me for."

"I don't *need* you at all. Yours was one of seventeen names on their officially approved list that they gave me. In all of India they could only find seventeen gem experts. Four hundred million people in this country, and they give me *seventeen* names."

"I'm not surprised. It isn't a vigorous market in India just now—"

"Vigorous?" She tapped the table with her finger. "I'll tell you something, it isn't vigorous enough to be mortally wounded."

"I'm sorry if—"

"Look, all I'm interested in is a warm body. When I checked on you, they said you were a very well-respected diamond cutter. Well, that's fine, Mr. Romanovna, but frankly I don't really give a damn who I get. I'm not looking for an expert. I can't get the travel authorization unless I take an expert along. So . . ." She shrugged. "Anyway, it's good money for a short trip."

"How much did you say was—"

"Five hundred dollars, American," she said, then quickly added, "That's not negotiable. It's a take-it-or-leave-it offer."

"Actually the money isn't important. I'm interested, I'm very interested but—"

"But? What's but?"

"I'd like to know what it's about. What are you looking for?"

She shook her head. "All you have to do is come along. The rest of it is my business. Obviously, it has to do with gemstones, but I don't have to tell you any more than that."

"Historical gemstones, according to the consul's office."

She frowned. "Who told you that?"

"A Mr. Simpson, from the consul's office, said this was, officially, an archeological expedition. He also said it was an expedition without much purpose." Yurev leaned forward slightly. "He called me, wanted to fill me in on what little he knew of the project. He said he wasn't sure it was something I'd care to get involved in—"

"Those *bastards.*"

"The British aren't keen to have to come looking for you if you don't come back. They don't want the responsibility for an American—and a woman at that—crossing into the Himalayas and possibly never returning. The notion of you in Nepal, for whatever reason, is at odds with the image that they hold of an adventurer. As a matter of fact, the honorable Mr. Simpson said—and I'm quoting—'The high hills is no place for a socialite from Chicago.' "

"Simpson is an ass."

"*Are* you a socialite from Chicago?"

"Who the hell does he think he is, the son of a bitch. . . . This isn't even his country, for chrissakes."

"He thinks he's looking out for your better interest, I'm sure. And as a matter of record, India *is* British. They run this country, or hadn't you noticed?"

She took a breath, obviously a prelude to some loud, rude assessment of British diplomacy. Yurev held up his hand to interrupt her. "I'm interested in your expedition, Miss Abbaye . . . I think I know what you're really looking for, and I'm curious about it myself."

"What I'm *really* looking for?"

"Simpson mentioned a photograph."

"So?"

"May I see it?"

Abagail said nothing. She stared at him.

"If you'll let me, Miss Abbaye, I may be in a position to help you. Everyone else you've talked to has turned you down, I understand. I'm willing to go on the condition that you tell me the truth. Simpson thinks you're looking for artifacts related to the history of the Koh-i-noor diamond. That makes it of archeological interest, at least as far as Mr. Simpson is concerned, but I think that there is more to it than that."

"Oh, you do?"

"Yes, I do."

"And what do *you* think I'm after?"

"I think you are looking for Shelkagari."

Abagail Abbaye glanced quickly at the waiter, who stood patiently across the balcony, waiting for her to extinguish another cigarette. He was the nearest person who might have heard Yurev.

"Shelkagari?" She lost her angry tone. "I don't know what you mean."

"Shelkagari is a Sanskrit word that means crystal-clear mountain. It's a diamond, truly the largest diamond that ever existed, if it existed at all. No one knows for sure if it was simply a legend created by the Ancients or if, indeed, there was a stone the size of a calf's head. Supposedly it disappeared in the third century, B.C., when Alexander came to India. The legend goes that the Macedonian king tried to bash it with his sword. He managed to cleave a corner surface. That section broke into three pieces, each of them said to be about the size of a woman's fist. They were called the Three Sisters of Light, and the half-dozen or so chips were made into a necklace that came to be known as the Pearls of Light. There are some who believe that the Koh-i-noor diamond, now among the crown jewels of England, was one of the Three Sisters." Yurev studied Abagail Abbaye's face. "Any of this sound familiar to you?"

She was staring at her wineglass, rolling the stem between her fingers.

When she looked up she didn't smile. "I don't know what you're talking about."

"No?" Yurev rested the palms of his hands on the edge of the table. "Then I've made a mistake, and I apologize. I won't take up any more of your time." He leaned back in his chair. "I want to get the label of this wine before I leave. What we get in Bombay has no elegance." He turned and glanced toward the Indian waiter.

"No, wait . . ."

Yurev looked back at her.

"I'm not a treasure-hunter, Romanovna. I—oh, Christ."

The waiter arrived with another clean dish for her cigarette.

"Will you tell this idiot to leave us alone." She opened another pack of Lucky Strikes and lit another cigarette with the gold lighter. When the Indian was gone, she said, "Okay, so maybe you know about the diamond. So what? What makes you think it has anything to do with this expedition?"

"The photograph," Yurev said. "Simpson told me you showed him a faded photograph of a Bhot wearing an amulet."

"What's a Bhot?"

"A Tibetan Buddhist . . . a wandering monk. They're called *bairagi*. They travel all over the north country. Is the necklace what you're looking for?"

She said nothing. She rolled the lighter in her hand.

"If the necklace is the Pearls of Light, then it would be a monumental find," Yurev said. "And priceless beyond dollars."

"I'm not looking to make a fortune," she said quickly. She reached down to the briefcase beside her chair. "Money isn't exactly what I need." She came up with a folder and removed the jacket. The photograph slid onto the table. "Don't bend the picture, please . . . it's nearly thirty years old."

The faded sepia photograph was slightly off balance, as if the tripod that held the camera were mounted on uneven ground. A portion of the photographer's shadow fell to one side at such an angle as to indicate that he was a tall man wearing a hat. At the bottom an unsteady hand had written in heavy black ink, "Ratnapa," and below that "1901/HCH." The image in the photo was of a middle-aged man in a patchwork robe squinting solemnly against the sun. He held himself erect with both hands clutching an enormous walking stick before the bleak backdrop of a Buddhist stupa. Standing barefoot on an outcrop of rock, his gaze was intent on the lens of the picture-taker. His robe was tied at the waist and from it hung an iron pencase and rosary. The tarnished amulet was visible in the folds of the robe around his neck. Strung together on a leather thong were six stones, slightly smaller than walnuts, that seemed to be black or covered with a dark tarlike substance. At the center of the necklace was a coin with a figurehead in relief. The photo was too grainy to make out details, but even so, there was no question in Yurev's mind about the figurehead. It was Alexander, son of Philip, king of kings.

"Amazing," was all he could say.

"It's the necklace," Abagail said. "No question."

"You're so sure?"

"I have another confirming source."

Yurev frowned. "Confirming? Who?"

"Sorry." She stabbed her cigarette out and gave a fiery warning look at the waiter. "I will tell you about the photo. It's from a collection of Stuart Tooke prints from his expedition just after the turn of the century. I bought it for six dollars. It's the best buy I ever made."

Yurev stared at the man in the photo, then glanced up quickly. "Nineteen-oh-one? But"—he pointed to the sepia figure—"this man is already fifty years old. Probably older."

"Probably."

"How do you know he's alive?"

"I don't. That's the risk I'm taking. Many of the people who live in the Himalayas often survive well into their nineties and older."

"And many more of them don't," Yurev said.

"He's alive, and I'm going to find him." Abagail nodded at the photograph. "He was born in that village . . . Ratnapa. That's where I'll find him . . . and I am going to find him."

"Where is this village, exactly?"

"Exactly?" She shook her head. "I couldn't tell you, exactly. Ratnapa is beyond the lowlands, is all I know. In the foothills of the Dhaulagiri range. That's my best guess. I—oh, there's my guide now." She nodded at a man who'd just entered the main dining room. He waved as he started up the stairway.

"He's an ex-corporal with the British surveying team in the Annapurna-Dhaulagiri region of Nepal—where we're going. He really knows the country." Abagail slid the photo back into its folder. "He doesn't know about the necklace, and I don't want him to know."

"You don't trust him?"

"I don't trust anyone, Mr. Romanovna." She folded her hands together on the table. "You haven't told me if you want to come along."

"Am I hired?"

"You are if you can follow orders and keep your mouth shut. It still pays five hundred dollars."

And the chance to find the Pearls of Light, Yurev thought. "Yes, I'd like to come along."

"Good." She lit another cigarette as her British guide approached the table. He had a distinctly military look about him, Yurev thought—a purposeful stride, straight back. He wore a khaki shirt and trousers and tall black boots. His belt buckle caught Yurev's eye. It was a solid brass British army hook-type buckle, highly polished, with a raised Maltese cross centered on a shield. The scroll was imprinted: "The King's Own." Yurev had heard stories of brawling British soldiers, swinging their belts like chains. The buckle could be a vicious weapon.

"John." Abagail smiled at the Englishman. "We can leave whenever you're ready." She indicated Yurev with a wave of her cigarette. "Mr. Romanovna is coming with us."

Yurev stood up. "Yurev Romanovna." He held out his hand.

"John Barbaree," the man said. His grip was firm, dry. He had a quick easy smile. "Welcome aboard. You'd be the stone man, then."

"Yes, I suppose I am."

"Russian, are we?"

Yurev nodded.

"Well, well." Barbaree smiled. He had very blue eyes. "Quite an international flavor we're taking on here . . . a Yank, a Brit and now a Bolshie. Should be very interesting, our little trek into the hills. A real adventure, eh, missy?" He laughed then. It was a thin, nervous sort of laugh, as if he didn't practice it much. And while he laughed John Barbaree had his eyes on Abagail.

◆ FOUR

"UTRAULA IS HERE . . . BUTWAL is here . . . where we'll hire the pack animals."

Yurev tried to follow the route Barbaree traced with his finger on the survey map but his eyes watered from the acrid pipe smoke. They were in a train compartment with six Indian travelers—a sheepherder and his wife, a soldier, two Sikhs and a barefoot old man who sat cross-legged on the floor chewing *pun* and fingering his rosary beads.

Yurev had not traveled by train in northern India, and it was as foreign to what he was used to in Bombay as if he had suddenly been plucked out of time and sent backward a hundred years. Train travel in southern India was relatively comfortable and uncrowded. The compartments were clean with cushioned seats and polished brass window slides. The ticket-takers were accompanied by porters who sold cigars and took orders for refreshments. They were wide-gauged tracks in Bombay—five and a half feet wide—which meant spacious cars, with compartments that seated six and even eight comfortably, and all of them pulled by powerful steam locomotives.

But this was not Bombay. This was a narrow-tracked, northern frontier train pulled by a wood-burning engine that belched black smoke and smelled heavily of oil. Its windows were open and its seats were wooden benches polished smooth by the rumps of pilgrims and merchants who didn't mind the soot and dirt. The frontier trains often made unscheduled stops so that the engineer (and anyone else quick to find an isolated bush or tree) might relieve himself, as there were no such conveniences aboard.

The sheepherder and the soldier lit their pipes as soon as the train had left the station. The sheepherder's wife, a tiny woman who wore a bright green sari, fell immediately asleep once the train began to move. Her head hung down on her chest with her mouth open, and Yurev, sitting directly opposite, could see her gold-crowned molars.

"At Butwal I'll hire a Tamang I know who speaks the local dialects," Barbaree was saying. He sat between Yurev and Abagail Abbaye with the map across his lap. The smoke seemed to have no effect on him. "He'll take care of the packs and two coolies, serve as cook and interpreter when required. I figure five rupees a day will satisfy him. We'll change money for silver coins and be off by midday tomorrow."

That Barbaree was in charge here was taken for granted by no one more than Barbaree himself. He was dressed in tans—the British summer uniform—without military insignia. His leather boots were old, but polished, and he carried a baton tucked under one arm. At the station he'd used the baton like a cattle prod when they had arrived, poking a path through the mass of Indians, yelling like a sergeant major. The train compartments were completely packed, but Barbaree harangued and managed to make space. His brutish manner was offensive but Yurev said nothing. Abagail Abbaye was, after all, the one who had hired him.

"Show me where Ratnapa is," Abagail said. She was staring at the map, a mass of swirling contour lines and elevation marks, none of which made any sense to Yurev.

"I make it right about here." Barbaree pointed out a space between contour lines northwest of the penciled x that was Butwal.

"You make it?" Abagail glanced at him. "Don't you know?"

"Look, Missy, where we're going there aren't any roads or signposts. Ratnapa is like a thousand other villages in the hills—a wide spot on a dirt path with maybe a mud hut or two. We'll be on trails most of the way, but everyone up there knows how to get to everywhere else. You hired me to get you there, and I will." He smiled. "Not to worry."

"Look, I want to get this Missy business straight right now. My name is not Missy. I'm not a child or some itinerant plantation hand from Georgia. Don't call me that again. Clear?"

Barbaree folded the map. "No offense, Mi . . . eh, *Miss* Abbaye."

"Let's just make it Abagail or Abby. We might as well get started on a first-name basis."

"Abagail?"

She frowned. "Never mind Abagail. Just call me Abby."

Barbaree nodded to himself. "Right, Abby it is. I'm Jack, then. It's what I usually go by. Too many Johns, I say. A bit stuffy, John." He was smiling again. "Yes, I like that, Jack and Abby."

She leaned forward slightly to see Yurev. "How about you, Mr. Romanovna?"

Yurev nodded. "Yes, of course, whatever you prefer." The smoke wasn't as dense as before. Most of it was being drawn out through the windows.

"I meant how would you like to be addressed? Romanovna is a mouthful of syllables for a girl from Chicago. It's Yurey, isn't it, your first name?"

"Yurev."

"That's very formal sounding—Yurev. Do you mind Yurey?"

Yurev hadn't been called that since he was a boy in Russia. His mother called him Yurey. It seemed a very long time ago.

"Do you mind it?" Abby said again.

"No. Yurey is fine. It is . . . o-kay."

Abby smiled. She held out her hand to him. "Good." She pumped his hand once, firmly. "Good. Welcome aboard, Yurey."

From across the narrow aisle the sheepherder nodded and smiled with them. He took the pipe out of his mouth. "Yurey," he said cheerfully. He leaned across the space, his hand outstretched, mimicking Abby. "Yurey." Yurev shook his hand, and the sheepherder seemed delighted. He turned to one of the Sikhs, held out his hand. "Yurey," he said again. The Sikh responded in kind. "Yurey." When Abby laughed, it encouraged all the Indians to smiles and shaking each other's hands. "Yurey . . . Yurey . . . Yurey . . ."

From his place on the floor the old man set his beads aside. No one had offered a hand to him but he was unfazed. "Yurey," he said happily. He clasped his hands together and shook them vigorously. "Yurey, Yurey, Yurey." When he smiled a toothless smile, *pun* juice rolled down his chin.

One could not call the stopping place at Butwal a train station. There was a long, narrow platform for unloading, nothing else. Goats grazed in the thick nearby grass, and several had to be shooed off the tracks before the train finally ground to a stop. A dozen ox carts filled with goods stood beside the platform, their drivers happily waving at the engineer. The long train ride had started off from a dry dusty place, but the further north and west they traveled, the lusher the scenery, the more humid the air. It was not what Yurev had expected. Nepal was the home of the great Himalayas, the vast mountain range of ice peaks capped with snow, of barren rocky landscapes. But these last hours they had traveled into jungle terrain, heavily vegetated with mango groves and enormous leafy plants, and more often the train passed over narrow bridges above crystal-clear streams. The trip might have been pleasant except for the stifling heat and the train's slow pace, which allowed biting flies as large as a finger joint to invade the compartment. It wasn't what he'd expected at all.

"Here we are, then," Barbaree said, swinging open the compartment door. He stepped down and turned to offer his hand to Abby. "Welcome to the roof of the world."

Butwal was not, apparently, a place people longed to visit, Yurev noticed as he climbed down from the train. No other passengers disembarked. There was only himself, Barbaree and Abby. The rest of the passengers had gotten off before the train reached the Nepalese border. Many departed at Gonda, but the greatest number left at Utraula. And, it seemed to Yurev, people didn't swarm to this place for good reason. There was only jungle here and a million attacking flies. And goats.

"This is Butwal?" Abby said. She held the newspaper she had used as defense against the flies to the short brim of her safari hat to shade the sun from her eyes. The underarm of her khaki shirt was dark with perspiration. "This?"

"The village is there." Barbaree pointed over the trees, north to a line of hills on the horizon. "We'll hire a cart to carry our supplies the rest of the way. It's not far. About eight miles."

Abby stared in the direction he had pointed. Yurev shaded his eyes and looked, too. The hills made a narrow valley, and from it came at least three streams. He saw a faint layer of smoke but no buildings.

"What do they call those mountains?" Abby said, still searching for some sign of civilization.

"Mountains?" Barbaree gave a short laugh. "Those aren't mountains, luv. We're in the Tarai, the lowlands. That's the Churai Range, the foothills of Nepal. They're nothing . . . twenty-five hundred feet or so. We'll be climbing twice that before we get to where we're going." He nodded to Yurev. "C'mon, old man, we have supplies to unload. I want to have a look at the pack animal livestock before it gets dark." Barbaree started off toward the boxcar that contained their gear. He was whistling.

Yurev stood beside Abby at the edge of the platform. They both stared for a long while at the hills. Past the hills the horizon faded into a haze, hiding whatever lay beyond. "They don't look like nothing to me," Abby said finally.

Yurev glanced back at the train. A pair of stokers shoveled coal into the mouth of the engine's furnace. Ahead, the track looped back on itself in a wide oval, proof that Butwal was the end-of-the-line turnaround. He thought briefly about the sheepherder and his wife who had left the train at Utraula. Only a few hours ago he had been standing in the shade of the station there, drinking cool tea while the train took on water. There was a hotel in Utraula, and the flies were not a carnivorous breed.

"I say, old boy." Barbaree was standing in the open door of the boxcar, tapping the baton in his free hand, smiling. "Whenever you're ready."

"Yes," Yurev said. "Ready . . ." He hoped he didn't sound as uncertain as he felt.

Butwal was almost too small to deserve a name. The village, following the contours of the river that snaked through the pass, consisted of less than a dozen one-room stone houses crowded between the river and the steep slope of a rocky hill. The houses had flat roofs, where several villagers were at work twisting grasses into twine. Rickety stick fences separated the houses into courtyards which were used as gardens or barnyards. There were goats and children everywhere.

The children were first to greet them, running down the ox path and jabbering like magpies. They were round-faced, sturdy little ragamuffins wearing drab, coarsely stitched homemade clothing. All wore beads around their necks, and their coal-black hair was made into braids. Those that weren't barefoot wore low-cut felt and leather boots.

Barbaree strode ahead of the ox, his baton tucked snugly under his arm. Yurev and Abby walked a few paces behind. Yurev had learned his first lesson in this hill country after only a few minutes of walking behind the cart: one walked ahead of or beside beasts of burden unless one didn't mind filthying his boots.

"Why are they doing that?" Abby's cheeks were flushed. Tiny beads of perspiration dotted her forehead beneath the brim of the safari hat. They hadn't spoken for nearly an hour. It had been a long walk in the sun, all uphill. She pointed to one of the children who trotted alongside them. Yurev couldn't tell if it was a boy or a girl; they all dressed the same. The child smiled and made a face, sticking out its tongue. Yurev had noticed, too. All the children were doing it.

"It isn't what you might expect," Barbaree said. "Up here it's a sign of greeting, extending the tongue, like saying hello." He glanced over his shoulder at Yurev. "Roll up your sleeve, old sport. They're Mongols up here . . . fascinated by arm hair."

The path wound through the village, and people stood on the rooftops to wave and greet them with their tongues. Barbaree stopped at a three-level shanty that seemed to lean against the rocky cliff, supported by hand-hewn timber beams piled almost haphazardly one atop another. He called out, and a short, stout fellow appeared at the opening on the top story. The man let out a whoop when he saw Barbaree, skittered down two ladders to the ground, yelling the whole way, and shook Barbaree's hand like a brother he hadn't seen for half his life.

"Ah, Jack-bishy, Jack-bishy. Good to see you, boss. Very good-dom to see you again . . ."

"This is Kancha," Barbaree said, disentangling himself from the energetic Nepalese man. "He served as cook and interpreter for the regiment."

"Kancha pretty good-dom cook, you bet you life."

"We're going north. Ratnapa. Four, five days I figure. We'll need ponies, coolies, rations. You can do?"

"Ah," Kancha nodded his head vigorously. "Ratnapa, four day, maybe. Two mules. No coolies. I cook." He smiled, exposing large, crooked teeth. "You pretty good-dom boss, Jack-bishy. Me pretty good-dom cook, you bet your life."

"I want two coolies," Barbaree said firmly. "We won't be packing." He nodded back at Yurev and Abby. "Three sahibs, you and two coolies. You can do?"

"Ah, you bet you life, boss." Kancha glanced at Yurev, then looked at Abby. He'd been hopping from one bare foot to the other, a hill welcoming dance, Yurev assumed, but when he noticed Abby his gyrations stopped. His eyes got round. When he spoke he spoke to Barbaree, but his eyes were on Abby.

"Jack-bishy. This is a . . . female memsahib person?" A stunned expression came over his face. "From below the hills?"

"From across the far sea," Barbaree said. Yurev was standing beside Abby, in front of the ox, feeling suddenly uncomfortable. He noticed that the villagers had followed them through the village. Now they were all around them, not terribly close, but surrounding the cart. And they were all staring at Abby.

"Would you mind removing your hat?" Barbaree said to her.

"What?"

"It's all right, luv. They've never seen a white woman before."

"Look, I didn't come up here to be displayed—"

"Please," Barbaree said. "This sort of thing is going to happen from now on. You'd better get used to it."

She looked at him defiantly for a moment until she noticed the crowd that had gathered. "My God . . ."

"It's all right. You're wearing trousers and a hat, a man's outfit. They're curious is all. Just turn around and smile at them and take off your hat. Let them see that you're not a threatening presence."

Abby looked at Yurev. He shrugged self-consciously. "I expect he's right," is all he could think to say.

She turned quickly on the heels of her boots—so quickly that the nearest villagers jumped back—and stared into the mass of brown faces. She smiled, then unbuckled the leather strap of the safari hat. "I feel like a goddamned vaudeville act," she said from between clenched teeth. She pulled the hat off in one swift motion, and red hair, glistening in the afternoon sun, tumbled around her shoulders.

"Ahs" rose from the crowd. They turned to one another, pointing, nodding their heads. The women clucked and extended their tongues. Even Kancha was impressed. "Ah," he said, nodding and smiling.

Abby looked at Yurev. "What's—"

"Your hair," Yurev said, remembering. "Red hair is a very good omen or a very bad one, depending on where you are."

Barbaree patted her shoulder. "Keep smiling, luv." He went to the cart and opened one of the rucksacks.

"How did you know red hair was a good sign to these people?" Yurev said quietly.

Barbaree shrugged. "I didn't, but I figured we might as well find out." He withdrew a carton of Lucky Strikes and handed it to Abby. "Now show them your generosity." He tore open the lid. "Toss these to them."

"*My* cigarettes?"

"Call it a sign of good faith, luv. If we show them that the first white woman to travel in these parts is generous and kind, we're less likely to have problems hiring porters. Cigarettes are worth their weight in gold in the hills. If you—"

"I get the picture," Abby said shortly. She flung a pack high in the air over the crowd that landed in the midst of them. The reaction was loud and immediate. Suddenly dozens of hands were outstretched in the air, reaching for the packages as Abby emptied the carton.

"Okay," Abby said, turning to Barbaree, "anything else? Card tricks? Cabaret? I'm not much for singing."

Barbaree's glance lacked sympathy. "You won't miss the cigarettes," he said. "Anyway, you won't feel much like smoking in a few days."

* * *

"They do not want to go so much, the coolies, Jack-bishy," Kancha said, staring self-consciously into his cup of barley beer. He held his head down so that the dim light of the butter lamps cast his face in shadows. "It is because of the fire, like I told you."

They were in Kancha's house, sitting in the main room on mattresses stuffed with hay. Yurev, Abby and Barbaree sat together across a low table from Kancha, who was now wearing an old British army blouse with faded corporal stripes, apparently in honor of his former sergeant. Kancha had taken them on a tour of the village, more, it seemed, to impress the villagers with his friends than any other reason Yurev could make out. Evening had come quickly, and Kancha had dinner served here by three stout young women who were his sisters. There were other rooms, but as guests the three foreigners were invited only into this one. The living quarters were on this second level, as the ground floor housed the stable, where two cows, a pony and several of the most anemic chickens Yurev had ever seen were kept. Dinner was a wooden bowl of *tsampa*, a pasty, barley cornmeal, and *chang*, a thick, potent home-brewed beer. Local etiquette required the host to offer guests three cups of this barley-based drink. Yurev welcomed the alcoholic content, though the taste was something else. It was bitter, and after the second cup, Yurev thought, had a kind of hairy flavor, as if it had been strained through the coat of one of the animals below. Rancid butter was generously smeared around the lip of the cup to intensify the flavor, Kancha had volunteered happily.

"We need the coolies," Barbaree was saying. "I will pay ten rupees a day."

Yurev held his cup of *chang* in both hands, sipping and trying to follow the conversation, and caught a slow-eyed glance from Abby that betrayed her impatience.

"I do not know, Jack-bishy," Kancha said, shaking his head. "I will see. I cannot say what will be the answer."

"All right then, twelve rupees."

It had been going like this for, it seemed, hours, starting at five rupees. Barbaree would make an offer, and Kancha would give him that sad look and explain about the fire. It had happened, the fire, several days ago, and two huts had been destroyed. What available manpower there was in the village was working to rebuild the huts before the monsoons began, which naturally reduced the coolie population. It was all very plain to Yurev, but

Barbaree pressed on, offering a few more rupees, oblivious to Kancha's commentary.

"I'll go fifteen rupees," Barbaree said, "but no more. If we have to we will carry our own."

Kancha's head bobbed. "Perhaps, yes, Jack-bishy. Perhaps not yes. I will see." He rose from his mattress. "I go to see the *pradhan panch.* The wise one will decide." He bowed to Yurev and Abby, filled their cups with more *chang,* bowed again and left after touching the altar at the base of the wooden Buddha.

Abby stretched her back, making a face as she rolled her neck. "Give it up. I'll carry a pack if it comes to that. I need some sleep."

Barbaree's smile was slow. "Think you could manage eighty pounds on your back every day for forty miles?" He took a long swallow of *chang* as Abby's frown turned into a grimace.

"How can you drink this stuff?" She looked into her cup. "God, camel urine would be an improvement."

"Camel urine isn't this sweet," Barbaree said.

"Oh, Jesus . . . look, you don't have to prove anything to me, Jack. And if we can't get coolies, we can't get them. Let's not beat a dead horse."

"Not to worry, luv. We'll get the coolies."

"Really? How long have we been sitting here, two hours? Three? All I've been hearing is the poor man explain that he can't get coolies. And all you do is up the price."

"We will get the coolies. The price is right now."

"Oh, c'mon, I—"

"Have you ever dealt with hill people before?"

"Of course not."

"Then let me handle this, luv, because I have. It is in their blood, haggling. They're better than Arabs at it. Kancha is only doing what is expected of him."

"Expected? By whom?"

"The *pradhan panch,* the village chief elder. We're Kancha's guests, but we want something from the village. It's his duty to make the best bargain he can."

"What about the fire? You saying there wasn't a fire . . . that this has been a great charade to pump up the price?"

"I haven't any doubt there was a fire, but, then, there are fires hereabouts constantly. You saw the village. Tinderboxes. He's using the fire as leverage . . . I expect to impress you, luv. Kancha will accept fifteen rupees because it's a fair wage. He isn't greedy, you know."

"Then why the business about seeing the prad-whatever? If—"

"*Pradhan panch*," Barbaree said. He nodded, smiling, then finished the last of his *chang*. "The *pradhan panch* of this village happens to be Kancha's father," he said with a smile. "That's why he has the biggest, most comfortable house in this settlement."

Abby glanced around at the dark bare walls. Cracks were filled in with dried mud. From below came the now familiar sound of dung splatting on the ground. A cow bell clanged dully. Chickens squawked.

"Drink your *chang*," Barbaree said. "It's like everything else up here . . . it isn't so bad once you develop a taste for spoiled butter."

She glanced at Yurev, sighed, then took her cup in both hands and drank it down, all of it, in huge gulps, some of it trickling down her chin and neck as she tilted her head back. When the cup was empty she brought it down hard on the table. She gasped violently several times, wiping her mouth with her sleeve. She waved off Yurev when he tried to help. "I'm all right, I'm all right," she said hoarsely. Her eyes watered.

Barbaree laughed and slapped Yurev on the back. "You see, old man, we'll make her a hill woman yet . . . a red-haired Pahari."

◆ FIVE

Yurev woke with a slight buzzing in his head. The taste in his mouth was slimy and bitter. He was in the same room where they'd eaten last night; he could still smell it, the food and the smell of the animals below. He remembered the final round of bargaining with the chief, an old man with a neck swollen with goiter, and that the old man had insisted on filling all their cups with one more drink of *chang*. He remembered lying on his mattress, resting his head on the crook of his arm and closing his eyes. Nothing else.

Now he scratched his shoulder and rolled on his side, still dressed except for his boots. Abby lay asleep on her mattress, knees pulled up, shoulders covered with a light blanket. Her boots stood neatly together near her mattress. Yurev sat up, certain his head would pound, surprised and relieved when it didn't. He heard Barbaree's voice from outside, barking orders. He reached for his boots with one hand, scratching his chest with the other, and realized what made him itch. It was another fact of life in this land of Asian bargainers. Fleas.

"Morning, old man. It's about time you rolled out. From now on we all rise together." Barbaree was fresh and alert, standing on an outcrop of rock, directing villagers in packing a pair of ponies with the gear they'd brought from the train. Yurev held his hand over his eyes against the sun that was already hot and brilliant.

"How long have you been up?" Yurev asked.

"Since dawn." He slapped the baton against his leg, motioning to one of the packers. "Easy there, watch what you do . . ." To Yurev he said without looking at him, "Sleep well, did you?"

"The mattresses have fleas in them."

"Yes, everything here has fleas, old man." Barbaree glanced at him. "You'll live. And from now on wear your hat."

Yurev nodded, then turned, following a black harrier eagle as it soared across the cloudless sky, and saw the mountains—they were mountains unlike anything he'd ever seen. White peaks rose like jagged teeth against the blue depth of sky across the horizon. In the morning light they were white to the point of silver, like the foam of sea after a violent storm. In the center, nearly due north, were two enormous peaks that towered over the rest with majestic grace.

"That's Dhaulagiri on the left, the taller," Barbaree said. "Annapurna on the right. The Kali Gandaki gorge between them. Deepest canyon on the planet."

"Incredible. How far are they?"

"Eighty miles by line of sight. Three times that on foot. I suggest you eat something, not a lot, mind. Want to get moving within the hour. Kancha has eggs and butter tea. Wake the madame while you're about it."

Yurev trudged back to Kancha's house. Abby was up, staring at the mountains. "Have you seen?"

"Yes." Yurev glanced back at Barbaree, standing on the rock, issuing orders. He wished the Englishman wasn't so British. He, it seemed, never scratched.

"Magnificent, isn't it?" Abby said.

It was one of those moments from the past that came to him at irregular times and caught him by surprise. He was standing with Celeste at the rail of the ferry that crossed Bombay Harbor. It was dusk, or nearly, and the slanting rays of the sun cast a copper sheen over the waterfront buildings, the dome of Victoria Terminus lit like a solid gold ball in the gathering haze. "Isn't it magnificent?" she had said, at his side. Yurev could smell her at that moment. She was beside him, an invisible flower.

"Yurey?"

Abagail's voice broke the spell. Yurev opened his eyes without realizing he'd closed them. Celeste was gone, and he was left with the stench of flea-ridden beasts and the conviction that he'd made a mistake coming to this place.

"Yurey, what's the matter?"

Yurev started back down the ladder. "Kancha is waiting breakfast for us." He nodded toward Barbaree. "Oh . . . don't come out into the sun without your hat. It wouldn't be bloody proper."

They were Tibetan ponies, unshod and laden with yak-hair bags stuffed with tents, blankets and Kancha's cooking utensils, an array of pots and pans that clanged together at the tiniest movement. There was a short ritual before they left the village, and though Barbaree was impatient to leave, he stood by stonily while Kancha's father, the chief elder, blessed the ponies, sprinkling vermilion powder and rice over the animals. The old man put a red *tika* mark on Kancha's forehead and on the two coolies, who, to Yurev's amazement, were young women. The old man also made marks on Abby and Yurev, chanting according to the puja ceremony, but when he turned to bless Barbaree, the Englishman had already started up the trail.

Kancha took the signal, and the little caravan began its trek. He poked the animals with a crooked stick, moving them toward the path, and hurried the two women coolies to move out. They were both eighteen— their names were Lagna and Kalu—with round brown faces and strong backs on muscular legs. They carried tall wicker baskets braced on their backs by a tumpline around their foreheads. They walked barefoot and wore ragged pants, vests and an assortment of beads that hung to their waists. They moved up the path without complaint and, Yurev noticed with some perverse pleasure, without hats.

The walk to the crest of the ridge took two hours by Yurev's reckoning. Barbaree, of course, led the way in a pace that was not especially grueling. Yurev and Abby went next, followed by Kancha and the animals with the coolies last. It was a beautiful day and hot, with a strong scent of the heavy foliage in the humid air. There were mosquitoes, but they seemed less bloodthirsty than their cousins along the train route. Even the fleas seemed not to be restless. Yurev and Abby made small talk along the way, but as the walk stretched on, conversation became less important. The path, a ribbon of caked mud and tough, entwined roots, became the focus of Yurev's attention. A dozen times he stubbed his toe or misstepped into a hollow while talking when he should have been watching the way. The last half-hour before reaching the crest was the worst. Trees and tall vegetation were becoming sparse, so Yurev and Abby were increasingly exposed to the sun. Yurev's back and knees ached from leaning forward, moving up this malicious trail. His mouth was dry and his underarms soggy with perspiration. The only sounds now were the stamp of his own footfalls and the ever-constant clanging of Kancha's pots and pans.

"Here, take a look."

Yurev glanced up to see Barbaree standing beside a boulder on stony, level ground. They'd actually reached the top. He stumbled to a large rock and sat down. A few moments later Abby moved up the path to join them. She leaned against the boulder and slowly lowered herself to a sitting position. Her boots were scuffed at the toes from a hundred encounters with the trail's protruding roots.

Barbaree held his canteen by its leather strap, offering it to her. "Water?"

Abby took it eagerly.

"Not too much."

She gulped down several mouthfuls, then brought the canteen into her lap. The water refreshed her voice. "Jesus," she said. She took another drink, slower, then held it over the bridge of her nose and let it trickle down her face.

"Well, luv, what do you think so far?"

"My knees . . ."

"Better let Yurey have some of that."

Abby passed it over. Kancha and the pack animals now clattered up the path, the little Nepalese poking them along with his stick, jabbering at them as if they were recalcitrant children. Lagna and Kalu came along after a few minutes, continuing, following Kancha. They didn't pause or glance about for a spot to rest. They just kept their pace, eyes cast at the ground ahead, their wide brown faces expressionless and, amazing to Yurev, who'd been sweating since he got up, dry.

"How do they do that?" Yurev said. He looked at Barbaree. "Don't they perspire, ever?"

"They will later," Barbaree said, "when it gets hot."

Abby groaned into her hat. She'd pulled it down over her face as defense against the sun and was sprawled against the boulder, head back, feet splayed out. The water she'd poured over herself had soaked her shirt so that the wet fabric clung to her skin. The line and lace of her bra showed clearly through and gave shape to the fullness of her breasts. If he weren't so tired, Yurev might easily have been aroused. Yurev noticed that Barbaree had noticed, too.

"How much further today?" Abby said into her hat. "I'm not complaining, just curious." She wasn't panting anymore.

"We'll do eight hours today," Barbaree said, "since it's your first day.

Tomorrow ten. Then fourteen, fifteen depending on the light. We'll—don't take off your boots."

Abby was picking at the rawhide laces. "What?"

"Keep your boots on until we make camp. You won't get your feet back in. Unless you prefer to walk barefoot the rest of the day."

She began retying the laces. Barbaree had pulled a pack from one of the animals as it passed, and now hefted it over his shoulder and walked ahead several feet. "Here. Take a look."

Abby gave Yurev a tired look. "I take it our rest stop is over." Yurev pushed himself off his rock. His knees were weak, and his legs felt as if they'd gained twenty pounds. As he gave Abby a hand up, his legs nearly buckled under him.

"It's better when you stop to stay on your feet," Barbaree said. "If you sit, the blood settles in your arse—'cuse me, luv—and takes the strength out of your legs. Also, if you'll suck pebbles, it'll help you not to get so thirsty. Small pebbles, smooth if you can find—"

"Oh, my God . . ."

Yurev had been staring at the ground, out of habit, when Abby stopped dead. He looked up to see what had startled her. She was staring straight ahead. The path widened for the short distance that it was level before sloping back down into jungle vegetation. Through the clearing lay a panorama of inner Nepal. Hill upon hill upon hill stretched ever higher before them in light and dark greens, as if in a watercolor, climbing one on top of another. Further on jungle foliage changed to piney forests and windswept pastures on rounded peaks. The ravined foothills crossed back on themselves, making successions of closed valleys and winding streams, while above it, rising out of mist, white against the clear sky, stood the high Himalayas. The giants. Where the gods lived.

"*Shita kypo*, eh?" Barbaree said. "Means 'very pretty.' "

"Magnificent," Abby said.

Barbaree slung the pack from his shoulder. "And not a little dangerous, I should tell you." Yurev watched him take out a sidearm in a holster. He rolled out the belt and strapped it around his waist.

Abby made a face when she saw the gun. "What's that for?"

"Protection." Barbaree retrieved two other sidearms in holsters from the pack and tossed one each to Yurev and Abby. "There's all manner of mean things hereabouts. Didn't want to get them out down at the village . . . scare anybody. Put them on. Get used to the weight. We'll carry them from now on."

"Mean things like what?" Abbey said. "This isn't tiger country."

"No? You know the wildlife indigenous to this area, do you?"

"I read about it," she said, a bit defensively. "In Lucknow." She glanced at Yurev. "Tigers aren't supposed to roam in the hills, that's what I read."

"Too bad tigers can't read."

"Look, I don't need—"

"It isn't just the odd tiger," Barbaree interrupted. "There's wild boar, black bears, jackals, a dozen kinds of vipers. Lots of snakes. Not all of them poisonous, mind, but do you know the difference? And always, of course, there's the unexpected." He patted the sidearm. "That's why we'll carry one of these, each of us . . . Enfield, British army issue, revolver, number two, Mark One. It'll be twelve pounds you won't mind having along if ever something comes up."

"Why do *we* have to carry it?" Abby said. "*You're* the guide."

"Yes. Well, luv, it's like a sergeant major I used to know. Sergeant Major Webley, Twelfth Regiment, Royal Engineers, Pokhara. Didn't have much use for the revolver either, the sergeant didn't. We were surveyors, not bloody infantry, he was fond of saying. The country was too beautiful to be vicious, that was his thinking. Went off to answer the call of nature while we were bivouacked near a waterfall up in the rhododendron forest." Barbaree shook his head.

"You're going to tell me the sergeant was attacked because he didn't have a—"

"We all heard him scream," Barbaree went on. "Even above the waterfall we could hear him screaming. Tigers are supposed to be nocturnal hunters, you know, unless they can't find food. We found the sergeant major, dragged into the bush about a hundred meters. Most of him we found. I never saw such—"

"All *right.*" Abby was strapping on the belt. "We'll wear the goddamn guns."

"Pistols, luv. Point four-five-five caliber. Cock it with your thumb, two clicks. It's bloody loud when it goes off."

"Thank you," Abby said, not looking at him, and, adjusting her hat, moved down the path after Lagna and Kalu.

Barbaree, watching her go, said, "Damn handsome woman, our Abagail Abbaye, eh, sport?"

Yurev scratched at one of the creatures beneath his shirt. "How *do* you tell the poisonous snakes from the harmless ones?"

"You don't, old boy. You kill every bloody one you see."

The caravan walked on, following the rocky, winding path uphill until it turned and slanted down and the whole process began again. Yurev's legs became numb to the soreness as long as he kept them moving. Gradually the jungle foliage gave way to pine and rhododendron trees and spiny barberry bushes and then to long stretches of grassy slopes populated by rape flowers in bloom and here and there villages in the distance, a cluster of thatched roofed huts in wide tidy compounds surrounded by low stone walls. Livestock grazed inside near the shade of banyan trees, giving them the serenity of parks. There was a strange poetry to this landscape, Yurev thought . . . it had a sense of beautiful isolation and no urgency. The massive peaks that crowded the horizon gave him a feeling of peaceful awe, something like looking at the stars and realizing what an insignificant dot this tiny world made in the cosmos. Then his hand brushed the butt of the revolver, warm from the sun, and he was back on the path, sweating under the heat, the chafing gunbelt riding heavy on his hip.

They stopped at a mountain hamlet in a valley where the path followed a diked stream. It was a small village of Paharis—hill Hindus—who lived in reddish clay huts with crude handmade shutters. Yurev passed women beside cribs of maize, pounding grain in stone mortars as children played at the edge of the stream. Flattened mounds of rice lay on straw mats, drying in the sun. There was the smell of civilization here, smoke and dung and chickens. Beyond the village, ascending in green terraces, swirling steps of rice fields followed the contour of the slopes to the blue sky, water gleamed in sunlight like transparent silver. To the other side, steep foothills narrowed the valley and blocked the view of the great snow peaks.

A giant banyan tree marked the village center, where the stream was channeled into a simple fountain, water cascading over smooth rocks. Kancha was up to his knees in the pool, talking to his ponies and dipping a felt hat for them to drink from. Around the tree was a stone rest wall; travelers would carry their loads to the wall, turn and rest their load while still standing. A breeze cooled Yurev's face as he made his way to the shade of the banyan tree. Abby was already there, sitting against the stone wall, arms resting on top of her pulled-up knees. She'd taken off her hat. The sweat band had left her hair matted and dark with perspiration in a line around her head. She acknowledged Yurev with a tired wave, a slow wrist movement. He didn't see Barbaree as he leaned against the wall.

"Which is worse for you?" she said without really looking at him. "Going up or down?"

They hadn't spoken since the rest stop at the top of the first ridge. Abby's place in the procession had been between Barbaree and Kancha. Yurev followed the ponies, and behind him were Lagna and Kalu with their wicker baskets. The caravan, over the hours, had become strung out so that at times Abby was already at the top of one hill before Yurev was down from the last. He'd become accustomed now to the clanging pack animals and followed the sound of them, letting his mind wander as he trudged along the unending path.

"I think down is worse," he said. His toes were sore, and he was sorry she had mentioned it, reminding him. Coming down the steep inclines, each step jammed his legs at the knees and into the toes of his boots.

"When I'm climbing up it kills my back and I can't wait to start down," Abby said. "When I'm going down my knees are screaming and all I can think about is going up again. You taken a look at that yet?" She motioned with her eyes toward the mountain ahead. The path disappeared into a forest of pines. It seemed to go straight up. "There's another one just like it on the other side." She gave him a weak smile. "Jack says it's a little higher." She tilted her head back against the stone wall. "You know what I've been thinking about for the last hour? I've been thinking, after we get to Ratnapa—three more days of this—we have to turn around . . . and come back."

"Do you want to stop?"

"Stop?"

"Go back." It was a thought that had occurred to Yurev more than once in the last hour.

"Jesus, no! The necklace is in Ratnapa. The Pearls of Light. We're going to get it, Yurey. Christ, no, we're not going back. Not without it."

"And if it isn't there?"

"It's there, it's *there.*"

Yurev glanced up as Barbaree walked across the square, baton solidly under his arm. The sun glinted off his brass belt buckle. It was a comfort to see his shirt front sweated through. It made him, somehow, less British.

"I told you about sitting down," he said with weary indulgence. "You'll only—"

"I know, I know. The blood rushes to my ass." She straightened her legs, plopped the hat on her head and pulled herself upright with the help of the wall, waving off Barbaree's hand.

"The memsahib is sore and stiff, is she?" Barbaree said. The shade of his hat covered his eyes.

"The memsahib," Abby said, brushing her pants, "is about as god-damned stiff and goddamned sore as a memsahib can expect to get after walking up and down goddamned goat paths for six hours in this goddamn sun."

"There's a teahouse over here if you're thirsty. It's not what they make in Lucknow but it's not bad. They say it has pain-killing properties."

"So does Jack Daniels. I don't suppose . . .?"

Barbaree smiled. "Sorry, no. *Chiya*, it's called. We'll have a bit of rice and start out again when the coolies show up."

Yurev hadn't paid much attention to Lagna and Kalu because he had his own worries on the trail. He assumed they were not far behind, but there was no sign of either of them even now as he looked down the path. They didn't carry weapons, he remembered, just baskets.

"Shouldn't they be here by now?"

"They? Oh, the coolies. No, no. Don't worry about them. Coolies are always slow, you know. Like camels. They'll be along." Barbaree slapped the baton across his palm. "Well, then, shall we have some tea?"

The teahouse was a hut with an open front and a thick plank of wood for a counter. Crude benches in the shade of a pipal tree were meant for patrons. The woman who operated this establishment was lean and ageless with large Mongol eyes and tiny ears. The muscles in her calves tightened as she bent over a large clay-mound oven in the floor. An opening in the side of the oven accepted twigs and small bits of wood for the fire inside. Water from the fountain was poured into two holes at the top for boiling rice. The same water, dipped out with a large wooden ladle, was used for the tea. She poured the hot water through a strainer containing tea dust and into brown earthen cups. She added coarse brownish sugar, mixed in buffalo milk and banged her ladle against the wood plank when it was ready.

Abby sniffed at her cup and gave Barbaree a look. "Tea?"

"*Chiya*," he said. "Really, it isn't bad." He raised his cup in toast to her and drank from the side that wasn't chipped. "You see? Actually, it grows on you after a few days."

"That I believe," she said.

Yurev drank his without a formal inspection. There was a familiarity to the taste that reminded him of tea. Also the buffalo milk was quite sweet. Kancha joined them and drank his tea sitting cross-legged on the ground.

"Good damn tea, Jack-bishy," he said happily, nodding vigorously. "No rotten bad smell like some times."

When the rice came it was steaming from a large bowl. Barbaree and Kancha ate with their fingers, dipping them like spoons into the mound and tilting their heads back, in the Indian way, to receive it. Yurev tried it, too, but more rice dribbled down his shirt than went into his mouth.

Abby declined to eat and sat stoically with her *chiya*, staring at the slopes on which they would soon advance.

Lagna and Kalu finally appeared, plodding up the path to the rest wall. They were each wearing leaves of a sal tree tucked under the tumpline across their foreheads to shade their faces from the sun. They walked to the banyan tree, turned and lowered the baskets onto the rest wall. Kancha delivered tea, which they drank standing at the wall, still harnessed to the baskets. Neither looked tired.

"When do you figure we'll make camp?" Abby said. She'd finished her *chiya*, most of it. Sitting on the bench in the shade she almost looked refreshed.

"Depends," Barbaree said. He brushed rice off his fingers. "Plenty of day left, you know. Depends on how much more you think you can do. I must say, you've surprised me already. I wouldn't have thought you could do eight hours the first day. Women don't usually have the stamina. Bully for you."

"Thanks . . . Jack-bishy."

"No, truly." Barbaree glanced at the sky. "If you think you're up to it I'd say we could do another four, maybe six hours." He nodded to the foothills that rose before them. "Tinau Khola is just over there, two, three kilometers. We cross it, and we start making altitude. Yes, five hours I'd say. Terrain's a bit rugged toward the end." He turned to her. "Depends on how you feel."

"Rugged?"

"Oh, nothing formidable. A bit rocky is all." Barbaree looked at Yurev. "The legs holding up all right, are they, old man?"

Yurev was thinking what five more hours would do to his knees, but he answered with a nod.

To Abby he said, "And you, luv?"

"I think this walk is making me shorter."

"Shorter? Ah"—he smiled at that—"yes, shorter, very good. Tell you what, I'll have Kancha cut you a stave. Makes these mountain trails a bit easier on the back. What do you say then? Across the Tinau Khola?"

"That's a river, right?"

"Won't see a river until we get to Kali Gandaki, two more days. Tinau Khola's more a tributary. Nothing spectacular."

Abby gave it a moment's thought. "Sure, why not?"

Barbaree got to his feet. "Good show." His face brightened. "At this rate we'll reach five thousand feet by dusk."

Abby pulled her hat on, stood up, testing her legs. "Bully for us," she said.

This foothill was steepest thus far and heavily overgrown with brush along the trail. Yurev lost track of time except that the sun was almost directly overhead, which he supposed put it around noon or after. They'd made it to the top of the ridge and he could see the next hill that rose even higher though the valley was not so deep. He had Kancha cut him a stave and waited some minutes to allow the ponies to move well ahead. The clattering pack animals were getting on his nerves even though he was getting used to the monotony of walking. Barbaree had been right about sucking pebbles, he wasn't so thirsty, and it gave him something to do, running his tongue across the smooth surface of the small stones and rolling them over in his mouth. After a while he'd developed a rhythm that allowed him to let his mind wander and at the same time to walk without tripping over every twig or tree root that happened on the trail.

He daydreamed about the dining room of the Avadh Hotel in Lucknow, remembering the cool wine and the boy on the bicycle fan and the smell of waiters passing with trays of covered plates. He remembered thinking how musical the name Ratnapa had sounded and how intrigued he'd been with the faded photograph of the lama with the piercing eyes. He also remembered when he first set foot in India and his first meeting with Fa Shing. He was here, he realized, nearly sweating blood on a footpath past civilization, because of the Chinaman. The Chinaman, who taught patience and humility. He brought into his mind's eye a vision of the necklace from the photograph, an almost unimpressive string of stones around the lama's neck, and remembered the night when he saw into Fa Shing's other life. It had been a long time ago, the Chinaman's other life. There had been love and suffering there, and, finally, enlightenment. It was the other thing they had in common, suffering. He might never have heard of Shelkagari if not for that.

It was after Celeste had died that the Chinaman told Yurev the story of his other life. It was when he was working without relief to drown his guilt, and Fa Shing was not unaware. It was a late afternoon when he came into the cutting room where Yurev was marking a stone, hunched over his workbench, squinting through his loupe at a six-carat brooch that was to be sized and recut as two brilliants.

"It is difficult, this one?" the old man had said, peering over his shoulder.

"The difficulty is not the cutting." Yurev relaxed his face and caught the loupe in his hand. "The difficulty is cutting at all. It is already a beautiful stone—good clarity, nearly perfect. See for yourself." He moved aside for Fa Shing to take a closer look. "A gift to the viceroy's wife from the Raj Ranstani. She thinks it is too big. She wants to cut it—for dinner rings."

Fa Shing studied the stone. After a moment he said, "Tell the viceroy's wife that it cannot be cut. Tell her that it may shatter under the blade."

"She'll just take it somewhere else."

"Perhaps." His small shoulders shrugged. "One cannot be responsible for the conscience of others . . . or the fate of each stone that passes before us, young friend. You have been working very much with the stones."

"It's what I do," Yurev said. After Celeste died he had found a rooming house by the bay, though he was seldom there except to sleep. He spent his days and nights in the small bungalow that was Fa Shing's diamond workplace. It had become his real home. "I have several sizings and some estimates—"

"You bury yourself in work but you do not look after other needs. Do you eat? Do you sleep? Do you sit for an evening to feel the night or consider the heavenly bodies as once was so?"

"I don't have time to sit, people are waiting for me."

"Ah." The Chinaman nodded to himself, his half-lidded eyes scanning Yurev's face, then moving on. It was the way he had of understanding more than was said. "Your industry is admirable, young friend. I wonder, if it is possible, that you might have dinner with me tonight. I have wine from France and a mood to share it."

Fa Shing had been his tutor almost three years but not once had he invited Yurev into his house. No one of Yurev's acquaintance had ever been asked inside the main residence. What guests he had were entertained in the garden or on the lawn. Always. It was part of the mystery of Fa Shing—the Roman Catholic Chinaman in India. Celeste had called him an enigma.

"You will come then?"

"I have—"

"At seven, please," Fa Shing said quietly. He touched the brooch lightly with a delicate finger. "The stones will not mind."

* * *

The walls of Fa Shing's house were covered with an odd assortment of framed watercolors and tapestries—odd because they were a mix of Chinese, Hindu, Moslem and some of Persian influence. Delicate hand-painted dishes and vases and glass figurines were displayed on Chinese Chippendale antiques. In all of it, Yurev realized, there was the same recurring theme—the lotus flower. The only art representing Western persuasion was an oil painting of Christ healing a cripple, and next to it was a crucifix.

Fa Shing wore a flowing kimono with large sleeves, red with cream-colored lotus flowers. The Chinaman cooked and served the meal on a hibachi, and they drank dark wine afterwards, seated on cushions at a small table that allowed a view of the harbor. A gentle evening rain had started, giving the lights of the harbor a soft glow in the darkness outside. They had started the evening talking about diamonds, it was the thing they had in common, but Fa Shing was interested in Yurev's life as a child, his other life, as he called growing up in czarist Russia. There was a parallel in their two lives. He had grown up under an autocratic regime—the Ch'ing dynasty, the Manchus—in his other life.

Born in a village near the port city of Tsingtao, Fa Shing had never known his family. A smallpox epidemic in 1855 all but wiped out his village, and as a baby he was found by French missionaries who had come to help burn the dead. Raised by nuns in a Roman Catholic orphanage, he had been brought up with Christian values in a Confucian, antiforeigner China. Until he was twenty-two he worked for a French blacksmith setting inexpensive stones in metal crucifixes for sale to European merchants. A German jeweler from Tientsin, on a buying trip, took notice of his work and offered him a job as a lapidary. For the next twenty years Fa Shing worked for the jeweler. His gem-cutting work was exceptional, but his skill as a diamond cutter set him apart from all others, and in 1898 he was summoned to Peking by Tz'u-hsi, the empress-dowager, ruler of all China.

"Peking was divided into three parts, one walled city contained another and that another," Fa Shing said. "Inside the great Peking wall was the Imperial City, which itself contained the Forbidden City, palace of the Son of Heaven and his mother, the empress, who was known also as the Old Buddha. I stood at the Gate of Western Flowering and saw across the Jade Canal the yellow-tiled roofs of the Inner City gleaming in the sunlight. It was a sight I shall never forget, so magnificent a city I had never dreamed of. It was summer when I first walked across the moat, through the Gate of Military Prowess. Velvety leaves and pink chalices of the lotus floated above the water. It was in the Imperial Palace that I first saw Wu Pen-Li. She was a maiden of the empress. And my heart was struck with her." Fa Shing's frail hands lay still on the marble tabletop. He sat straight on his cushion, toward Yurev, his wrinkled face lit by the glow of a candle, but he looked past Yurev, into his other life.

"Even then I was not a young man—forty and six. Wu Pen-Li was the flower of youth. She was from Pao T'ou on the Huang Ho River, daughter of a Manchu magistrate. Her skin was smooth like her people's. Her feet were large because Manchu women do not have their feet bound as children. For two years I was in the Forbidden City and often at the Summer Palace at Jehol—the Mountain of Ten Thousand Longevities. It was during this time that I met the American Bert Hoover, a mining engineer with the British company Bewick and Moreing. As he was a geologist, and I also had some knowledge of rocks, we passed many evenings together, and he told me of his adventures in the great desert of western Australia, where he mined for gold. It was he who gave me encouragements about Wu Pen-Li. But he did not understand our ways. Many times I saw Wu Pen-Li, and always it gave lightness to my heart to look into her face, but more than that was not possible. She was a concubine in the imperial household, and I was a peasant Chinese, not even Manchu. A nod, a look . . . for me it was enough. One evening at the Summer Palace as I watched the sun set over the lakes and streams from the Thousand Colonnade Promenade, the Old Buddha came with her entourage. I knelt as they retired. It was Wu Pen-Li's hand that touched my shoulder, passing softly as a petal lights on the pond. Forever after it was a secret—the one who cut stones and the handmaiden who could not smile. Only Bert Hoover knew."

"You never once saw her alone?" Yurev asked.

"It was forbidden to even speak to members of the entourage. In the Imperial Palace, every place I went I was escorted, even to and from my sleeping quarters . . . I was taken to this room and that room by eunuchs of the palace guard. Only Chinese were allowed into the Imperial Palace and even then no one was allowed free movement. It was a bad time then. The I-ho t'uan—the Righteous and Harmonious Militia—were everywhere killing foreigners and Christians. It was a very bad time."

"The Boxers?"

"Everyone wore something red, their sign, even the eunuchs. I did not know then how it was outside the city . . . the killings. We inside the palace did not hear about the troubles until the springtime. It was soon after that my past was discovered, that I was raised by foreigners . . . by Christians. The chief eunuch, Li Lien-ying, was enraged. Chinese Christians were being killed everywhere, and now they had uncovered one living in the same palace with the imperial family.

"My execution was ordered. I was led to steps at the side of the palace where beheadings were performed. Above, from a palace balcony, the Old Buddha watched. I knelt. A eunuch bound my arms behind me and cut off my pigtail—a sign of dishonor to Chinese. He pointed my head down, exposing my neck, and ordered me not to move. As the executioner prepared the blade there came a great fury beyond Wu Gate. It was, I learned later, the first great assault on the foreign legation. Thousands and thousands of Chinese militia charged the foreigners' compound. So much shooting that spent bullets fell around me, pinging against the palace walls. Terrible cries and black smoke went up from beyond the gate.

"Then, I was alone. My executioners ran off. I had never heard the sound of firearms or cannons. Dying by the blade of the executioner's sword was a thing I had accepted. But in the cries and confusion of this surrounding war I felt lost. I could run, even bound up I could run, but did not know where to go. Then a hand touched my shoulder, guiding me to an unguarded gate at the west of the palace. I could see across the empty Park of Intimate Harmony, beyond the White Pagoda to the Gate of Western Flowering, where I had first entered the city two years before. Outside the gate was Peitang Cathedral, the Catholic mission. I turned to thank my benefactor and looked into the face of Wu Pen-Li."

Fa Shing stared at the harbor for a long moment, and Yurev felt like an intruder. The old Chinaman had never talked to him this way before.

"The mission was very crowded," he said finally. "There were a few dozen French and Italian priests and some soldiers, and about three thousand Chinese Christians. There was very little food. Every day there was shooting and many fires and at night some of us left the mission to look for food. It was on one of these forages that we were discovered by a band of red-sashed ones. They fired their long guns and many of us fell. I ran and hid until daylight. I was afraid to go back to the mission, afraid I would be caught, so I waited until night and escaped from the city. I walked for three days, hiding from the roaming bands that searched for Chinese Christians. I walked to Tientsin, to the International Settlement, a place I thought would be safe." Fa Shing looked at Yurev. "It was not safe, young friend. It was worse even than Peking. Cannons bombarded it at all times of night and day. The brown waters of the Pai River became choked with the bloated bodies of Chinese Christians. I found my American friend, Bert Hoover. He was a rock among his compatriots, taking in many hundreds of Chinese for protection, repairing barricades, fighting the endless fires. His wife helped, too, riding her bicycle in the midst of bullets to help the wounded and dying.

"When the relief army came from Taku and the siege was lifted, I went to Bert Hoover. The army was preparing to move north to Peking. I could not know, of course, how it was for Wu Pen-Li in the palace. I asked Bert Hoover to find a way that I might go with the army. At first he tried to discourage me, but when he saw the deepness of my sincerity, he found a way.

"Along the route north my prayers were for Wu Pen-Li. I tried to imagine what was happening, if there was food enough for her . . . I had heard stories that the people in Peking had no food, and they ate horses and dogs and rodents and even insects. I knew that many people were dying there, Chinese people, and my heart went out to them, but my prayers were for Wu Pen-Li.

"When the army arrived at the city there was celebrating everywhere, the Chinese were so happy to see them. The red-sashed ones fought briefly and withdrew. In victory there were spoils to be had, but I did not believe the Christian soldiers would act in that way. They had come to relieve the city of the antiforeign militia, not to plunder and abuse their Chinese Christian brothers. I was wrong. It was when I knew that the time of China was over. The foreigners had won a great victory. Old Buddha and the Son of Heaven had fled from the Forbidden City in a cart, disguised as common folk. When the tree falls, it is said, the shade is gone. The time of China was over.

"I searched for Wu Pen-Li. Most of the palace servants had fled because they feared what the foreigners might do. Because the imperial family had left in such haste, I thought that Wu Pen-Li would be there. I had to save her from the vengence of the Christians. There was very much confusion. Peking was not the city I had known when I first arrived. Great sections had been burned and bombarded into rubble, and the dust of it was everywhere. For weeks I searched, wandering the streets, looking.

"I went to the Summer Palace, to the Mountain of Ten Thousand Longevities, where we first touched, but there were only soldiers there. I was told that many from the palace had gone to a village near The Great Wall in Shansi province. Winter was coming, and the cold dry winds from the desert of Mongolia would be soon with us. I walked there, thinking if Wu Pen-Li were safe she might come with me, south to Macau. I could work there, cutting stones, and teach her a quiet life.

"In Ning-wu I found a Manchu family that had known Wu Pen-Li. They had not seen her but another Chinese from the palace was also living in the village. He had been a palace eunuch, and when I went to see him he could not rise from his pallet because of the wounds he had received fighting the foreigners. He first told me he was never in the palace. He thought I was helping the foreigners search out members of the Righteous and Harmonious Militia for punishment. But I knew him . . . he was the same eunuch who had cut my braid for the executioner. I told him I was not with the foreigners, I was only searching for a maiden of the court. I also told him I had looked for her because she had saved my life.

"The eunuch's name was Li-te-hai, and now he seemed a different person. He told me I should not have come, he said his brain was tormented by a thousand devils since the first day of the siege against the foreigners. He ran away after many weeks of fighting. He had lost two brothers and was himself wounded. He told me to go away. He said he was dying, and that he would not talk to me. I should go, he said, and let him die in peace. But I would not go, and then, finally, he told me about the death of Wu Pen-Li . . ." Fa Shing stared into the candle. "This is what I want you to know, young friend. Our lives are parallel, our old lives. The lands of Russia and China, our Celeste and Wu Pen-Li. Parallel, yet different."

Fa Shing had been talking for a long time—the candles had melted down to stubs—but he never looked at Yurev as he remembered his other life. Rather, he stared out toward the blurred lights in the harbor. The light rain falling on the stone walk outside made a sound like a low fire. Everything else was still . . .

"Wu Pen-Li was executed in my place," Fa Shing said. The chief eunuch had seen her betrayal, releasing me, and called for her destruction as the dying cries of dancing Chinamen filled the streets. For touching a Christian inside the Imperial City, her hands were cut off at the wrists. For delivering a condemned prisoner from death, her feet. For the time it took her blood to run out they left her outside the palace. Li-te-hai had witnessed it all. He said she did not once cry out. Guilt, shame took me over. I despised myself for surviving. I despised my race, my religion. A merciful God could not be. It was a very bad time . . ."

Fa Shing's eyes now moved slowly to Yurev. "We have parallel lives, young friend. The wheel of life turns, and we must make our own way.

Like Moses, I was for a time lost in the wilderness of frustration and guilt. As you are now. One day you will come out and leave the other life behind. I know it is a hard thing to understand, but the truth of what I say lies in patience."

"Patience?"

"Our times were meant to touch, yours and mine. There is purpose to the suffering."

"What?"

"You have heard the story of Job?"

"I don't believe in a superior being—God or gods." Yurev looked at the harbor. The rain had stopped. "In any case it's rather unlikely that one would pick me to test my faith."

"Do you know the story of Shelkagari?"

"I don't read the Bible, Fa Shing."

"Shelkagari is not related to the Christian faith. It is a story as old as India. It was told to me by an old one in the high hills. I had heard of it once in China where it was called the Stone of Forever Shining."

"Stone?"

"A diamond, some say. As large as the head of a cow's calf."

"You were in the Himalayas?"

"Home of the Ancients, yes. It was in my other life. After I left China. I went south, first into Szechwan, then west across the great Yangtze and Mekong. For two years I lived in Lhasa among the Bhots, and many times saw their God King who lives in the great palace called Potala. It was there I learned patience from the Buddhists. It was my wilderness of sadness. I sold cloves of garlic in the streets.

"When I went away from there I was cook's helper with a pony caravan, traveling west and south toward the high snow passes. It was a great surprise and pleasure to me when, as we met another caravan returning from the passes, I saw my American friend Bert Hoover. He had accompanied a British geological expedition into the high hills. We sat together by the fire and talked into the night. My friend nearly cried when I told him of Wu Pen-Li. He pleaded that I return with him to China. He said I should come with him to America of the United States and begin again. He said I should not waste my life traveling nowhere in the high hills covered in the juice of the garlic bulb. My knowledge of stone would be welcomed in his country. But my heart was still clouded in the mist of despair. I told him that I could not, and at morning light we parted and I watched until his caravan was one with the horizon. I never again saw my American friend. This was the twilight of my other life."

"Before you came here?"

A nod. "The caravan went on for many days," Fa Shing continued, "into the high plains. It was when we were attacked by the dogs with the smooth coats. They are much feared, the blue dogs. They are very large and so fierce that the Bhots carry a charm portraying this savage beast fettered on a chain. The chain is clasped by a *dorje,* a holy stone, and the inscription reads, 'The mouth of the blue dog is bound beforehand.' Scores of dogs attacked, led by a great black bitch. They circled the ponies, sending them running for their lives in all directions. I was terrified. There was much confusion. Ponies and dogs were everywhere. The barren ground became slippery with blood. I ran like the ponies, wildly, not knowing where to go. Then they were around me, dogs with bloodied teeth, their jaws snapping. They circled at a trot, around and around. I was too paralyzed to move. They came closer, moving in and out like jackals, but they did not attack. Then, slowly, they moved away. All of them. They left the carcasses and were gone. It seemed a miracle. What else was there to explain it? That they had gorged themselves on the ponies? Perhaps, but more likely not . . . at least so said the leader of the caravan."

"The cloves," Yurev said. "You were wearing the garlic cloves. That's why they didn't attack?"

Fa Shing's eyes fastened on Yurev. "Surely so." He folded his long slender fingers together. "At the next village the story of the dogs spread quickly. This was when I met the old one, the *bairagi.* It was thought that my *dorje* was very powerful to have protected me from such numbers of blue dogs. The old one wanted to see it. But I am not a Bhot, I told him. I had no charm. Hearing this he was very troubled. He said I must be a devil or a god. I told him that I was only a man and had no powers. Then he asked me if I had come for The Stone of a Thousand Miracles."

"The what?"

"It is how the Bhots call the Shelkagari, the Compassionate Stone of Ushas. He told me the legend . . . and it has been with me since that day."

"Ushas?"

"Goddess of Dawn in the time before time, when gods walked with men," Fa Shing said. "In all the world there was one kingdom, below the snow hills, ruled by a just and merciful king who had three sons. Ushas was in love with the youngest prince, a frail boy born with a deformity of the foot. The young prince was benevolent and wise beyond his years. He sang his songs of love to Ushas from a rock at the edge of a glistening pool each morning. The goddess honored the young prince with favors and prolonged the daylight to hear him sing. Her preoccupation with the prince angered the other gods, but nothing they could do persuaded her to end the consociation. When the king died Ushas decided that her prince, because he was wisest, should ascend to the throne over his brothers. She persuaded her reluctant poet-prince that it was a just claim and went to the gods to demand that they give aid to her prince in the challenged combat. He must be imbued with strength and power to overcome his infirmity, she said. The gods, seeing only an opportunity to teach Ushas never to interfere in the affairs of men, agreed.

"The combat began, and the young prince, invested with the raging powers of a warrior god, slew his eldest brother in a furious battle. Standing over the bloody body the young prince turned to face his next brother. At that moment the gods instilled in him an emotion more powerful than duty—guilt. For mortal man to be responsible for his actions he must pay the price of enlightenment. If justice were to be a virtue then conscience would be the counterpoise. To the horror of Ushas, the young prince suddenly threw aside his weapon and was killed by his remaining brother with a single blow.

"The goddess of dawn was tormented by the death of her prince. The gods had betrayed her. In her grief she refused to allow dawn's light over the kingdom. Without dawn crops withered because there was no sun. Without crops to feed the people there would soon be starvation. To console Ushas the gods combined their powers and transformed the body of the dead prince into a dazzlingly clear stone of such hardness as to never erode and that would reflect sunlight in brilliant colors forever. But only in the light of dawn would its beauty be realized. In this way, the gods hoped, Ushas would allow morning's light to return to the kingdom. So Ushas accepted the stone. She placed it among the peaks of the sacred high hills where she would be first to see its radiance for eternity. If ever touched by mortal man, so it goes, his soul would know the terror of ten thousand devil dogs and his life cursed. Thereafter, until restored by the son of the third-born son of a prince, only a god or a woman may touch it without suffering." Fa Shing looked directly at Yurev. "The Stone of a Thousand Miracles. It is called Shelkagari, its sanskrit name—Crystal Clear Mountain—from the Ancients."

"A myth," Yurev said.

"Truly."

"You don't believe such a tale?"

"I believe many things . . . Christian things, Hindu things, Moslem—"

"There are hundreds of stories like that. Diamonds with curses . . . Buddha's third eye. All that. India is full of folk tales."

Fa Shing merely looked at Yurev, then went on.

"The old one, after he told me this story, sat on the ground. He closed his eyes and rocked back and forth chanting. All night. When I came back to see him he said he'd had a vision. He said the attack of the blue dogs was a sign. In his vision he saw a walled fortress on an island. Inside the fortress lived giants whose tails grew out of their heads. One day a clumsy giant crushed the litter of a blue bitch. The blue bitch ran around and around the walled fortress, snapping its teeth but the giants were not afraid. Then the blue bitch swallowed its dead young and grew ever larger until it became a great beast with seven heads and seven tails. The beast crashed through the great walls of the fortress and, spewing fire from its heads and swinging its spiked tails, destroyed the walled fortress and every house inside it. It killed every giant of the fortress, all except one. It spared one who had no tail from his head. To this one the beast gave a mission —go to the land beyond the red-faced devils and send back a man with the heart of a lotus blossom. The old one said the blue dogs did not harm me because I was the messenger, friend of kings and princes and potentates."

"He was talking about the siege of Peking—the walled city?"

"A city surrounded by a moat."

"No tail from his head . . . your pigtail?"

"An interesting dream from a man so remote, wouldn't you say?"

"He probably heard of the siege from another wanderer," Yurev said. "He might have heard it from a hundred different people. It wasn't a prediction, just a fanciful dream. They're all storytellers, the hill people."

"Truly," Fa Shing said, nodding. "The old one, he interpreted his vision to be that the ancient stone of Ushas would be returned but that I was not the one. A day would come, he said, when a man would come to me. The son of a prince this man would be, and he would be the first ring in the chain that would return the Stone of a Thousand Miracles to the land of Bhots. A man fired by suffering. A man"—Fa Shing leaned slightly forward—"from beyond the All Encompassing Sea. A *gorah* sahib . . . a white foreigner. An American foreigner—"

"*Me?*" Yurev looked at Fa Shing, waved his hand quickly. "You don't really *believe* any of that?"

"There is much worth considering. True or false, it is very interesting, I think."

"Consider what? Old friend, it's a story. Embellished over generations. You don't really—"

"Ah." Fa Shing nodded his head gently. "And was the great Alexander also a teller of stories? The Macedonian warrior-king, conqueror of his world."

"Alexander the Great?"

"It is said—and written, I have seen it—that the boy-king Alexander was given a great gift when he subdued India. A great stone that light shone through. He struck three large pieces from it and several smaller. Of the original stone and the three large pieces, nothing more has ever been heard. But of the smaller stones, six in all . . . of them came a necklace that was fashioned for his queen. Whether you believe or not that the stone was Shelkagari, it is recorded that the great Alexander won not another battle. His soldiers would not follow him further into India. They died by the thousands crossing the vast Gedrosia Desert. And of Alexander himself, on reaching Babylon he went insane and died there."

"Driven insane by ten thousand devil dogs—whatever they are?" Yurev smiled at his mentor. "All because he touched a mythical diamond?"

"Defiled might describe it better."

"You *do* believe it." Yurev stared at him. "You really do think it's true, about Shelkagari?"

The Chinaman was silent.

"Why?" Yurev said. "Because an old man in the Himalayas had a dream? Only that?"

"It is, as I said, a subject worthy of consideration."

"By me, you mean?"

"Does it make you wonder how this old one knew, thirty years ago, that you would come to me?"

"No," Yurev said quickly. *"No."*

Fa Shing shrugged his bony shoulders. His eyes were on Yurev. "Later, young friend, perhaps you will. Perhaps in your next life . . ."

Yurev stumbled now but caught himself with the stave Kancha had cut for him. This plus the pony's clattering pots and pans brought him abruptly back to the present. The path, overgrown again with roots, wound down through heavy jungle foliage. He could hear the sound of rushing water, the smell of it heavy in the air.

"You call that a bridge? That is *not* a bridge. A bridge is anchored. A bridge has something to hold it up. A bridge does not drift in the goddamn wind," Abby was saying to Barbaree.

Yurev made a turn on the path and found them in a clearing beside the mouth of a bamboo suspension bridge that stretched fifty feet to the banks of a clearing on the other side. A hundred feet below was the brown Tinau Khola, its swift current bubbling around rocks. Kancha, already halfway across the bridge, was slowly leading one of the ponies.

"It's the only way," Barbaree said impatiently. He held the remaining pony by its tether. "Ratnapa is that way which you bloody well can't get to unless you move your arse from here"—he pointed to the other side —"to there. Be a good girl now and come along."

"It's goddamn dangerous—"

"Of course it's bloody dangerous. Just hold on and walk carefully. Look at Kancha. If he can make it with a pony, surely you can manage. You're not carrying anything, you know."

Abby turned to Yurev, who'd moved to the edge of the bridge. He hadn't taken his eyes off it. The bamboo walk was about three feet wide and lashed tightly together. The thick rope handrails were weathered but sturdy. It did sway a bit, though.

"I don't like heights," Abby said. "I don't like—oh, Jesus. Yurev . . . you're *bleeding.*"

"What?"

"Your neck. It's . . ."

Yurev felt his neck. His hand came away bloody.

"Jesus, *I'm* bleeding!" Abby dropped her stave. "Something's *on* me . . ."

"We're all bleeding," Barbaree said. "Not to worry. They won't take much."

Abby's eyes were round. "*What?*"

"Leeches," Barbaree said. He pointed back into the jungle. "They drop off the leaves."

Abby swung at her neck. "*Leeches?*"

"*Don't pull them off,*" Barbaree said quickly. "Their suckers are imbedded. You'll only cause a wound."

"Get them the hell *off* me." Abby tore at her sleeve. A trickle of blood on her forearm had soaked through her shirt leaving a thin red line.

Barbaree caught her hand before she could slap the leech. "Wait." He unbuttoned the wrist and gently shook her arm. A leech about an inch long dropped to the ground, engorged.

"Oh, *Jesus* . . ."

"Leave them. Ripping them out makes it much worse, believe me.

You're losing very little blood. It's the serum they inject with their suckers that keeps the blood from clotting. By the time you see any blood they've already had their fill. Don't worry, luv, they're practically harmless." Barbaree drew back his shirt below his neck. Two small black leeches were fastened to his skin above the collarbone. The larger one dropped off, and blood oozed from a pair of tiny incisions. "You see?"

Abby turned her head, closed her eyes tightly. *"Get them off me . . ."*

Barbaree looked at Yurev. "Truly, old man, they're harmless buggers. You can spare a bit of blood, eh?"

"Please?" Abby was crying now.

"Right, then." Barbaree unbuttoned his shirt. "Like this." He found a tin of salt on the pony and took off his shirt. "A pinch of salt over them like this." He rubbed salt between his fingers, sprinkling it where the leech's suckers attached to his skin. "They don't like it much, and it stings a bit when they pull out quickly." The salted leech fell off after a moment. "There. All right luv, shirt off. You too, Yurev."

Abby didn't hesitate. She unbuttoned her shirt, pulling it down to uncover her shoulders. Yurev saw a leech on her back, below the shoulder blade. A small one. Another leech was attached to her left breast, above her bra.

"Off, I said." Barbaree nodded at her shirt. "Leeches don't understand modesty."

Abby gave him a hard look. "Just the leeches." She let the shirt fall to the ground, holding her arms out from her sides. "Do it, and hurry up."

Barbaree sprinkled salt on five leeches, brushing them with his little finger until they fell off. There were three at her belt line, black against her white skin. They looked very much like slugs, Yurev thought. They'd left a faint trail that glistened on Abby's skin. Barbaree seemed very much to enjoy removing the leeches, especially the one on her breast and another curled in her navel. Abby grimaced as each of them dropped off. Then he did Yurev. Four leeches. They shook out the shirts before putting them back on. When Kalu and Lagna appeared from the jungle path Barbaree waved them on toward the bridge.

"Not likely any got past the belt in your trousers," Barbaree said. "Even so, they'd be very small and probably already had their fill." He pointed across the bridge to the top of the hill. "I told Kancha that we'd camp up there. All you have to do, luv, is make up your mind about the bridge. It's—"

"Are there any leeches up there?" Abby was staring at the next summit. The terrain was rocky near the top with few trees.

"Not there, no. We may be in jungle again tomorrow. But after that we'll be out of leech territory, so to say."

"Thank God for that at least."

"There will be other bridges—"

"I can handle the bridges."

"Can you now?"

She picked up the stave, measuring its weight, and watched the two Nepalese girls making their way across the bamboo. Lagna and Kalu walked almost like a team on the bridge. They grasped the rope handrail about a foot ahead of themselves and pulled, forcing their legs onward. If anything, their wicker loads seemed to give them balance. When Abby turned to Barbaree, her eyes were dead calm. "You bet your limey ass I can," she said, and handed him the stave. "You can give this back when I meet you over there." She grasped the rope handrail, tested her weight on the bamboo and started across, moving slowly, grabbing the handrail and pulling herself as Lagna and Kalu had done.

"That is sweet determination, that is," Barbaree said to Yurev. "All right, mate. Off you go. I'll follow with the pony once you've reached halfway. Keep at least ten paces' separation . . . and don't look down if heights bother you."

Yurev grasped the rope. Heights did bother him, but he'd already looked down at the river. His mouth felt suddenly dry, and rolling the pebbles over his tongue did nothing to relieve it.

"C'mon, then. You're not going to give me trouble, too?"

Yurev shook his head. At the other end Lagna and Kalu stepped onto solid ground. Fifty feet. Yurev swallowed and stepped out onto the bamboo. He was nearly across when he realized that the smooth pebbles, to fight thirst, were now in his stomach.

"Pretty good damn grub, yes?" Kancha's smile was caught in the flickering light of the campfire as he squatted beside Yurev.

"Yes, it was very good, Kancha." Yurev sat close to the fire on a smooth rock. His cup of *chang* warmed his hands, and for the last several minutes he'd lost himself staring at the night. He'd never, he decided, seen so many stars in his life.

"Kancha good damn cook, you bet you life."

They had made camp among the rocks at the top of the hill. Yurev and Barbaree had unloaded the pack animals and pitched the two small tents they would use, one for Abby and the other for Yurev and Barbaree. The coolies and Kancha would sleep by the fire. Darkness had come quickly, and Kancha had used easily a dozen of his pots and pans preparing the meal, which turned out to be *tsampa*, his specialty, and hot *chang*. As soon as the sun was gone the evening turned quickly chilly, and it occurred to Yurev that sleeping in a tent twenty feet away from the fire might not be the luxury he'd thought.

"What time do you make it, Kancha, eight, nine o'clock?"

"Time?" Kancha shrugged. "No time, Yurev-bishy. Night."

It was another of the measurements he'd left behind, Yurev realized.

"You like coolie girls?" Kancha had moved closer to the fire, raising his hands to it for warmth. He looked extremely uncomfortable, Yurev thought, squatting like a duck with only flat feet to support him. "They never saw white sahibs before."

Yurev nodded. Lagna and Kalu watched him from across the fire, smiling, then giggling to one another. Teen-agers. He'd never seen two people eat so much—they'd consumed at least half of Kancha's *tsampa* between them and easily as much *chang*. They'd put on shawls and sat side-by-side, drinking their *chang* from tin cups, occasionally tossing woodchips into the flames. Abby lay back against a rock, feet toward the fire. She hadn't moved for several minutes, and Yurev assumed she was asleep. Barbaree had gone looking for dry firewood, and Yurev was relieved he hadn't asked him to come along. They'd walked twenty-odd miles today. It was enough.

"You like to have coolie girl?" Kancha refilled Yurev's cup with *chang*. "They pretty good damn girls, Yurev-bishy."

Yurev stared at the little Nepalese. "Are you serious?"

"Indeed, yes," Kancha said. "Very great honor for coolie girl."

"Now, look—"

"Folks say white sahib blessed with much big compassionate member. More bigger than Nepalese man. Lagna and Kalu never seen white sahib before."

"Compassionate member . . ."

"The limb of life," Kancha said poetically, then pointed to his groin.

Yurev glanced at the teen-age pair across the fire and saw eager smiling faces.

"Yurev-bishy, they think you very pretty. Strong, too. Can have one or both. One times, two times, no matter. Whatever you want."

"I *don't* want."

"Long walking making you tired. They understand. Maybe you lie down. Coolie girl, she can fix. Make you strong, hard like stone. Other coolie girl, like this"—he indicated his squatting posture—"make happiness."

"Look—"

"Problem?" Abby moved to the fire. She dipped her cup into the pot of *chang* beside the hot coals. "Don't let me interrupt."

"I thought you were asleep."

"And miss this?" She sipped her drink. "It's almost worth the trip."

Yurev turned to Kancha. "Tell them, too."

"Yurey-bishy not liking coolie girls?" Kancha's expression was sad, confused.

"Yes, I like them, I mean . . . I don't *want* them. Just tell them no . . . thanks. I mean—"

Yurev glanced at Abby, who was smiling into her cup.

"I'm sorry," she said, still smiling.

She wasn't, of course, at all sorry. Yurev could see that. She was staring now at the fire, drinking her *chang,* but even in the darkness he knew she was still, damn her, smiling . . .

Barbaree had returned with a load of wood, dumping it into the pile Kancha had gathered earlier. He knelt beside Lagna, feeding dry branches into the low flames. From somewhere beyond their hill an animal's cry reached the small circle of flickering light. A moment later came another, in answer.

Abby's attention came away from the fire. "What was that?"

"Jackals," Barbaree said. "Hunters. It's their time of night."

Abby gave him an anxious look.

"Not here, luv. They're after smaller game."

"How small?"

He patted the weapon at his side. "Anything not carrying one of these."

Abby licked her lips. "Oh, well, I suppose that's comforting to know."

"You two better shove off." Barbaree indicated the tents with a nod. "Tomorrow we'll be moving to higher, rockier terrain." His glance touched Abby. "And some bridges. We'll strike camp shortly after dawn. Better sleep now. Those yak-hair blankets, make sure you have one under you. You won't get cold. And take your boots off. Your feet need a rest."

Abby stood up. "Anything else, general?"

"One thing. Relieve yourself now, luv, within light of the fire. It'll be safer now rather than later when the fire is low."

"Within the light of the fire?"

Barbaree smiled. "I promise I won't look, luv."

* * *

Yurev fell asleep almost the instant he lay down. It seemed hours later when he woke up to Barbaree crawling into the small space of the tent beside him.

"Sorry, didn't mean to jostle you."

The glow of the fire only outlined shapes in the darkness. Someone tossed branches over the fire, producing a shower of embers. Yurev recognized Kalu in the flickering light.

"What's the time?" Yurev said, only half-awake.

"No time." Barbaree's breath was heavy with the aroma of *chang*. "Go to sleep."

"Is that Kalu?"

Barbaree kicked off his boots. "You had your chance, old man."

"Where have you been?" Fully awake now.

"Making happiness, old man." He pulled the heavy yak blanket up over his shoulder and rolled on his side. "Bloody sweet, too."

Yurev lay awake for a long time, listening to the sound of the Englishman's snoring and the far night cries of jackals at work. A light wind caused the tent guy ropes to hum. Even with the yak blanket, Yurev felt a chill.

◆ SIX

LIGHT DAWNED LUMINOUS ACROSS the sea of mountains ahead, creeping slowly down the peaks as Yurev endured Kancha's breakfast and the morning cold. There were still stars in the sky, fading like candles in the spreading pink blush of day. The way they had come was still shrouded in mist below, and rainbows fell away into ravines as they set out toward the rising sun.

Yurev was given a pony, Barbaree took the other so that Kancha could lead the way. The trail turned quickly rocky with only a few trees, which made walking up more difficult because they faced into the sun.

The soreness Yurev had expected after a day's march inexplicably had not developed except high in his back around his shoulderblades. His legs, to his amazement, were not stiff.

"How did you sleep last night?" Abby had caught up with him as he paused while his pony relieved itself at the crest of a treeless hill. The sun now was vibrant in the cloudless sky.

"Aside from a spell of cold, very well. And you?"

She nodded. "Same here. I never slept eight hours straight before in my life until last night. I don't know if it was the exhaustion or the air or what. You don't suppose there's something actually medicinal in *tsampa?*"

"Maybe." Yurev prodded his pony with a stick the way he'd seen Kancha do. The clatter of pots and pans was beginning to have a certain rhythm to it that was nearly musical. Abby walked on the other side of the pony, using her stave like an oar, pushing it out ahead and pulling her body to it. "Maybe it's the *chang,*" Yurev said.

"*Chang?*"

"Medicinal."

"Oh, God forbid."

"I'm getting used to it, I think."

She gave him a compassionate look. "You're getting sick, Yurey-bishy." She tapped a finger against her temple. "Very golly damn sick."

At least, he thought, she smiled when she said it. . . .

Late in the morning they negotiated two wooden bridges that traversed shallow rocky streams with swift currents. They forded another stream, wading barefoot through hip-deep, incredibly cold water. Yurev wore his jacket against the resulting chill for an hour in spite of the sun's heat. It was a new sensation, sweating and freezing all at the same time.

By afternoon the terrain changed again to vast grasslands and hills of wild flowers, and Yurev succumbed to another of Kancha's examples— talking to the pony. He dubbed the pony Niro, which liberally translated meant unconscious one, a suitable name, he figured, for an animal that, short of beating, had to be constantly reminded where the trail was. They passed by several villages where people came to wave, the men chattering unintelligibly and the women and children smiling and sticking out their tongues. At one point Yurev had to steady Niro for several minutes as a caravan of sheep and goats passed coming the opposite direction. There were scores of animals, most with tinkling bells strapped around their necks and many carrying packs—two haphazardly tied bags of salt to be traded in the lowlands for grain. To the side of the path among the wildflowers were large patches of wild strawberries that attracted Niro, and Yurev indulged the animal until he discovered that along with the patches of strawberries were also hordes of leeches.

Now the hills were becoming less steep and the trail made its way lazily around them through wide valleys where brilliant green rice paddies contrasted with the dark muddy water in which they grew. By late afternoon they were skirting a thick forest lined with walnut trees and then moved into a grove of tall leafy plants and chinook trees. Abby was waiting, swatting mosquitoes that infested the grove, as Yurev rounded a bend in the trail. Niro was getting especially obstinate, stopping to nibble at the spiny leaves in spite of the mosquitoes.

"Our intrepid leader says there's a village about a mile ahead where we'll spend the night." Her face was liquid with sweat, attracting carnivorous insects. "He also says not to let the pack eat this stuff."

"Niro doesn't know the meaning of the word restraint . . . unless it has to do with moving forward."

"Niro?"

"You don't spend a whole day with an animal like this without calling it *something.*"

"Well, you'd better have a quick talk with your friend," she said. "She's eating ganja leaves . . . marijuana. There must be tons of hashish out here."

Yurev poked Niro with his stick. "Come, Niro. *Come.*" He pulled on her harness, and she finally plodded onward, chewing happily.

Abby strode along beside Yurev, using her stave to push back the overhanging leaves. "God, what I'd give for a hot bath and a cold drink. If my father could see me now he'd probably have a stroke. Abbaye women aren't supposed to be the adventurous type.

"What is your father?"

"What is he?" Abby shrugged. "A tycoon, son of a tyrant, grandson of a genius. I'm not sure what that makes me . . . sure as hell not what my father wanted."

"And what is that?"

"A male heir. I'm the youngest of five girls. He stopped trying after me." She smiled. "There's no son to continue the Abbaye tradition."

"You find that amusing?"

"You'd have to know my father. Actually, if you had to meet an Abbaye it should have been my great grandfather—Samuel Joseph Abbaye."

"He was a genius?"

"What he was was a thief, but a lucky one. He and John Rockefeller. My great-grandfather was a gambler, and when he won he bought land. He won a lot because he cheated. When railroading seemed to be the coming thing he put his money into it and sweated blood building the Northwestern Railroad Line. My grandfather made it into an empire, San Francisco to Chicago. My father . . . well, my father just makes money and worries about his image. He's afraid of dying and not leaving a son. That's *my* heritage."

"And you live in Chicago."

"Yes, with the bootleggers and the crooked politicians and the gangsters." Abby glanced at Yurev. "It's a very cozy crowd."

"I have never been to America. One day I would like to go there."

"It isn't all Chicago."

"I've read of the American west. Plains Indians and outlaws. Do you still have trouble with the red men?"

Abby laughed. "I wouldn't say trouble, no. They're still paying for Custer, I think."

"And outlaws?"

"In Chicago we don't have outlaws. We have gangsters . . . my father's friends."

"I have heard of the gangsters . . . Sacco and Von . . . von . . ."

"Vanzetti? Sacco and Vanzetti weren't gangsters. Christ, they weren't even killers. The biggest crimes they committed were being Italians and living in Massachusetts. No, I'm talking about big-time hoods. Real rough crowd that wipes out flowershops and garages with machineguns. Like Capone—a dumpy little creep. They call him Big Al. Always has his goons with him so some other creep's goons don't blast him while he's having lunch. You don't know what bloodthirsty is until you've seen the handiwork of a bastard like Capone."

"Bloodthirsty?"

"I guess you never heard of the St. Valentine's Day massacre."

Yurev shook his head.

"You can believe me," Abby said. "They don't come any more vicious than Big Al."

"Ah." Yurev pulled on Niro's harness to keep her straight on the path. "I wonder, have you ever heard the name Joseph Stalin?"

There was a sound like an explosion ahead, and Niro stopped dead when she heard it, pricking up her ears. The sound rumbled like thunder, and a hundred flapping birds, hidden before in the forest of leaves, were suddenly airborne, the air filled with their high-pitched screeching. And then another explosion—gunshots.

Abby looked quickly at Yurev. "Jack." She started off in a near run up the trail, striking through the thin branches that overhung the way. Yurev grabbed a fistful of Niro's rein and, surprised that the animal followed dutifully, crashed into the whipping ganja leaves after her.

"Abby . . ."

The trail curved this way and that, and ahead he could see the grass-covered slope of the next hill. Kancha was there, waving his arms. The sky was alive with the panicked motion of the birds.

". . . Wait . . ."

The leather holster flapped against his leg as he moved, reminding him it was there. When he heard another report, echoing like a cannon across the valley, he let loose of Niro's rein and ran, hands up against the whipping leaves. A thick green branch caught him above the fore-head, scraping his hat off his head. He passed Abby's stave where she'd dropped it in the trail. When he did catch sight of her she was out of the ganja forest, running up the slope, fighting to get her weapon out of its holster.

Barbaree was standing just off the trail in a grove of rape flowers, one foot propped on a large rock. There was blood from his knee to his boot. He was smiling, his revolver in his right hand.

"Well, then"—he nodded at the sky full of circling birds—"that woke them up a bit, eh?"

Abby, out of breath, held her gun at her side. "What happened, what was that shooting?"

"Noisy bugger, isn't it? I told you it was."

"You're *bleeding*." She turned to Yurev as he came beside her. "He's shot himself—"

"Me?" Barbaree's smile widened. "No, not me, luv." He reached down beside the rock. "Here's the bloke got shot." He raised a large porcupine by its tail. Blood dripped across Barbaree's pant leg. The animal's head had been blown away. "Thought you might like a change of diet."

The porcupine meat was roasted over an open fire in a village called Dura Dam, a scattering of thatched-roofed huts in a valley of the Tinau Khola. The village chief, through Kancha, had invited the three whites to stay in his home. Yurev had watched Barbaree skin the porcupine— quill pig, Kancha called it—which was not made more appetizing when he learned that porcupines were actually rodents that ate almost anything, including ganja roots and cow dung. He was grateful to discover that the meat was edible if a bit stringy. Abby ate it, happy that *tsampa* was not on the menu. Yurev spared her the details of her dinner's frequent diet.

"The chief say"—Kancha pointed to Abby's breasts—"why memsahib wear cloth around there . . . under garment."

They were seated around the fire, the chief and several of his villagers with Abby and Yurev and Barbaree. A group of wandering ascetics, nine Buddhist monks with musical instruments who had come from the west, were also on hand. Everyone drank hot *chang* from a community pot on the fire. It was the tradition here to be hospitable to travelers.

The monks, Kancha had explained, lived by begging from one village to another, singing songs of blessings. They wore rags patched together and ate very little. Some chewed *pun,* spitting the juice into their palms and rubbing it over their hands like lotion. Others chewed the root of the ganja. One of the monks, Yurev noticed, the eldest one, seemed the most observant. While his companions stared into the fire or gazed stoically into the night this one had taken to staring at the sahibs across the fire. The old Hindi watched Barbaree for a long while, never letting his eyes wander from him. Then he studied Abby. He almost never blinked. When it was Yurev's turn, and their eyes met, Yurev felt a decided uneasiness.

"He wonders if it is because they are too big, the breasts," Kancha continued, "or if they are injured." The little Nepalese sat in his squatting position between the chief and the sahibs. His eyes sparkled in the fire-light as he waited for a reply.

Barbaree cleared his throat. "What he wants to know, luv—"

"I *know* what he's talking about," Abby said, and to Kancha: "Tell his goddamn holiness that it's none of his friggin' business."

Kancha frowned without understanding, looked to Barbaree.

"It is the way of memsahibs in the south," Barbaree said with a smile. "Not too big, not injured. Just fashion."

Kancha nodded, but by his expression he wasn't convinced. He spoke to the chief, who passed on the news to the monks, who seemed most interested. There was much conferring and shaking of heads.

"Jack, do you think we could get the honorable chief to move on to another subject? I think we've pretty well covered the anatomy of the white sahib—red hair, blue eyes, white skin . . . and the rest."

"I told you to expect this sort of thing. You're an oddity up here. Hill people have never seen a white woman before—"

She looked at Yurev. "You hear that, an oddity? Hey, this isn't so funny, you know."

"Of course not." Yurev covered his mouth with his hand. "But almost worth the trip." He was getting a little back, which she seemed to realize when she'd calmed down.

She held out her cup. "Give me some more *chang.*"

"Begging your pardons, memsahib." Kancha, eyes bright, had another question. "The chief say—"

"I'm not taking anything off, if that's what he has on his mind."

"No, by jove, indeed not, memsahib. The chief say only what is the color of a white memsahib's sweetmilk?"

"What?"

"The chief say—"

"Suckling milk," Barbaree said.

"Suckling—all right, that's it. What am I now, a goddamn cow?"

"Don't exercise yourself, luv. They're only curious. It's their nature to—"

"Screw that. Before we get around to breeding habits, tell his honorable self to buy a ticket to Joliet if he's so interested. I'm not—"

"Kawali baul bhairavi."

Abby turned toward the monk who had spoken, the first one who had uttered a sound all evening. It was the old one, the one who had been watching them. Another monk raised his reed instrument, a *sahnai*, and began to play.

"What—"

The chief spoke to Kancha as the ragged Hindis began to rock side to side to the sound of the music. The old one, darkly wrinkled and without teeth, started a chant, and after a moment the others joined in.

"The chief say that the wise ones, they wish to sing a most pious song," Kancha said. "To lift the anger from the night."

Abby glanced at Yurev, who shrugged.

"This most pious song, it is to honor the memsahib," Kancha said.

The monks' song gathered some volume, though it was still not really loud.

"This most pious song, it is called the White Goddess."

The Hindis' chant became animated as the monks began making gestures and clapping their hands. They sat in a row and rocked, their shoulders rubbing together as they leaned to the left and to the right. It was only then that Yurev saw the medallion that the old one wore around his neck. It was a small metal disk, on a metal chain, worn and darkened with age. It contained the image of a beast tangled in chains.

"What do the words mean, Kancha?" Abby said.

"It is praise to Shiva, the One to Become Many, lord of destruction." The Nepalese listened a moment, concentrating on the group across the fire. "It goes . . . 'In his hair the Ganges plays . . . and seated on his lap the White Goddess caresses him . . .' "

The chant was louder now, the sound of the *sahnai* pitched high.

" 'Holding in his hand the garland of skulls . . . day and night he drinks the cup of poison . . . and seated in his lap the White Goddess caresses him . . .' "

Yurev looked into the old man's pit-black eyes that reflected the flickering flames between them.

" 'Wearing at his waist the skin of a beast . . . a scorpion tied as an armlet . . . this merciless youth spends his life . . . and seated on his lap . . . the White Goddess caresses him . . .' "

"Sha sa ma . . ."

The old one spoke fast and loud, and then the chanting abruptly ended. The other monks bowed their heads, but the old one stared at Yurev.

Abby looked at Kancha. "What—"

"*Om mani padme hum,*" the old one said. The monks repeated his words, touching their heads to the ground. "*Om mani padme hum . . . Om mani padme hum . . .*"

"What are they doing?" Abby looked to Barbaree. "Jack?"

"I don't know."

"It is mantra," Kancha said.

"*Om mani padme hum . . .*"

"What's mantra?"

"A prayer, memsahib." Kancha set his cup down. He touched his head to the ground. "To invoking the compassionate one, Avalokitesvara, the Buddha To Come . . . for protection."

The old one spoke to Kancha, but his eyes were still on Yurev. "The old one is afraid, Yurey-bishy," Kancha said to Yurev. "He says . . . he says you have been here before . . ."

Yurev said nothing. He just watched the old man.

"*Om mani padme hum.*"

Now the chief was touching his head to the ground, and the gathered villagers followed his example.

"What the *hell* is going on?" Abby said. She looked at Yurev.

"It means 'hail to the jewel of the lotus,' what they're chanting," Yurev said.

"Hail . . . to *what?*"

"The lotus is a symbol of man . . . man's heart. The jewel"—he took his eyes off the old man and looked at Abby—"represents the wisdom of man through which he may achieve deliverance."

"You know about this stuff?"

"Someone explained it to me once. It's interpreted several different ways. Basically it represents the unity of male and female principles."

"What was that about you being here before?"

Yurev shook his head. "No, he doesn't mean me. He's talking about someone else."

"Another white man?"

Yurev frowned. Abby's sudden probing interest made him uncomfortable. Of course she could not know about Fa Shing's encounter with Hoover thirty years ago . . . "I don't know." And to change the subject he pointed to the medallion around the old one's neck. "Kancha, ask him where he got that."

Kancha did, then said, "The wise one say it is charm against evilness. Come from Back of Beyond."

"High hills mumbo-jumbo," Barbaree said, getting to his feet. He flicked his cup and *chang* splashed into the fire, sending embers flying. Kancha moved back, brushing his pants leg. Barbaree walked between Yurev and Abby and squatted down. "Don't let's get into telling superstitious stories, old sport," he said in a low voice. "Kancha's a good man but he spooks easy. I don't hold much to the myths and legends that come out of these hills . . . and we don't need to hear talk of devil dogs and sacred stones from a band of drugged-up monks."

Abby scooted slightly closer. "Devil dogs?"

"Tibetan hounds," Barbaree said. "They roam wild up in the high hills. Fearless as a mongoose and ten times bigger."

"There's some religious significance—?"

"Everything up here is invested with religious import, luv." Barbaree reached to the communal pot and dipped his cup into the *chang*. "What say we have one more go here and turn in. We're off again at dawn, you know."

"It was just getting interesting."

"Interesting?" Barbaree shook his head and sipped the *chang*. The monks were quiet now, their heads bowed before the fire. Barbaree smiled. "I'll show you something interesting. Tomorrow."

Abby glanced up. "And that is?"

"We reach the Kali Gandaki tomorrow. I think you'll find it more than interesting, luv."

"Why's that?"

"It's sacred to Hindus, like Ganges. Even its river stones. Some of them are more valuable than gold. But it has other interesting qualities." Barbaree turned to the Nepalese guide. "Isn't that so, Kancha?"

"Oh, yes, by jove, indeed, yes," Kancha said, nodding vigorously. He had moved back into the circle of conversation, squatting beside Barbaree. "Kali Gandaki mean river of black womans, very sacred. From Kali, female side to Shiva. Big damn river. Long time falling."

"I've seen big rivers," Abby said.

"Not like this one, luv. It's black."

"Black?"

"Close enough." Barbaree gave Kancha a conspiratorial smile. When he looked at Abby again he nodded. "There's also a bridge, luv."

◆ SEVEN

It wasn't a bridge at all. It was a rope.

They had climbed all day up the rocky trail through scrub pines and stands of bamboo, and when they reached the summit of the last hill even Niro was tired. She had stopped often after the midday meal, sweat-lathered, and eaten dandelions and morning glories wherever she could find them, and Yurev had broken several sticks across her rump to get her attention back on the trail.

Mercifully, the sun hung behind heavy clouds most of the day, and a few times Yurev felt raindrops, but nothing came of them except that the air became oppressively humid. But it was not Niro's recalcitrant ways or the humidity or the backbreaking trek up that combined to make life hell. It was the porcupine. Yurev had thought about it since dawn. It had to have been the porcupine. Somewhere in his gut something disagreed violently with the rodent meat. When he finally joined Abby at the ridge of the hill he was sore, tired, and wholly unprepared for what lay before them—the Kali Gandaki gorge.

It stretched west to east like a giant tear in the planet, disappearing in a gray mist downstream. The walls on both sides were steep and dark, falling away to the monsoon-swollen torrent at least three thousand feet below. The water thrashed between narrow banks like a storm at sea, crashing over dark boulders and showering dingy spray thirty feet above its own ashy mist. The river seemed to swallow light—nothing at the bottom of the gorge had a color lighter than pewter. And the sound that rose up from there was like a hundred trains speeding into hell. Barbaree was right. The river was black. At this height, looking down into that raging fury, it could be nothing else.

"He should have told me about this." Abby was seated on a boulder, her stave across her lap. She was staring across the gorge. "Christ."

Yurev tied Niro's harness to the branch of a cotton tree where the other pony was tethered. He moved carefully to where Abby was perched. Just below, the stump of a tree hung tenuously to the side of the cliff. Tall, wicked shards of splintered wood, weathered to black, poked out from its center as if some enormous creature had broken its spine and ripped it in two. He glanced across to the facing cliff. All along the ridge were other stumps, and the view reminded him of what Kancha had said the night before about the black goddess Kali—Devourer of All Things.

Yurev sat beside Abby. "Well, he said it would be interesting."

"The son of a bitch."

Yurev glanced around. "Where is Jack-bishy?" He looked at her. "You haven't heaved him over?"

The sound of the river nearly drowned her words. "Down there," she shouted, pointing with her stave. "Inspecting the Brooklyn Bridge."

Yurev followed the line of the stave. A thousand feet below on a ledge that jutted out from the face of the cliff wall he saw Kancha testing the timber anchors that held the bridge in place. The bridge—so-called—consisted of three parallel rope lines attached to form a V. It spanned the 150-foot gulf across the gorge. The rope bridge sagged fifteen to twenty feet below level at its middle. It didn't sway in the breeze like the bridge at Tinau Khola. It swung in the wind.

Yurev leaned back. His stomach felt suddenly heavy.

"It's a big joke to him," Abby said. "Something interesting, he says. It's not like other rivers, he says." She glanced down into the rapids. "The bastard."

"It would be pointless, I suppose, to ask if there were another—"

"The only way we get our *arses* from here"—she pointed to the opposite ridge—"to there, in the immortal words of our honorable guide, is on that *bit of hemp.*"

Yurev watched the rope bridge swing in an updraft. "What about the ponies?"

"They stay here," Barbaree said. Yurev turned to see the Englishman climb up the steep footpath that led down the face of the cliff to the bridge. He used his hands on his knees to get the last few steps up. "From now on we pack our own." His face was glistening with sweat.

"You're a real comedian," Abby said. "Why didn't you tell us about this, this crack in the earth?"

"Never mind that." Barbaree looked at Yurev. "How far back are the coolies?" He wasn't smiling.

Yurev glanced back down the trail. "Ten minutes. Not far. Why?"

"We have to move quickly." Barbaree nodded at the sky. "There's a storm moving down from the hills. I want to get across before it arrives."

Abby slid down from her boulder. "Storm?"

"Rain squall," Barbaree said. "Start unpacking the ponies. I'll leave one of the coolies with the pack animals. Kancha will rope the gear together, and we'll start across as soon as it's done."

"Wait a minute." Abby looked up at the sky. Massive clouds to the north blotted out the high hills. "We're going now? I thought you said we'd cross in the morning. When there was more light."

"Plans change."

"Why?"

"Luv, there isn't time to—"

"Goddammit, I'm getting tired of you only giving me bits and pieces! What the hell's the rush?"

Barbaree pointed at the dark clouds. "We're going to have a bloody cold rain in less than an hour. In these hills that means we could have rain for two hours or two days, and we can't cross the bridge in a rainstorm. I don't fancy sitting on this bloody hill waiting for it to stop. Ratnapa is only half a day from the top of that ridge; we can be there this time tomorrow. Kancha says there are caves on that side of the gorge. If we move we can sit nice and cozy in a dry place with a fire. Now, luv, what would *you* like to do—wait out the weather here or over there?"

"Look, I just wanted to be kept informed—"

"You just do what I tell you and we'll get along fine, luv. You hired me as a guide, so trust me to guide."

"If we stay here . . . if we wait, what are the chances that the storm will only last a few hours?"

"I don't know. You can't ever tell in these hills. But I do know two things. One, hemp rope absorbs water like a dry camel. It's up to ten times heavier wet than dry, and when it's stretched out nearly two hundred feet —like this bridge—we're talking about tons. That kind of weight makes rope stretch, which has an unfavorable effect on its tensile strength. I'm not keen to test it further with the added weight of four people packing gear across it—most particularly if I'm one of them. All clear?"

Abby only nodded.

"All right, then, I suggest that you and Yurey unload the packs. Send the coolies down as quickly as they get here. I'm going back to help Kancha with the harness. Leave the tents."

"Harness?"

"I'll explain it when you get to the bridge." Barbaree gave Abby a challenging look. "Unless you'd like it explained *now.*" No answer. "Anything else?"

Yurev cleared his throat. "What was the other thing?"

Barbaree turned quickly to look at him. "What?"

"You said there were two things—"

"Mineral deposits," Barbaree said impatiently. "The hills around here are full of ore—iron, zinc, boron, copper . . . you don't want to be sitting on top of one when a storm passes over."

"Why not?"

"Because of that . . ." Barbaree pointed to the splintered remains of a large pine tree like those Yurev had noticed scattered across the opposite ridge. "The river is only Kali's unruly tongue," he said. "Lightning is her bloody bite."

Walking a rope bridge, Barbaree had said, was not dangerous unless someone told you it was. No one had ever told Kancha. To the little Nepalese, crossing bridges made of ropes and bamboo was as routine a way of life as paved streets and sidewalks were to sahibs. He didn't think twice about crossing one. It was not even an adventure.

"A piece of cake," Barbaree was saying as they all stood on the wide ledge in front of the bridge. A shelter about six feet deep had been chiseled into the rock face as a resting place for travelers. Lagna had been chosen to stay behind in this crude shelter, fortified with the gear that was not to be carried further, including most of Kancha's pots and pans. It had taken twenty minutes to unload the ponies, and the sky was already gray with forbidding clouds.

Yurev squinted across the gorge at the mist the ropes disappeared into, searching for some confirmation that the bridge actually was attached to something solid on the other side. Barbaree's claims about the harness as a safety factor gave him little comfort. Abby, from the set of her jaw, had similar thoughts.

"Kancha will go first," Barbaree was saying, "then you, luv, then Kalu, Yurev, and me. Lagna will stay at this end and play the rope out from the anchor."

The safety harness consisted of five utility ropes knotted together into one length. At fifty-foot intervals it was made into waist loops for each of the crossers. When Kancha reached the other side he would secure his end to a support timber before Barbaree left, ensuring, Barbaree promised, that at all times the harness would be anchored. There was, he said, no problem.

"I get the theory," Abby said. "Just tell me how the hell we're supposed to walk on that thing." She nodded at the bridge. The wind was holding it to a thirty-degree angle.

"She'll flatten out once there's weight on her," Barbaree told them. "You see all those vertical ties between the handrails and the spine? They're two feet apart all the way across. Use them like steppingstones. Hook the heels of your boots over them as you move across. Really, there's nothing to it. The hill people have been doing this for centuries, luv."

"You say that like you figure they've got a leg up on civilization," Abby said. "The almighty hill people, who recently discovered the wheel."

Little Kancha, in his corporal's blouse, moved tentatively at first, stepping in his bare feet from one tie to the next. His was the heaviest pack, and it rode high on his back, obscuring his head. Barbaree was right about the bridge: the further Kancha moved out from the ledge, adding weight toward the middle, the less the oscillation effect of the wind. Barbaree played out the rope, keeping it from fouling until the slack was used up. Kancha twisted himself to look back, gave Abby a smile of encouragement.

"All right, luv." Barbaree thumped the top of her pack with his hand. "Just one step at a time. Keep the same pace as Kancha. Keep the rope as taut as—"

"Christ, do you *never* shut up." She took her first step, her gloved hands gripping the handrail ropes tightly. To Kancha she yelled, "Go."

Yurev watched as the two figures moved slowly above the gorge. As Kancha took a step, Abby did the same, following his lead. The rope between them drooped slightly because of the distance, but Abby kept it taut. Below, the water churned ferociously. Even the whitecaps were gray. The bridge swayed even less now, but with the new weight it sagged more, forcing Kancha and Abby to walk, in effect, downhill.

As Kalu started out, Yurev felt a raindrop. And another. Kancha was halfway across, the bridge sagging directly above the river, and Yurev realized that the rain would start long before everyone was on the other side. He looked at Barbaree.

"I know," Barbaree said as he glanced at the sky. "It's moving faster than I thought."

"We're going to be out there when it hits . . . all of us."

"You're not bothered about getting wet?"

"I'm bothered about rope as thirsty as camels and tensile strength and ten-to-one-weight ratios."

"I wouldn't worry about that, old sport. Anyway, if anyone should worry it should be me. I'm the last to cross."

"But you said—"

"I can't very well call them back, now, can I?" Barbaree said as he handed the harness rope over. "Keep this tight on Kalu. You're next."

The rain started just as Yurev moved to the mouth of the bridge, beginning gently, washing over him, pinging against his hat. When he felt the tug of the rope around his waist, as Kalu took up the last of the slack, he made his first step, holding tight to the handrails. Barbaree said something but Yurev didn't hear . . . his whole concentration was now on the coolie girl ahead of him, waiting for her to take a step, reaching out his foot and catching his heel in the tie and pulling himself another two feet closer to the opposite wall. He fought thinking that he was two thousand feet above a raging black river or that the rain was increasing, making his leather gloves slippery on the thick hemp. The only thing in the world real to him was Kalu, and following her precisely.

When the storm broke, Yurev heard it before he saw it. And then it was all around him, nearly blotting out all light. Not only could he not see the cliff wall ahead of him, but Kalu was at best a vague blur. The sensation was terrifying. He could feel the heavy rain pounding the ropes through his hands and feet. His clothes were instantly soaked, and his pack quickly took on double its weight. A stream of the bone-chilling wetness rolled off his hat down his neck, but the image in his mind was of something else—broken jagged tree trunks, split and splintered by fire from the sky.

. . . Now he heard Barbaree's voice through the din, but knew he couldn't turn to look at him or even hope to see him if he did. He assumed Barbaree was urging him forward, yelling at him to move, but he couldn't move. Kalu wasn't moving. Nobody was moving. They were all stranded there, frozen, waiting for Kali's death kiss.

"Turn away from the storm." The Englishman's words penetrated the icy rain. *"Turn your pack to the rain."*

He must have been yelling at the top of his lungs, Yurev thought. Abby was right, the man was a lunatic. But what difference did it make—he was soaked, his hands were numb even with the gloves. He badly wanted to yell something back at Barbaree, something obscene and fitting, but of course it was pointless. Doubly so when from the corner of his eye he saw a glimmer of white, and his breath caught in his throat as a sheet of whiteness came crashing toward them down the gorge. There was only time to duck, twisting his back toward it. What he saw, he realized, wasn't rain and it wasn't snow. It was hail.

The rope under his feet twanged with each impact. The bridge swayed and creaked. Through his feet he could see the hailstones pelting the river and exploding against the black boulders. The hail was enormous, easily as large as his fist. One struck his pack, jolting his chin into the handrail. Another disintegrated against his safari hat, hitting it squarely in the center, making his head ring. He knew if one hit either of his hands he'd be finished, he'd never be able to pull himself along the rope with crushed knuckles—

The jerk on the harness punched the air out of his lungs and he gasped, losing the heelhold of his left boot. For a terrifying moment one leg dangled between the ties, and he nearly pitched forward from the weight of the pack. Panic gave him strength, and he pulled himself up, frantically trying for and finding purchase in the next tie. The pull on the harness forced him to move forward again. He could see nothing except streaks of hail slashing with the rain ahead of him. Kalu, with an incredible burst of strength, was actually able to pull him.

Yurev moved as fast as he dared, stepping from one tie to the next, wanting to get a solid hold with one boot before committing the other. The tension on the harness was sawing at his waist, slivers of the rope cut into the skin at his back. He remembered that Kancha by now had tied his end off at the other side. He didn't think it was likely that the little Nepalese could be pulling all this weight, but anything was possible in these hills. To maintain his balance he had to move in an awkward, nearly sitting position, his feet rigid ahead of him, his body bent at the waist and his hands well back, gripping the handrail ropes at eye level. He felt as if he were the anchor in a tug-of-war contest, and his side was losing.

As he was reaching with his left foot, probing for the next tie, a hailstone struck his leg in the meaty part above the knee. The sudden pain had a paralyzing effect . . . the senseless leg shot through the space between the ties, pitching him forward, ripping the handrails out of his grasp from the momentum. With nothing to hold him back he nearly flew forward . . . tie supports spinning past as the harness dragged him across the bridge's coarse, hairy spine. He tried to catch hold of the ties but was dragged too fast, and his wet gloves slipped away at every attempt. When the jolting stop came it nearly broke his back, and for a time—he could not tell how long—his mind was black. It was Abby's voice that roused him out of it.

"Yurey . . . *Yurey*. For chrissake answer me . . ."

Yurev opened his eyes, and the world was upside down.

"Yurey?"

It took a moment to realize his situation, and when he did he was too frozen with fear to talk. He'd fallen through the bridge, at least partly. Something held him at the waist, caught in the spine of the bridge. The harness loop cut into his back, under the pack, and the rope was tight against his chest. Dangling below him, fifty feet down, was Kalu, spinning slowly in the rain. Her limp body was doubled over in the waist loop, head down. One strap of her pack had ripped along the seam. It hung below her, swinging back and forth like a pendulum. Kalu hadn't been pulling him at all, Yurev realized. A broken tie hung down beside his head. She'd stepped on it, and it broke. She'd dropped through the bridge, and her falling weight had dragged him to this point.

"Yurey!"

He tried to look up but his pack was jammed against the back of his neck. His hat was gone. Rain matted his hair. Only after staring at the river several seconds did he realize the hail had passed.

"Yes . . . I'm stuck." He couldn't see Abby, rain dripped into his face from his clothes, but she was very near. He suddenly realized that if he'd been dragged to this place by Kalu's falling weight then Abby must have been, too. She had been on the other side of the girl. It also occurred to him that one hundred feet of the harness hung below him, which meant that Kancha hadn't yet reached the other side and that Barbaree, behind him, was fifty feet or more from the ledge. It meant that the harness was not anchored to either side.

"Give me your arm." Abby's voice was remarkably calm. "C'mon, Goddammit, you want to die on this frigging thing?"

Yurev moved his right arm. It seemed a monstrous task. Raising his arm tightened the rope at his back. The bridge creaked. Water rolled down his sleeve into his face.

"More."

He raised his arm and felt her hand. She pulled, guiding his hand to something thick and solid.

"That's the spine," she said. "Can you pull yourself up?"

"I—"

"Don't think about it. *Do* it."

Yurev tried but there was just too much weight. He heard Barbaree's voice but couldn't make out the words.

"Hold on, Yurey. Jack says to cut the straps off your pack. Hold on."

Yurev waited, staring at the river, and at Kalu. She'd turned herself and looked up at him. A flicker of understanding passed through her eyes. She wriggled her body, trying to work the pack straps off her shoulders. He nodded, trying to encourage her. She was doing the right thing, every bit of weight they could eliminate was that much less to lift. Meanwhile, Abby was cutting; he could feel the sawing motion of her knife, and when it was done he could reach higher on the spine and have better leverage.

"Okay, Yurey, hold on, I'm going to kick the pack over your other shoulder. Let it drop off."

"No . . . it'll hit Kalu."

"Then bend your arm. When it rolls off your back, swing it out and away from her."

Abby kicked, and the weight of the pack slid over his head. He caught it by the other strap and, swinging twice, let it drop, saw it just sail past Kalu. The coolie girl, her face shiny with rain, gave him an acknowledging grin. She'd almost worked out of her own pack when Yurev realized that it was all wrong—

"No, *no. Wait.*"

Kalu glanced at him with a questioning look as her pack dropped away, tumbling through space. The harness loop was positioned midway on her chest, riding up, as it had, from her waist. The pack had been a counterweight, balancing her in the harness, but as soon as it was gone the equilibrium was upset.

Kalu slipped out of the loop, still looking at Yurev.

The bridge gave a short bounce, the harness snapped up at the loss of weight, and Kalu was falling in a lazy half-somersault, down and down, following the pack. . . . She hit the water nearly upright, slightly ahead of a large boulder, the beads around her neck trailing after her body into the churning blackness. Yurev stared at the river. The rain pelted over her grave. Her body did not return to the surface. Kali Gandaki had swallowed her whole.

"Yurey . . . Jesus . . ."

Yurev pulled himself up onto the spine with Abby's help. There was a rope burn alongside her right eye, her hair hung down over her face, whipped by the wind and rain.

"Yurey, I . . ." She swallowed. If she was crying he couldn't tell. "I'm sorry, Christ . . ." She looked down into the river.

"Give me your knife."

Abby pushed the hair out of her face. "What?"

"The knife." He held out his hand.

She handed it to him and watched as he cut the harness that still dangled below them. It dropped, squirming like a snake, and disappeared into the water.

Yurev nodded toward Kancha. "Go on," he said to Abby. "Jack and I will wait until you two are off the bridge."

"But—"

"Nobody else is going to die today," Yurev said. "Go on."

He watched her move up the bridge, stepping carefully over the ties. When she was little more than a blur in the rain he hauled himself up and signaled to Barbaree to move. It had been the weapon at his side that saved him from following Kalu through the broken tie. The holster had caught on the spine. It was only dumb luck, he realized, that he hadn't been the one to drop into the abyss.

Fa Shing, and an ancient old man, would not have agreed.

◆ EIGHT

THE CAVE WALLS FLICKERED in the light of the fire, the air smelled of wet yak blankets. Scratched and gouged into the rock, the names and artwork of previous travelers loomed darkly on the walls, accented by shadow in the glow of fire. Outside, rain attacked the cliff with unabated fury. Kancha's crackling fire and Kali's incessant wind were the only other sounds.

For an hour after they had found the cave, conversation was limited to accomplishing the tasks at hand. Kancha built a fire from a pile of dry wood stored by previous tenants. Barbaree set about looking after the casualties. Abby had simple rope burns on one arm and above her eye. Yurev's abrasions were more severe. His waist was raw where the rope had sawed across his skin, and his back was scraped behind the shoulder blades, where it bled. Barbaree plucked bits of the rope's hairy fiber from Yurev's back. The medical kit had been in Kalu's pack so Barbaree used Dewar's Scotch whiskey, poured from his flask over Yurev's raw skin, as antiseptic. As painkiller, Kancha boiled rice and ganja—a popular hill treatment— mixed it with mud and applied it to Yurev's wounds. Barbaree bound them up with one of Kancha's turbans. Afterward, they placed their boots before the fire and wore yak blankets while their clothes dried, steaming in the flickering light. Huddled around the fire, they ate Kancha's rice cakes in silence while the rain drummed outside.

"I've taken stock of things. We have enough water and rice to get us through tomorrow, so food isn't critical. We're only half a day's march from Ratnapa." Barbaree had taken inventory of the remaining packs. He held the list to catch the light while he read. "We've lost the blankets except these, the binoculars, half the ration of cigarettes, eight of twelve boxes of cartridges, the balance of our marching clothing, rope and the medical kit." He glanced around at the figures in front of the fire. "It could have been worse."

"Could have been?" Yurev looked up at him. "How?"

"I know we're all exhausted," Barbaree said in a subdued tone. "We've been through something . . . I think the more rest we can get, the better."

Abby's face was golden-red in the wavering light. She smoked a cigarette, her first since they'd left Butwal. When she spoke she did not glance up from the fire. "Are we going to say anything about that girl or just ignore the fact that she's dead?"

"It wasn't anyone's fault, what happened," Barbaree said.

"That doesn't make it any less horrible." She looked up. "What will happen to her body?"

"It isn't for you to worry—"

"What?"

"It was an unfortunate accident. You have to be thick-skinned about this sort of thing. Sometimes it happens. You can't allow yourself to take it personally."

"Thick-skinned? I walked up and down these miserable hills for three days with that girl. I shared food with her. She rubbed lotion on my blistered feet and showed me how to massage the soreness out of my arms and legs. She wasn't my best friend in the world but I liked her. Then I watch her fall two thousand feet into a black river and disappear." Abby looked at Barbaree. "Don't tell me not to take it personally."

Barbaree sighed.

"What will happen to her body?"

"It will wash down river."

"And?"

"Someone will find it and do the proper thing."

"Someone?"

"What do you suggest, that we scale down the cliff and search ourselves? Jeopardize our lives in *that* river? We can't do that. I'm sorry, but there it is. The body is miles away by now. There isn't anything we can do . . . nothing."

"And what do we tell her family when we get back to Butwal? Go look down river?"

"This isn't accomplishing anything, luv. Death is accepted up here. It's—"

"Will you stop with that hill-people-understand-everything crap? They're human, aren't they? They *feel*, don't they?" Abby looked at Kancha, squatting on the other side of the fire, but he only stared back at her. "Christ." She threw her cigarette into the coals and ran her fingers through her tangled hair. Her eyes glistened in the light of the fire. "All right, forget it."

"Abby—"

"I said skip it." She rolled her blanket under one arm and got to her feet. "My clothes are dry. I'm going to sleep."

Yurev watched her find a place at the rear of the cave. She doubled the blanket and lay between the folds, her back to the fire. In a few minutes Barbaree retired, too. He moved to the mouth of the cave and sat against a rock, his blanket and his flask to keep him warm, and stared at the rain.

Kancha stoked the fire with a few more branches, then gathered the boots and set them together with the packs. When he returned, he got into his corporal jacket that had been propped on sticks beside the fire.

"You sleep now, Yurey-bishy. Heal fast. Kancha watch fire."

Yurev nodded. His back didn't hurt as much as it had earlier. The rice and ganja treatment worked, but only when he didn't move. He decided to sleep beside the fire.

"I'll just lie here, Kancha."

The little Nepalese settled into his familiar pose. "Can fix *chang*. You sleep good."

"No, I'll be fine."

"Kancha pretty good damn cook, you bet you life." He smiled but there wasn't any life in it.

"I know . . . good damn cook." Yurev waited a moment, trying to find the words. "I'm sorry, Kancha. I am. I tried but . . . I'm sorry . . ."

"Thank you most courteously, Yurey-bishy. You pretty good damn boss, I think. Strong here"—he touched his head, then his chest—"and here also." He pushed a charred branch deep into the fire. "It is great sadness to memsahib, but should not be," Kancha said, glancing back at Abby. "Coolie girl free now. Kalu good coolie girl. Maybe in next life have good karma, be like memsahib."

Yurev nodded. "Yes. Maybe, yes." He lay his head down and stared at the flickering ceiling. For the first time in two years he slept without remembering Celeste.

◆ NINE

At dawn Yurev woke sore and itching. Kancha's treatment had soothed the pain of Yurev's scrapes during the night but the rope burns were alive again and simply getting to his feet was painful as the exercise stretched his raw skin. The muscles in his legs and upper body were sore as well, and the spot where the hailstone had struck his leg was bruised and tender.

Kancha prepared a new painkilling solution, this time *chang* and ganja. He soaked the turban bandage in the mixture and wrapped it around Yurev's chest so that it covered the burns on his back.

Breakfast was two rice cakes washed down with *chang*. Yurev's pain had fueled his appetite, and he ate without commenting on the sand that invariably accompanied Kancha's cooking. The meal was quiet. Abby, who had usually something to say about the chill of early morning, sat with her blanket around her shoulders, staring at the fire, and afterward smoked a cigarette. Barbaree was the busy one, eating and moving at once, preoccupied with loading the packs so the weight would be equally distributed among the travelers and hurrying Kancha as the Nepalese moved in and out of the cave gathering firewood to replace what they'd used.

The rain had stopped during the night, and as they left the cave, climbing along the ledge of the cliff toward the summit, Yurev was struck by the freshness in the air. The sky was clear and still slightly pink with dawn. Hoopoe birds chirped busily from branches of red-blossoming cotton trees, and the water at the bottom of the slate-colored gorge slid downriver with silent grace. There was nothing to mark the nightmare that only a few hours ago had visited this place.

* * *

At the top of the ridge, sixty-five hundred feet, Barbaree reckoned, the vista ahead was at once magnificent and disconcerting. As far as Yurev could see were hills of vivid shades of green. Further on, rising in the mist of morning, were the gray-blue foothills of the high hills. Flanking the orange sun, the white majestic peaks of Annapurna and Dhaulagiri overshadowed the landscape like colossal icebergs floating with the clouds. The view gave Yurev a sudden uneasiness, as if from somewhere beyond those peaks Ushas, Goddess of Dawn, was watching. He shook his head to exorcise her.

"Mind your step," Barbaree said. He'd had Kancha cut new staves for each of them, and now stamped his into the soft soil. "The trail may be a bit slick from the rain. Watch also for the odd viper. They'll be out looking for a warm spot to sun themselves, away from the moist ground."

"Snakes?" Abby glanced at the ground.

"Not so much on the trail as on rocks. Just mind where you sit."

"What do we do if we see one?"

"Leave it alone. That's the first rule. Some of the blokes up here believe snakes are godly creatures. Many's the time a native has been bitten trying to woo one, and been dispatched to his next life."

"Leave it alone," Abby repeated. She nodded. "Right. How do you know when they're angry?"

"Normally a snake will coil before it strikes. But they aren't very quick. Even so, if necessary, kill the bloody thing if you have a clean shot at its head."

"Shoot it?" Abby glanced at Yurev. "With this pack I'm going to wrestle out my twelve-pound cannon, cock it twice, aim with both hands and shoot a goddamn snake *before* it bites me?"

"No, no." Barbaree indicated his stave. "Crush it . . . like this." With a quick overhead motion Barbaree sliced the air with his staff, smashing it against a rock. The report echoed in the trees, sending several birds into the sky.

Yurev gripped his stave. He tried to imagine himself using it as nimbly as Barbaree had demonstrated. His back was on fire under the weight of the pack as sweat seeped into his burns. Just carrying the stave was going to be a burden. "And if the unfortunate happens and we're bitten—"

"Don't *let* it happen," Barbaree said quickly. "Not that it would do any good for snake bites, but we don't even have our medical kit anymore."

Yurev nodded. He glanced across the hills before them. It wasn't such a magnificent sight after all, he decided.

They marched for six hours, Barbaree leading. It hadn't been as hot as the previous days even though there were no clouds, but Yurev sweated his shirt through anyway. His waist chafed from the weight of the gunbelt, and his back was raw. Finally he took off his shirt, tied the pack to his stave and carried it on his shoulder, careful to keep up with Kancha. It wasn't so bad, walking bare-chested. The bandages weren't tugged back and forth by the sweaty shirt, and he felt cooler. In six hours he saw a variety of beetles and other insects, also a tree toad, but not a single snake. He also quit sweating. It was a sign, he felt confident, that he was acclimating to the hills. . . .

"There it is. Yurey, c'mon, we're here." Abby beckoned from along the trail, waving Yurev on. "Ratnapa."

They had approached the village from the southwest, over a grassy rise that sloped toward a narrow stream. Yurev was relieved to see it; his legs were becoming heavy and his breathing labored. It was a prosperous-looking village sprawled on alluvial terraces. Beyond were small fields of buckwheat and barley. Ratnapa was larger than the other villages they'd passed through and was surrounded by a low stone wall that followed the contours of the rolling terrain. There were several white-washed stone houses and, on a higher elevation, a building three stories tall.

"That's the monastery," Abby said excitedly. "The tall building."

Yurev walked until he stood beside her. He felt a bit embarrassed that he was shirtless in front of her but was too tired to care. He leaned on his stave, dizzy and panting. He looked around the stave to give her a weak smile.

The breeze was warm on his face. Without a hat his head was exposed to the heat of the sun and now after only a half day's march he felt suddenly weak. Ratnapa was the goal he'd had in his mind for several hours, an oasis, and now that he was here the sense of relief he had been suppressing overpowered him.

"Yurey, look at . . . Yurey?"

It was the thirst that struck him first. His tongue seemed to fill every part of his mouth. Words slid apart on his lips.

"Do ou hab . . . wah-der . . ."

"Yurey? What's the matter?"

Then all his muscles rebelled all at once. His knees were helpless to hold him. Even as he saw the villagers coming to greet them he felt his hands slipping down the stave. He was looking at the rocky ground, his hand supporting him. It was his hand, he was sure it was but it looked so far away. The stones on the trail grew before his eyes into boulders, then balls of fire. That's when he felt the pain. It began at the top of his back, and in his mind's eye he saw strips of meat, sizzling in one of Kancha's pans, turning red and blistering over the fire from the stones. Despite the pain it was a ridiculous vision, Yurev thought. Stones didn't burn. He tried to look up to tell Abby. She would understand what nonsense it was. Kancha was a Pahari, a Buddhist hill man. He almost smiled at the very idea of it. Everyone knew Buddhists didn't eat meat. Not even porcupines. The whole idea was terribly silly . . .

"Keep his head up!"

Yurev recognized Barbaree's voice before his eyes focused. He was very cold, and he could hear the gurgling sounds of water running. When he opened his eyes he found himself sitting chest-deep in the stream. Dozens of villagers, many of them children, squatted on the banks watching.

"Wha—"

"Hold still, Yurey." Abby was behind him, keeping his head above water. Barbaree was standing in front of him, using his hat like a bucket, pouring water from the stream over Yurev's head. The water was shockingly cold.

"Did I not tell you to wear a hat, man?" the Englishman was shouting at him. "You don't expose yourself in these altitudes, you bloody fool. And you *never* take off your shirt."

His head spinning, Yurev tried to respond but got a mouthful of water for his effort.

"His face is cool," Abby said. Her voice was anxious. Yurev could feel her fingers at the back of his neck but couldn't understand what was happening.

"Pull him out, Kancha."

A hand dragged him by the hair over a muddy bank. He closed his eyes when he looked into the sun and rolled on his side to cough the water out of his lungs. Someone dropped a blanket over him. By the time he caught his breath Barbaree was beside him on one knee, in his face.

"Tell me your name?"

Yurev blinked water out of his eyes. "What?"

"Where were you born?"

"St. Pe . . . Peters . . . burg."

"Do you know where you are?"

Yurev saw Abby over Barbaree's shoulder. Her expression was grim.

"Answer me, you stupid sod."

"I—" Yurev glanced around him. Dozens of villagers seemed interested in the question even if they didn't understand the language. "Ratnapa . . . isn't it?"

Barbaree looked at Abby. "He'll probably be all right. I ought to bash him."

Yurev waited a moment until his breathing slowed down. He was still terribly thirsty. "Can I have water . . . to drink?"

"Later."

"I don't understand what hap—"

"You've almost cooked your own brain," Barbaree shot back. "Have you never heard of heatstroke? Bloody fortunate for you there was a stream nearby to lower your body temperature."

"Heat . . . stroke?" Yurev's head was still swimming. "Is that serious?"

"You stopped sweating," Barbaree said as if it should be obvious. "Without a hat or shirt to collect the perspiration and cool your skin it just evaporated. You used it all up, your sweat." He shook his head again. "Five more minutes and your brain would have fried, ten and you'd have been dead. Yes, as it happens, it is serious."

Yurev tried to get up but he hadn't the strength.

"Don't move." Barbaree motioned to Kancha, indicating the villagers. "Get a litter. Have some of these carry him the rest of the way." To Abby he said, "I'll go ahead and find the chief. This isn't exactly the sort of entrance I had in mind."

"Why the hell are you so angry?"

"Because it's a bad sign. Sahibs are supposed to present an impression of power to these people. Carrying Yurev in like this doesn't exactly promote that image. It undermines our bargaining edge."

When Abby looked down at Yurev he tried to apologize. "I'm sorry, Abby, I didn't—"

"Just, please, keep quiet. Okay?"

The little Nepalese helped Yurev onto a blanket and with six wiry villagers each clutching an edge lifted him and set off toward Ratnapa as dozens of villagers walked along beside, peering down at him. Yurev shaded his face from the sun. The sky was incredibly blue. Somewhere, before they put him down again, he closed his eyes.

* * *

"Boiled. Do you understand? Boiled? I'm not drinking it if it hasn't been boiled."

Yurev pushed the ladle away as the old woman tried to bring it to his lips. He was in a hut, sitting on a bed pallet with his back against the cool wall. The room was not lit except from sunlight that spilled in from the open doorway. He'd been awakened by this woman who smiled and jabbered and offered him water from the ladle. There was no one else in the hut and communicating with her was impossible.

"No. Only boiled water." He pushed the ladle away again. He did not know how long he'd been asleep. "Where are the others? The sahibs?"

The old woman shook her head. She held the ladle up. *"Chiya."*

"Tea?"

"Chiya." She shook her head again and raised the ladle slightly above her lips. She tipped the ladle, and the liquid poured into her mouth. When she looked at Yurev again she smiled. *"Chiya. Raamro chiya."*

Yurev recognized the word for good, meaning tasty. He also remembered that shaking the head was often an affirmative gesture. He tried to remember, but could not, the Nepalese word for boiled.

"Where are sahibs? Jack-bishy? Kancha?"

She shook her head. *"Khaanu . . . chiya."*

It was no use. Yurev took the ladle and drank. It was the most horrible liquid he'd ever tasted, but it was cool, and he realized that his body needed water.

"Raamro chiya," the old woman said with a smile.

"Raamro," Yurev said in surrender. He finished three ladlefuls. The taste didn't improve.

The old woman brought Yurev a large wooden bowl of *daal*, chickpea soup over rice. His thirst had affected his appetite, and he ate it all. He got up twice to look outside for the others and was met at the door by dozens of children eager to touch his arm and marvel at the hair. Yurev didn't know where Barbaree and the others were but assumed they'd gone to find Abby's Buddhist monk, the one from the photo. The simple exercise of getting up was very tiring. He decided that they'd left him here to rest so that was what he should do. The old woman lit some butter lamps and brought more *chiya* before leaving him alone. The rope burns on his back were not as painful as they had been on the trail but it worried him that he was so weak. His arms were like lead weights; just drinking tea was an effort. He tried to think about Lucknow and returning there

on the frontier train. The train compartment would be a place of luxury
compared to this. Even considering the man-eating flies.

It was nearly dark when Barbaree and Abby returned. Yurev heard
them arguing even before they reached the hut.

"No, it isn't possible. You hired me for Ratnapa and here we are."

"Look, if it's money I'll pay you double."

"No."

"What we agreed, plus a thousand."

"No."

"Pounds, I mean, not dollars . . . pounds."

"No!"

Barbaree came in first. He looked at Yurev and scowled. "This woman
is insane . . . bloody insane." He plopped down beside the vat of tea and
dipped the ladle in, gulping down the stuff, then wiping his mouth with
his sleeve.

"You're supposed to be the goddamn guide," Abby said. She remained
standing, hands on her hips. "You can take us there."

"I don't *want* to take you. Do you understand? It's six days one way,
easily that. It means two weeks just to get back here." Barbaree shook his
head. "No. The contract was to Ratnapa, and here we are."

"I'll pay—"

"*No.*"

Yurev looked at Kancha, who had taken a place against the wall, out
of the lines of fire. The little Nepalese stared at the dirt floor.

"Wherever you've been," Yurev said, "I take it that it didn't go altogether well." He stared at Abby. "Did you find the man in the photograph?" He was certain he already knew the answer.

Abby sat down cross-legged beside Yurev's pallet. "He isn't here."

"Dead?"

"No. He's at a monastery," she said, glaring at Barbaree. "A place our
so-called guide doesn't want to go."

"If you had the slightest appreciation for these hills you wouldn't want
to go there either," Barbaree shot back. "Especially not to Tramar-Dri."

"I'm the one who decides when we stop. You're just the hired—"

Yurev held up his hand. It was a chore, like raising a boat anchor.
"Please."

Abby gave him a fiery glance. "We're not going back."

"Please. I don't know what's happened. What's Tramar-Dri?"

"Tramar-Dri *gumpa*," she said. "It's a monastery." She pulled the
photo from her pack. "It's where *he* is, Yurey. He's *alive.*"

"But that doesn't explain—"

"We've been meeting with the village chief for hours. He spent most of the time giving us a history lesson. Ratnapa used to be the site of a small monastery but several years ago it was abandoned." She pointed to the middle-aged man in the picture. "He went to Tramar-Dri, our wandering monk. Ratnapa is his home but now he's the head holy one at that monastery . . . and he's got the stones. I showed this picture to the chief. He recognized the necklace."

Yurev nodded. "Six days? One way?"

"I don't care how far it is."

"You'd bloody well better consider it," Barbaree said. "You can't get there without me."

Yurev looked at the Englishman. "What does it matter? She said she'd pay for—"

"Tramar-Dri is up the Kali Gandaki gorge, around Dhaulagiri," Barbaree said. "Where we've been is a bloody picnic compared to the climb into those hills. I've seen Tramar-Dri. It's a rocky fortress sitting on a cliff, up a very dangerous mountain this time of year."

"But the monsoons are over."

"Don't you know what follows the rainy season?"

"You said winter wasn't for another two months," Yurev said.

"I was talking about here, in the foothills. It's all very cozy here." Barbaree held one hand near the floor. "Look, mate, we're here, see. Ratnapa. Sixty-five hundred feet elevation. It's still warm, green grass, flowers, all that." He held his other hand about a foot above the other. "Tramar-Dri is here. Another ten thousand feet up, see. That's above the timberline. There aren't even pines. No flowers. No green grass. Just bloody rocks and glaciers . . . and winter. Nobody goes *up* Dhaulagiri in winter." He glanced at Kancha. "Tell them."

Kancha wet his lips. He looked at Yurev. "Indeed, yes, Yurey-bishy. Tramar-Dri *gumpa* very high. Very cold place now. Many hill peoples come down. Go back after coldness."

Yurev looked at Abby.

"We're too close to stop now," she said.

"Maybe you'd better tell him why it's so important to you."

"Tell *him?*"

"That or go back."

Abby sat down against the wall, pulling her knees up and hugging them with her arms. "Goddammit!"

"It's the beads, isn't it?" Barbaree offered a smile. "In the picture you showed the chief. The rosary beads."

Abby glanced up.

Barbaree nodded to himself. "You're after the beads. I figured as much when you made such a fuss about them to the chief. All this archeological business is just a lot of rot. It's something to do with Alexander the Great, isn't it? The beads are artifacts, yes? What are they? Two thousand years old . . . more? You think it's worth your life to track down a handful of sweaty ancient beads?" The Englishman laughed. It was the first time he'd laughed since he shot the porcupine. "You're a pip, you are, luv." He smiled at Kancha. "Bloody beads!"

Kancha, almost in defense, returned the smile, even if he didn't understand.

"They aren't beads," Abby said quietly.

"Oh, no, course not. They're emeralds, aren't they? Rubies, maybe. Remnants of a great Greek treasure left behind, right?" Barbaree shook his head. "If you'd told me what you were after in Lucknow I could have saved us all a lot of exercise. There aren't any treasures in these hills, luv. No golden idols or fabulous gemstones fashioned as Buddha's third eye. Just Paharis and goats and a few poisonous snakes."

"They aren't beads." Abby sighed, glancing at Yurev before facing Barbaree. "They're diamonds."

"Diamonds? Oh, that's better. Much better." His amusement was contagious. Kancha was grinning now, too. "Yes, diamonds, I like that."

"Look, you asshole, they *are* diamonds. Alexander had them made as a necklace for Roxanne . . . his wife."

"How sentimental of him." Barbaree began laughing again. His eyes were watering when he got control of himself. "I'm sorry, luv. Truly. But you don't know how many centuries kings and potentates have been looking for such things in these hills. Nobody ever found any fortune . . . emeralds, rubies or diamond rosary—sorry, diamond necklaces. It's all fantasy, luv. Just fascinating stories to amuse the sahibs."

Abby turned to Yurev. "Will you say *something?*"

"Why, am I more credible? I think nothing we say will convince him to change his mind." Yurev raised an eyebrow toward Barbaree. "Yes?"

"Bloody right."

"You *want* to go back and start this all over again?" Abby's expression was more surprised than angry.

"I can wait until spring. I'm sure he's right about the danger. At least we know the necklace exists."

"Wait five months?"

Yurev shrugged. "Six, I think. Anyway, I think it may take that long to find another guide."

"We?" Barbaree cocked his head at Yurev. "You don't *really* believe this story of hers? I mean, diamonds, old boy? On a Buddhist priest?"

"There is evidence enough for me at least to be very curious."

"What evidence?"

"You saw the photograph. The fact is Alexander *did* have a diamond necklace made for Roxanne when he came to India. There were several historians who accompanied Alexander on his eastern conquests who wrote about it and some who made drawings. Anyway, I've seen the drawings. Whatever you think, they do at least match the necklace in that photograph."

"That's not proof."

"I didn't say it was proof, Jack. But it is very interesting. When Alexander left India, when he returned to Babylon, he didn't have the necklace. For twenty-three centuries the fate of Roxanne's necklace has been a mystery. Not a great mystery, I grant you that, but if the necklace in Tramar-Dri is the same one, then it opens the door to a truly great mystery."

Barbaree squinted. "And that is?"

"Shelkagari."

Kancha perked up. He'd been following the conversation with only polite interest, but when he heard the name his eyes found Yurev.

"All right, Yurey, that's enough," Abby said. "We don't have to tell him a goddamn thing."

"No, no, I want to hear this," Barbaree said. "What's Shelkagari?"

"A stone," Yurev said. "Quite a large one. Possibly the oldest ever found . . . and the largest."

"A diamond, you're saying?"

"Yes. According to some historians the stones in Roxanne's necklace were cut from it."

"They were called the Pearls of Light. I don't suppose you've ever heard of them."

"No, mate. Diamond necklaces don't come up in my circle. How big a rock are we talking about, this, this . . ."

"Shelkagari," Yurev said. He moistened his lips. He saw a glimmer of interest in Barbaree's eyes. "I don't know precisely. No one has ever seen it. I mean not since 326 B.C. The only physical description has it about the size of a calf's head." He held his hands out about twelve inches apart. "Perhaps this size."

"What!" Barbaree's mouth fell open. "Diamonds don't get that bloody big."

"Diamonds are rocks," Yurev said impatiently. "They don't grow. They get crushed. A billion years ago there may have been diamonds the size of Cheops' tomb inside the earth. They get heated, cooled, crushed and pulverized in their million-years journey to the surface. India was once the only diamond-mining area in the world, if you didn't know. A stone that size is not impossible."

Barbaree held his hands out, visualizing a stone between them. "A stone that big . . . it would be what, a thousand carats? Five thousand?"

"More," Yurev said. "It would be hard to speculate."

Barbaree looked at him. "Try."

"Possibly . . . thirty thousand carats."

"*Thirty*—"

"Maybe more. There is no way to know. That's why the necklace is so important. Yurev nodded at the photograph. "If that is Roxanne's necklace, then Shelkagari may actually exist. It's the key, you see."

Barbaree took the photograph and studied it. "And these diamonds—if they really are diamonds—how big are they?"

"Ten to fifteen carats each."

"And how much are they worth?"

Abby cut in quickly. "They don't have a value. The necklace is priceless, just as the artifacts from Egypt's Tutankhamun tomb are priceless. You can't put a price on it."

"Oh, sure you can, luv." Barbaree smiled. "They're diamonds, aren't they?" He looked at Yurev. "How much, just guessing now?"

"That's impossible to say. Abby's right. It isn't the commercial value of individual stones that is important here, it's the necklace itself."

"And you'd risk your life to find them?"

"At this point I'd say that depends on you," Yurev said. "Are you interested or not?"

The Englishman rubbed the line of his jaw. He stared at Abby for some time. "And you were going to pay me five hundred American dollars for the privilege, weren't you? To find a fortune in bloody diamonds. You walk away with a treasure while ole Jack Barbaree gets stuffed."

"I would have paid you more," Abby said defensively. "I *will* pay you more. Still, we haven't found it yet. We don't know for sure that—"

"How much is it worth to you . . . to get it now?"

"What?"

"If I take you to Tramar-Dri. Say we find the necklace. How much is it worth to you?"

Abby shook her head. "I told you I'd pay—"

"I'm not talking about a thousand bloody pounds," Barbaree said angrily. "A priceless artifact, that's what it's about. The lost necklace of Alexander's queen, full of diamonds. You don't think that's worth something?" He looked at Yurev. "Millions, I'd say."

"I'd pay you what was fair," Abby said.

"Oh, would you?" Barbaree smiled. "And what do you think is fair, I wonder?"

"Ten thousand dollars," Abby said quickly. "Paid when we return to Lucknow."

"You have so much money in India?"

"I can get it. But that's only if we find the necklace. If Yurev says the stones are not the Pearls of Light, then—"

"I'll take you to Tramar-Dri for five thousand American dollars," Barbaree said. "I'll risk my neck for five thousand. Take you up and bring you back. Five thousand."

Abby glanced at Yurev. When she looked back at Barbaree she nodded her head. "Done. I'll pay—"

"If we find the necklace, I want more."

"More?"

"If we find the necklace"—Barbaree stood, dusting off his pants—"I'll take one of the stones."

"One of the stones? You're out of your goddamn mind!"

Barbaree shook his head. "I don't think so. I don't think I'm out of my mind at all."

"I'm not giving you a diamond, for chrissakes."

Barbaree pointed a finger at her. "Don't talk to me that way . . . ever again. You're not *giving* me anything. You haven't got anything yet. It's me that's doing the bargaining. And I say that Jack Barbaree gets what's fair." He looked at Yurev. "I'll leave you to make your own deal, old man. There's plenty to go around." He started for the door, then stopped and turned to Abby. "By the by, luv, in case you were wondering . . . I have the revolvers."

◆ TEN

THE MORNING SUN WAS warm on Yurev's face as he walked across the courtyard to Barbaree's hut. Several of Ratnapa's barefoot children scuffled along beside him, smiling and jabbering at him as his boots kicked up dust in the street. He had been thinking since dawn what he would say to the Englishman. Last night had not gone well, and Yurev had had a restless sleep, bothered by Abby's stubbornness and Barbaree's greed. He'd lain awake since early morning, trying to find the words to persuade Barbaree that a share of the necklace was an impossible demand.

The Pearls of Light, if they were in Tramar-Dri, did not belong to any man or woman. They were a treasure, truly, but not to be divided among adventurers. The stones were a national treasure. They belonged to these children as much or more than to a group of sahibs. It was something he had to make Abby see as well. Fa Shing, he knew, would have understood. The stone chips of Shelkagari were meant to remain in these hills, not to be booty of yet another foreign enterprise as had happened to so many gemstones across the span of history since Alexander. He had to make Barbaree see that.

Yurev knocked, then pushed open the door. "Jack? Jack, we have to talk."

The room was unlit, and Yurev waited a few moments for his eyes to become accustomed to the faint light. A figure lay on a pallet covered with a blanket against the wall. "Jack?" It occurred to him how odd it was that Barbaree would be still asleep. Barbaree never slept past dawn. He knelt beside the figure. "Jack?"

The man on the pallet moaned when Yurev shook him and rolled him on his back. Even in this light Yurev could see the bloody, battered face. "Oh, my God!"

Kancha opened his swollen eyes. Blood had dried caked around his mouth. "Please . . . not hitting Kancha some more." The Nepalese's voice was strained with pain as he raised a hand to protect his face. "Please, sahib-bishy . . ."

"Wake up." Yurev shook Abby again, harder. "Wake up!"

She turned over to face him, still groggy with sleep as she propped herself on an elbow. "Huh . . ."

"Get up. There's trouble."

Abby exercised her eyes. "What?"

Yurev pushed her boots to her. "Barbaree's gone."

"Gone?" Abby sat up, still disoriented. She rubbed her face with her hands. "Who's gone?"

Yurev took a wet rag and squeezed it over her. Brownish water splashed onto her face.

Abby jumped back. "Jesus, what the hell—"

"Wake up."

"Christ, I'm awake. What's the matter?"

"Barbaree is gone. Sometime last night."

Abby wiped a sleeve across her face. "Jack? What do you mean he's gone? Gone where?"

"He didn't leave a note, but it shouldn't be a great mystery where he's headed."

Abby was suddenly alert. "The monastery? Without us?"

"I expect he's decided one diamond isn't enough."

"That son of a bitch!"

"He told Kancha to take us back to Butwal. Apparently, sometime in the night, Jack got up to leave. When Kancha tried to stop him Jack beat him." Yurev got to his feet. "I cleaned him up. He's very angry, Kancha is. Jack-bishy did him a bad turn. One thing these hill people do very well is survive."

"How bad is he?"

"Nothing broken, but he's battered up. Barbaree used his belt."

"Oh, Jesus."

"He's going to be okay."

"Yurey, we can't let Jack get that necklace." Abby quickly pulled on her boots. "We have to stop him."

"We can't *stop* him from getting to Tramar-Dri. He took everything with him, including the weapons." Yurev folded the rag and set it back in the water bowl. "I think he'd kill us if we tried."

"Goddammit, I'm not going to give up. I can't—"

"What *we* cannot do is fight him," Yurev said quickly. "But there might be something else. Barbaree went west, toward the gorge. The normal route is along the west face. But there's another way, on the east face—more dangerous, but shorter."

"How do you know?"

"Kancha," Yurev said. "He wants to take us. Shelkagari is not unknown up here. It is sacred, which means the necklace is, too. Kancha doesn't want Barbaree to take it away."

"But we don't have any supplies or—"

"It's being looked to now," Yurev said. "These people are not all that trusting of sahibs, but Kancha is one of them. They want to help."

"Do *you* think we can do it?" Abby looked at him. "Last night, I recall, you had your doubts. Besides, your back is—"

"The burns will heal whether I'm moving down the mountain or up." Yurev glanced out the door of the hut. Dhaulagiri was white against the morning sky, challenging. "I don't want Jack Barbaree to get his hands on those diamonds," Yurev said grimly. "They just weren't left there for him."

◆ ELEVEN

FOR MOST OF THE trek the walking was simply difficult because it was all
uphill. They followed the Kali Gandaki River, moving along the eastern
ridge, and when the trail wandered away from the gorge the roar of the
gray water was always in the air. They passed through lush oak forests,
crossing dozens of small streams that emptied into the gorge, and forests
of rhododendron, and finally, above eight thousand feet, scruffy pine.

They spent most nights on the trail, camped in the forest or beside large
rock formations above the gorge. The higher they went, the less wildlife
they encountered. As the forests became less dense the monkey population dropped proportionately. Nights were dreadfully cold, and even with
the fire Yurev could not rest comfortably. It was the altitude, Kancha told
him. "Higher is less air, so less heat," Kancha said matter-of-factly. "But
also firewood last more times longer. Some good things, some bad things
. . . all even out."

At villages along the way they bought food and warmer clothes. Eventually they entered Bhot country populated by Tibetan Buddhists, from
whom Yurev and Abby each acquired the cold-weather garment of these
altitudes, the *chuba*. Much like a coarse, heavily lined dressing gown, the
chuba was also cut twice as big. The robe hung to the ground in folds and
the sleeves were knee-length.

"Most easily fixed," Kancha explained. He held the wide sides of the
robe up, slipping a twisted belt around his waist. He pulled the material
up through the belt, letting it drop outside, then cinched the belt tight.
Folded this way, the robe was now a manageable length and contained

large pockets. He rolled the sleeves back to show his hands. "Much simple, Yurey-bishy. Good damn warmness for nights, you bet your life."

The single advantage to traveling into these higher elevations, Yurev noticed, was that the cold discouraged fleas and ticks. By the morning of the fourth day, at an altitude of roughly eleven thousand feet, he'd actually stopped scratching.

As the route gained altitude the wind became stronger. It blew from the south up the gorge during the day. At night and in the early morning it was from the opposite direction—always brisk, always frigid.

On the fifth day, with the sun straight above, Yurev stood on a boulder beside a stream that cascaded into the gorge, and holding a tree branch against the wind, looked over the edge. It was some two miles to the bottom, he calculated. The sun made the Kali Gandaki a sparkling ribbon, silver and silent. High to the west, Dhaulagiri's peak rose another fifteen thousand feet above him, and to the east Annapurna's twin summits glistened white against the pale sky. It was a moment of exhilaration, like standing on a plateau between heaven and earth; the only spot on the planet where death and beauty became a graceful, living painting.

"Yurev, look over there."

Abby was pointing across the gorge. Yurev followed her finger. The gorge was a mile or wider at this height, and the opposite side was difficult to make out in the strong light of sun.

"There," Abby shouted against the wind. "Somebody is there."

Yurev shaded his eyes, searching the distant mountain. Finally he found two figures, an animal and a man, plodding up the rocky trail. The animal looked like a buffalo but it was too far away to see more than outlines.

Yurev climbed down from the boulder. Kancha was staring across the gorge.

"Kancha?"

"A yak, Yurey-bishy, and a man."

"Is it Barbaree?"

Kancha looked hard, squinting.

"Is it?"

Kancha shook his head. "I cannot say, but he is a curious fellow, I think. He is walking in frontwards of the yak." He glanced at Yurev. "Most peoples in these countrysides are walking behind their animals."

"It's him," Abby said. "Who else would be going *up* the mountain? He's going to get there first."

"He isn't there yet," Yurev said.

"Indeed not, by jove, Yurey-bishy." Kancha was nodding. "Yaks being very slow-walking creatures. Also, if it is Jack-sahib, he will have climbing over rocks at Benithog. Very many rocks."

"You're saying it's going to slow him down?" Abby said.

"Most surely. A yak, it does not like climbing rocks. Very difficult for such large animal. For one man, one yak, it is one half day climbing."

"And where do we cross?" Yurev said. "How do we get from this side of the gorge to that side?"

"Oh, same place, sahib." Kancha pointed north, up the Kali Gandaki. "That way, the gorge narrows, at Benithog. It is a place where part of the west mountainside broke . . . a most enormous large bigness of rock. It came falling across the gorge to the east mountainside. Very misfortunate for Benithog village when large rocks falling upon heads of peoples. Happening seven hundreds, eight hundreds years ago."

"A slab of rock?" Abby glanced over the side of the gorge. "Across that?"

Kancha held his hands apart, slowly bringing them together. "Gorge getting smaller across. You see. At Benithog."

"Well, thank God for that," Abby said. "At least we'll have something substantial under us. I don't think I could face another rope bridge, especially not over that. A rock, that's different. Something safe for a change."

"Oh, by jove, not safe, Abby-memsahib. Peoples always falling into gorge and screaming most horrid. But is only crossing from east mountain to west mountain in these countrysides."

Abby looked at Yurev. A gust of wind swallowed her short exclamation.

They saw Benithog the next morning, a village of flat-roofed huts spread across the narrow slope on the opposite side of the gorge. Yurev realized what Kancha had meant when he said a man and a yak would take half a day, coming from the southern trail, to reach the village. Rockslides had made the trail a tortuous path between enormous, cracked boulders up a steep slope. The direct distance looked to be possibly three-quarters of a mile, but climbing along the winding trail the distance was easily four times that. Barbaree, even if he appeared now, would be hours behind them.

The gorge itself angled to the west, making a bend where both sides became steep cliffs. The space separating them was over five hundred yards, and, just as Kancha had said, there was a land bridge across it. But it was not simply a slab of rock as Yurev had expected. An entire ridge of the Dhaulagiri range had crashed down this slope, leaving in its wake a saddleback of crushed boulders, and depositing a sliver of itself—forty feet wide, Yurev guessed—wedged in the gorge. Exposed to rain and constant wind over the centuries, the granite's gray surface had been worn so smooth that, from a distance, it had the appearance of an enormous whale's back.

"Jesus God almighty!" Abby stood back from the edge of the cliff, holding the trunk of a pine tree for support, her hair and *chuba* flapping wildly in the frigid wind. Narrowed from a mile wide to a few hundred yards, the gorge produced a tunneling effect on the compressed air as it raced between the steep cliffs. The result was an icy, near-gale-force wind that rushed against the granite bridge. Across the gorge, sure-footed, happy villagers had gathered, waving their arms in familiar greeting. Abby spun to face Yurev. "No! No, *no.*" She almost had to shout to be heard in the wind.

"It's only dangerous," Yurev said. He tried to smile but the wind only made his teeth hurt.

"Don't humor me. Jesus, look at that. One bad step and it's a two-mile drop. Two goddamn *miles.*"

"Tramar-Dri *gumpa*"—Kancha was pointing across the gorge, at the saddleback between the ridges—"that way. Not so far, five mile, maybe. Easy walking."

Abby stared at the whaleback of granite stuck in the gorge. "There's still *that.*"

"We've done this sort of crossing before," Yurev said. "Not this high, of course, but—"

"And not in a goddamn hurricane. There's nothing to hold onto. How the hell are we supposed to walk across that?"

"Not walking," Kancha said. "Too much strong wind for walking on feets. Only way is walking on belly."

"Crawl?" Abby looked across five hundred yards of stone.

"Also, tying supplies inside *chubas.*" Kancha made a pushing motion with his hands. "Tie very much tight and pushing frontwards ahead."

"Take this off? C'mon, it's the only thing keeping me from freezing to death."

"Can put on again," Kancha said. "Other side." He pointed to Abbey's robe, flapping violently in the wind. "Wearing *chuba* on rock, then wind catching, Abby-memsahib flying away, falling into air. Not so good idea, I think."

Abby looked at Yurev. "Not so good idea." She began untying the belt around her waist. "And what the hell are they waiting for?" She nodded at the villagers across the gorge. "Why don't they help? I thought hill people were supposed to be so goddamn friendly."

"Oh, Benithog peoples very friendly," Kancha said. "Make you some good damn hot tea. But Benithog peoples not cross enormous bigness of rock . . . not polite to show courage to adventuring sahibs."

"We *want* them to help."

Kancha shrugged his little shoulders. "They help plenty—pray for sahibs. Pray for Kancha. Sing to keep evil spirits away. You see. They pretty good peoples, you bet your life." His smile was genuinely confident. Sensing Kancha's belief modified none of Yurev's dread. Prayers meant something to Kancha.

The wind was intensely cold without the heavy *chuba*. Their khaki shirts were no protection. Yurev's skin was suddenly numb except for the rope burns on his back, which felt as if they had split open. Kancha made three flat bundles of the *chubas* and secured in them their few supplies. The goat-skin water containers gave the bundles ballast to keep them from blowing away. Instead of single file they moved out onto the rock three abreast, Abby in the center. To his surprise Yurev found the smooth granite surface warm under him. Even with the chilling wind the constant sunshine kept the rock warm to touch.

"Yurey . . . look . . ."

They'd crawled a hundred yards, pushing the bundles ahead as Kancha had instructed. They hadn't spoken because it was an effort merely to breathe in the wind.

Yurev pushed himself forward, head down, to escape Abby's hair whipping his face. She was pointing with her finger, palm down against the rock, toward the south, into the wind. The view of the gorge opened up from this angle, and he could see miles and miles of it stretched out before him. The sun reached down into the depths and lighted the Kali Gandaki with reflective powers that showed against the dark walls like shimmering mirrors. Even from miles downstream the river was like a mirage of itself.

Halfway across, Yurev heard the clapping. It had started as a faint echo until he realized that it wasn't the wind or the sound of his body scraping across the rock. Looking around his *chuba* bundle, he saw the villagers sitting in rows at the end of the granite bridge, like ducks in an arcade, dozens of them. They were clapping and singing—though he could barely hear their voices—and rocking from side to side as the wandering ascetics had done before the campfire at Dura Dam.

With less than fifty yards to go, Yurev's back was on fire. His shirt, billowing and collapsing in the flailing wind, had beaten his healing skin raw again. Every movement of his arms, pushing the bundle ahead, was painful exercise for his shoulders. He tried to ignore the pain and concentrate on reaching the rows of little brown men ahead of him. There was safety there and wet mud to soothe his burns. When Abby's bundle suddenly rolled in front of his face it was a startling distraction. Yurev turned to see Abby reaching for the bundle. In a moment he realized what had happened. Abby had gotten tired of pushing her bundle and had tried rolling it, turning it end over end until it lost its flat shape and became rounded. It was only a matter of time before the wind took it. In the same moment he knew what Abby's instinctive move was—she was already up on one elbow.

"Abby, *don't.*"

She had risen to her knees and grabbed for the bundled *chuba* as it rolled past Yurev. Her lunge in the wind gave her lift, and she tumbled backward over Yurev, arms and legs spread like a human kite.

"*Yurey!*"

Yurev grabbed for her, catching a handful of hair. He saw her *chuba* bundle roll across the smooth rock, gaining velocity until it turned sideways and began bouncing. In a few seconds it was airborne and sailing straight out into space, hanging for a moment beyond the rock, then disappearing silently into the gorge.

Abby's momentum jerked him onto his back and started them sliding toward the gorge. Yurev held her hair tight, bending his knees, using the soles of his boots as brakes on the pitted stone surface, desperately trying to keep his body flat. He knew that if they started rolling, nothing would keep them from following the *chuba* over the edge. His left hand found his right, and he pulled with all his strength to stop the slide. He knew his back was a bloody mess as his shirt had torn, exposing his burns to the scraping grit of stone, but he held on, closing his eyes, anticipating the sudden rush of air, the feeling of weightlessness, and wondered how long it took a body to fall two miles—

Yurev opened his eyes when he jolted to a stop. Away from the leading edge of the rock bridge the granite surface was rougher, and his left boot had caught and held in a crack. He was looking at a mass of clouds, watching them move across his line of sight, making him dizzy. His back was a sheet of flame, sticky and suddenly cooled by the wind. His arms ached with the weight in his grasp but held tight to Abby's hair.

"Yu-Yurey?"

Her voice was a sleepy sound from beyond the pain. He could not raise his head to look down at her.

"Yurey . . . don't move."

He made a sound from his throat that was barely a noise in the wind. By moving his eyes laterally he could see only part of the rock. Beyond were only steep cliff walls and blue sky.

"Yurey . . . I'm half . . ." her voice faded. He tried to tighten his grip but his fingers were getting numb. "Don't let go," Abby said. "Please, Jesus . . . don't let go. I'm . . . halfway over the side, my feet are dangling in air."

Yurev swallowed, trying to get moisture into his mouth again. He moved his right foot gently, using his toe to feel for the crack. When he found it, there was just enough to get the edge of his boot in for a foothold. He wet his lips with his tongue. "Take leg . . . ," was all he had strength to say. He rested a moment for the burst of energy he needed, then yelled into the wind, "Take hold of my leg."

A hand slapped the leather around his ankle, and another, and her full weight was suddenly supported by the instep of his boot. Yurev pulled her hair, and she moved up several inches, her grip around his calf. His foot was slipping, he could feel the grit under his boot give a bit. If she slid away from him now he knew he couldn't hold her.

"Hand," he yelled, "now!"

Yurev let go of her hair with his left hand and reached down as his foot slipped out of the crack. For a moment he was sure he'd lost her, the grip on his leg was gone, and he heard her scream. Her hand slapped into his in the next moment, and the weight of both their bodies rested suddenly on his right leg, on the tiny purchase his boot had found in the slightly larger crack.

He pulled with his last ounce of strength, and her free hand found his wrist. Her hands were ice cold. It was a bizarre detail to note, he thought, as they were a breath away from tumbling into clear blue space. It was odd how the last thought before death should be such a mundane thing as that. His arms were numb with pain and cold, and he knew there wasn't any strength left in them. It was a final effort he'd made, a proper sahib gesture, and altogether futile. He hoped Abby appreciated it just the same.

"Not moving, please, Yurey-bishy." Yurev felt strong hands roughly grab him under each armpit. He moved his eyes only and saw Kancha's face straining above him. "Not talking, too." Then he felt himself moving, scraping along the rock, pulling away from the ledge. Kancha's small hands were like vices, incredibly strong.

His shoulders scraped ten feet up the whale's back, holding Abby with both his arms, Kancha holding him. Every inch was a victory. Abby was yelling to him but the wind was stronger now, throwing her voice back into her face, and he had nothing to say to her anyway. Kancha was the one doing the work, speaking only to urge him to hold tight. I'm trying, Yurev wanted to shout back.

Yurev felt a drop of rain on his head. The sky was absolutely clear now, the clouds had moved away. It couldn't possibly rain. When he felt another he glanced up and realized it was sweat dripping from Kancha's nose. It was the first time he'd known him to perspire.

Twenty feet.

Yurev's arms had no feeling. He took a chance and glanced down. He saw only the top of Abby's head, her dark red hair blowing wildly, and the emptiness beyond.

"Holding memsahib tight, please," Kancha said beside his ear. "Some little bit more."

Yurev closed his eyes, concentrating on his fingers, willing them to hold. Then he heard voices. When he opened his eyes again, there were arms all around him, short strong brown arms. Then faces, mouths working, making a litany of undecipherable sounds. Kancha sat a few feet away, loosening a rope from around his feet that had been used to lower him. It was only after several moments that Yurev realized he was surrounded by villagers, safe on the Dhaulagiri side of the gorge, and that what they were all trying to persuade him to do was release Abby's arms.

"It was dumb, stupid . . . *stupid.*"

Yurev sat on a laundry rock to the side of one of the village's flat-roofed huts, Abby pacing before him with a striped blanket draped over her shoulders, as Kancha dressed his back with some local ointment that cooled the fire. They were out of the wind though not out of the chill. A score of villagers sat nearby, quietly studying the sahibs, particularly taken by the red-haired memsahib who clomped this way and that, occasionally kicking small stones in her path, angry as a demon.

"I wasn't thinking," Abby said, turning again and passing in front of Yurev. She kicked at another stone. "We could have died today." The knee of her left pant leg had been torn, and it flapped open and shut as she moved, exposing raw, scraped skin.

"Better have Kancha do your knee when he's finished here," Yurev said.

"Jesus Christ, Yurey, I'm trying to apologize."

"Then do it in one place, please. I'm getting dizzy following you."

Abby stopped and turned, hands on hips.

"Thank you," Yurev said. "Anyway, it was Kancha and these people saved *us*. I just happened to be in the way. You should thank them." Yurev winced as Kancha touched a spot high on his shoulder.

"Pardon, Yurey-bishy." The little Nepalese shook his head. "Not thanking Kancha, please. Thanking Benithog peoples for helpful prayers."

Yurev tried to smile. "There, you see? It was the gods pulled us back from the precipice."

"All right, then, just forget it." She paced again. Finally she stopped, her face suddenly concerned. "Is it very painful, your back?"

Yurev shook his head. It was an easier lie than speaking.

"Can you walk? I mean, we can stay here until—"

"No. We've only five miles to go. Better move on. I don't want to be here when Barbaree arrives."

"I almost forgot about him."

"I suspect he's forgotten about us, too." Yurev glanced at the trail ahead. "When he remembers, I want to be up there."

Abby traded her last carton of cigarettes for a faded red *chuba* that nearly matched the color of her hair, and the three of them set out on the last leg of their journey. Considering the way they'd come, Yurev thought that this march would be easiest. But by Kancha's reckoning they were above seventeen thousand feet, and every breath became labored in the thin air of the high hills. With Kali Gandaki behind them, the landscape turned rocky and barren. They were surrounded by far-off mountain peaks and glaciers. Rising majestically on their left was the white summit of Dhaulagiri and to the right was another for which Kancha had no name. At their backs, in the east, were Annapurna and a hundred lesser peaks, receding in a bright blue sky.

Kancha had no problem with the altitude. He led the way up the rocky landscape, picking his path through the boulders as if it were a Sunday outing. The little Nepalese took the opportunity, in light of the labored silence of his panting sahib companions, to become tour guide. This pass, he said, was called the Valley of Weeping Winds. It had earned the name

because of a siege that had taken place a thousand years earlier when India
—"Land of the Five Rivers"—had been invaded from the west by Sultan
Mahmud, the Mohammedan. "An army of the Mohammedan had been
coming this way," Kancha demonstrated, indicating the pass, "killing hill
peoples because they were nonbelievers. All hill peoples most afraid, going
to Tramar-Dri *gumpa* for praying to Most Holy One, high priest of
monastery." Kancha helped Abby through an area of loose rock, continuing his storytelling without missing a step.

"Army coming through here with horses and all much battle weapons,
chasing hill peoples to holy place. At *gumpa,* army demanding Most Holy
One to come down, surrender priests and all peoples hiding in red city.
But Most Holy One saying no. Most Holy One saying please go away. But
army of Mohammedan not going away, try to attacking *gumpa.* Then hill
peoples dropping large and most heavy rocks on soldiers' heads, driving
soldiers away from walls. Army saying stop doing that and Holy One
saying will stop when go away."

Yurev tried to imagine the besieged hill people at the walls of the
monastery, throwing rocks at heavily armed soldiers, protecting their own.
It didn't change, he thought. Women and children were slaughtered in
the name of God even here.

"So Mohammedan army begin lopping off heads of Benithog village
peoples. One day pass and Holy One not come down, then one head
lopped off. Dead village peoples hanging from feet by ropes and all insides
coming out. This goings on for many weeks. Then snows coming and
army having no foods, and freezing in darkness. Finally Mohammedan
army they say fighting finished. They say to Holy One, please giving foods
and warm robes because toes freezing and turning black and falling off
feets. So Holy One tell soldiers to throw away battle weapons. Then Holy
One giving foods and warm robes while priests finding heads for bodies
of dead village peoples and burn in large fire."

They stopped again to rest. Abby's face was wet with perspiration
despite the cold. She shared her water with Yurev. Kancha continued his
story as soon as Abby nodded she was ready to go on.

"Then Holy One had soldiers tie ropes around waists, all together, and
leads to Benithog. Then Holy One say go home please, not coming back.
But soldiers not pleased, beating on chests, saying many unpleasant things
and kicking dirt at Holy One. This unpoliteness make hill peoples very
angry. They hit soldiers with sticks and poking out eyes and make soldiers
running in snow. When first soldier falling and slipping into gorge, next
soldier falling also because of rope around waist. Soldiers then screaming

and biting with teeths on rope, but cannot stop from falling into gorge. Then soldiers all gone, all falling long time, tied together like fishes, making very much screaming until hitting rocks. Then Holy One returning to Tramar-Dri *gumpa*."

They'd been walking for three hours, and as they picked their way around an enormous boulder, Kancha stopped.

"There, Yurey-bishy . . ." Kancha pointed ahead. His smile denied his excitement. "Tramar-Dri *gumpa*."

Yurev glanced up to see where Kancha was pointing. Less than a mile away the valley cut between steep cliffs. On a rock shelf two hundred feet above the valley floor Yurev saw the low-slung red buildings of the monastery. He steadied himself against a rock, nodding to Abby, who just stared past him at the holy place. "We made it," he said in a dry voice.

They walked the rest of the way without stopping, passing pens of livestock and, Yurev was surprised to see, Nepalese ponies. The walls of the cliff below the monastery had been whitewashed, and stone steps cut into the rock face zigzagged to stone-hewn ramparts at several landings before arriving at the main level. The stairway entrance was flanked by a pair of red-and-white-painted stupas—large white domes on a square red base—monuments to the Buddha-to-come, Kancha said. The steps, also, were stained red.

Kancha led the way up, bowing to monks, mostly young men, who were sweeping the stairway. Along the way tiny white prayer flags fastened into holes in the railing fluttered in the cold light breeze. It was the most well-swept stairway Yurev had ever seen—at every half-dozen steps was another monk with his straw broom, busily at work on his portion. The monks greeted them with silence, some taking no notice whatever. Kancha explained that it was their vow of silence. There were men here, he said, who had not spoken in thirty years.

An elderly monk in a flowing robe stood at the top of the stairs leading to the monastery as Yurev and the others reached the final rampart. Beside the monk, unharnessed, sat a large, powerful dog. The dog's black, short-haired coat was so dark it appeared blue in the sunlight. It made no sound whatever, not even baring its teeth, but kept itself intently attuned to the presence of the three strangers. It was the most ugly and terrifying animal Yurev had ever seen. It was, he realized, a Tibetan mastiff, an animal feared more than any other in these hills for its viciousness. A devil dog.

Kancha greeted the monk with a deep bow, touching his knees to the bottom stair. As the holy one listened to Kancha's introductions, the monk's eyes darted back and forth between Yurev and Abby, the mastiff rose to all fours, a graceful and frightening movement. The dog's black stare was on Yurev, and though he tried not to look at the animal, afraid to show his fear, he was drawn to it as if behind those dead eyes were a secret. Finally, the monk made a brief comment, nodded toward the sahibs, turned and walked across the open court to the monastery. The mastiff followed, looking back once and exposing its canine incisors, then moving off at a slow gait.

"Most reverent one saying please wait," Kancha said, sitting down on one of the wide steps. "Going to get *unze.*"

"Who's Unze?" Abby said.

"*Unze* name for next high monk to high lama. Much important monk at *gumpa.* Taking care of most business." Kancha pointed at Abby's boots. "Most reverent one also saying please taking off boots. No walking on boots in *gumpa.*"

Abby sat down beside Kancha to unlace her boots. The prayer flags at this rampart, just below the entrance to the monastery, were larger and made of silk. The sound of them in the breeze was like small cracking whips. "That was the scariest-looking dog I've ever seen," she said.

"Dog friend of holy ones. Protect *gumpa.*"

"Mastiff?" Yurev said. "Devil dog?"

"Not devil dog anymore times, Yurey-bishy. Used to be. But now all-watching dogs—protectors of Holy One."

Yurev glanced at the buildings above. "There are more?"

"Oh, by jove, yes. Many dogs here, but all dogs being quiet. Holy ones removing throat box but keeping teeth, so no barking. Pretty good damn all-watching dogs."

"Jesus." Abby shook her head, tugged on her boot until it came off. "When are we going to see the high lama?"

"See *unze* first."

Abby gave Yurev a look, then pulled off her other boot. "They certainly keep the trainees busy."

"Many *trawas* here," Kancha said. "Tramar-Dri very prosperous *gumpa.*"

"What's a *trawa?*" Abby said.

"Oh, *trawas* new monks . . . students, very low in order."

"These people don't look very prosperous to me."

Kancha bowed to a monk who descended the stairway carrying a basket heaped with red robes. "Not prosperous of monies, Abby-memsahib. Monastery own lands, grow crops, give to poor. Also, many scholarly monks here. Study all religious manner of things."

"That's what they do . . . study? All of these—"

"Oh, by Jove, no, memsahib. Some monks keeping land, some keeping kitchen, some working for other monks. Others building villages, saying prayers"—he pointed to the monk with the basket—"cleaning clothing. Much different jobs in *gumpa.*" Kancha nodded toward the monks sweeping the rock stairs on the rampart below. "These ones—*trawas*—they sweeping monks, always keeping *gumpa* clean. All monks working for Holy One, the high lama of Tramar-Dri."

Abby glanced at Yurev. "Sounds like some of my father's friends."

"Monks come, go as they choose. In eleventh month, all holy ones returning to *gumpa* for thirty days, give lessons, hear high lama. Many holy ones here already."

"I haven't seen any women." Abby shaded her eyes, looking across the livestock pens below. "Where are they?"

"No womans in Tramar-Dri. Only mens."

Abby gave him a sharp look. "What? None?"

"Womans not allowed in *gumpa.*"

"Not allowed?"

"Only holy ones. No womans. Womans not being monks. Womans stay in Benithog, cook foods, clean—"

"Wait a damn minute. What the hell are they going to think *I* am?"

Kancha pondered the question a moment. It hadn't occurred to him until now. Finally he resolved it. He smiled. "You not womans. You memsahib."

Yurev turned away to smile and glanced back at the way they'd come. The valley pointed east and opened to the peak of Annapurna filling and towering above the horizon. When he saw the yak his smile disappeared.

"Someone's coming."

Abby swung around. "What?"

Yurev pointed at the trail they'd just come by. A man and a yak were moving past one of the pens below. "There."

"Oh, Christ . . . Barbaree."

"Wait, please." Kancha moved to the low wall of the rampart. He watched the man and his animal for several seconds. "Not Barbaree-sahib." He turned back. "Forgiving me, please, but not Barbaree-sahib. A hill peoples."

Abby squinted at the two figures. "That isn't the same one we saw yesterday? Across the gorge?" She looked at Yurev. "If it isn't Barbaree, then . . . ?"

Yurev shook his head. "I don't know."

"Where the hell is he? You don't think he turned back?"

"Not bloody likely, luv."

Yurev felt a sourness in his stomach when he heard the voice and the thin laugh that followed it. He turned to look at the top of the stairs.

The monk had returned, but without the guard dog. Instead, outlined against a wisp of cloud in the blue sky, a head taller than the Tibetan monk, stood Jack Barbaree. He wore a sheepskin jacket and had six days' growth of beard. He was barefoot, his khaki pant legs rolled above his ankles. He nodded at Yurev. To Abby he smiled.

"Well, now," he said, "isn't this a surprise?"

Behind him, a row of prayer flags snapped in answer to a quick gust of wind from the rock valley below Dhaulagiri's silver peak.

◆ TWELVE

"WHEN DID YOU GET here?"

The monk had led the sahibs to a small stone courtyard inside the monastery walls. In the center was a dish-shaped pool made of polished pebbles painted blue that gave the water a bright turquoise hue. The monk offered mats to each of the visitors except Kancha, who bowed at every opportunity to the revered holy one. When the sahibs were seated he excused himself, explaining the *unze* would be along shortly. As soon as he disappeared into the shadows of the monastery, Abby came angrily to her feet.

"When the hell did you get here?"

Barbaree stood, too. He walked to a narrow railing that afforded a view of the valley. "Been nearly a week since I spoke English," he said. "Not that I've been talking much at all since I left Ratnapa, you know. Long climb, alone. But—" He waved it off. "I don't suppose you brought any cigarettes, eh, luv?"

"*When did you get here?*" Abby demanded.

"Yesterday . . . toward sundown. Just in before they took up the drawbridge, so to say. They have dogs here, you know." Barbaree looked at Yurev. "How's the back, old lad? Six days on the trail must have been an adventure for you."

Yurev shaded his eyes from the sun at Barbaree's back. Barbaree had been a day ahead of them all along. "You didn't take the Dhaulagiri route." He meant it as a question.

"No other way except up the gorge, mate."

"You didn't go through Benithog."

"I've seen Benithog. The tea's all right but the view's a bit monotonous." Barbaree pointed at a narrow valley that cut into the cliffs from the south. "See that? Through there—six, seven miles—is a glacier, coming down Dhaulagiri. From the gorge you have to do a bit of climbing to get to it. It's cold, but it's a shorter walk. Locals don't care for it much due to the odd carnivore that prowls about." He looked at Yurev. "You came up the east side, right? Crossed at Benithog." He smiled. "People have been known to fall off there, old lad."

"We managed," Abby said quickly, "and without you."

"I felt bad, I did, leaving you in Ratnapa."

"But not *too* bad." Abby was controlling herself better than Yurev expected.

"Greed will lead men to do the most audacious things, luv."

"Yes, I saw what you did to Kancha."

"He's had worse." Barbaree looked directly at the little Nepalese. "You remember Chandrakot? What was it, '27? Corporal Cavanaugh used his cartridge belt, right?" Kancha was silent. He stared at the cleanly swept patch of stone in front of him. "Same thing then," Barbaree said to Yurev, "disobeying a superior."

"You're not in the army anymore."

Barbaree gave Yurev a sharp look. "No one is ever *out* of the British army, old lad. Not that it matters. *I* hired Kancha, didn't I? He was paid from my kit, wasn't he? I told him to take you back. The little bugger gave me some lip about it. I don't take kindly to insolence. Anyway—" Barbaree moved away from the railing. "We don't want to dwell on what's past. As a matter of fact, it's fortunate we've hooked up again. We can help each other, we can."

"*I* should help *you?*" Abby said. "Not bloody likely . . . old *lad.*"

"Now, now, luv. We're partners again, that's all."

"We were *never* partners."

"Well, true as that may have been, partners is what we are now, luv. I'm here, you're here, and, what we're all hoping, our necklace is here too."

"*Our* necklace!"

"The right one, of course. Any trinket won't do, will it?" He glanced at Yurev, who still remained seated on his mat. "That's your department, right? Examining it, I mean—to be sure it's the one?"

Yurev only stared back. "I know why I'm here," he said. "The question is, why do we need you?"

"Have you learned Bhot in the last six days? Can you speak to these people without an interpreter? You need me for several reasons, old lad, not the least of which is to bargain with his holiness for the necklace."

"We have Kancha."

"Kancha?" The Englishman laughed. "Oh, that's rich, that is, mate. Little Kancha, working a deal for a pair of sahibs with the high lama of Tramar-Dri. I'd like to see that, I would."

"What's so wrong with Kancha speaking for us?" Abby said.

"Oh, nothing, luv. Nothing wrong with it at all. I'd just like to watch it. I can just picture it. Kancha, a Tamang from Butwal in the foothills, prostrate before the high lama, the most religious figure of his world, negotiating for two *bedeshis*—foreigners. That would be a sight to see. Something akin to a a Vatican choirboy, kneeling before the Pope, asking to buy his signet ring for a pair of African Muslims." Barbaree shook his head. "The Buddhists here are a polite lot—they won't embarrass you by laughing in your faces."

"You can do better?"

"I've been here before, luv. I know something about these holy men, you know. For one thing it strokes their vanity when a sahib comes asking for something. And for another thing they don't often have money offered to them—nobody up here has money—and they don't turn it down either, I can tell you." Barbaree glanced at Yurev. "So you see, old lad, the question isn't why do you need me, but why do I need you."

"To identify the stones," Abby said.

"There, you see," Barbaree said, "we've come full circle. All of us back at the same place."

"Stalemate," Yurev said.

"Ah." Barbaree held his finger in the air, making the point. He smiled. "Partners."

The *unze* was called Tupjuk-se, and he received them in a room with a low ceiling. The walls were painted black with white and silver line drawings of fierce Tibetan divinities. There was one window, facing west, behind the *unze*, who sat cross-legged on an orange carpet. Butter lamps in brass pots illuminated the room, filling it with a heavy odor. Barbaree leading, the four visitors were led by two young monks to mats arranged in a semi-circle before the *unze*. Tupjuk-se wore a faded yellow robe and occupied himself with a parchment on his lap, though it was obvious to Yurev that the old man was not reading it. He wore round spectacles with wire struts. There was a dark patch of discolored skin high on his forehead. When all were seated, Tupjuk-se glanced up. He looked at Kancha directly, speaking to him only. They exchanged words, Kancha bowing at every utterance from the *unze*. Finally Kancha nodded toward Barbaree and the conversation took a less formal turn. The Englishman's voice was stronger, deeper, and he did not bow.

Barbaree drew a white silken scarf from his sheepskin jacket, offering it to the *unze* as he spoke. Tupjuk-se accepted the scarf indifferently, as if he'd expected it. They communicated for several minutes, the *unze* responding often with wide arm gestures. Even though Yurev didn't understand what was said, he felt Barbaree's grasp of the language was, to his ear, rather more technical than smooth, the way Germans spoke French. At one point Abby leaned toward Yurev and asked what the scarf meant but Yurev only shook his head. Barbaree was right about one thing, Kancha would have been useless as a negotiator. From the moment he took his place on the mat the Nepalese was mesmerized by the presence of the holy man before them, bowing whenever Tupjuk-se spoke, even when the words were directed to Barbaree.

The audience was over in ten minutes. Having listened, Yurev had no idea what had been agreed to, if anything. Neither the *unze* nor Barbaree's expression gave hint to what they had discussed.

The monks who had escorted them into this rather small, dark room led them out. They were taken to another room lit also by butter lamps, but with a fireplace and a low wooden table. Four places had been set— *tsampa* and *chang* for each guest. One of the monks spoke to Barbaree then moved back to the doorway with his companion, but did not leave.

"Well, then," Barbaree said proudly, sitting down to one of the places, "it's on for tomorrow." He glanced up. "C'mon, sit down, sit down. They're feeding us."

Abby folded herself in front of the table. "The lama?" Her voice was full of anticipation. "We're seeing him?"

Barbaree took his cup, swallowed some *chang*. "Righto, luv. Himself. Where's that photo?"

Abby gave him a suspicious look. "Why?"

"I told Tupjuk-se. He wants to see it, pass it on to the high holy one. They've never seen photographs in these parts, you know. Probably every monk in the place will see it before we get it back." Barbaree scooped rice from the bowl with his fingers. "Best eat, luv. Sundown comes early up here." He pushed the rice into his mouth then held his hand out to her as he chewed. "C'mon, then."

Abby glanced at Yurev before reaching inside her *chuba*. The photo was carefully wrapped inside a waterproof pouch. She stared at it a moment, not wanting to hand it over.

"This is the original—the only copy."

"We're in a Buddhist monastery," Barbaree said impatiently. "Surrounded by bloody pious monks and the high lama of Tramar-Dri on the eve of their most reverent meeting. Do you really think someone's going to steal it?"

Abby handed it over with a quick gesture. Barbaree in turn handed it to one of the monks from the doorway who quickly disappeared with it. Abby stared after him.

"Don't worry, luv. Tomorrow you'll see the real original."

Yurev sipped his *chang*. If anything it was stronger than any he'd had before. "What—" he paused to clear his throat. "What was that about . . . with the scarf?"

"The *kata?*" Barbaree helped himself to more rice before continuing. "A ceremonial gift. It's the custom. It's considered bad form to visit a *gumpa* and not have a *kata* for his holiness. A courtesy. Just that. You'd better eat. They only serve one meal here. I missed it last night, and I don't fancy another cold night on an empty belly."

Abby glanced into her bowl. The rice was gray. She drank the *chang*. "When tomorrow?"

"Whenever the old boy decides," Barbaree said. "Tomorrow is a vague notion to people who don't own clocks. Tupjuk-se's eyes lit up when I told him the three of us had come great distances. That impresses them, travel. I said we came from England, Russia and America, the three great powers beyond the All Encompassing Sea. Could be we'll see him tomorrow. Could be in two days. But it won't be long. When I mentioned the necklace the old boy seemed intrigued, if I'm any judge. Anyway we've stirred their curiosity."

"Two days!"

Barbaree finished the rice, washing it down with the last of his *chang*. He nodded to Kancha. "If it was him asking, you'd be waiting till their holy days were over. I don't think you'd like that, luv. Bloody thing doesn't start for two weeks."

"So we wait?"

"And pray it doesn't snow. You sure you didn't bring some cigarettes? I could do with a smoke."

Abby gave him a look. "They're at the bottom of the Kali Gandaki River, remember?"

Barbaree nodded. "Right."

Abby ate her bowl of rice, scraping a bit at a time out into her cupped palm and shoveling it into her mouth. It reminded Yurev of Celeste, taking medicine that didn't cure.

Yurev spoke to erase the memory. "Are we sleeping here?" He glanced around the room. Sitting on mats had made his back sore again and the single cup of *chang* made him light-headed.

Barbaree shook his head. "There's the bad news."

Abby glanced up quickly.

"Last night I slept in a room with thirty of these boyos," Barbaree continued, "every one of them snoring or breaking wind. I should have counted myself lucky."

"We're sleeping with monks?"

"No. We're sleeping with the goats and other livestock. Tonight and until we leave this place." Barbaree motioned with his finger, pointing at the window. "Outside the monastery."

"What!"

"It is at least a roof and four walls, to keep the wind off. Also a fire, I expect. They'll be along for us directly, to escort us out."

"They're kicking us off this rock?"

"Us?" Barbaree gave her an impish smile. "Not precisely. Unfortunately, you make the difference, luv. The high holy one will meet with you, but he draws the line at a woman staying inside the monastery—even a memsahib."

"Oh, for chrissakes, I never heard of such nonsense—"

"Yes, well, that may be in America, but you're light years from that here." Barbaree turned as a pair of monks entered. Yurev noticed one of them carried Barbaree's backpack. "And here they are now."

"This is ridiculous," Abby said. "I didn't walk six days to get to this rockpile to sleep in a cold goddamn stable."

Barbaree cast a solemn eye on Abby. "Be a good girl, luv, and don't start a row. We're guests, remember, try to act like one. Think about the diamonds. That should keep you warm."

The sky was losing its light as they moved down the long deserted stairway to the valley floor. Two monks led the group with two monks taking up the rear. Each of them carried a torch even though it was not yet dark. Prayer flags flapped continually in the chilling breeze.

"Why the procession?" Yurev said.

"We're honored guests," Barbaree replied, "they don't want us to get lost, I expect. Besides, it is nearly dusk. They will be letting the dogs out soon."

"I don't understand that. What are they guarding against? Who would harm these people?"

"They're protection against evil spirits, for one. These Buddhists are a superstitious lot, I told you. The dogs have protected Tramar-Dri for centuries, since the Moslem invasion. Their real usefulness is against the rogue leopard or lion that wanders down into the valley on the scent of the livestock. Don't get many Moslems bent on enslaving the populace these days."

Abby, walking beside Kancha, looked back at Barbaree. "Leopards?"

"Not to worry, luv. A dozen or so dogs is more than their match."

"And what about your protection?" Yurev said. He remembered the revolvers and that the Englishman had all of them. "Where are the weapons?" He nodded at the backpack carried by the monk ahead of Abby.

"You think I'd bring a sidearm here—to the monastery?" Barbaree looked at him as if he were an idiot.

"Then . . . where?"

"A safe place," Barbaree said. He glanced across the uneven terrain to the valley that led toward Dhaulagiri. "A very safe place."

◆ THIRTEEN

A GROUP OF MONKS came at dawn. The valley was still cast in cold darkness though the tip of Dhaulagiri was silver with sunlight. Yurev marched silently behind Barbaree, aware only of the vapor his breath made in the chill of morning as they marched past the prayer flags on the stone steps.

They made their way through small dark rooms in the *gumpa*, passing stores of barley and butter, red peppers and dried dung. In a room without windows or decorations, they were offered hot *chang* and *tsampa*. It was a prayer room, lit by large butter lamps in pots at each of the four corners. The *unze* would be along soon, Barbaree said. It would be the *unze* who would make the introduction to the high lama.

"We might wait here all day," Barbaree said. "Make yourselves comfortable. Sleep if you want. It could be a long time." With that advice, he made himself a place against the table, crossed his arms and, tipping his hat down, closed his eyes to sleep. Abby was too restless to sleep. Unable to find a comfortable sitting position, she paced, walking in and out of the glow from the lamps. Kancha, the only one who had not touched the food, bent into that awkward crouch, pressed his hands together between his closed eyes and prayed, swaying slightly as he did so.

Yurev sat beside a butter lamp, where it was warm, with his knees drawn to his body, too tense to sleep. Less than two weeks ago he had left Bombay and entered a world he had not known existed. He had joined a quest which from the outset was a search for a fantasy. He had not believed in his heart that Abagail Abbaye's mission was anything more than a diversion in his life, a time-filling exercise to escape the plague of guilt that haunted his soul. But something had changed. He had been, until now, little more than a diffident observer, aware of himself in the past tense. All of his travails these past days were, he sensed, a test, a trial, as if it were prelude to some role he was to play. He remembered Fa Shing, sitting in his house the night it rained. *A day would come when a man would come to me. A man fired by suffering. A man from beyond the All Encompassing Sea. A gorah sahib. This man would be the first ring in the chain to return the Stone of One Thousand Miracles.*

Yurev blinked back the vision. Fa Shing had known it all along? Some freak of destiny had brought him here? From the time he stumbled across the first Himalayan ridge he'd felt watched. The feeling was with him still but stronger now. It was a presence he felt, a vital, powerful presence. Somewhere in the flickering dimness of this room watchful eyes seemed to measure him. Time became an object he could feel. It pressed into his chest until he could not breathe. He felt cold, and rain. The floor beneath his feet turned clammy and soft. A storm built in his mind's eye, and he felt the rain, matting his hair, streaking down his cheeks. Thunder broke like rolling drums from black, boiling clouds and clumsy, distant trumpets sounded across a bleak marshland of mud. Lightning flashed over a sea of twisted faces. Bloodied beasts, eyes turned skyward with panic, crushing, erupting bare bodies underfoot. And above it all, gentle as the whisper from an angel, came a soft voice . . . *Rivet thine eyes to the violence and tenderness of the divine faces . . . Hail the jewel of the lotus . . .* Yurev knew that voice. It was familiar as life but now it was, suddenly, terrifying. It was Celeste—

And he came awake, short of breath. He'd fallen asleep in the warm glow of the butter lamp. His eyes stung with sweat from his forehead. The shirt beneath his *chuba* was damp with perspiration.

"Yurev?"

He recoiled from the woman's voice, jerking his head around. Abby was kneeling beside him.

"God, you look like hell," she said. She sat down against the wall. "You're mumbling in your sleep again."

Yurev stared at her. The sounds and visions were gone, swallowed in the shadows of the small room. He wiped the long sleeve of his *chuba* over his eyes. The wool garment was warm against his face. "Sor—" he moistened his lips. "Sorry."

"You've been doing that lately, you know—talking in your sleep. I think we're all going a little batty."

"We haven't been getting enough sleep," Yurev said. He meant he hadn't. The nightmare he'd just awakened from was proof. He realized the tormented beasts he dreamed of were elephants.

"I haven't slept a full night through in days," Abby said. "Last night was worst. I kept thinking about those goddamn dogs, prowling around in the dark. Those are the ugliest animals I've ever seen. The fact that they can't make a sound makes them seem even scarier."

"Have you been bothered lately by nightmares?"

Abby leaned back slightly to look at him. "What?"

"Bad dreams. I wonder if the altitude somehow has anything to do with it. Low content of oxygen or something."

"The only bad dream I have is looking into another bowl of *tsampa*. On the other hand—" she nudged Yurev's foot with her own. She was looked away from him, across the room. "Tell me if I'm hallucinating, Yurey, or . . . is a man standing in the shadows over there, in the doorway?"

Yurev sat up. The figure took a step forward, into the flickering light. He was wearing a dark red cloak or *chuba* and he was very old. He moved again, coming straight toward Yurev, and stopped at his feet. "Come, please. It is time. Your coming has been much longed for." Then he turned and moved back to the door. Yurev's mouth was suddenly dry. The old man's face had changed only a little in thirty years. He was the monk from the photograph, the Holy One who owned Roxanne's necklace. The high lama of Tramar-Dri. And he was speaking to Yurev *in French*.

Yurev stood and Abby rose beside him, each of them speechless.

"Rejoicing are we that the One Who Would Come Later is arrived at last," the lama said. "We have been waiting a great while."

◆ FOURTEEN

Seeing the lama so suddenly, unannounced and without the *unze*, was a mild shock to Barbaree, if his expression was any indication. He rose quickly to his feet, unsure at first to whom the lama was speaking or in what language. The look of surprise on Abby's face was worth a thousand pictures. Kancha—poor confused little Kancha—was already on his knees, head bowed to the floor.

"Please, with your friends, come in," the Holy One said, motioning with a sweeping gesture toward his chambers. That his French was stiffly formal did not surprise Yurev. If the syntax was disjointed, and the inflection and pronounciation of his speech wrongly accented, the lama could hardly be faulted. The miracle was not his delivery.

"*Merci, mon—*" Yurev's voice faltered. He suddenly could not find, in his adopted language, a salutation fitting for a high lama. "*—mon ami,*" was all that he could come up with.

The old man smiled. He was at least as old as Fa Shing, Yurev judged, and his hands were the same, delicately wrinkled with long slender fingers. But even his advanced age and frail body could not deter an imposing presence. He had a long hawklike nose, unusual for a Tibetan, the chiseled facial features of a Greek and dark, copperish skin. His dark hair was tied in a braid, and he wore an extra long sleeveless *chuba*, red the shade of simmering coals, over a faded red and gold brocade silk shirt. But it was the eyes that drew Yurev's notice—they were clear and aware, alert to everything. The lama executed a short bow and turned, leading the way into his inner sanctum.

"What the hell's going on?" Abby whispered, moving beside Yurev as they met at the narrow doorway. "Was that French what he said?"

Yurev nodded.

"*French?* But how—"

Yurev took her arm. "I don't know," he said. "I don't know at all."

Barbaree followed behind them. "I don't know what his game is, mate, and I don't like it. Just be careful what you say." The Englishman's expression was at once solemn and wary, and beneath it, Yurev sensed, was anger. Barbaree had suddenly lost his leverage. All along he had been the one with the answers. Now, for the first time, he was simply an observer.

The room Yurev entered was lavish compared to what he'd seen of the monastery up to now. This was the lama's prayer room, and it contained an altar complete with incense burners, wax paper flowers and several brass and bronze religious figures. On the walls were hung *thankas*, vivid cloth paintings recording scenes of historical importance to the *gumpa*. Behind the altar was a fresco depicting the wheel of life, held in the jaws of Mara, god of death. The wheel portrayed the six hells into which man is reincarnated according to his deeds. In the center hub were painted the three causes of man's suffering—a bird, a pig and a snake—passion, ignorance and wrath.

A pair of stuffed Tibetan dogs, propped up with sticks, flanked the altar and drew a gasp from Abby. Their mouths were open in sneers exposing yellowed vicious teeth, no doubt to protect the altar from evil spirits. Leaning against the center of the altar, as if by accident, was another small painting. Yurev recognized it as the figure of Boundless Light, the Buddha of Enlightenment, holding in his hand the glowing stone of virtue.

The lama seated himself before the altar and gestured for Yurev to sit. Pillows instead of mats had been provided. Yurev sat, with Abby and Barbaree on either side. Kancha knelt on his pillow and put his head to the floor, hands together in supplication.

"My God," Abby whispered, "look at these books."

Yurev glanced to his right. The entire wall was made of shelves that contained manuscripts, long, rectangular bundles wrapped in silk and held together between thin wooden covers. Hundreds of them.

"*Tramar-Dri*"—the old man opened his hands—"*friendly to gorah sahibs.*"

"*Very friendly,*" Yurev agreed.

"And you are One Who Would Come Later, seeker of the small stones left in great times past by the baron gorah sahib." Someone had taught him poor French, Yurev thought, probably from one of these books. What he didn't understand was why. "You have come a far ways. Across the All Encompassing Sea . . . like the one before. So it is?"

Yurev only stared at him. He didn't know how to respond.

"What's he saying?" Abby said.

Yurev ignored her. "How did you know we were coming, Holy One?"

"It was written." The lama took a parcel from beneath the altar. He unwrapped the silk binding revealing three manuscripts. The topmost he touched to his head and handed to Yurev. The first page was simple and written in a florid style:

Le Septième et Final Voyage
Aux les Himals
de Jean-Baptiste Tavernier
Baron d'Aubonne
MDCLXXIX

Yurev stared at the brittle yellow parchment. Jean-Baptiste Tavernier. Yurev was stunned. Tavernier was the greatest diamond and gem trader of all time, the Marco Polo of the seventeenth century. He was a French jewel merchant who traveled six times to the Orient—Turkey, Persia and India. King Louis XIV of France had bought, in all, forty-four diamonds from him, including the Great Blue, to be known as the Hope Diamond. And Tavernier had known the two most famous Mogul kings, Shah Jehan, builder of the Taj Mahal, and his son, Aurangzeb, from whom Tavernier bought the greatest number of diamonds.

"What is it, mate?"

Yurev glanced through the first few pages of the manuscript. After Tavernier's last trip in 1676 he wrote a book on the subject of his diamond finds in India, required reading of every apprentice diamond cutter in Europe. *The Six Voyages of Jean-Baptiste Tavernier* described the gems of the great Mogul he had seen in Industan. It was full of fascinating stories of legendary stones and mysterious spiritual tales, including one about a diamond that was called "Stone of the Chakravartin"—The Stone of A Thousand Miracles.

"Yurey? What does it say?"

Tavernier became a man of mystery near the end of his life. In 1687 on account of political and religious turmoil in France, he left on what would have been his seventh trip to India at the age of eighty. But instead of reaching Bombay, his port of call, he disappeared. Nothing more was heard of him for nearly two hundred years. In Moscow in 1885 a grave-stone with Tavernier's name was discovered in a Protestant churchyard. Yurev remembered seeing the chiseled name on a simple granite stone worn thin by ten generations of Russian winter winds. His uncle Niko-layev had taken him to see it. No one could explain how or why Tavernier came to be buried in Moscow when he had last been seen in Paris, traveling in exactly the opposite direction.

Yurev looked again at the page before him, at the words Jean-Baptiste Tavernier had written nearly two and a half centuries earlier:

October 17, 1689—

   The journals herein contain the full account and detailed portrait of my travels in the Himals of which these words are the last. In a brief time I shall leave this parchment in the gentle care of the kind and generous Lama of Tramar-Dri who has promised faithfully to stand by its good repair until one, whose name I know not, will come for it. To the one who reads this missive I beseech but one request. Let it be known that my labours of the last months, as I have traversed these grand and treacherous slopes in the eightieth year of my life, have been with ever constant zeal in making known the heroic qualities and humble genius of His Most Royal Majesty, Louis XIV, Sun King of Europe. And to His Majesty express, in gracious and polite language, that this most recent quest was accomplished in His service and for the honor of France.

   As I will soon depart for the north, on the route of the great salt caravan toward the frontier of Russia, I know I shall not touch again French soil, lifeblood of my heart. Such is the travail of age for one not of this land. Even so, in these journals I leave behind the secret of an age bygone. The Little Sisters have I found and left them here for one who follows me. The mystery of Chakravartin's stone, the greatest treasure to the brotherhood of men, is, in these pages, solved. The truth is in Buddha's hands.

Yurev's hands trembled. The Little Sisters were the necklace, he had no doubt. The Pearls of Light. But the necklace was only a portion of the treasure. Chakravartin's stone had to be The Stone of a Thousand Mira-cles—Shelkagari. And Tavernier had found it.

"For chrissakes, Yurev, what does it *say?*"

Yurev looked at Abby. His mouth was dry. "Someone was here before," he said. He wet his lips. "A Frenchman named Tavernier."

"He didn't take the bloody diamonds?" Barbaree said quickly.

Yurev almost smiled. "No. He was here more than two hundred years ago. He left the necklace here. He expected someone would come for it—"

"Two hundred years?" Abby said. "They've kept it all that time?"

"Safekeeping it for the One Who Would Come After," Yurev said. "For whoever came to claim it. As far as the lama is concerned—me."

"Hold on, mate. Don't get yourself swept up in this mumbo jumbo. We're partners, all of us." Barbaree nodded at the lama. "Just tell his reverence that we're here for the necklace. The quicker we get out of here the better. I don't fancy getting snowed in. That stable isn't a place I figure to rest up through winter."

Yurev tapped his finger on the manuscript, ignoring Barbaree, trying to contain the emotion building inside him. "It's in here," he said to Abby. "Tavernier found the Shelkagari—"

"*Shelkagari.*" The lama repeated the name. "*Stone of a Thousand Miracles.*" He bowed his head. "*Hail the jewel of the lotus.*"

"What's he on about now?" Barbaree said. "Why doesn't he speak a proper language? We're not interested in—"

The lama rose gently to his feet, holding the two remaining manuscripts, gesturing that Yurev should also rise. Yurev stood and the lama touched the manuscripts to his head then handed them over. "*Hail the first ring of attainment. Hail the blue dogs, custodians of mercy. Hail the jewel of the lotus. Om mani padme hum.*" He opened the folds of his *chuba,* revealing around his neck the necklace that Alexander the Great, son of Philip, had made for his queen two thousand years ago.

The necklace was magnificent. It hung down to the middle of the lama's chest, ending in a large, wine-red garnet in which a cameo of Alexander had been carved. On each side of the red stone were alternating gold links connecting sculpted lotus petals, also gold. Rubies were mounted in the center of each petal except for the last three on either side of the garnet. In these were mounted what appeared to be black stones—the jewels of the lotus. Alexander had ordered the walnut-sized stones dipped in the juice of the beetlenut, a hard tarlike substance which was not to be removed until the necklace had been delivered to his Roxanne. Only Roxanne was to look on the brilliance of their everlasting light. Even with the black covering Yurev recognized the primitive Indian facets. They were diamonds, of course, cut three hundred years before Christ.

The Pearls of Light.

Bowing his head slightly, the lama removed the necklace and placed it over Yurev's head. " 'Godspeed to you,' " the high lama said, " 'for the honor of his French majesty, Sun King, protector of the faith.' "

"Français?" Barbaree was on his feet. "What's that about France?"

"It's all rote," Yurev said. "The lamas of this monastery have been waiting for generations to hand this over. It's what Tavernier told them to say. While he was here he must have taught them a bit of French. They've been practicing it, generation after generation, for two hundred and forty years . . . and waiting." Yurev touched the garnet in the center of the necklace, felt the figurehead of Alexander. He turned it over between his fingers. The reverse startled him because it was cut exactly opposite to the obverse side. It was an intaglio cut, a relief, and the design was the *dorje* symbol, a devil dog fettered in chains, charm against evil. He remembered Fa Shing's story of his trek into these mountains from China and the monk who had forecast a dream.

"Holy One," Yurev began. He was confused and unsure how to proceed. Fa Shing was the key to the events here, he was sure of it now, but exactly what it had to do with him he still didn't know. If Fa Shing was truly a messenger, a link between Tavernier and the Shelkagari to him, then this holy one would know, wouldn't he? "*Holy One, there have been many gorah sahibs here before, yes?*"

"*Many gorah sahibs.*"

"*Why haven't you shown these stones to them?*"

"*One other,*" the lama said. "*But it was not to be him.*"

Yurev's mouth was dry again. The lama had to be talking about Fa Shing. "*Was it a man from the north? He came many years ago to these hills. A holy one revealed a vision to him. Are you that same holy one?*" Yurev could feel his pulse beating in his head. "*A Chinese?*"

The lama's eyes held Yurev's for several moments.

"*The holy one said he was to be the messenger,*" Yurev continued. "*That one day a man would come to him—*"

"*Long time past,*" the lama said. "*Gorah sahib come to Ratnapa, saw stones, but was not One Who Would Come After. He use picture box on sticks, dig in ground, look at rocks, make drawings from stones, then leave.*" The lama moved to the shelf of manuscripts, searching through them. He withdrew a stack with charcoal smudges outlining Devanabolic characters. From one of the pages fell a scrap of paper. "*Drawings from stones,*" the Holy One said.

Yurev's attention was suddenly drawn to the scrap on the floor—a torn photograph, years old. Even from a distance he recognized it—the missing half of Abby's Ratnapa photo.

"Yurev, would you *mind* telling us what's going on?" Abby said, her patience gone. "Does he know where Shelkagari is?"

Yurev waved her off, his mind on the photo. Fa Shing was the figure in the missing side. It *had* to be Fa Shing. Yurev restrained himself from rushing to it.

The lama retrieved the torn photo, then produced Abby's half from the folds of his *chuba*. He touched them together. The two parts matched exactly but the second figure was not Fa Shing. The man in the picture was tall and wore a mustache. His arms were crossed and he was smiling, his hat shading his eyes, one foot forward on an outcrop of rock. The lama handed the complete photograph to Yurev. "*Ratnapa, from some time past,*" he said. "*Gorah sahib Bert Hoover, Drawer of stones.*"

Bert Hoover! Yurev stared at the angular face. Fa Shing's American friend from China. It was Hoover who had seen the stones, not Fa Shing. The only sahib since Tavernier to see the Pearls of Light turned out to be a geologist, an engineer who wasn't even looking for them. So destiny hadn't brought him here; there was no great plan. Fa Shing wasn't a messenger from the gods, just a sentimental old Chinese with a weakness for superstition . . .

The lama had moved to the door. "Come," he said, bowing and gesturing for them to follow. "Some drink."

"Yurey?" Abby's eyes were inquisitive.

Yurev felt cheated, and embarrassed by his own pretensions. He had wanted to believe Fa Shing, to be part of the old man's dream. "That way," Yurev said, glancing at Abby. He nodded at the lama. "We're to have *tea.*" He'd rather have had a strong shot of whiskey.

The balcony was adjacent to the high lama's private quarters, the highest point of the monastery. Below, the smooth surface of the monastery wall angled two hundred feet to the valley floor. Pillows had been set out for them in an orderly fashion, centered on the square blocks that were the balcony floor. Beside each pillow was a cup of steaming tea. Otherwise the balcony floor was bare, well-swept. They spent the better part of the morning there drinking tea. Abby was quiet, Barbaree bored. He paced around the balcony, studying the blocks as if he had an abiding interest in stone craftsmanship. Yurev and the high lama sat facing each other as Yurev read Tavernier's manuscript, occasionally asking something in French of the Old One. Twice they left the balcony to refer to other texts in the book room.

As Yurev returned from the second trip, Abby was sipping her tea beside the wall, staring at the rocky terrain below. Barbaree was asleep, using a pillow to shade the sun. Kancha was where he had been from the beginning, squarely on his pillow as if attached to it, prostrating himself whenever the Holy One appeared.

Yurev knelt beside Abby. "Tavernier didn't find Shelkagari," he said in a low voice.

Abby looked up dully. "What?"

Yurev sat with his back against the wall. He held the manuscript in his lap. "Tavernier never actually saw Shelkagari. What he found were scrolls." He felt very tired and turned his head slightly to catch the breeze. The book room had been like an oven.

"Scrolls? What scrolls?"

"It's a bit involved."

Abby turned to face him, elbows on her knees, supporting her chin. "I'm listening."

"May I?" Yurev pointed to her cup of tea. "It's very dry inside."

She handed him the drink. "What have scrolls got to do—"

Yurev held up his hand. He emptied the cup. "It has to do with Kancha's story about the siege of Tramar-Dri," he said. Yurev shook his head. "Let me start at the beginning."

"Thank you."

"Early in the eleventh century India was invaded by Moslems. Do you know your history?"

"Bastille Day is in July, and Sherman burned Atlanta in eighteen sixty something. On Moslem invasions, I'm not exactly current."

"India has been ripe for conquest since before Alexander," Yurev said shortly. "The Moslems honed the practice to a science."

"All right, sorry."

"Early in the eleventh century the Sultan Mahmud of Ghazni made several raids into India. He came through the Punjab but his armies went everywhere. Hindus and Buddhists were considered unclean infidels and so were slaughtered by the thousands, their temples and holy places ransacked and burned. From a Buddhist temple in Shanjahanabad— middle north India—the Holy One sent a monk into the hills with the temple's holy light. A stone, a very large stone. The monk had one duty . . . to protect the stone, to keep it out of the hands of the advancing Moslem army. It was his life's mission. His name was Ayrub Ravi."

"The stone was Shelkagari?"

"Well, Tavernier thought so."

"Jesus."

"Ravi was a Brahman, a priest," Yurev continued. "He was educated to be a recorder of events."

"A scribe."

"Exactly. And as he traveled he kept a diary so that when he returned to his Holy One he could show not only where he had gone but, more important, where he'd hidden the holy light. His diary was written on parchment about seven inches by two inches, several leaves—the scrolls." Yurev opened to one of the pages of the manuscript. "In all of Tavernier's notes there's only this one bit of translation from Ravi's text." He glanced at her. "Would you like to hear it?"

Abby shrugged. "Don't leave out any dirty parts."

" 'Hear ye all, mighty potentates, covet not Shelkagari. For he who embraces the Mountain of Light, shall he inherit the Island of Jewels, yea also suffer the violence of the divine faces. Until heir of the third princely son loosen the hounds of azure, shall only the Divine One possess the Miraculous Gift.' " Yurev looked up from the page. "It's called the Promise of Ushas."

"Ushas?"

"Goddess of Dawn."

"So what does it mean?"

"I don't know, but Tavernier thought it was important. He found the scrolls here."

"*Here?* Tramar-Dri?"

Yurev smiled. "You're sitting on them."

◆ FIFTEEN

YUREV LADLED TEA INTO Abby's cup. He drank it, surveying the view from the top of the monastery.

"All right. Tell me what the hell you're talking about." Abby's hair rippled, touched by the breeze. "*What* am I sitting on?"

"First, the siege," Yurev said. "You see, when Ayrub Ravi left his temple in India it wasn't without notice. The holy light was, after all, a very precious thing. People knew it was gone. And it didn't take the invaders long to figure out that something important was missing, accustomed as they were to stealing everything of value before torching places."

"So?"

"They sent an army after Ayrub Ravi," Yurev said. "An army . . . three hundred warriors, carts, horses . . . everything."

"For one priest?"

"A formidable sight, I would think, a mob like that clanking up these valleys and passes. And slow, too."

"That was the army at Tramar-Dri. After the priest."

"After Shelkagari," Yurev said. "Listen." He turned to a passage in Tavernier's manuscript. " 'To the holy city of the Red Cliffs, Tramar-Dri in the hidden valley beyond Benithog, came again the Reverent One to rest after his worried travels. A short while only did this journeyer pause a second time before the valley vibrated under the heavy beat of Sultan's war gongs. Three score and nine days did the Moslems attempt to broach the holy city without victory. The valley below the walls ran scarlet with the blood of innocents in such horrid and vile manner as cannot be here

162

described. And still the valiant defenders refused to give up their brother from below the hills.' " Yurev closed the manuscript. "The siege."

"The army caught up with the priest here."

"Right, but *after* he'd hidden Shelkagari." Yurev nodded at the monstrous peaks these people called hills. "Somewhere."

"After? But if the army followed him here, surely he still had the diamond?"

Yurev found the page again. He looked at Abby. "Ayrub Ravi stopped here twice. Once on the way up with the stone. Then again . . . on his way back. I told you that an army that size had to have been slow. They must have been weeks behind his trail. When they found him at this monastery Ravi was on his way back to his temple. He'd already hidden the stone. He was going home."

Abby considered it, nodded. "Okay. But that still doesn't explain the scrolls. If this priest was on his way home why didn't he take the scrolls with him? I mean, if this horde of Moslem soldiers took a swan dive into the gorge then there was no one to stop him. Right? You *did* say the scrolls are here. Right?"

"But Ayrub Ravi died here," Yurev said. "Winter killed him. Tavernier says he wasn't a young man when he started. He's walked up here from the plains of India. Walked. No frontier train, no porters. Three hundred miles barefoot into these hills with an army at his back. Just Ravi and a twelve-pound stone. Yurev glanced at the high lama. "The Holy One read to me from the texts of their own *mollas* . . . history books. Ayrub Ravi was sick, but before he died, he had the scrolls copied. The original was buried with him."

"Buried! Jesus, you said Tavernier found them."

"So he did," Yurev said. He opened his hand, gesturing to the balcony's stone-block floor. "Right here. Ayrub Ravi had the scrolls copied here . . . carved into the stones." He glanced at Abby. "You're sitting on his tomb."

Abby's fingers trembled. She touched the warm square of stone beside her pillow. The hard edges had been worn down, but the impressions were there, the classical Devanabolic script, like a beautiful faded pattern.

"It's Sanskrit," Yurev said. "But I think we could persuade our host to have it translated for us."

"I didn't even notice." Abby ran her hands across the surface. "It's almost worn smooth."

"I'm not surprised. It's been here a thousand years . . . and swept every day."

She glanced up. "This is it," she said slowly. "Jesus . . . *this is it.* A map to Shelkagari!"

"Not quite a map is it, luv?" Barbaree moved from under his pillow, squinting in the sunlight. "Just some scribblings, I make it."

Abby turned to him. "You heard what Yurey discovered?"

"Discovered? I'd hardly call it that." Stone carvings and ageless myths did not arouse his imagination. The Pearls of Light were real—six diamonds, any one of which could make him rich. Money was reality.

"You don't believe it?"

"Have you ever heard why the water buffalo holds its head up?"

"What?"

Barbaree grinned. "The water buffalo. You see, the water buffalo and the yak were good friends. They both loved salt, but in the lowlands there wasn't much salt. So the yak said he'd go into the high hills to find some if the water buffalo would loan him his coat of hair. The water buffalo agreed, and the yak went off and never returned. To this day the water buffalo has no hair, but he holds his head up, searching, waiting for the yak to bring him salt." Barbaree glanced from Yurev to Abby, smiling. "Poetic little bit of tripe, isn't it? These people have a gift for making nonsense alluring."

"This isn't tripe," Abby said angrily. She pointed to the stone floor. "For godsakes, it's written right in front of your eyes."

"Ah, you're the expert now, are you, luv? You interpret ancient classical Sanskrit back in Chicago, do you?" Barbaree pointed at the necklace around Yurev's neck. His smile had disappeared. "There's what's in front of *my* eyes. Diamonds. *Real* diamonds. All the rest is rot. That mumbo jumbo is Bhot nonsense. It's nothing to do with eleventh-century priests or eroding blocks of stone or bloody turnips for that matter!"

"Shelkagari is real," Yurev said. "It exists. We're standing on the proof."

"Bloody proof—"

"We can find it."

"Find it? Look, mate, you're wearing *six* fortunes around your neck. That's two for each of us. I'm a rich man, I am. And rich men do not risk their necks acting like fools. Not *this* one, I can tell you."

"We aren't going to split up the diamonds," Abby said. "The necklace isn't a goddamn treasure chest full of coins. But Shelkagari is more important. It's the mother stone. Finding the necklace is nothing compared to finding Shelkagari."

"Good. You look for your mythical stone, and I'll keep these . . . the little buggers."

Yurev climbed to his feet. The high lama, sitting cross-legged in the shade on his red pillow, had patiently listened to this conversation, understanding none of it. Yurev made his decision abruptly. There was only one way to make Barbaree see that they were not finished. He spoke to the lama in French. The lama rose, his face curious, eyes alert.

"What's this, then?" Barbaree said.

Yurev kept his eyes on the lama. "*A gift, Holy One. To safekeep a short time longer.*"

The old man moved beside the railing, in front of Yurev. He held his hands together, bowing his head as Yurev placed the necklace around his neck.

"What the bloody hell are you doing?" Barbaree was on his feet.

"I'm giving it back."

"What!"

To Abby, Yurev said, "Until we return with Shelkagari."

She was startled at first, then her face smoothed into a smile. "Perfect."

"The *hell* you say." Barbaree charged toward the lama, kicking a pillow across the patio. "We're not doing any such thing." He held out his hand to the Holy One. "Let's have it. They're bloody maniacs, they are."

The Holy One bowed to Barbaree. "*Om mani padme hum.*"

"The necklace will be safe here," Yurev said. "We're going to find Shelkagari."

"Not with me, you're not." Barbaree stepped closer to the Holy One. "C'mon."

The high lama took a step back. His bare foot touched the patio wall. His eyes flashed at Yurev, suddenly questioning. Kancha came instantly to his feet as Barbaree pressed in.

"Jack-bishy, Jack-bishy! Not touching Holy One. Not touching Holy One. Jack-bishy—"

Barbaree grabbed the garnet at the center of the necklace and jerked it away, snapping the gold clasp that held it around the lama's neck. He turned to Yurev, holding the necklace up in his fist. "You had no right to do that. No right!"

"Jack, for chrissakes—"

"A third of these stones belong to me. You have no right—"

"*Aha! Hundaaina! Dinos phirtaa!*" The lama, stunned by Barbaree's action and suddenly inflamed by the chatter, stood on his toes, reaching high with both hands raised to the necklace. "*Dinos phirtaa!*"

Barbaree's reaction was protective, pushing the old man away with his forearm, forcing the lama back another step, off balance.

"Jack—no!" Yurev rushed forward, realizing even as he did that he was too late.

The Holy One tumbled over the wall in a flash of red as he passed from the shade of the patio into bright sunlight. Yurev's fingers closed on air as he lunged to catch the holy *chuba*.

He became spectator to death once more as the man cartwheeled away from him like a spoon down a well. It seemed an eternity before the high lama's body struck the rocks below, bouncing once against the wall, the red cloak flapping madly, before ending in a quiet, sickening bump and a flutter of dust. He didn't scream. Tramar-Dri's most holy one didn't make a sound in his very last moment before nirvana.

◆ SIXTEEN

ABBY WAS BESIDE YUREV, looking down at the broken body sprawled over jagged rocks. The edges of the *chuba* flapped lazily in the breeze, covering the old man's open, sightless eyes. Yurev remembered his mother, crumpled in the snow, killed by Russian patriots.

"It was an accident." Barbaree was still holding the necklace. His face was drained of color, and his voice was weak. "I didn't mean . . ." He looked over the wall, then at Yurev. "He came after me. You saw it." He looked at Abby. "You saw what happened." She could only stare back at him.

It was a new side that Barbaree was showing, Yurev thought. "Give me the necklace," he said.

"What?" Barbaree eyes were wide.

"The necklace."

Barbaree looked at it in his hand as if it were something evil. "Yes, yes, here." He handed it over quickly. "Take the bloody thing."

"Holy One . . ."

Yurev saw Kancha get to his feet. The little Nepalese's eyes looked glazed, as if he couldn't believe what he had just witnessed. "Most Holy One . . . dead?" He looked at Barbaree. "Jack-bishy?"

"It was an accident—"

"Holy ones coming soon, Jack-bishy," Kancha said, obviously frightened. "Throwing Kancha on rocks also."

Cries rose from below as red-robed monks gathered at the foot of the wall. Yurev watched as they moved close to the body, touching it, terrified of the blood. Some of them were already raising their faces to the patio, shading their eyes from the sun, looking up to the top of the long wall.

"We've got to get out of here." Perspiration beaded on Barbaree's upper lip. "Kancha's right. They'll kill us for this." He scrambled to the door, peeking inside.

"*Us?*" Abby regained anger from shock. "*We* didn't do anything."

"Right. You explain it to them—three foreigners, *gorah* sahibs, alone with the Holy One when he falls two hundred feet from his own patio. I'm sure they'll understand that. Me, I'm getting out." Barbaree opened the door. When he turned back his eyes were on Yurev. "You coming?"

Yurev glanced down at the crowd that had gathered around the corpse. Many of them were on their knees, wailing to heaven. The rest were looking at him. He looked past Abby. "Yes."

They moved quickly through one dark room after another, retracing their steps from the high lama's chamber. Monks ran to answer desperate calls from the south end of the cliff. Barbaree led the way, waiting in doorways until it was clear, then darting ahead. In one of the grain depositories Yurev found a goatskin bag filled with dry barley, quickly emptied it and placed Tavernier's manuscript and the necklace inside, slipping the harness over his shoulder.

"Don't stop, don't talk, just keep going," Barbaree said. "When we get to the first rampart put your boots on fast."

When they reached the main terrace of the *gumpa* twenty yards of open court remained to be crossed to the stairway down. Monks were scattered everywhere, hurrying up and down the stairs like busy termites.

"But our packs—"

"Leave them. We're just out for a stroll. Nothing suspicious in that."

"Just walk away?" Abby looked at him incredulously.

"Brass it out. They're still confused, unsure exactly what's going on. The *unze* is the only one who really knows we were with the lama. Just smile if anyone speaks to you but don't stop. We'll make it out of here, luv." He stripped off his belt, wrapping the thick leather around his hand. The buckle faced outward, making a vicious weapon. "I've cleared out a few pubs with this before, I can tell you."

"Where the hell are we going? Not back to Benithog?"

"No." Barbaree pointed to the narrow slit in the cliffs across the valley. "That way. I buried the revolvers and packs under a stupa. No one's going to follow us to the glacier."

"You wouldn't shoot them?"

"Two hundred angry monks? With sticks and rocks? Bloody right
. . . and so would you." He looked around the door. "All right . . . let's
go."

Prayer flags stood out from their stanchions, whipped by the cold
morning wind as the four walked briskly across the courtyard and down
to the first rampart.

"Just take your boots," Barbaree said with a fixed smile as they came
on their gear stacked together. He nodded politely to one of the sweepers.
"Smile, luv."

Abby pulled her boots on. She showed her teeth to the monk, and the
sweeper, respectfully, extended his tongue.

They moved down the wide stairs four abreast, Barbaree on the outside.
Sweepers stood aside as they passed, and Yurev avoided looking any of
them in the eye, focusing his attention on the terrain between the *gumpa*
and the cliffs across the valley. He guessed the distance to be a mile,
possibly less, and every foot of it strewn with rocks. It was a long way to
run.

"*Basnu Bedeshi.*"

The shrill voice came from behind, from a balcony high in the monastery. Yurev glanced at Barbaree from the corner of his eye.

"Don't stop," Barbaree said. "Don't look back. Whatever happens,
don't stop."

The voice cried out again, pitched high with rage and mourning,
competing in the wind against the flapping of the prayer flags. It was
Tupjuk-se. Yurev recognized his voice. The *unze's* tirade continued until
others joined in, making a growing chorus of angry voices. Beside Yurev,
Kancha, his short legs hurrying to keep up, gasped and glanced back.

"Jack-bishy—"

"Shut up!" Barbaree unleashed his belt, letting out half its length, and
swung it. The buckle cut through the air, forcing aside a sweeper who
stood in his way. As they walked across the last rampart, turning down
the final set of stairs, two young sweepers were already moving up to meet
them. They held their thick-handled straw brooms horizontally in front
of them, a passive gesture of restraint. They looked bewildered, as if they
were untrained soldiers unsure of their duty.

"*Basnu! Basnu!*" they said together.

Barbaree yelled at them, motioning with his arms to let them pass. The
voices behind them were now the chaotic cries of a mob, echoing across
the cliffs. Yurev could barely hear Barbaree's barked order.

"Take the broom!"

Barbaree grabbed the broom of the monk in front of him with both hands, twisting it savagely to his left, knocking the startled sweeper to his knees. It was a fluid motion executed with the skill of a man who was never really out of the British army. But by training it demanded more. With a quick powerful overhead thrust, just as he had shown Abby how to kill a snake, Sergeant Major Barbaree swung the thick blunt end at his enemy's forehead.

"Jesus, Jack, don't—"

The cracking skull was like a muffled gunshot; a soft, mushy explosion. Yurev felt warm blood splatter on his cheek. The monk's body was propelled backward by the crushing blow, flip-flopping down the stairway, bumping down each step, tumbling down and down, coming finally to rest against one of the large red stupas that marked the entrance to the monastery. The trail of blood was marked by splotches where the monk's head had squashed against the cleanly swept stone steps. The silence that followed came slowly, like a wave, moving up each level until it reached the highest balcony. For a moment the only sounds were the prayer flags, wildly flapping, beating out a rhythm like a palpitating heart.

"Biraami chhu."

Yurev looked back at the second monk. Mouth open, eyes wide, the young monk dropped his broom, held his hands back, palms out, cowering against the wall.

"Keep moving," Barbaree commanded. He pushed Kancha forward with the bloodied end of his weapon. "Yurey, pick up the broom, you may need it before this is done. Head straight for the cliffs. When I tell you, run."

"I don't—"

"Don't argue with me. Move. *Now.*"

Yurev took the broom and with Abby moved quickly down the stairs, his bare feet sliding once in the blood. The voice from the top of the monastery started again but this time it contained no shrill anger. It was a chant, and it started slowly, pounding in resonance as the rest of the holy ones added their voices. Yurev and Abby were two hundred yards from the monastery, the chant echoing all around them, when Yurev realized that the pounding cadence was the monks beating their feet against the stone. When it suddenly stopped, Yurev turned back to a grisly spectacle. Barbaree, twenty yards behind, was carrying the dead monk over his shoulder. The body was nude, stripped of its red *chuba*, and Barbaree's jacket was covered with blood.

"My God, what are you doing?"

Barbaree waved him on. "Don't stop. Keep moving." He glanced back at the monastery as the echoes of the chant died away, then straightened, dropping the body at his feet. He pulled off his jacket, tying the sleeves around the waist of the corpse. "Now," Barbaree yelled at Yurev. "Run."

But Yurev's attention was diverted by the movement at the monastery. The courtyards, the ramparts, the stairs were crowded with the figures of Tramar-Dri's holy monks—hundreds more than he thought possible, their red robes blended in the distance with the color of the painted buildings. Yurev watched until a cry went up and suddenly the monks were pouring out of the monastery, an angry red stream of vengeance.

Abby gasped. "Oh my God . . ."

Barbaree was pounding toward them. "Run. Damn you—*run.*"

Yurev ran. With Kancha's help he kept Abby in front of him, pushing her, encouraging her whenever she fell, pulling her up and pushing her on. It was impossible to run on the terrain, even wearing boots. Every step was a fight for balance. The rocks were like knurls of cut glass. Yurev's hands bled, and his knees and shins ached. But he kept running, urging Abby, moving ahead.

Barbaree caught up. His shirt was wet with blood and sweat as he fought to get his breath. "That way, Kancha," and he pointed to a small stupa at the mouth of the cliffs fifty yards away. "Take memsahib . . . two packs buried . . . under monument. Revolvers inside."

Kancha nodded.

Barbaree held Yurev's shoulder, waiting until Kancha and Abby were gone. He put his hand on the goatskin bag. "You have the diamonds . . . in there?"

Yurev couldn't talk. He was looking at the stupa. Fifty yards might as well be fifty miles.

"You *do* have them?"

Yurev nodded. His legs were jelly. He shouldn't have stopped.

"Good." Barbaree wiped sweat from his eyes. He glanced toward the stupa. "Remember"—he swallowed, forcing air into his lungs—"remember to aim for the mouth."

Yurev looked at him. "You haven't killed enough of them?" He shook his head. "I won't shoot unarmed men—"

"You bloody idiot. The monks . . . they aren't going to lay a hand on us." Barbaree twisted Yurev around to see what was behind them. "*Look.*"

The multitude of holy ones moved like a slowly advancing army. They seemed to stretch across the whole valley. Barefooted, they had to pick their way through the sharp rocks and had not yet reached the place where Barbaree had dumped the body. But something else was moving ahead of the army.

"The dogs, man, the bloody dogs."

There were nine of them. At a dead run the smooth black beasts were terrors from hell racing across the uncertain ground like dark apparitions, not slowing or stopping until they reached the monk's body.

"Now we'll see," Barbaree said.

Deceived by the *gorah* sahib's jacket, the animals attacked the body, tearing at the remains like jackals over a carcass, their teeth flashing in the sunlight. And through it all they did not make a sound. Yurev watched, repulsed and fascinated. But one of the animals, larger than the others, held back. It trotted back and forth, oblivious to the melee, ears up, dark eyes searching.

"Bloody black bitch," Barbaree yelled. "The *keti*'s not buying it."

"*Keti?*"

"Runs the pack. Female. Biggest, smartest of the bunch."

Yurev watched the female mastiff trot back and forth—she stopped, her searching black eyes drawn to the spot where Yurev rested on his haunches. The dog bared its teeth, and in an instant the *keti* was on the run, a streaking black specter heading straight for them.

"*C'mon.*" Barbaree shoved Yurev forward. "Before they're all on our necks."

Yurev tried to keep up with Barbaree but his legs wouldn't obey. He stumbled over the rocks, the heavy goatskin bag banging against his hip with every step. Ahead, Abby and Kancha were on their knees, digging with their hands at the base of the Buddhist monument. When Barbaree got to them Yurev was still far behind. A brisk, frigid wind was coming from the opening in the cliffs into Yurev's face, and he had to bow his head, fighting for every breath.

"*Yurev . . .*"

Yurev glanced up. Barbaree was digging now, pulling on the strap of a pack, but Abby had stopped. She was frozen, looking past Yurev.

He didn't hear the dog, only saw it when he turned. The *keti* stood no more than ten feet away, its black eyes locked on him. The animal was monstrous, larger even than the stuffed demons in the lama's prayer room. Saliva hung like string from the corners of its open mouth, blown back on its powerful shoulders by the wind. The animal still didn't move. In the near distance the others were coming, bounding over the rocks.

The wind blew up around Yurev, penetrating his *chuba*, his sweat suddenly a cold film on his skin. Still the *keti* didn't move. Closer now, Yurev could see the wild eyes of the pack. Their broad snouts and teeth were red with the blood of the dead *trawa*. Within seconds the rest of the pack arrived, mouths snapping as they hurdled the last few yards to where the *keti* stood. Yurev braced himself. But they did not attack. Instead, they positioned themselves in staggered formation on either side of the *keti*, panting, eyes wary.

Barbaree spoke now from behind. "Move to your right a bit, mate. I'll blow her bloody head off."

Yurev heard the double click of the hammer drawn back. "No." He held his hand up. The *keti*'s eyes followed Yurev's movement. Across the plain the horde of monks were still coming, their incessant cries now like the din of rain echoing in Kali Gandaki's gorge.

Yurev swung into the wind toward Barbaree. "Don't shoot, they won't—"

The explosion from Barbaree's gun overpowered the whistle of wind. Flame leapt from the muzzle in a brilliant flash of light. "No . . ." But Yurev's voice was swallowed in the sound of gunfire. The wind carried the smell of burnt cordite. Barbaree held a revolver in each hand, firing them alternately. Abby had the third pistol, holding the heavy weight of it with both hands, shooting in panic.

Four dogs went down without a sound, killed instantly by the large-bore weapons. The rest, whipped into frenzy by the gunfire, attacked. Two animals fell on Yurev, ripping at his arms and legs as he tried to fend them off. He screamed as teeth slashed through his boot, gouging out leather and skin. Another bit into his arm below the elbow, sinking teeth to the bone. Yurev tried to roll away to protect his face and caught a glimpse of Kancha rushing toward him with a broom.

The little Nepalese proceeded to wade into the dogs, swinging the broom handle like a club, striking the dogs on their heads and hind quarters, driving them back.

"Be running quickly," Kancha called out.

Yurev tried to move, lurching forward on his hands and knees. The tattered sleeve of his left arm was soaked red. His hand was slick with blood. He fell, slipping off a rock as he tried to support himself to stand.

The dogs attacked again, now focusing on Kancha. Yurev heard the crack of the broomstick as it snapped in the jaws of a dog. Kancha went down, his blue corporal's jacket flapping in the wind. His screams echoed off the cliffs. Like jackals, the dogs were on him.

Yurev felt himself being dragged across the rocks, Barbaree had him by the collar, pulling him away from the melee.

"Get up," Barbaree ordered. Yurev tried to get to his feet. A wounded dog jumped at Barbaree, its slashing teeth ripping at his head. Barbaree shot it through the spine, splashing blood into Yurev's face. "Hold on to me." Barbaree reached for him.

Yurev held tight to Barbaree's shoulder, and half-running, half-stumbling, they moved into the wind of the canyon behind the cliffs. Blood ran down Barbaree's neck. The dog had ripped a notch in his earlobe.

"Kancha." Yurev tried to look back but Barbaree pushed him on.

"He's done," Barbaree called. "Keep moving, keep *moving*."

They ran on for several minutes, following the steep winding walls deeper into the canyon. Abby ran beside them, often backwards, screaming against the wind that her revolver was empty. Finally Yurev could go no further. He pushed himself away from Barbaree and dropped against the smooth canyon wall. Blood dripped from his fingertips.

"My arm . . ."

Abby dropped to her knees, literally panting. She pulled Yurev's hand away from the wound and blood spurted on her cheek. "Oh, Jesus . . ."

The dogbite was a jagged gash; strings of flesh hung from the wound, stiff with dried blood. "Tie it off," Yurev said between clenched teeth. "Rip the sleeve."

Abby folded back his *chuba* and ripped Yurev's shirt sleeve into strips, tying them over the seeping wound in a compress.

"Give me a pistol," Barbaree said. He was on one knee, reloading his revolvers, watching the way behind them. "Quick."

Abby handed it over. Her face was dirty with dust and streaked by dried tears. "They tore him apart," she said in a voice barely a whisper. She looked into Yurev's eyes. "Kancha. The dogs . . . they just tore him . . . they tore him . . ."

"He's dead and we're not," Barbaree said. "Be thankful for that." He reloaded her pistol, snapping the cylinder shut with a flick of his hand. He nodded to Yurev. "And he doesn't look too good." He shoved the pistol into Abby's hand. "I don't think the dogs will come after us, but if they do aim for the mouth. It'll go right through the brain."

Abby held the weapon limply in her hand. "What have we done . . ."

"We've survived, is what."

"God, Jack . . . your ear . . ."

Barbaree touched the rip in his earlobe. "Bloody lucky, I say . . . bugger was going for my neck." He pointed down the canyon. "We have to move on, a different way. We can't go back to Benithog. There's a way down the glacier, west then south. Two, maybe three days to the snow line—"

"The gorge?"

"No, not the bloody gorge. It isn't safe."

"Safe? Jesus Christ, it was never safe. Why can't we go the way we came?"

"Because of what happened," Barbaree said angrily. "These hill people have a peculiar respect for their holy ones. They'd kill us if we went back. I've seen hill justice. I don't fancy being tied up alive in a burlap bag and rolled off a cliff." He turned to Yurev. "I'll have the stones."

"What?" Yurev glanced up quickly.

"We'll leave you a revolver." Barbaree stared at him without expression.

It took a moment for Yurev to realize what he was saying. "You don't think you're leaving me *here?*"

"You're too weak. Look at yourself, you can't even stand."

Yurev pushed himself to his feet, balancing on his good leg. "I can walk, of course I can walk." The pain from the bite through his boot made him falter. "You aren't going to leave me here . . ." He took a step and stayed upright through sheer will. "You see?"

"You're a bloody marathoner, you are, mate," Barbaree said. He held out his hand. "The stones."

"I don't think so." Abby's voice was suddenly strong. She stood braced against the raw wind, her hair and *chuba* caught in the draft. "Nobody's getting left behind, Jack. Unless you want to stay." She held the gun now with both hands, aimed at Barbaree's chest.

Barbaree looked at the gun. "Just wait, now, don't be a bloody fool, luv. You and I can get out but he's done—"

The double-click hammer action of her weapon cut through the drone of wind. "You get us out of here, damn you. *All* of us. Or we end it right here. You decide, *luv.*"

Barbaree nodded. "Sure, why not, we're all partners." He glanced at Yurev. "Just remember, old boy, it's a long walk down. A very *long* walk."

"I'll make it," Yurev said. His eyes were on the Englishman. Yurev had never felt such a rush of hatred. It absorbed him even beyond pain. "I'll make it."

"This way, then." Barbaree offered his wooden smile. Behind him the canyon whined. The Valley of Weeping Winds moaned its monotonous song with ancient complacency.

◆ SEVENTEEN

No more barren terrain exists on the planet than the soundless, windless landscape of a Himalayan glacier.

Yurev was awed from the first moment he saw it. Barbaree's narrow canyon opened onto a massive tongue of ice and rock that sloped steeply between isolated peaks. It seemed to have no beginning or end, just a frozen river, stuck in time, that moved only as a consequence of its own immeasurable weight. Hour after hour as he made his way down the slope the view did not change—treacherous ice and patches of smooth rounded sheepbacks, bedrock scarred and cracked from an eon of glacial tides. During the day the view was devoid of color, only gradations between white and gray against the burnished metal hue of far-away, snow-crowned summits. At dusk the sky became a rainbow of flames, the Dhaulagiri peaks turned purple, then black, as twilight faded to night, unveiling a million stars.

The sterile beauty masked an unforgiving nature. Stepping down a glacier was monstrous work that required agility and conditioned legs. Yurev had neither. His trek across the craggy ice was a walk through hell. Barbaree set a blistering pace, Abby and Yurev lagging far behind. The first casualty was conversation. The arid atmosphere combined with the physical exertion made their mouths dry out. Breathing expelled visible plumes of air, each breath a piercing labor that seared the lungs. Eventually the distance between Yurev and Abby stretched out and walking became an individual challenge.

The first night's camp was the hump of a sheepback rock twenty feet square in bitter cold. Without food to eat or kindling to burn their nighttime goal was to keep their feet from freezing. The heavy, coarse weave of their *chubas* was just enough protection for their bodies but not their feet.

"Take your boots off and hold them under your robes," Barbaree said. It was only the third time that Yurev had heard him speak all day. "We'll sleep head to foot, Abby in the middle. She'll hold our feet, and our bodies will keep her from freezing. Keep your hoods over your faces, or your noses and ears will frostbite."

"Is this really going to keep us warm?" Abby's voice was weak with exhaustion.

"No, luv. It's going to keep us alive."

And it did. At sunrise they were off again. The second day was a repeat of the first, an endless vista of ice and rock. Yurev fell further and further behind, stopping often to adjust the binding over the dog bite above his ankle. His leather boot had saved the bone but the skin had been ripped in parallel gashes. The wound bled very little, on account of the cold, Yurev decided, which seemed to speed the clotting action. Still, the binding chafed his leg, and the blood-saturated cloth had frozen, eventually working free and slipping down inside his boot.

Several times during the day Yurev noticed that Barbaree would stop and wait for Abby, resting on a slab of bedrock. Then, as Yurev approached within a few hundred yards, the Englishman was up again, moving against the horizon. Yurev thought perhaps Barbaree was concerned, that his stopping was a show of encouragement. Abby set him straight.

"He doesn't want you getting lost," Abby told him. "You've got the diamonds."

Their second night on the glacier Barbaree burned his pack. It was a useless item, he said, since it only contained the gunbelts, ammunition, a small cookpot of Kancha's and a thirty-foot rope. The burning pack produced almost no flame but the heat warmed the rock. The hemp rope, however, was Abby's idea. It burned and crackled with tiny sparks of flames for almost an hour. Barbaree chipped ice into the cookpot, and they stewed strips of the leather gunbelt. The water never came to a boil but it was hot, and for a time the liquid warmed their stomachs. After chewing the softened leather for whatever nutrition existed in its juices they slept in the warm ashes of the fire.

When they reached the snow line the next day Yurev noticed that the rocks were showing signs of vegetation, sprigs of sandworts and edelweiss appearing in the cracks of bedrock. Around midday he caught up to Abby resting on a patch of rock and eating a plant.

"Yurev . . ." She handed him a small yellow flower. Her lips were cracked from the cold but she managed to smile. "I saved this for you, Jack says it's okay to eat."

The flower had no taste except a slight bitterness. Yurev ate it quickly, then pulled at the patch of grass beside the rock. He had to chew quite a lot before his saliva started running.

"Jack says we'll be in the trees tonight," Abby said. She was still panting slightly, her breath visible as she spoke. "That means a fire." She held up the cookpot she'd been carrying. "I'll make pine-cone tea or bark tea or some goddamn thing."

Yurev nodded with a mouthful of jasmine roots.

"How's your leg?"

"Well enough."

"Arm?"

Yurev raised his bandaged arm. He hadn't noticed the pain in hours. "Better." He looked downslope, shading his eyes. "Barbaree?" He saw a tiny dark figure in the distance.

"Forging ahead," Abby said. She touched Yurev's shoulder. "He's crazy, you know. The only thing he thinks to talk about is the diamonds . . . how he'll kill you if you drop them."

Yurev pulled the goatskin bag around by its strap, holding it on his lap. "It's safe . . . the necklace and the manuscript."

"I don't think we're safe."

Yurev watched the figure in the distance. "He's kept us alive. He could have killed both of us a dozen times and taken the stones."

"He just doesn't want to freeze to death. He's only needed us to keep warm. And something else—I think maybe Jack can read Devanagari script."

"What?"

"Back at the monastery—while you and the high lama were deep in French, Jack walked around the balcony several times. I thought he was just bored. Now"—she shrugged—"I don't know. Maybe I'm just nuts." Abby stood up. "I'm just saying that we need to be careful, Yurey. When we get to the lowlands—if we get there—he won't need us anymore."

Yurev nodded and kept moving, aware of the goatskin bag and the bulge of the necklace inside. He thought about Jack Barbaree. To the extent that the cold and the loneliness of two days on this empty barren icescape made one crazy, then they were all slightly insane. But something more than survival drove Barbaree. Yurev adjusted the bag's strap on his shoulder. He would have to do something about the Englishman. He'd known that since their confrontation in the canyon. What to do exactly, he hadn't yet decided. But staying alive, Yurev was convinced, meant more than surviving the elements.

The glacier penetrated the mixed conifer and broadleaf forest like spiked fingers. Abby and Yurev saw it hours before reaching the first trees. What for days had been an ash-colored sky due to low, misty clouds was now dark blue in the late afternoon. Beyond the forest was a green sea of lesser hills sprawling across the horizon, spilling one over another into lush valleys and tropical plains. Yurev could see some thirty miles. Ahead he could see the intermediate range of mountains below the Himalayas where they had toiled up and down ridges and cursed every step. He didn't curse them now.

"Yurev, down there." Abby was pointing to a faint line of smoke rising from among the trees. "Jack."

The distance was deceiving. What appeared to be near took half an hour to reach. Barbaree had built up quite a fire, five or six feet across, and was hacking at a branch with his knife when Yurev hobbled into the small clearing alongside Abby. The warmth of the fire radiated twenty feet. Even the ground felt soft.

Abby went straight to the fire, raising the skirt of her *chuba* to catch its heat. "Oh, God, thank you, thank you, Jesus."

"Was me that built it, luv." Barbaree splintered the branch across his knee and tossed it onto a pile of dead wood. He'd taken off his *chuba*. "It'll be cold again tonight, and we'll have to keep it going. You brought the cookpot?"

Abby held it up for him to see and turned to warm her backside. Yurev found a rock and lowered himself to it.

"Don't get too comfy, mate." Barbaree pointed his knife at the sky. "It'll be turning dark in an hour. We need more wood. We'll all rest once the work's done." He flipped the knife toward Yurev, and it clattered against the rock. "Can you manage it, old boy?"

Yurev picked up the knife. Barbaree smiled, arms folded across his chest. "I'll get the heavy bits, mate. You just find the branches with leaves for Abby's tea. We don't want to tax you, now do we?"

Yurev let it pass. Anyway, the bastard was right.

Night came quickly and with it the promised cold. Barbaree had built a lean-to affair from green leafy branches that caught and held the fire's heat. Beyond the radiation of the fire the air was frigid.

"I expect we're somewhere in this vicinity," Barbaree said, using a twig to point out a spot in the map he'd drawn in the soil. They sat in a semicircle, exposed to the fire. The cookpot rested on two charred logs pulled from the fire. Torn leaves lay in the bottom of Abby's slightly green tea. "If I'm correct," Barbaree continued, "then our course will be to guide on the rising sun and move south. In a few days we'll find a village where we can take a new bearing."

Abby ran her finger along the line that was to be the Kali Gandaki gorge. "We're safe . . . on this side?"

"Nobody's *safe* in the hills, luv. Not with winter coming on. Plenty of beasts hereabouts, scavenging for food."

"I was talking about the people. You said they'd—"

"We've come down the backside of Dhaulagiri, on the *west* side of Gandaki. There's a whole range between us and the river. This isn't a route that anyone takes. We might as well be on another continent as far as the monks from Tramar-Dri are concerned."

Yurev nodded beyond Barbaree's map. "How long before we reach Butwal? Will there be a train?"

"We aren't going to Butwal."

"What?"

"We're going to Bilaur." He poked the dirt with his stick. "Here. Further west."

"Why?"

"Less people to ask questions, for one . . . and Bilaur is where we pick up Rapti Khola."

"Who the hell is that?" Abby said.

"A river, luv, at the base of the Mahabharat range. On a boat we can be in Utraula two days before we would have gotten to Butwal. The frontier train stops in Utraula."

"So why didn't we go that way in the first place?"

"I didn't know we were looking for a bloody diamond fortune, *and* I didn't know we would wind up on the other side of Dhaulagiri . . . if you recall."

"How long?" Yurev said.

"To Bilaur . . . normally, I'd guess about four and one-half days. With you, six. We'll be cutting across a bit more rugged mountains than before but there are less of them. I don't think—"

The explosive noise of the gunshot startled everyone. The excited flurry from the brush was brief. Then quiet. Abby reached for her pistol, upsetting the cookpot of green tea.

"Easy, luv—"

Abby held the pistol with both hands, eyes alert, searching beyond the fire.

"Unless I'm very off my mark," Barbaree said, "that was a marmot or mouse-hare drawn by curiosity to the fire. I think now he's dinner."

Barbaree had rigged a cocked revolver in the brush with whittled branches. The tiniest movement of the barrel would set off the trigger.

"We're in luck," Barbaree said, returning with his victim, carrying it by its hind legs, dripping blood. It was a stone marten, a catlike squirrel that lived in the high forests. "Sharpen your sticks, stone man, tonight we feast on roast."

The meat was spare but they chewed every bone clean. When they lay down to sleep wrapped in their *chubas* they had food in their bellies, a warm fire, and a plan of action. And all provided by Barbaree. Yurev stared into the fire, letting the flames mesmerize him toward sleep. The Englishman had all the answers, damn him, knew all the tricks, but Yurev couldn't bring himself to put his trust in a man whose conscience was clear in the wake of three violent deaths. Yurev also didn't like the way he looked at Abby, the way he touched her with his eyes, and he detested his swaggering self-assurance. Jealousy? He couldn't discount it. This mountain trek had changed them all, but Barbaree most. The Englishman was a survivor. He would get out any way he could . . . and take with him exactly what he wanted.

The trick with the revolver drove the point home for Yurev. The weapon was hidden in the area where he'd been sent to fetch branches. Shooting the stone marten was just a pleasant surprise to Barbaree. Yurev closed his arms around the goatskin bag, and remained awake long into the night.

◆ EIGHTEEN

THE FORTRESS JUST APPEARED. They had been moving up and down trails for two days, Yurev limping along at his own pace with the aid of a staff he'd cut from a black juniper. At mid-afternoon, winding around a bend in the trail, they came on a small squat building made of cut stone perched on the side of the ridge. A young boy of about six was laying out dung patties in the sun. When he saw Barbaree, a fearfully pale stranger with hair on his face, the youngster bolted up the steps, waving his arms in warning.

"They're Gurunds," Barbaree said after a brief conference with the leader of the small band of villagers. Yurev and Abby sat on the edge of the trail while Barbaree laid out the situation. Behind him, arrayed on the steps to the isolated building, was the entire population of the settlement . . . seventeen men, women and children. "Nomads, they are, wandering around the hills, probably one family. That fellow there is their shaman. He says we're welcome to stay. They've never seen sahibs before." Barbaree smiled at Abby. "They think you're a white goddess from the high snow hills."

Abby touched her hair, smoothing the tangle of red strands back from her forehead. "Do white goddesses eat?"

Barbaree folded his arms across his chest. "Whatever they want, luv," he said with a grin. "Whatever they want."

As best Yurev could gather, this clan had been on this spot about two years. Barbaree figured the structure was an abandoned fortress constructed in the previous century by British or Nepalese hands as a winter outpost. The villagers raised a few crops on the slopes below, mainly barley, and had some goats. They saw very few people, especially at this time of year, though in the spring the men traveled to another village called Lum that was near the Dara Khola, a tributary of the larger Mayagdi Khola. They traded their grain for salt and other goods but for the most part they were a self-sufficient bunch.

The Gurunds waited on their guests hand and foot, literally. On finding Yurev's wounds, the women cleaned the bites with a brownish solution that smelled worse than it burned. They bathed his arms and legs, finishing with a mud pack bound over the dog bites, similar to what Kancha had done for his back. In the meantime a meal was prepared befitting honored visitors—tea, turnips, barley bread and, Abby's favorite, *tsampa*. By nightfall the sahibs were clean and fed, sharing these peoples' home as if they were family. Inside, the house was what Yurev had come to expect of a hill Buddhist home—butter lamps, small altar, fire and sleeping mats. The goats, fortunately, remained outside.

"We're fixed up," Barbaree said. They were sitting in the center of the room near the altar, with Barbaree doing all of the talking with the shaman, drinking *rakshi*. "We're about two days' march from the Dara Khola. Beyond that, another half-day, is Lum village. I can get a pack animal there, and then it's no more than two days to Rapti Khola." He was beaming. The *rakshi* agreed with him. "Inside a week it'll be Utraula."

"The train," Yurev said.

"Right. This time next week I'll be back in Lucknow, sipping Scotch on the balcony of the Avadh."

"You mean the three of us," Abby said.

"Ah, right, luv. Of course." A wicked smile. "The shaman's giving us packs, a bit of food, and his best blessing."

"Giving?"

The Englishman looked at Yurev. "Actually not giving, old boy. Trading."

"What the hell do *we* have to trade?" Abby said. "There isn't anything."

"Don't underestimate yourself."

"Myself? *My*self!" She looked hard into Barbaree's eyes. "Look, smiling Jack, if that son of a bitch puts a hand on me," she patted the revolver beneath her *chuba*, "I'll blow his goddamn compassionate member straight into nirvana. And you next!"

Barbaree laughed. "No, not that, luv." He pointed to her hair. "Some of that. He wouldn't dare touch you—not the white goddess from beyond the snow. Just a bit of hair. For good luck. He is their shaman, after all."

"That's it?" Abby eyed him suspiciously.

Barbaree took another long sip of *rakshi*. He set his cup down empty. "For now. Still, there's always the unexpected."

"Meaning?"

"You're a damn handsome woman, you are, luv. Even for a white goddess." He poured himself another cup of rice liquor.

"Maybe you'd better lay off that stuff."

"That was good, what you said," Barbaree continued. He smiled to himself. "Shoot off his compassionate member, indeed. I like that." He held his cup to her. "I'll bet you're a pistol, luv. A bloody tigress."

"Don't press it," Abby said sharply.

Barbaree glanced over his cup at Yurev. "You wonder, too, don't you, old man?"

"Enough," Yurev said, leaned over and took the container of *rakshi*, setting it out of Barbaree's easy reach. "It's still a long walk ahead."

The Englishman stared at Yurev for a moment. "Maybe not as long as you think, stone man." He drank the rest of his *rakshi*. When he looked back at Yurev he wasn't smiling.

◆ NINETEEN

THEY LEFT SHORTLY AFTER dawn, winding down the slope past the barley field still in the shadow of the high hills. The shaman had blessed them before they departed, singing a prayer, touching each of them with a red *tika* mark, even sprinkling a bit of vermilion powder over Yurev's staff. All of the villagers stood on the sun-bleached steps waving goodbye, the shaman at the forefront proudly holding his hank of red hair.

They'd come down nearly ten thousand feet in elevation since leaving Tramar-Dri, and the hills now were alive with sounds and motion. Dozens of birds were constantly in flight—swifts, thrushes, titmice—and from the forests came the rattling intensity of woodpeckers and the twittering chatter of rhesus monkeys. The weather was mild. Only Barbaree's pace and the up-and-down terrain made Yurev's walking on a bad leg grueling. More and more often, as they came to the top of a ridge, they found piles of rocks and prayer flags blown ragged with the years. The custom of the hill people was to toss a stone onto one of these piles out of respect for the mountain they'd just climbed. The more devout Buddhists also left a prayer flag and sometimes a *mani* stone. It was all hill nonsense to Barbaree, but Yurev liked the gesture, paying tribute.

"Yurey, you'd better carry this." Abby held out her revolver. They were at the top of another ridge where Abby had waited, leaning against a giant oak. Barbaree was not to be seen.

"What's the matter?"

"Jack is drunk, or nearly," she said. "He's been drinking that goddamn *rakshi*. Take it."

"*Rakshi?*"

"His pack is full of it. He stops along the trail to relieve himself. He knows I can see him. He's also playing games with his pistol, aiming back down the trail toward you, making popping sounds and laughing. Haven't you noticed?"

Yurev shook his head. "He's so far ahead I don't see him half the time. I have my own worries just keeping up."

"Your leg's not bleeding again?"

"I don't think so. I'd rather not look until we make camp."

"Take the gun." She shoved it into his hand. "In the shape he's in he could be dangerous. Hell, he *is* dangerous. Just be careful, Yurey."

"What about you?"

"I'm okay."

"Now, look—"

"Whatever danger I'm in is not life-threatening," Abby said quickly. She held his eyes for several seconds. "I'm a plaything. You're expendable. That's the difference. Okay?"

Yurev nodded, stuck the pistol into the deep pocket of his *chuba.* For the rest of the day he ignored the wildlife and the view and the pain. He kept his attention focused on what lay ahead, his thoughts on how to deal with it.

They made camp on a ridge at a large *door-chorten,* its red ocher paint flaky and faded after generations in the sun. It seemed an oddity to Yurev to find a *door-chorten* in such a remote spot. Usually they were found at the boundaries of districts or before the gates of an important village. And this one was large, easily fifty feet high, its domed top commanding a view of the valleys on either side of the ridge. The massive base included a passageway ten feet tall, and across its stone face were dozens of eroded Buddhist symbols. Inside these solid structures were said to be the relics of saintly lamas or religious texts. There was no clue to how long it had been here, solitary bastion against time.

"Build the fire inside," Barbaree snapped, pointing to the *chorten's* passageway. He stood beside the base, an arm out to hold himself steady. The *rakshi* made him slur his words. "Be quick about it. The wood, too."

"Inside?" Yurev carried a load of dead wood under his good arm. "*Chortens* are supposed to be sacred, like temples. I don't think—"

"I don't give a bloody damn what you think." Barbaree stuck his thumb toward the sky. "I don't want to get wet."

Yurev glanced up. Heavy clouds were forming to the southeast, moving their way.

The downpour began shortly after dark, whipping against the stone monolith. Abby and Yurev cooked while Barbaree sat propped against the wall staring into the darkness. They ate in a silence prompted by the rain and Barbaree's sullen mood. The Englishman loaded and unloaded his two revolvers, breaking them down, cleaning them with his shirttail. Over and over. He didn't speak and only occasionally glanced up to look over the flames where Yurev and Abby sat together, keeping the fire alive. The flickering light cast Barbaree in shadows, his eyes hollows of darkness above the unkempt beard.

"What are you talking about?"

Yurev was groggy with sleep. He'd awakened to fuel the fire because his feet were cold. The rain had not let up, and Barbaree had not moved from his spot. Yurev didn't know how long he'd been asleep.

"What?"

"You think I don't know, don't you? You two, bloody cozy, aren't you? You think I can't hear?"

Yurev noticed the *rakshi* goatskin open beside Barbaree. "I was just stoking the fire, Jack. Abby's asleep."

"Talking about me, aren't you, old man? Scheming a way to keep what's due me."

"No. I told you, I—"

"I'm not a bloody fool, you know. I have ears, don't I?" Barbaree leaned forward slightly and belched, nearly falling over.

He's drunk, Yurev thought, sitting in the darkness, drinking *rakshi*, fantasizing a plot. "You heard the rain. Nothing else."

"I know what I heard." A revolver was in his hand. He pointed it lazily at Yurev. "I could shoot you now and nobody would ever know. By rights, I could. You'd be dead ten times over if not for me." He placed his thumb on the hammer. "I don't like you, mate. From the beginning I didn't like you. And I was right. You want the diamonds for yourselves, you and her. I bet you had her, too . . . on the trail. I'll bet she was sweet, eh, that lily white arse banging a bed of pine needles and you sticking her. Isn't that how it was, mate? You and her?"

Yurev licked his lips. His revolver was behind him, useless beside the bag with the necklace. Reaching for it would be idiocy. He tried to look past the gun into Barbaree's eyes. "That's not the way it was," he said in a voice that was steadier than he felt.

"You figure to do me, don't you, old boy? Somewhere between here and Rapti. Bash poor old Jack and keep the diamonds for yourselves." The hammer clicked. "Killing you would be an act of self-defense."

"For godsakes, don't be crazy." Yurev felt absolutely helpless. Making a run for it on his leg would be suicide. Barbaree would cut him down even before he could get wet. Besides, where could he go?

"Crazy, is it?" Barbaree's dark eyes glowered with impatience. "Crazy was giving that necklace back to the Holy One. Everything wrong that's happened has been your fault. You're the one killed him, not me. Now you want to get me out of the way. The diamonds and the girl, that's your thinking. It won't work, old boy, because I'm onto your little game."

"God, man, do I look to be in any shape to strike into these hills alone? It would be crazy. You're the guide. You know these hills. You speak the language. How would I get across a bridge without your help?" Yurev's mouth was dry with fear. The gun in Barbaree's hand wavered, the barrel drawing little circles in the air. From the corner of his eye Yurev saw a tiny movement. Abby lay on her side, eyes shut, but her left hand inched toward their pistol a foot away. "Shooting is not an answer," Yurev said quickly, riveting his attention on Barbaree. "It can only create more problems."

Barbaree didn't respond. For several seconds there was only the sound of the rain.

"You must see that," Yurev said finally. "If you weren't so full of *rakshi* you'd—"

"Shut up." Barbaree lowered the gun, setting it down beside his leg. "You talk too bloody much, you do." He waved at Yurev. "Lie down and shut up. Just remember, I can do you whenever I like."

Yurev leaned back away from the fire and caught Abby's hand as she grasped the pistol. He took it from her and slid it inside his *chuba*. Abby's look was murderous. "Shoot . . . him . . ." She mouthed the words.

Yurev said nothing. He turned away from her, positioning himself so he could see Barbaree and feel the warmth of fire on his face. He held the pistol in his strong hand, his finger beside the trigger guard. If Barbaree got up or made any move toward Abby or himself, he would kill him. Just aim for the chest. At this range it didn't matter where the bullet hit him. He had seen what a British issue Enfield could do close in. They were all the same now, capable of, even eager for a killing. Yurev stared into the rain. Somewhere beyond the darkness came the mourning howl of a solitary jackal. The sound was miles away, and Yurev imagined the animal crouched on a stony outcrop, its muzzle dripping with rain, crying for some relief. He wasn't alone. Yurev closed his eyes, tired of the struggle. Tomorrow would see an end to it, one way or another.

* * *

"Pack the *chubas* or leave them. From here they'll just be in the way."

First light had wakened a sober Barbaree. Whatever effect the *rakshi* had had on him last night was gone. He'd made tea and set out the last day of the barley bread. His actions displayed nothing of his outburst only hours ago. He was all business, checking packs, issuing orders, cursing the weather. The rain had lessened in intensity but had not stopped. Gray, dreary clouds hung overhead like wet sackcloths. It would be a hard march to the bridge at Dara Khola, he repeated. His paranoia seemed replaced with a nervous anxiety to move on.

Abby was silent as she drank her tea, keeping her eyes on Barbaree. When time came to leave she gave Yurev a look of warning.

The rain soaked their clothes before they were five minutes on the trail. Barbaree kept a reasonable pace, often looking back to check on Yurev, whose feet squashed water inside his boots with every heavy step. His staff, dependable on dry terrain, slipped on smooth rocks or broke the rhythm of his walk by sticking fast in the soft mountain soil. Whether oak or rhododendron forests or terraced, treeless hills, the drudgery remained the same. Only tactics changed. Barbaree had been right about the *chubas*. Drenched with rain, the garments would have been an exhausting burden. Barbaree was always right about such things. . . .

Yurev heard the river before he saw it. They were on a rocky downslope full of trees. Craggy uneven boulders made the trail a winding alley strewn with loose gravel. Above the rain came the sound of rushing water. They'd been on the move for hours, and reaching the river meant finding a bridge and stopping to rest. Yurev was ready to stop. The wrapping on his leg had come loose. The hard, knotty scabs that had covered his wound had softened and, chafed by the constant action of his trouser leg, were bleeding again.

"There. Dara Khola." Barbaree pointed into the canyon from the edge of the trail where it turned against the ridge. The pathway now was solid rock, a shelf above the churning white water five hundred feet below. "There's the bridge." Barbaree's face ran with rivulets of rain from his hair as he gestured toward the rope and plank suspension bridge.

The span was little more than fifty feet, and the bridge itself looked sturdy enough with its planks and handrails. For one who had survived the rope crossing over Kali Gandaki, Yurev thought smugly, this was nothing. He flashed a smile at Abby, squinting through the rain.

"No problem."

The plan was for Barbaree to go first, then Abby, Yurev last. "You watch us cross," Barbaree told Yurev, raising his voice against the sound of water. "Mind where we step. Keep an eye out for loose or cracked planks. We don't want you stepping through something with that leg." It was an unusual display of concern by Barbaree. Yurev felt a rush of gratitude, then reined it in. Barbaree's concern had more to do with diamonds than Yurev's health and welfare.

Barbaree carried all the packs himself—he was the strongest—but it gave Yurev a moment of hesitation. He'd stuffed the pistol inside his pack because it was too heavy to lug around in his waistband. Still, he'd only be without it briefly. Anyway, Barbaree had packed his revolvers, too. Yurev had watched him.

The bridge sagged slightly under Barbaree's weight, but he crossed without trouble. Every plank looked securely set, which was as much a relief to Abbey as Yurev. Barbaree waved her on and, smoothing the plastered strands of hair back over her head, she started out, holding tight to the handrails, taking careful, measured steps. As she reached the half-way point, Barbaree held up his hand.

"Hold it, luv."

The Englishman was smiling, standing between the bridge anchors. He held a knife in his hand.

"What the hell?" Abby took another step.

"I said stop." Barbaree sawed on an anchor line with the knife.

Abby froze. "Jesus Christ! What're you doing?"

"We have a bit of business to discuss. Just stand fast, luv. This is for Yurev and me." Barbaree looked past her. "You hear me, stone man? I told you last night, didn't I? I told you your game wouldn't work."

Yurev just started across the narrow span. The moment had finally come. "What do you want?"

"What do I want?" Barbaree laughed. "*What do I want?* What the bloody hell is there?"

Yurev pulled the goatskin bag off his shoulder. Rain rolled into his eyes. He wiped his face on his sleeve. "This?"

"Yurey, don't." Abby half-turned, clinging to the handrails. "He's bluffing."

"Bluffing, do you think?" Barbaree began sawing on the anchor line again. "Tell me when you think I'm not." Severed strands of hemp flayed back from the cut as the knife sawed deeper. The rope creaked, stretching. The bridge yawed slightly—

"All *right.*" Yurev held the goatskin by the strap.

Barbaree held the knife away from the cut. "There's a sensible fellow. I told you the stones would be safer with me."

"Yurey, Christ . . ." Abby turned away from the rain. When she spoke again her voice was hard. "Throw the goddamn thing in the river. I'd rather do that than give it up to the son of a bitch."

"I wouldn't, old man," Barbaree said. He touched the rope with the knife. "I really wouldn't."

"Let Abby cross. I'll bring you the stones."

"We'll deal on *my* terms, mate." He held up his free hand. "Just fling the bag over here. Very carefully. If you miss . . ." Barbaree pressed the knife into the other anchor line. The taut rope began to splinter. "You see how it is, then?"

Yurev saw.

"You miserable bastard," Abby shouted. "I'll kill you, I swear I'll kill you myself—"

"Not from there, you won't luv." He looked at Yurev. "The bag, old boy. Now."

"Yurey, no . . ."

Yurev held the bag by its leather thong straps, measuring the weight of the stones inside, judging the distance to where Barbaree stood. A schoolboy could have made the toss easily; it was only fifty feet. But Yurev wasn't a schoolboy. He was bone-weary with a bleeding leg on a granite cliff slick with rain. And life depended on his accuracy.

"C'mon, Lum is only a few hours away. Let's don't waste time."

Yurev swung the bag underhand by its leather drawstrings, back and forth, building momentum until it was swinging in a circle, a clockwise motion, over his head then back down, millimeters from the rocky cliff.

"Easy, mate."

It was all in the timing of the release. Too high it would have altitude but not distance. Too low it would smash into the cliff below Barbaree's feet. Only Yurev could know the moment. The timing, for a change, was his to decide . . . The goatskin bag flew. Its leather drawstrings trailing like the tail of a kite, the bag described a gentle arc above Abby's head. Barbaree took a step back, reaching up. He caught the bag by the neck. A schoolboy couldn't have thrown it better.

Barbaree beamed. Rain dripped from his chin as he slung the bag over his shoulder. "Thanks awfully, old boy."

"Now let Abby cross—"

"You still don't get it, do you?" Barbaree picked up Abby's pack, then Yurev's. He held one in each hand. "We end it here. I told you last night. I'm only acting in self-defense." With a slight push, he dropped the packs over the cliff. Yurev watched as they fell, bouncing against the rocks, careening, spinning—dark, heavy raindrops swallowed by the river.

Abby looked on helplessly, stranded in the center of the bridge.

"I would have liked to give you a go," Barbaree said. "I will miss you, I will, at the Avadh Hotel." He put his knife to the anchor line. "Sorry, luv." He started sawing.

Abby turned toward Yurev. "Yurey—"

"Run." Yurev scrambled to the mouth of the bridge, hooking his bandaged arm around the anchor post, reaching out to her with his other hand. "Run *now*."

◆ TWENTY

BARBAREE DIDN'T HAVE TO cut through the rope. As he reached the halfway point, weight and strain on the weakened hemp took their toll, and the line began unraveling on its own. When it separated, the anchor line snapped like a broken bow string, its frayed end whipping back against itself the instant it was free. The corresponding handrail, suddenly without tension or support, gave way, and the entire right side of the bridge collapsed like a wave of falling dominoes, racing Abby to the opposite cliff.

She was running, gasping in the rain, when the bridge planking simply dropped from under her and she grabbed for the nearest lifeline.

Yurev saw her stumble, thought for sure she was gone. But she was there, dangling from the bottom handrail, her knuckles white around the rope. No longer a suspension bridge, the web of ropes and planks resembled a grotesque smile hung between the granite walls of the canyon. She was fifteen feet away, too far to reach.

"Pull your legs onto the rope," Yurev called out. "Swing them up."

"I can't . . ."

"You *have* to." Yurev crawled as far as he dared over the edge of the cliff, locking his legs around the support post. "Pull yourself to me until I can reach you."

Abby swung her legs out and back, kicking them toward the rope. On the fourth try she hooked a heel over it, then the other. But her jerky movement had caused the whole tangle of ropes to swing as well. The smile over Dara Khola began losing teeth. Planks, straining under Abby's swinging weight, began popping out of their tie-downs. With a wet crack the planks slipped away from one knot, snapping up and out of the other and spinning end over end like wild propellers into the canyon below. Every loosened plank created a bit more slack, which made Abby's handrail sag even further, putting more strain on the next plank in line. In a few seconds the air was filled with cartwheeling wood, and Abby was falling, clinging to the rope.

"Hold on." Yurev scrambled back to the anchor post, where the handrail was taut, and began pulling the rope, walking backward around the post until he had enough slack to wrap around his waist. He pulled hand over fist, dragging Abby up the slick wall of the canyon. His arm was on fire under the bandage. The rope, even wet, splintered his hands, but he kept pulling and calling to her to hold on. God, he couldn't lose her now, after he'd beaten Barbaree.

A hand appeared on the ledge, grasping for purchase, then the other. Yurev reached for her and caught her hand, hauling her up. They fell together beside the post, exhausted and panting. Yurev looked across the canyon, squinting through the rain. Barbaree was gone.

"Is he . . ." Abby tried but couldn't raise her hand.

"No."

"Why didn't he just shoot us last night?" Abby covered her eyes with her arm, against the rain. Her hand was bleeding.

"He thought about it," Yurev said. "I guess he wasn't quite up to it. Here." Yurev scooped mud from beside the post, smoothing it over her palm. "It helps take out the sting."

"You shouldn't have done it, Yurev. Giving him the stones. You shouldn't have."

"You'd rather be dead?"

She pulled herself up, wrapping her arms around her knees. She stared at the rain. "Hell, we are dead. At least we could have kept them from him." She looked at Yurev. "He's got the necklace, and we're dead. The only link to Shelkagari is going to be butchered in India and sold to the highest bidder, diamond by diamond. In the meantime we get to starve or fall off these Godforsaken mountains."

Yurev dragged himself to his feet, found his staff and put his weight on his good leg. "Can you walk?"

"Walk?" Abby glanced up at him. "Sure . . . where would you like to go?"

"Home."

"You're crazier than he is."

"Maybe. But he's going to be very angry when he comes back. I don't think we should be here."

"Barbaree? Come back here? Why the hell should he bother? He's got what he wants."

"I buried the necklace," Yurev said. "Last night. At the *chorten.*"

Abby's look was incredulous. *"What?"*

"Wrapped in the manuscript."

"You *buried* it?" She glanced at the opposite cliff. "But . . . what was in the bag?"

"Rocks, stones. I felt sure after last night that he would do something. I didn't want him to have the necklace. I thought I had to do something."

"You *buried* the necklace," Abby said again, still amazed.

"He'll kill us if he finds us. I think we better go."

Abby got to her feet. "It's still ours," she said quickly. "We can—"

"The necklace was never ours." Yurev had thought he was going to be telling that to Barbaree. "It belongs here, in these hills."

"What the hell are you talking about?"

"I'm talking about Bert Hoover," Yurev said. "The drawer of stones."

"Hoover? The geologist in the photograph?"

"I didn't realize what the lama meant until last night . . . 'drawer of stones.' That's what he called Hoover. I think he was talking about tracings. Hoover made charcoal tracings of the balcony floor." Yurev remembered Fa Shing's story about the last time he had seen his American friend. *He was coming from the hills with a present for his memsahib, who collected ancient things.* The yellowed stack of pages with charcoal smudges that the Holy One had retrieved from the book room shelf were preliminary scratch sheets.

"Tracings? You mean, someone *else* knows about Shelkagari?"

"I doubt it. Hoover didn't come here looking for anything except rock samples. He was just a geologist who happened on this place. The year before he was in China during the Boxer Rebellion. No, I think he probably just kept them, keepsakes. Pretty pictures . . . ancient script from a Himalayan monastery. Anyway, it's a pretty good theory." Yurev tested his staff. He pointed to the river. "We'd better go. That's our way out, I think. The Dara Khola flows south. It has to wind up somewhere in the lowlands."

Abby stared into the canyon. "You mean some geologist who was here thirty years ago has the text of the scrolls"—she looked up—"as a goddamn *souvenir?*"

Yurev nodded. He was suddenly very tired. Wet, tired and bleeding. But he was alive, and so was Abby. Shelkagari wasn't lost, it was just waiting . . .

* * *

Alone, Yurev and Abby were four days in the hills following the river. The water was drinkable, and there was food—berries and fruit and nut trees. The days were warm and, except for daily stops to rebandage Yurev's leg, pleasant. The evenings were cool but the nights were chilly. Even in the lowlands there was winter, but it wouldn't get terribly cold until February. It was early November, Yurev guessed, probably the first week. They would be out of here in a few days. That's what he told Abby and hoped it was true. As for Barbaree, they never saw him. If he had followed them, he was a shadow that never appeared.

Without implements to make a fire they slept side by side for warmth on the bank of the river. Yurev built a test raft. If it floated, he figured, the current would move them faster than they could walk. They spent a whole morning on the project, gathering bamboo, tying the contraption together with vines. By midday, when it was finished, the thing looked reasonably sturdy. Under way, they floated for an hour, paddling down the Dara Khola with heady confidence, until the craft shattered against the rocks of the first rapids it encountered.

Soaked and feeling lucky that their bruises were not worse, they made camp, propping their boots to dry on the few sticks of bamboo that had survived the rapids. The supply of berries smashed to jam on the rocks, they slept in their wet clothes, tired and hungry. Abby had little to say. The raft had been Yurev's idea.

"Yurey . . . Yurey . . ."

Yurev woke on his back. He opened his eyes to an enormous moon. Abby was beside him, her hand on his chest.

"I hear something." She was looking into the trees. Her voice was a whisper. "In there."

Yurev rolled over, blinking. "Where?"

"There . . . in there."

This had been the routine over the last two nights. The further south they traveled the more animals they came across, especially monkeys. They also were back in mosquito territory. Without a fire to keep the monkeys at a distance the curious ones got closer. For a woman who had survived these last few days, Yurev thought it funny . . . if anything at this point could be thought funny . . . that mere monkeys that were easily dispatched with a few stones could frighten her.

Yurev sat up, gathering a handful of stones. "You could do this, you know."

"I'm a rotten thrower." She pointed. "There. Right in there."

Yurev listened a moment, heard nothing but the buzz of insects. He got up on his knees and threw five or six stones, one after another, into the brush.

"There. I hope—"

The bellowing roar of the tiger burst from the darkness like a sudden thunderstorm, sending monkeys screaming. In an instant, the forest was alive with frantic noises; every animal within range of the deathly sound was running for its life.

"Jesus . . ."

Yurev grabbed Abby's wrist and ran for the river, skipping on his bad leg, hauling her, splashing into the water. He fell and came up gasping, still holding her. "Rocks . . ." He pointed to the white water bubbling over the rapids. Pulling himself onto the gray boulder was tricky, slippery business. Getting Abby up after him was even more of a job.

"Climb," Yurev cried, pulling her arm, trying to balance himself so as not to fall back into the water. The river bubbled around her head, and Yurev found her other hand. He put all his weight into heaving her up, and she slipped, sputtering and coughing water into his arms. He pressed her down quickly, his eyes searching the shore.

The huge cat moved silently out from the shadows of the trees, its golden coat orange in the moonlight, slit black with stripes. It held its ears up, head low between massive shoulders. The tiger prowled back and forth on the river bank, making ever-shorter passes until it was directly on the spot where Yurev and Abby had lain. It was a magnificent beast, ten or twelve feet long, plus the tail. Easily six hundred pounds. Yurev could not help but feel awed by its presence. It moved with a grace that he had never seen in an animal that size. Its slow, deliberate manner, the way it carried its head, the swagger in its walk, left no doubt as to why hill people called it *gaida*—king.

"Do tigers . . . swim?" Abby was fighting to catch her breath. The slanted boulder stood two or three feet above the churning water, and she lay at Yurev's side, an arm tight around his waist.

"I don't know."

"I think it can," Abby said. "I think tigers . . . swim." Her eyes were wide. "What do we do if it comes?"

"I don't know."

"*Think* of something, for chrissake."

Yurev glanced at her. Abby's face was beaded with water, her hair plastered over her ears. She looked back at him with panicked eyes.

"Scream," Yurev said. He turned to watch the tiger, squirmed out of his shirt, wrapping it around his hand to make a wet fist to smash it on the nose if he got a chance.

"Scream? Do you think that will—"

"I don't *know*," Yurev said quickly. He lay his head on the rock, exhausted, turned his gaze to the shore.

The tiger now attacked the boots, knocking them from their drying sticks, sniffing, testing each one. Like a giant kitten playing with a toy, it pawed the boots, slapping at the leather with its huge claws. Yurev heard leather split as the tiger's ripping incisors tore into a sole.

A second tiger appeared from downstream. Yurev did not see this one, smaller than the first, until it announced itself with a roar. It had dropped something, and now picked it up again, trotting forward to where Yurev's boots lay in shreds. It was a monkey that the tiger carried in its great mouth, and seeing it, the first tiger lost interest in boot soles. There was a scuffle, not really a fight, though Yurev saw claws flash. The result was a dead monkey in two parts. For several minutes the two cats ignored each other, ripping at their own small meals. The moist noise of tearing flesh and crunching bones was all the sound Yurev heard from the river bank.

The monkey now devoured, the smaller tiger raised up, shook itself, then casually walked back into the forest without once taking further notice of the other. The remaining animal lay for some time in the same place. When he finally stood, powerful hindquarter muscles rippling beneath the smooth coat, the cat urinated on a scrap of boot leather, sniffed the monkey remains left by the other tiger and moved to the edge of the river for a drink. It lapped water for several seconds, then became rock still, its head low between its shoulders, hind legs posed as if to leap. It stared across the water, twenty-five feet to the boulder, its eyes shining like copper in the glow of the moon.

Yurev tightened his fist and felt the fabric of the shirt strain around his hand. In all of his morbid imaginings about how he might die since leaving Butwal, none included confronting a Bengal tiger . . . He took a deep breath, stood up, feet spread wide on the cool granite.

"All right, damn you . . . come on." He yelled the words as loud as he could, his arms held out from his body, fists hard. His voice echoed slightly, rebounding in the night from the cliffs behind him. He didn't know if an animal like this could sense fear—at this moment, the air was full of it. His.

The huge cat did not move, eyes steady.

Yurev slapped his bare foot on the rock, crouching down.

Standing at the water's edge, the tiger roared, jaws wide open, exposing yellow teeth.

Yurev fought to keep his legs under him. Thoroughly unnerved, he roared back, and for a time the cat just stared at this mad creature on the rock. Yurev stared back, eyes stinging with perspiration. Slowly, the tiger turned away. It made two passes around the camp leisurely, as if to display supreme indifference, then, without looking back, strode into darkness, swallowed by the trees.

Yurev waited, watching, expecting it to be a trick, searching for some sign that the big cat would leap out of the shadows and charge into the river. But everything was still, except the river and his pulse. Now, drained, his legs gave way, and he collapsed on the rock.

Beside him, Abby rolled into a ball, her knees pulled up to her chest.

"It's gone," Yurev said, not sure it was true. She flinched when he touched her shoulder.

"Jesus." She uncoiled, turning to Yurev, arms around him, pressing her head against his bare chest. "That sound . . . it . . . ."

He thought she was talking about the tiger's parting roar, then realized she meant the sucking, crunching sound of monkey meat being consumed.

Abby tried to speak but the fear and frustration she had held back for so many days finally broke through, and she cried uncontrollably, unashamed of her tears, clinging to Yurev, who closed his arms around her shoulders, rocking. He stroked her matted hair until he felt the tension begin to drain out of her. When he tried to lift his arm from around her she mumbled something and tightened her hold on him. Finally, she was asleep, her breath warm against his chest. He rested his chin lightly on her head, protecting her from the buzzing mosquitoes, caressing her, keeping an eye toward the river bank. If the tigers returned, then they did. He was too exhausted to worry. Instead he thought about Kancha smiling beside an open fire in his faded corporal's jacket, happily dishing up *tsampa*, and about the buffalo in the lowlands, waiting for his salt . . .

Abby slept in Yurev's arms through the night, legs tangled together on their granite island. She stirred just before dawn, that magic time of morning when the sky was not yet pink, and purple clouds rode a sea of falling stars.

"Yurey?" Her hand moved on his back, warm against his cool skin. "Are you awake?"

"Yes."

She was quiet for a time, then: "We're still alive."

"Yes." He'd been awake all night. Not fully alert but awake. No more tigers, just insects.

"Have you slept?"

"No, it wasn't my turn." He started to move, to untangle himself, but Abby held him.

"Don't. It's all right." She ran her fingers over his back. "You're cold."

"It'll be light soon. The sun will warm us up." He raised his head slightly to see her. "How are you feeling?"

"Embarrassed. Guilty. And stupid . . . for the way I yelled at you last night." She touched his face. "I'm sorry."

"Well"—he glanced at the river bank—"at least they didn't come back. After a whiff of those boots they probably figured to stick with their usual diet. I guess *gorah* sahibs just aren't—"

She pulled his head to hers and kissed his mouth. "Thank you for saving my life." She kissed him again. "And for the dozen other times, too."

"I—"

"You don't mind, do you?"

"Mind? No, but—"

"What was it Kancha called it on the trail? Making happiness? You turned it down then, with Kalu and Lagna. How about now?"

He tried to find the words. "You don't owe me anything—"

"I owe you a lot. A helluva lot, but not this. I'm not offering you a reward. I *want* to . . . with you." Her eyes were bright and serious. "Make love to me, Yurev. Make some happiness with me." She unbuttoned her khaki blouse and guided his hand inside.

Yurev leaned down and kissed her, holding her head in his hands. She helped him shed her blouse, and they worked together on the rest, peeling off each other's wet trousers as if they were molting skin. Intensity created delicious harmony, and at sunrise and after, their own passionate cries aroused a mindless chatter in the trees. . . .

Yurev shaded his eyes from the sun, settling his shoulder blade to the smooth contour of the granite rock beneath him. Abby lay on his chest, her breathing normal again.

"Don't move," she said as she adjusted to him. "There, right there."

Yurev kissed her neck. Her hair was now dry. "We need to be moving on, you know."

"I know."

"While we still have our strength."

"Speaking of strength . . ." Abby tilted her head to see his face. "Is that you . . . again? How do you do that?"

"Berries."

In a short while their voices echoed in the valley, startling the wildlife again. . . .

An hour later they were back on the trail, and, hobbling barefoot with his staff, Yurev nodded to the chatterers in the trees. "Do you think we've shocked the monkeys in this part of the country?"

Abby pointed to a couple in the trees. "Look there . . . monkey see, monkey do."

Walking without boots was a new and unpleasant experience. Every stone Yurev stepped on was sharp or angular and every twig a thorn. He felt as if his back and shoulders had been a testing ground for a breed of starved mosquitoes. In the middle of the afternoon, though, where the river wound around a forest of birch, they managed to reach Kali Gandaki.

Half a mile further was a village. It was small, half a dozen thatched-roofed houses and a few boats, but after five days alone and lost, the place was beautiful.

Children were first to greet them, swarming around, tongues out in welcome, touching the sahib's hairy arms. Then came a village elder. He might have been a shaman. Yurev couldn't decide. Language turned out to be the problem.

Yurev and Abby sat in the shade of a banyan tree. The village spokesman was an old one whose hair was still black despite his age. He directed his comments to Yurev, punctuating the end of his sentences with a friendly smile. He ignored Abby except to glance at her hair. The villagers had formed a circle around the tree. Spectators. No one spoke for them but the old man.

"Can you make out any of it?"

Yurev shook his head. "No. I've tried French, English and Hindi. The few sentences I've been able to pick up these last few weeks have to do with tea and stubborn ponies."

"Great."

The old one pointed in the direction they had come. He spoke animatedly then smiled, waiting for a response.

"I think he wants to know where the hell we came from," Abby said.

"That may not be a good idea, telling him." Yurev pointed at the river. "Kali Gandaki." He pointed south, following the river, then to himself and Abby. "We . . . going . . . Butwal." He used his fingers, walking them in the dirt. "Butwal. You . . . know . . . Butwal?" He raised his eyebrows to the old man.

"*Butwal . . .*" The old one pointed also, but slightly west of the river. "*Butwal.*" He glanced around to the villagers, his face triumphant that he'd made a breakthrough. "*Butwal.*" Several of the people nodded, acknowledging the news with smiles and clucking sounds. They also pointed. Now everyone knew. Butwal was that way.

Yurev pointed at the river again. "Kali Gandaki . . ." He walked his fingers. ". . . to . . . Butwal?"

The old one shook his head. He pointed in the direction he had indicated before. "*Butwal.*" Then he used his fingers as Yurev had done, smiling, like he enjoyed this game, pointing to the river. "*Ibanawi.*" He pointed out one direction, then the other, so Yurev would understand. "*Butwal . . . Ibanawi . . . Butwal . . . Ibanawi . . .*"

"The river doesn't go to Butwal," Yurev interpreted. "It goes to Ibanawi."

"Brilliant."

"Maybe you'd like to try this," he said.

"No, no. Sorry. Go ahead."

It took the rest of the afternoon and a gallon of hill tea to sort things out. This was the village of Ketni-Tooke. Ibanawi was south, two days by boat. A train from Kathmandu to the Indian frontier stopped in Ibanawi.

Abby perked up. "A train?"

"We can be in Lucknow in three days," Yurev said with a smile, and added, "having a drink at the Avadh Hotel."

That night Yurev's fever began. First he was attacked by chills and vomiting. Then his temperature rose, and his coloring turned jaundiced. By morning he couldn't stand or hold any food. Abby stayed with him, wiping his face, pouring water over his chest and head to reduce the fever. She was present during his hallucinations and the torment of his delirium as he called out and cried for the one person who would not come. Celeste.

◆ TWENTY-ONE

BENARES, INDIA

"I DON'T REMEMBER TRAVELING by boat, although I know I did. My last recollection before I woke up in the British hospital at Faisbad was the dirt floor of a village home. Malaria is what it was, probably something I drank."

Yurev's back and neck ached. He had been talking for hours, sitting across the low table from Fa Shing, reliving a lifetime that had begun only weeks ago in the dining room of the Avadh Hotel. He had been to the high hills and survived. It was the story Fa Shing had come to hear, and the old Chinese had listened without interruption.

Yurev changed his position on the pillow, stretching his legs. "When I came here to Benares I came for Jack Barbaree. I didn't find him. That's when Mahbub Ali, your Afghani friend, found me. The rest you know."

Fa Shing sat with his hands folded in his lap, a position he had not changed in hours. For several seconds he said nothing, simply staring at the low table between them. Finally he unfolded his hands, placing his delicate fingers on the polished table top.

"And the American woman? What has become of her?"

"She's gone. Went back home to Chicago." Yurev remembered the hospital. The doctor in charge would not talk about Abby or even acknowledge that she had been admitted there. Yurev found out later during the interrogations. "She was sick, too," Yurev said. "The British transferred her to Lucknow, then Delhi. Someone from her family took her home. I didn't see her again."

"Not since the village of Ketni-Tooke?"

"I had fever," Yurev explained. "I don't remember afterwards."

Fa Shing nodded. "And at the hospital there was some trouble with the authorities?"

"The British," Yurev said angrily. "The British were the trouble. Barbaree had disappeared; they wanted to know what happened to him. I told them what happened, I told them he left us to die. They said there would have to be an inquiry. Barbaree was our guide, after all. The authorities hadn't been too keen on letting a memsahib go off to the hills in the first place. Coming back without Barbaree caused them a lot of trouble. But when Abby turned up at Faisbad, babbling deliriously about killings in the hills, the authorities couldn't get her out of India fast enough." Yurev glanced at the old Chinese. "Bad press, you know," Yurev said, affecting an accent. "Bad press, what with all this Gandhi business about the British being ineffective caretakers. Bad indeed, old boy, old son, old man . . ."

Fa Shing looked impatient.

"The inquiry would have ended there. The hallucinating American was sent home, and nothing more would have come of it except for one detail. They found Kalu's body."

"Kalu?"

"Our porter from Butwal. Her body had floated miles downstream. And with Abby gone, there was only me to explain it. I told them over and over what happened . . . that Barbaree had left *us*. They couldn't accept that. Not Barbaree. Not upstanding Jack. An Englishman wouldn't do *that.*"

"The authorities did not believe?"

Now Yurev looked impatient. "They had a body to account for. When I woke up in the hospital the British officer was there waiting. He accused *me* of negligence, even hinting that Abby and I had done away with Barbaree to cover it up. Only the damn British in India would pull something like that—diverting the guilt of foul play from one of their own."

"You escaped from the hospital?"

"I *left*," Yurev said. "I went looking for Barbaree. I'm the only one who knows he isn't dead. He's not going to show himself, not after what he's done. I wanted to kill him. I still do."

"You will not find him now. The authorities search for you still." Fa Shing leaned forward slightly. "You attacked a British soldier, not Jack Barbaree. It's time for you to leave India, young friend."

"I plan to."

"I have friends who can get you back to Paris. We have only to—"

"No. There is nothing for me in France. I'm going to the United States."

"Ah. The American woman. In Chicago."

"No. Someone else. *Your* American friend. Bert Hoover."

Fa Shing's smooth forehead wrinkled. "In search of the Buddhist's scrolls?"

"Ayrub Ravi's scrolls are the only clues to Shelkagari. I'm going to find them. Hoover has the texts. He *must* still have them. I have to believe that."

"But so much time has passed. How will you find him? How will you know him?"

Yurev remembered Abby's torn photograph of the Old One. On the back side were the initials HCH printed neatly by Fa Shing's friend twenty-eight years ago. Yurev might never have made the connection except for the British newspapers in Faisbad. The news was everywhere, Faisbad, Lucknow, Benares. The British were very worried. They were calling it The Crash, and Black Tuesday—the great American stock-market failure of October 29, 1929. Yurev was in the hills when it happened. At Tramar-Dri.

"Young friend?"

"Finding him will not be difficult," Yurev said. "He's not a geologist anymore." The British newspaper headline had said, "Great Engineer Faces Historic Crisis." The newspaper photograph had shown the president of the United States alone at his desk—a study of a man worried by time, trapped by circumstances.

Herbert Clark Hoover.

◆ TWENTY-TWO

HERBERT CLARK HOOVER HAD become a casualty of his own achievements. His rise from obscurity as an orphaned Quaker to international hero to president of the United States was a circuitous route that began in the East. In the aftermath of the Boxer Rebellion after geological expeditions to China's interior he was selected by his London employers to be the chief engineer responsible for reorganizing the mining operations in China, an enterprise employing over twenty thousand men. He was only twenty-five, a newlywed and four years out of college, but his inspired capacity for organization and efficiency was unequaled in China.

In a short time "Boy Hoover" was in constant demand, and his reputation as a doctor of sick mines spread from one continent to another. Before the age of thirty, he was one of the most sought-after consulting engineers in the world. By 1908 at age thirty-four he was a millionaire with offices in San Francisco, New York, London and Paris. He had become the "Great Engineer," a wunderkind, a flesh and blood Horatio Alger who went about the globe streamlining failing mines. He was a man in a hurry, driven to work, the quintessential rugged individualist. His worldwide reputation had been confined to a particular industry during the early years of the century, but that changed with an assassin's bullet at Sarajevo in the summer of 1914 that sent the world to war and committed Hoover to a life of public service he had not sought. In London at the outbreak of war the Great Engineer reluctantly accepted a plea from Belgium to use his organizational prowess to prevent noncombatants in German-occupied lands from starvation. The result was the Commission for Relief of Belgium, led by Hoover until the end of the war. He devised the greatest food-relief program ever, feeding ten million people in Belgium and northern France for four years.

By the war's end the Iowa Quaker was an international hero. He became a force in a world begging his opinion. Ten years later, after serving three administrations, Herbert Clark Hoover became the thirty-first president of the United States, and his 1928 election victory was the largest popular margin on record. Black Tuesday, October 29, 1929, crushed the dream and vilified the man. For his single four-year term Hoover was caretaker to the greatest economic reversal in history.

Hoover's election victory in 1928 was overshadowed by Franklin Delano Roosevelt's landslide victory in 1932. On his last ride down Pennsylvania Avenue as president, Herbert Hoover was escorted by Douglas MacArthur's Third Cavalry. Troops armed with machine guns were stationed on top of high buildings along the route, a presence to ward off attempted assassination. At the end he was a prisoner, his star extinguished. The ride was over.

Yurev Romanovna also attended Franklin Roosevelt's inauguration in 1933, one among the one hundred thousand spectators that chilly gray March morning who had come to witness the triumph of one man and the wake of another.

Yurev had arrived in San Francisco during the winter of 1930 with two thousand dollars pinned inside his jacket. Officially a French immigrant, he was processed with hundreds of Chinese immigrants and given a new name. A harried immigration officer, disdaining even to look at Yurev's face in the noisy and crowded processing center, interpreted Yurev Alexander Romanovna to be Alexander Romanov. His life in America began with a heavy stamp to his application papers, a scrawled signature and a loud "Next."

Diamond cutters were not in great demand in Depression America, so Yurev worked a steam press in a San Francisco laundry for a year, living above the establishment in a one-room apartment. Depositing his stake at the Bank of America, he made up his mind not to disturb it, and wrote to dozens of diamond dealers asking for work. Those who replied had nothing for him.

He also wrote to Herbert Hoover at the White House and at the president's Palo Alto residence only a few miles from San Francisco. "Would it be possible," he had written, "to meet with the president at some convenient time?" They shared, he wrote, a mutual friend from his days in Peking. All of Yurev's letters were answered by a secretary. A convenient time could not be arranged. The president of the United States was "pressed by more urgent matters." Perhaps at some future time. "Bert Hoover," Yurev was sure, never saw the letters.

In July 1931, Yurev heard from a firm in New York—Frederich DeHaan of DeHaan & Spahr needed a diamond appraiser.

◆ Yurev

◆ TWENTY-THREE

YUREV BEGAN WORK THE first day of August, moving quickly into the job of first cutter. His joining the firm brought about his introduction to Helen DeHaan, Frederich's daughter. Helen was a bright, clever woman who taught Yurev Dutch for his trips to Amsterdam and Antwerp. She was attractive if not beautiful, and passionate in her support for Yurev's new ideas about diamond setting. Gold distorted the color and fire of a stone, he had said. Diamonds should be set in platinum or iridium. The senior partners, though, were not convinced . . . until bad times got worse. Then, infused with two thousand dollars from Yurev, DeHaan & Spahr became DeHaan, Spahr & Romanov, and their first platinum diamond setting was an engagement ring for Helen, who became Mrs. Alexander Romanov in January 1933.

As Yurev stood in the chill that March day in 1933, listening from the steps of the Capitol to Franklin D. Roosevelt speak of "turning retreat into advance," his thoughts returned to the bitter cold of the hills and the message carved in stone at the Buddhist monastery. Bert Hoover, seated behind the new president, was his link to Shelkagari. The Great Engineer was his last hope of finding the Great Stone.

"Alexander Romanov?"

Yurev glanced up from his newspaper in the ornate lobby of the Wal-dorf-Astoria Hotel. A man in a plain gray suit stood above him. "Yes?"

"I'm with Mr. and Mrs. Hoover. Would you come with me, please?"

Yurev, excited, followed the man past bronze portals along the marble hallway to the bank of elevators. In one of the large rooms a gala tea was in progress celebrating FDR's inauguration. Another man waited at the elevator and the three of them stepped in. As the doors closed the first man said, "We're Mr. Hoover's security, Mr. Romanov." He stood slightly away from Yurev, one hand on his hip, revealing the holstered gun on his belt. As he spoke, his partner behind Yurev ran his hands over Yurev's clothes. "Just a precaution. The hotel has already received a death threat. I hope you don't mind."

Yurev said he didn't. "You're Secret Service?"

"Pinkerton. Mr. Hoover doesn't have Secret Service protection anymore." He pressed the elevator button for the thirty-third floor, and Yurev stood silently between the two detectives as the elevator creaked upward to the fading strains of cheerful violins emanating from the Roosevelt victory tea.

Number 31-A was a ten-room suite that overlooked Park Avenue in the shadow of the massive two-year-old Empire State Building. Yurev stood in front of one of the large windows, staring down at the traffic.

"Good afternoon, I'm Lou Hoover."

Yurev turned as a maid in the adjoining room closed the door behind the now former First Lady. Mrs. Hoover walked briskly to him, extending her hand, shaking Yurev's with a firm grip. "I'm sorry to keep you waiting." She indicated a large overstuffed chair and took a seat in the corner of a print sofa. "Please, sit down, Mr. Romanov." She was taller than Yurev had expected, and her features were softer than in the news pictures. She wore a blue-pleated jacket with side pockets and a wide-collared blouse that did not overemphasize her matronly figure. Her light graying hair was pulled back. Yurev remembered she'd worn a hat at the inauguration.

"I'm afraid I must apologize," she said, her eyes not avoiding Yurev's. "My plan has gone awry. I had arranged this appointment today with ulterior motive, I have to confess. I had wanted something to take my husband's mind off today's events, and when your note came, mentioning Fa Shing, I thought it would be a wonderful distraction. Have I insulted you?"

"Not at all," Yurev said self-consciously. He had written his last letter nearly six weeks ago. It was promptly answered, to his surprise, by Mrs. Hoover. She had set the date and the time quite specifically. "I am honored."

"It's kind of you to say, Mr. Romanov. Unfortunately this has been a trying week for my husband, tidying up. Then the train ride to New York . . . What I'm saying badly is that my husband won't be joining us. He's resting. I know it's a disappointment but it seems you'll have to endure a visit with me."

"Not in the least a disappointment," Yurev said, disappointed.

Lou Hoover smiled. "Thank you for lying." She leaned forward on the sofa. "Now, tell me about Fa Shing. It has been more years than I care to admit since the last time I saw him. Is he well? Have you seen him recently?"

"Not for three years but we correspond." Yurev produced a photograph from his jacket pocket. "He sent me this photo to give to you and Mr. Hoover."

The picture had been taken on the lawn of Fa Shing's estate, the bay in the background. He was dressed in white, just as he had been the first day Yurev met him. Mrs. Hoover held the photo for some time, studying the old Chinese. "He's changed," she said. "It was so long ago, China. Shing was so devoted to us." She laid the photo aside. "Did he tell you about our time in Tientsin? During the Rebellion?"

"Yes." Yurev tried to image a thinner, younger Lou Hoover, dashing behind the barricades on her bicycle, dodging bullets fired by fanatic Boxers. "He has always spoken warmly of his American friends, Mr. and Mrs. Bert Hoover."

Lou Hoover nodded. "It was very sad for us when we heard of Wu Pen-Li's death. So much human misery and destruction. Peking was such a beautiful city. I'm sorry, you didn't come here to listen to an old lady dredge up her past." Her eyes were suddenly bright again. "So, you were a student of Shing's? In Peking?"

"Bombay," Yurev said. It startled him that she remembered the name of Fa Shing's love after all these years. "He settled in Bombay after he left China."

"Is he still a Christian?"

"A Roman Catholic, yes."

"I'm glad of that. Chinese Christians had a bad time back then. Herbert will be pleased. They were close friends, as close as they were allowed to be."

The door opened, and a maid entered with a tray. Mrs. Hoover poured coffee for Yurev, tea for herself. When the maid was gone, she said, "I'm not sure when I started calling him 'Herbert.' Everyone called him Mr. President, even his friends. It just seemed strange to have a president of the United States answering to the name 'Bert.' " She stirred her tea a moment. "Anyway, it's behind us now. Did you listen to the inaugural address this morning?"

"I was there," Yurev said, not sure why he had to admit it. He remembered all the guns, all the soldiers. He suddenly remembered that the Pinkerton man had said that there had been a threat.

"Were you?" She seemed surprised. "I've read all your letters, Mr. Romanov—am I pronouncing that correctly? We've read every piece of mail that's come to us . . . and replied. I'm not sure that has always been the case at the White House, but you know, the Hoover presidency will always be associated with setting precedents." A small smile. "They were rather curious, your letters. They were polite, which was refreshing, but forgive me, you didn't seem to want anything. I mean, not money, not food, not a car or a house . . . just"—she opened her hands to him—"to meet." She held him with her eyes. "Why?"

Yurev moistened his lips. It had taken four years to reach this room, but for all his rehearsals of what to say, his mind was blank. He was talking to the wrong Hoover.

"Mr. Romanov?"

"China," Yurev managed to say. "It has to do with when you were in China."

"Yes? Something to do with Shing?"

"In a way, yes." Yurev set his coffee cup down. "I apologize for sounding mysterious, Mrs. Hoover. It's just that I have a question about that time in China, and I'm afraid of the answer. I mean, afraid that I might be wrong."

"Now you *are* sounding mysterious."

"In 1901 Mr. Hoover was in Tibet on an expedition, surveying rock formations . . ."

Mrs. Hoover smiled. "Yes, he did that quite a lot, you know . . . looking at rocks."

"But in the Himalayas."

"I remember it," she said. "He went to Lhasa on that trip . . . met the Dalai Lama. Found the boy-god riding a bicycle in a courtyard of his palatial monastery." She chuckled at the memory.

"He also visited another monastery. Further south. A cliff monastery. It was called Tramar-Dri. Beyond—"

"In the Valley of Weeping Winds. Yes, the red cliff monastery. The high lama was very generous. Bert spent several days there. Yes, that brings back memories. An impressive, eerie, desolate place, Bert called it.

They took several photographs, I recall. The high holy one in his flowing red vestments. It would have been grand to see that in person . . . He also described a magnificent necklace, black gems of some sort."

Yurev's elbows rested on the arms of his chair, his hand squeezed together causing the knuckles to go white. "Was there something he brought back?" He marveled at the calm in his voice.

"Oh, yes." Mrs. Hoover was looking past Yurev, remembering. "Scads of charcoal rubbings. Fifty or sixty sheets. Each one from a square of carved stone. Beautiful ancient text. Put together I think they would easily cover this room. As a matter of fact—"

"Do you still have the sheets?"

"What? Oh, yes, I'm sure we do. In storage, of course, at San Juan Hill. All of our collection of trinkets and such are there."

"San Juan Hill?"

A smile. "Our home in Palo Alto. Above Stanford University. It's my most favorite place in the world, though you could hardly tell it from the little time we have spent there. Now, I think, we will have time for it."

Yurev sat forward on the edge of his chair. "Mrs. Hoover, please, I would like to see those rubbings if at all possible."

"You're a student of Sanskrit, Mr. Romanov?"

"Just of that particular text," Yurev said. "I'm . . . especially interested."

"And that's what you wanted? All those letters? To see charcoal rubbings?"

"They are very important to me. I'm afraid the explanation would be long and tedius."

"Are they in some way important to Fa Shing?"

"Yes." And it was true. "Yes, important to Fa Shing as well."

Bert Hoover's wife pursed her lips. After a moment she stood, extending her hand. "Then you shall see them, Mr. Romanov. But you must come to Palo Alto. I'll make the arrangements but it won't be immediately. We haven't decided just yet what we're going to do with ourselves. Is that fair enough?"

Yurev took her hand. "Very fair, Mrs. Hoover," he said. "Very fair."

He felt like jumping in the air.

◆ TWENTY-FOUR

YUREV HAD LEFT THE Waldorf-Astoria buoyant with hope, confident that the enigma of Shelkagari was now within his reach. But the demands of the Depression would prick his balloon and push even Shelkagari to the side. DeHaan, Spahr and Romanov, like most other diamond jewelers, was now on a headlong path to bankruptcy. In the last three years worldwide production of diamonds had fallen from over two million to fourteen thousand carats, a staggering ninety-nine percent reduction. The wholesale price of diamonds plunged to half their former values, and hundreds of dealers simply disappeared.

Something had to be done and quickly. Banks everywhere were failing. No one had money for jewelry. "You must *do* something," Frederich DeHaan told Yurev.

Yurev's life wheel had brought him to the brink of ruin and, even worse, frustrated his quest for the great stone. DeHaan, Spahr and Romanov was sinking into the vortex of the Depression, and he was helpless to save it. And then the wheel took another, unexpected turn . . .

Diamonds are like snowflakes, no two are exactly alike. The range in quality is vast. The most valued, the rarest, are colorless, flawless stones of pure carbon—"pure whites." Every other grade of diamond is measured by its imperfections. Impurities in the chemical makeup of a diamond account for a range of colors from blue and green to red. Nitrogen, for example, results in yellow diamonds. The lowest classification, useless as a gem because of its size and color and poorly crystallized nature, is called bort. . . . "Bort is manure," said Sir Francis Kimberly in 1886, "useful only when it is ground into grit to polish decent jewels."

Sir Francis did not live to know how wrong he was. In 1931 the Krupp Company of Germany developed a tungsten carbide alloy that was many times stronger and harder than steel. The alloy revolutionized mass production—until then dies and steel blades used in cutting precision parts had to be constantly sharpened or replaced as they wore out. Tungsten carbide steel provided a quantum leap in the standardization of machining critically tolerant parts. The only difficulty that Krupp encountered was finding a cost-effective means of sharpening and honing the new metal into cutting dies and blades. Nothing was harder than tungsten steel, and there was the problem.

Yurev knew better. Diamond grit as an agent for polishing, grinding and cutting gemstones had been a familiar practice for hundreds of years. Yurev realized that the Krupp Company would eventually discover what every gem merchant already knew—nothing was harder than a diamond —not steel, not a tungsten carbide alloy. He also knew, too, that independent diamond mines were failing worldwide, strangling in the grip of the Depression. Their uncut stones were going begging for buyers, and as the cost of digging surpassed return on investment, diamond mining was becoming a ghost industry. But Yurev realized that they were digging for the wrong thing. Gem-quality stones had always been the prize. No one, ever, mined for *bort*.

Gambling on his hunch, Yurev astonished his partners at DeHaan, Spahr & Romanov when he bought a diamond mine, the Jagershoot Mining Co., Ltd., of the Belgian Congo, in July of 1933, which became the Romanov Mine, Inc. Yurev bought it for seven hundred dollars, one tenth its appraised value. The Antwerp banker who sold it to him thought Yurev was out of his mind. "Water is more precious than the stones that come from this place," he said. Yurev wasn't put off. The quality and quantity of diamonds mined at Jagershoot were inferior to marginal and, important only to Yurev, the mine was an alluvial deposit in the heart of the Congo. All the mines in that region were small, producing poor quality stones. But they produced bort by the ton. The invention in 1934 of the diamond grinding wheel using ground bort impregnated in a steel surface gave rise to a new industry, and almost overnight Kimberly's manure turned to gold. Bort, useless for centuries, became hugely valuable, and by 1937 industrial-grade diamonds were more important than gem-grade diamonds.

Yurev sailed for Africa with his wife Helen in October 1933. His Romanov Mine was on the Lulua River, one hundred miles from the nearest sizable town. From Leopoldville the trip took a week through rain forests and over the grasslands of long linear hills that separated the hundreds of winding streams and rivers. Reaching the savanna, the Congo's green plateau of wide meandering rivers, Yurev was awed by the wildlife . . . crocodiles and hippopotamuses populated the same waters, herds of buffalo wandered freely from one watering place to another, casually sharing the vast flatlands of grass with an occasional rhinoceros. The predatory cats—lions and leopards—roamed further east as did the jackals and hyena.

At their new home Yurev concluded the transition of ownership in an afternoon. The previous owners had never visited the mine, but the manager, Captain Munro, was a Portuguese who had lived in Africa all of his life and oversaw a mining staff of eight Bantu workers.

"That's all there is? Just eight of them?" Helen fanned her face with her hat. She'd already inspected the living quarters, a large grass-roofed house with an elevated hardwood floor surrounded by a shaded veranda.

"Eight is plenty," Munro said. He smiled at Helen, wiping his brow with a blue kerchief. "It's only a small operation." He pointed to the wooden sluice near the river where the bank had been excavated into long mounds of dirt.

Helen glanced at Yurev. "But where's the mine? How deep is it?"

Yurev shook his head. "Not deep, wide, Helen. This isn't kimberlite, it's a gravel deposit. We aren't going down into a hole, we don't have to." He pointed to the winding river. "The diamonds are right out there, you'll see."

Yurev also told Helen something about mining for diamonds, which he said was like mining for gold. There were two methods, he said. One was digging straight down, deep into volcaniclike pipes to the hard bluish rock matrix—blue ground or kimberlite. The second method was almost like panning for gold. During millions of years of movement inside the earth blue ground had been pushed to the surface, and erosion and rain had washed the crystals into riverbeds. Recovering diamonds became a matter of digging down to the gravel locked in the river sediment and sifting sand. At the Romanov Mine eight men could dig and sift about five tons of soil a week.

In the first month of production, with Munro directing the diggers, Yurev operating the sluice and Helen sorting gravel, they recovered twenty-one thousand carats of bort. Twenty tons of dirt moved for a sack containing little more than eleven pounds of black diamonds. At four cents per carat, the going rate for bort, the stones represented less than nine hundred dollars. But it was a start.

It was also backbreaking work that began at dawn and ended shortly before the savanna sunset. Days turned slowly into months, and the tiny stockpile of stones slowly grew. With the few flawed gem-quality diamonds discovered in the gravels, Yurev would cut and sell on his trips to Leopoldville every other month, covering their expenses for food and wages.

By the end of their first year Yurev bought an adjacent mine, doubling his output. The price of bort had risen to six cents per carat, but Yurev and Helen had much more than increased profits to celebrate. A son, Frederich William Romanov was born, delivered by a Bantu midwife. Fifteen months later Alexander DeHaan Romanov was born, bort was up to eleven cents, and Romanov Mines controlled three alluvial deposits. The next year the newly organized Belgian diamond consortium was buying Romanov bort at twenty-two cents a carat, sending their man around once a month to collect and paying in the cash of British notes.

By the summer of 1939 Yurev had been in Africa six years. Somehow finding Shelkagari did not seem the obsession it had once been. It was still a dream, but his work and his family seemed to be taking its place. Life on the savanna was simple and peaceful. The original grass-roofed structures beside the river were now replaced by stone and shingle buildings —the main house, a rambling single-story home, an administration building and a sluice/sorting building with a windmill-driven conveyor trough. With sixty men now working four Romanov mines, Yurev could make time for his sons. Frederich and Alex, now five and four, were incessantly curious, and Yurev taught them about diamonds and took them on wildlife excursions, identifying animals across the vast range of the savanna.

Bort was now at seventy-six cents a carat, and with the extra manpower and efficient means of sifting and sorting, the Belgian buyer in his dark gray suit left ten thousand dollars in British currency and a receipt for deposit on the Bank of London for another sixty thousand on each of his trips every month. The world beyond the Lulua River did not concern the Romanovs. How the nations of the world used his bort wasn't his concern. Yurev was insulated from the fears of the Depression by distance and wealth.

Until the rotating wheel turned once again.

◆ TWENTY-FIVE

"THERE'S GOING TO BE war, Mr. Romanov. I can promise you that. Germany has armed herself to the teeth. And when it comes we do not want to be unprepared."

The man's name was James Bradley, an American. He'd come in the morning on a truck from Leopoldville bringing gasoline for Yurev's generators. Yurev had been out on the savanna with his boys, photographing a rhinoceros wallowing in the mud of a watering hole. Bradley, a young man with serious brown eyes, was wearing a khaki shirt and trousers. Representing the U.S. State Department, he had brought an unusual proposition. As they sat on the veranda facing each other across a heavy wooden table Yurev had ordered from Stanleyville, Bradley did most of the talking. Even in the open air, his clothes smelled of gasoline.

"You want my diamonds," Yurev said, "to grind precision machinery for America's war machine."

"In a nutshell, yes."

"We only produce seventy thousand carats a year. Not very much, considering you want six and a half million."

"You're not the only producer we're talking to, Mr. Romanov."

"Yes, but all the independents sell to the Belgian consortium . . . those of us in the Congo. Why don't you talk to them?"

"We have. Our concern is that the flow of industrial diamonds to Brussels and then to London may be interrupted. We don't want that to happen, we would rather make our deals directly at the source."

"Interrupted?"

"Hitler's desperate for precision machinery for the mass production of airplanes, tanks, torpedoes, artillery, gyroscopes. And it all depends on diamonds. So will ours. We can't let this resource fall into his hands." Bradley referred to his notebook. "The United States government is prepared to buy your annual allotment of diamonds at ninety-eight cents per carat." He glanced up from his notes. "That's twenty-two cents over market value, Mr. Romanov. An increase—*above* current profits—of some hundred and sixty thousand dollars."

Yurev was impressed. "You know, I'm sure, that DeBeers in London has an inventory of industrial diamonds in excess of forty *million* carats. I don't understand, Mr. Bradley, why you're wasting your time with me."

"Exactly because DeBeers is located in London," Bradley said. If there's war in Europe, Belgium is immediately vulnerable. If Germany invades France successfully nothing will stop her armies on the continent. And if the continent falls England's not safe. Do you think the English Channel would slow down Hitler's war machine?"

"I don't think it should be up to me—"

"You are an American citizen, for godsakes."

"My wife is American," Yurev said, suddenly angry. "I was born in Russia, although I'm no longer a Russian. I grew up in France, but I'm not a Frenchman. I learned my profession from a Chinese in India, although I don't claim any love of that country from the experience. Just how do *you* measure allegiance, Mr. Bradley? To the highest bidder? I'm not at war with anyone, I live in Africa with my wife and two sons. The world outside can be insane, but I'm not part of it—"

Bradley closed his notebook. "You're rejecting our offer?"

"No. I promise to consider it."

"You do that," Bradley said shortly.

Yurev laid his hands flat on the table. "Mr. Bradley, I apologize for what may seem cold-blooded to you. But this life here has become like a second chance for me . . . and my family . . . I can't explain everything, but as I said, I'll consider it."

Bradley's prediction of war came true two months later with Germany's invasion of Poland. Hitler then moved against the west, turning his panzer divisions loose on Belgium in the spring of 1940, crashing through the lowlands in a matter of days. As Bradley had further predicted, industrial diamonds by the hundreds of thousands fell into Nazi hands. The Romanov Mines did not stop production, though the Belgian consortium representative to pick up Yurev's diamonds was replaced by an armed contingent. The war had pushed the price of bort to eighty-two cents by June 1940, and Yurev was visited several times by Americans, though Bradley was not among them. The American offer had increased to one dollar twenty cents. Several other independents had accepted the American's deal, and the Belgian consortium was receiving pressure from London to put a stop to it.

"I understand you're considering the American proposition," the man named Groote said. He was sitting in the same chair from which Bradley had predicted war. Groote had come with the Belgian contingent but he represented DeBeers.

Yurev nodded. "Its an interesting proposition."

"Yes, and we are aware of their persistence. They want us to move twenty million carats to Canada."

"Will you?"

Groote removed his spectacles, cleaned the lenses with a pressed white handkerchief. "We'd like to encourage you against accepting their offer. Their persistence is undermining the structure of bort's market value. We will begin to worry if Alexander Romanov changes his mind."

"We operate four very small mines. I explained that to Bradley, the man from the States. One way or the other our diamonds are insignificant compared to the overall picture—"

"Diamonds aren't at issue, leadership is. I've been to see all the independents. When I ask them what they intend to do they ask what is the Russian going to do? You are greatly respected, Alexander, for your knowledge of stones, your tenacity, your integrity . . . Did you not tell that American fellow that patriotism was not as cheap as diamonds?" He held up his hand. "No, no, don't answer. I'm happy to believe it, regardless. You resented him equating the two, and you were right." He took out some papers from his briefcase. "In any case, I have here a proposition from DeBeers in London for your consideration."

"I'm already selling to DeBeers," Yurev said. "Through the consortium."

"Yes, yes, but should you change your mind, the result could prove detrimental to the DeBeers interest. Whatever you do will influence the decisions of scores of other producers. I will put it to you bluntly, Alexander. Losing a block of small producers in Central Africa might begin a trend. And frankly that's a trend that DeBeers views as having extremely serious consequences on the world market. Not just industrial diamonds but gems, too. So we've decided to make you an offer of our own—"

"I won't sell the mines," Yurev said. "Not at *any* price."

"The mines? Oh, we know that, Alexander. No, no, we don't want to buy your mines. Our interest is in the product, not the source. Maintaining a stable price structure is our goal. No, our proposition is unique. If you will continue to sell your diamonds to the consortium for the duration of the war in Europe then we are prepared to grant you privileges in return."

"And you are not offering to raise your price for bort?"

Groote thumbed through the pages in front of him. "We will continue to buy your diamonds at market value, which is to be set by the DeBeers board. With demand, the price naturally will rise, but price will never be allowed to float . . . "

"Let me understand this. You're asking me to continue to sell bort to you at *your* price for an indeterminate period with no guarantee. While at the same time the United States is willing to pay thirty percent more with the very good chance they will go higher. You're right, your offer *is* unique."

"What we're offering you, Mr. Romanov, is the opportunity to become a client of DeBeers' Diamond Trading Company at St. Andrew's House, London. Your first love, we recognize, is the gem-quality stone. Your considerable talent as a cutter is wasted in African bush country. What we are offering you is an opportunity few men receive in a lifetime."

Yurev was dumbstruck. Invitation to St. Andrew's House was reserved to fifty or sixty diamond dealers. Since DeBeers controlled ninety-five percent of all diamonds, the London office was headquarters to virtually the world's stockpile of uncut diamonds. The Diamond Trading Company was the DeBeers distributor, selling its stones at twenty-five percent below wholesale to its elite list of clients.

"This offer," Groote continued, "is contingent on the Romanov Mines remaining under your ownership and management and your doing business exclusively with the consortium—that includes any and all gem-quality stones you may produce."

Yurev stared at Groote a moment. It was an amazing offer, but with a catch. "There is a war," he said. "No one buys quality diamonds during a war or a recession."

"Correct. We are extending this proposition to you in anticipation of the conclusion of hostilities, be it one year from today or ten years. To cover whatever temporary loss in profits you might incur, we will guarantee you a forty-percent discount from wholesale for a period of five years on all diamond parcels you accept. Also, we will allow you to have first refusal, for the same period, on any stones over ten carats." He pushed the papers across to Yurev. "Everything is spelled out in this contract. Other than the exceptions I have outlined just now, you would be obliged to follow the usual rules our clients follow."

"Which are?"

"That you take the entire parcel of diamonds assigned to you or none at all. That you pay in cash within one week with no bargaining about price. That you resell only cut diamonds—you may not buy discounted stones from us and then resell them in an uncut state. It's all in the agreement there."

"What if I can't afford your price of a parcel or decide not to accept a particular parcel? It's well-known that clients who have refused their parcel aren't invited again."

"That restriction is waived for the five-year period," Groote said. "If you don't want a particular allotment of diamonds then it will not be held against you. And before you ask, your allotment will be good stones, profitable for cutting and resale. Not macle, not twisted crystals. The contract also stipulates that when you submit your request for the number and type of diamonds that you want in your parcel the Syndicate will not exceed the value by more than ten percent. That's quite a concession. No other client has that guarantee. We need a stable market, and you are key to that."

"And if there's a German victory—"

"That's a risk we all share." He rose to his feet. "Please, read the contract at your leisure. If you have questions, I am here to deal with them." He smiled. "I am instructed to wait as long as your hospitality will allow me. I'd really quite like to see a hippopotamus while I'm here."

Yurev took a pen from his jacket. "I accept." He pushed the agreement back to Groote. "Your countersignature. My man Munro will witness."

The man from DeBeers signed the pages quickly. When he'd finished he looked up at Yurev. "You intended to sign all along?"

"I was waiting to hear what you would propose." Yurev stood up. He nodded toward the river, brown as coffee in the setting sun. "There's a bend that way, where the water spreads out into shallows. We'll have a look there tomorrow, before you leave."

"Tomorrow?"

"Hippos," Yurev said. "Great, magnificent, powerful animals but a bit shy. They love the shallows where the river isn't too fast. We'll have plenty of time to see them play before they realize that they're being watched. For all their size, they just don't see very well."

◆ TWENTY-SIX

WHEN THE LAST BOMB was dropped and the world had entered the Atomic Age nothing on the savanna had changed. The long green plains had not been scarred by skirmishes or tanks or screaming shells. News of the distant madness had been related through weeks-old newspapers from Leopoldville. Sitting beside a campfire Freddy and Alex listened transfixed as Yurev read aloud the progress of armies half a continent away. And, with his American wife, hoped for the Allies to win out.

The war had been a fascinating bedtime story to the boys, a glorious fantasy of warriors in uniform clashing together at arrows marked on newsprint maps. Never having seen an airplane or a tank or a U-boat they were held in rapt attention, imagining great battles in the deserts of North Africa and the combat ships at sea. The war had been a lesson in history and geography that augmented their tutored education in math and language from their mother. A large map of the globe hung beside the family fireplace on which were plotted the slow advance of the Allies in both theaters of war. Eisenhower and Rommel and MacArthur were as much a part of their studies as Caesar and Napoleon and Genghis Khan. The boys' keen appetite for news of the modern world also developed an interest in art and architecture, science and to Yurev's surprise, religion.

The boys were educated as if the world were a fishbowl, to be studied without getting wet. But with the end of war Yurev realized that a day of reckoning was fast approaching. And perhaps it was a needed corrective. He'd been in Africa twelve years, his sons chafed to see beyond the familiar plains. Then came the telegram from England, delivered with the mail in the fall of 1945: FIVE-YEAR ARRANGEMENT TO BEGIN

ONE JANUARY NEXT. SUGGEST COME LONDON EARLIEST
CONVENIENCE.—GROOTE

"It's time for a change," Helen said. "For the boys' sakes. We have to
think about school for them, after all."

She lay beside him in the master bed, her skin the color of frost from
the silver half-moon at the window. Gypsy geese squawked somewhere on
the river, the sound traveling like a shot in the cool African night. After
a moment she turned to him. "You know I'm right, don't you?"

Yurev had been staring at the dark ceiling, trying to imagine Freddy
at a public school in England, dressed in a suit and school tie. "Yes," he
said finally.

"We never planned to stay here forever." Her voice was soft. Helen
loved this place as much as he did. She'd borne both her sons in this house,
and that more than anything else made it home. "We'll come back one
day," she said. A lie, she knew. Yurev felt the warmth of her tears inside
his arm, and he held her closer.

The squabbling noise of geese subsided to silence. Yurev caressed
Helen's shoulder, his fingers drawn absently over her smooth skin, his
mind continents away.

"We won't come back, you know," he said. "We'll be caught up in it
again."

Helen lay still beside him. Silence was her acknowledgement.

"And if that's to be," Yurev went on, "then there is something I must
do. Something I set out to do years ago."

Helen stirred. She found his hand, interlacing her fingers with his.
"Shelkagari," she said. "Again?"

"I need to find it, I *can* find it." The Holy One of Tramar-Dri strode
through his memory, smiling from his pillow on the stone floor of the high
balcony. "I was so close to it . . ."

"When?"

Yurev didn't know. It was still too much a dream.

Helen squeezed his hand. "Promise me . . ." She covered his fingers
with both her hands. "Promise me that we will go together. Wherever
you are, I will be there with you. Home when we leave here will be
wherever you are. Promise me."

Yurev leaned down to her and kissed her mouth. "Yes." He kissed her
again. "I do very much love you, or did you know?"

"One more promise." Her eyes took in the room, all the things they
had acquired together. "When we leave . . . I want to burn the house.
I don't want to leave it. I can't bear the thought that someone else might

walk in these rooms, make love inside these walls. Strangers. I want to burn it down. Completely."

Yurev was quiet for a time. "All right. I'll have Munro see to it after we—"

"No, we'll do it. You and I and the boys. It's *our* home. We built it. She looked at him with tearful eyes. "Agreed?"

Yurev nodded in the darkness. "Agreed."

Smoke rose in black steamy clouds a hundred feet into the air then, pushed flat by the winds aloft, spread out over the river. Yurev and Helen watched from a knoll as the fire crackled through the roof, engulfing the entire structure quickly in flames. The west side collapsed first, beginning a chain reaction as the falling roof dislodged the near chimney, and the crumbling stones brought down one wall after another.

The boys stared in awe at the conflagration, sitting in the gray Land Rover that would take them all to Leopoldville. It was to be a short caravan, just the Land Rover and a small truck packed with their belongings—a tiny assortment of articles to represent twelve years.

Helen's eyes were dry when she turned away from the burning ruins. She walked quickly to Munro and kissed his cheek and without a word climbed into the Land Rover.

Yurev shook Munro's hand, clasping his shoulder. "Realign that sluice gear and don't forget to repack the bearings. We don't want the place falling down."

Munro gave him a smile. "We'll do our best. Good luck to you. It's been my pleasure to have worked with you, sir."

Yurev pumped his hand one last time. "And you, Cap. Take care of the boys." Yurev shook the hand of each of the Bantus assembled beside the Land Rover, addressing each by name, thanking them. Then he signaled the driver of the truck, and the engine belched to life.

He was leaving the only home he'd ever known for a future that was open, unknown. And Shelkagari was in his thoughts as he maneuvered the vehicle across the vast expanse of savanna. It had, after all, been a day like this—under a cloudless blue sky in brilliant sunlight—that he'd set out from the foothills on another continent in search of the great stone.

◆ TWENTY-SEVEN

"ENGAGEMENT STONES, THERE'S YOUR future, old friend."

Groote's office was on an upper floor of St. Andrew's House, the huge window behind his uncluttered desk admitting northern sunlight—the best light to study diamonds in.

Yurev was bent over the desk examining with a loupe the hundreds of stones on nonreflective white paper. The uncut diamonds had been brought in a white packet like a small shoebox with "Romanov, Alexander" handwritten on the label. The diamonds ranged between three to seven carats in weight and good to flawless grades of clarity. Not one of them threatened to be troublesome to a cutter. They were perfect.

Yurev had worked with bort for so many years he'd almost forgotten the power and beauty contained in gem-quality diamonds. The color and fire of even these rough stones made his veins race with adrenalin.

"So, what do you think of your first allotment, old friend?" Groote hovered over him like an excited father, proud and talkative.

Yurev was not Groote's old friend—they'd met only once, after all—but he let it pass. He stood up, handing the loupe to Helen, who sat quietly in an overstuffed chair, so that she could judge them herself.

"Fine stones," Yurev said. "How much?"

Groote smiled. "With your discount, two hundred fifty-six thousand dollars. As you grow the allotments will increase but we didn't want to start you out too high, even though the demand is already there."

"You mentioned engagement stones."

"Oh, yes. All the boys are coming home from war, millions of our boys.

And most of them are unmarried, left their sweethearts to fight Huns or Japs. Now they'll be coming home to settle down, pick up their lives. We're going to see an enormous boom in marriages in the next couple of years—just as happened after the First War. You are in an extremely fortunate position on that score, I would say."

Yurev glanced at Helen. She returned a blank look. "Why is that?" Yurev said.

"Why? Because the United States will be returning seven million men to civilian life, sixty percent of whom are unmarried or newly married." Groote waited for some sign of jubilation, but Yurev only stared at him.

"What in the world," Yurev said finally, "are you talking about?"

And so Groote told him. Diamonds for engagement rings were a tradition, he said, that had begun only in the late nineteenth century with the discovery of diamond mines in South Africa. Until then diamonds were mined only in India and Brazil and were truly rare stones—the world production of gem-diamonds was less than two pounds a year. Diamonds were jewels for the aristocracy because only they could afford them. But that changed with the mass production of diamonds from the mines of South Africa. By the beginning of the twentieth century world production of diamonds was in tons, not pounds, and the diamond as a natural resource was no longer scarce. The diamond was in jeopardy of becoming just another *mooi klip*—pretty pebble.

The Diamond Syndicate, Groote went on, led by the DeBeers company, feared a collapse in diamond prices. Production quotas were put in to maintain price stability. A centralized buying and selling organization was formed to which mine producers sold their diamonds and from which diamonds could be resold to the world in a controlled fashion. The organization, run by DeBeers, was a monopoly. Nearly every diamond mined in the world came under control of DeBeers, which by stockpiling an immense inventory of stones kept an effective rein on the supply of diamonds, thereby sustaining their high values. Diamonds were still scarce —outside the DeBeers diamond vaults in London.

But, Groote said, controlling supply by stockpiling and then selling only a fraction of inventory without controlling demand was a tricky business. The DeBeers solution was simple. Create demand. And the engagement diamond ring, almost singlehandedly, did that and saved DeBeers.

A betrothal is a promise to marry, Groote said, warming to his subject, and the time between promise and marriage is the engagement. Cows and goats lost their appeal as gifts. Jewelry replaced cattle as a symbol, and the engagement ring was born. DeBeers set out to refine the engagement ring tradition by adding a diamond, and by the first quarter of the twentieth century DeBeers had found a market where diamonds were a "gift of love" on a massive scale—the United States. But American men had tended to buy small, usually poor quality diamonds in the eighty-dollar range for their fiancées. The trend toward cheaper diamonds was not in DeBeers' interest so the diamond syndicate targeted the American market for a publicity campaign emphasizing the relationship between diamonds and romance in a new way—the larger and finer the diamond, the greater the expression of love. Diamonds were forever and so symbolized the promise of everlasting love. The bigger and more expensive the diamond in the ring, the more everlasting the love in the marriage. With the end of war, marriageable men returned home eager to restart their lives, settle down and get to work, and descended on jewelry stores like locusts.

Yurev and Helen, twelve years in Africa mining bort for an industry hungry for industrial stones, had missed DeBeers' American campaign that Groote was so proud of.

Yurev stood at the window listening to Groote's hour-long recital. In the street below a workman passed with a wheelbarrow loaded with bricks. London was still scarred from the war. In some sections of the city whole blocks were gone with only neat piles of rubble remaining like cemetery monuments. The sights brought back childhood memories of St. Petersburg, except London was cleaner, and there weren't any bodies . . .

"So, you see, old friend, that's why I say engagement stones are the future of the trade." Groote had been pacing between his desk and Helen's chair, bringing them up to date. Groote, Yurev realized, was not put off by the sound of his own voice. "If you'll forgive the reference, you are sitting on a gold mine, you are. As one of the few American cutters you also avoid the ten percent duty on cut diamonds." He glanced up from the patterns on the floor, beaming. "It's a fortunate time for you, old friend." He nodded at Helen. "*And* you, Mrs. Romanov."

Yurev stared silently at the street. After a moment he said to Helen, "We're right back into it, aren't we?"

"Look here," Groote said, "I should have thought this news would have been better received. You needn't dance or sing but good God, you might show some sign of . . . satisfaction."

"Sorry," Yurev said. "It's very nice."

"Nice!"

"I hadn't realized things had moved so fast."

"And about time, too, I say." Groote paused to clean his spectacles.

"You'll be hard at it for two years, I guess, perhaps three, just keeping up with demand. There's a prospect that should appeal to you, cutting stones again, I mean. Better than that bloody flat plain in the bush, digging stony blacks out of river sand."

"That bloody flat plain," Helen retorted, eyes of fire, "happened to be our *home.*"

Groote fumbled to catch his glasses. "Oh, of course. I didn't mean— damn!" As he reached down to retrieve his spectacles, Yurev saw the temptation in Helen's eyes to impress him with an open-toed shoe.

"We had discussed opening a cutting center in England," Yurev said, moving around the desk to his chair. "I'm not an American citizen. Not yet. I left for Africa before the naturalization requirements were satisfied."

"Oh?" Groote looked surprised. "Belgian, is it?"

"French . . . Russian exiled."

"I see. You're concerned, are you, about getting American citizenship?"

"I'm not even sure they'll let me go back."

"Is that all then," Groote sighed, relieved. "Obviously you've not been informed by the American Embassy."

"Embassy?" Yurev's glance touched Helen before going to Groote. "About what?"

"Or the Belgian representatives." A thin smile on Groote's lips. "I suppose it's because they hadn't realized you'd left Africa. No doubt a letter, actually two letters, wait for you"—he looked at Helen—"at your beautiful home beside the Lulua River."

"About *what?*" Yurev repeated.

"An award of recognition. Yes, truly, the Medal of Belgian Recognition, to be precise. All the member mines of the consortium were awarded the medal in appreciation of the war effort. I have seen it, and I must tell you that it is a truly handsome piece—not the O.B.E., of course, but impressive in its own right."

"In appreciation of the war effort?" Yurev stared at him. "Are you serious?"

"Oh, absolutely, old friend. And if that surprises you, this next will be stunning news. You see, you have also been conferred, as a civilian of an allied power in furtherance of the defeat of a common enemy, the Medal of Merit from the United States. So I really don't see any cause to worry about your welcome in the States. You're a hero of the war effort—"

"That's silly," Yurev said.

"Every war has its heroes. They're not all soldiers and fliers, you know. It's recognition of the homefront effort—"

"We don't want medals," Yurev said. "We weren't part of a war effort. We just mined diamonds."

"Nevertheless—"

"We didn't come to discuss awards," Helen said. She looked at Yurev. "We're just in the diamond business."

Yurev nodded. "Right." To Groote he said, "There is still the matter of the large stones. The contract gives me preference of the large stones over ten carats," Yurev said.

Groote wound the spectacles over his ears. "All the categories over ten carats, including the large colored fancies."

"There's only one stone we want to see," Helen said. She was sitting with her hands folded together in her lap.

"Yes . . . ?"

"The yellow octahedron from the Jagersfontein Mine," she said. "The one you've had around here for six years."

"The Jagersfontein?" Groote looked at Yurev. "You're interested in the Jagersfontein diamond?"

"It's here, isn't it?"

"Yes, but—"

"We'd like to see it, Mr. Groote," Helen said.

The Jagersfontein diamond, at 746 carats, was the third largest diamond ever found. It was discovered at the Jagersfontein Mine in South Africa's Orange Free State in 1939, the same mine that forty-six years earlier had produced the 995-carat Excelsior. The largest stone was also from South Africa. The Cullinan weighed 3,106 carats in the rough, dug from the Premier Mine near Pretoria in 1905. But unlike both the Cullinan and Excelsior, the Jagersfontein diamond was an amazingly clear stone. Hardly any inclusions, which made it a problem. Large diamonds were cut into small diamonds to eliminate flaws and impurities so as to make as many perfect stones as possible. The Cullinan was cut into 105 pieces, the four largest ranging from 530 carats to sixty-three carats. The trouble with the Jagersfontein diamond was its near perfection. Cutters were afraid of it. No one was willing to risk his reputation for the dubious distinction of smashing such a prize into fragments with a misaligned cleave mark. Until now . . .

"My God, it's magnificent," Helen said.

The diamond had been brought to them in a small metal box with a hinged lid. Even uncut the stone contained a dazzling fire and brilliance, light dancing from the faces of its octahedron planes.

"Kaplan was here to see it," Groote said. "Also Tolst."

Yurev recognized the names. They were diamond cutters from two of Amsterdam's most respected cutting houses.

"Representing buyers?"

"I couldn't say. They came before the war, soon after the stone was brought here. They have not come back."

"They're afraid of it," Helen said.

Yurev shook his head. "Tolst isn't afraid of any stone. It's the war. Kaplan and Tolst were paying their respects, looking at this diamond. They didn't have a buyer."

"Kaplan spent two days," Groote said. "When he left his only words were 'a difficult rock.' "

Yurev held the diamond in his hand. It was cool and heavy. "No one has come since?"

"We have shown it, of course, but there has been no serious interest."

"How much?" Yurev said.

Groote folded his arms. "You understand that the sale of this stone is by approval of the board. It is a most special—"

"The contract, Mr. Groote. All stones . . . no exceptions." That was Helen.

"But—"

"How much?" said Yurev.

"Three hundred seventy-one thousand pounds." Groote brought his hands together, rubbing them nervously on the desk. He avoided looking at either of them. "Approximately one million four hundred thousand dollars."

Helen looked at Yurev. "It would be the first major stone ever cut in the United States."

"*You* don't have to cut it," Yurev said. "Kaplan might be right to avoid this stone. If it shatters . . ."

"Then we will have four ounces of melee and take a huge loss. But it won't shatter. It will not. And cut by Alexander Romanov, the finest diamond cutter in the world. That's what they'll say. You know that."

She was right, and Yurev knew it. His hesitation came in discussing it in front of Groote. Helen's eyes were fastened on her husband, as if no one else existed.

Yurev relented with a smile. "Do you mind, Helen, if I study it for a while?"

"You're the cutter, darling."

Groote's handkerchief was balled between his hands. He touched the linen to his neck above the collar. "You don't have a buyer. I mean, you have no client to represent. How can—"

"We will find our own buyer, Mr. Groote," Helen said. "My husband will cut it, and we will find a buyer."

Groote dabbed his forehead. "I see, yes, an interesting notion."

"My husband will be world famous," Helen said, "but not just because of his cutting abilities."

"Oh?"

Helen looked at Yurev proudly. "He's going to find the greatest stone ever. It'll make the Cullinan look like an engagement stone by comparison."

"Have you discovered another diamond mine in Africa, old friend? Mining so large a stone as the Cullinan again is less than doubtful."

"No, this stone already exists," Yurev said, grateful to his wife. "A clear white. Shelkagari by its Indian name—Crystal Clear Mountain." Yurev glanced at Helen. "It's somewhere in the high hills of the Himalayas."

"Somewhere? It's lost?"

"Hidden . . . since the tenth century."

"Ah," Groote nodded as if he understood. "A legendary stone from the subcontinent. Like the Koh-i-noor. Also cursed, I suspect. Those mythical diamonds generally are, you know." Groote laughed. "Buddha's third eye. The Great Mogul. Jolly good, that. You nearly had me there for a moment. There are those who believe in that sort of thing, you know. In the East, of course. Our little brothers and sisters and their wonderful stories of fabulous riches."

"Stories, you think?"

"Entertainment for the gullible," Groote said. "Still, not unusual from a people who believe there is sacred virtue in a cow. Poor buggers. There's the distinction of the Christian West, breeding and culture. One day, in a century or two, we'll teach them civilization."

Yurev glanced outside at the empty blocks piled high with bricks. The red monastery at Tramar-Dri was already two hundred years old when the first bridge on the Thames admitted Christians to London.

"Yes," Yurev said, "what a day that will be." And in that moment he knew he was back . . . that finding Shelkagari was his only reality. The past twelve years had been a rest. An escape? It was time to renew the search, and the first step was in the United States. Lou Hoover still held the key.

◆ TWENTY-EIGHT

THE SIDEWALK ON LEXINGTON had been swept clean of snow. Yurev stepped from his taxi and walked quickly into the hotel. It was Sunday, a slow, quiet day on New York's East Side, for which Yurev was grateful. He never wanted to endure another day like the previous twenty-four hours.

The lobby of the Waldorf-Astoria did not look any different than the last time he'd visited it, the day of Franklin Roosevelt's first inauguration almost exactly thirteen years ago. The difference was that, if he'd liked, he could take a suite here now. Or even a floor.

The man at the desk was very tall with a deep soft voice. "I'll ring that you're here, Mr. Romanov. Just one moment, please." If he recognized Yurev he didn't let on. A copy of the Sunday *Times* lay behind the desk, open to the story about the diamond.

The million-dollar diamond story was an event that had excited the imaginations of hundreds of thousands of people in the city, and made the name Alexander Romanov, at least for a week, a household word. It began in the middle of January three weeks after Yurev and Helen arrived from London. The first news article had been a short piece in the *Times* financial section relating the sale of a large diamond in England to an American cutter for an estimated one million dollars. The avalanche of publicity snowballed after a *Daily News* headline stated: WORLD'S 3RD LARGEST DIAMOND BOUGHT BY NEW YORKER, and "Gem to Cross Atlantic on Queen Mary."

The *Times* dispatched a special correspondent to London to follow the stone on its journey to New York aboard the ocean liner. For days the city's newspapers published stories about diamonds. The histories of famous diamonds from India—the only stones old enough to have a history —were traced. The Hope. The Orlov. The Regent. And, of course, the most legendary stone, the Koh-i-noor. There was even an attempt to provide a history of the Jagersfontein stone, though it had none. Other articles explained the DeBeers diamond operation and its monopoly, mining in South Africa and speculation about Alexander Romanov, who was to cleave this enormous new stone—or shatter it.

The stone was referred to as the "Romanov Diamond" and it was called the first "major" diamond ever brought to the United States for cutting. Yurev was variously described as a world-renowned Belgian diamond cutter, an unknown Russian dealer, an African who had taught himself cutting in the river sands of the Congo and a German jeweler from Bombay practiced in the secret art of Indian cuts. By the time the Queen Mary docked in New York the fervor over the Great Romanov Diamond was white hot. Hundreds of New Yorkers crowded to see armed guards load a strongbox from the ocean liner into an armored truck. Hundreds more were on hand to watch the unloading at DeHaan, Spahr and Romanov on Fifty-first Street. Security had been tight for the thirty-block trip. A motorcycle procession, lights and sirens blaring, escorted the truck from ship to shop. In the history of the city no inanimate object had been the subject of such fanfare and publicity.

Which was the point.

The diamond from the Jagersfontein Mine in South Africa was never in a locked and guarded strongbox. It had never been aboard the Queen Mary. The stone had arrived two days earlier by registered mail wrapped in tissue paper inside a small cardboard box. The ruse had been Helen's idea. She said it would be fun creating a little mischief. By leaking to the press that the largest uncut diamond in existence had been sold to an American cutter, the game was on.

Yurev never dreamed publicity could create such a monster. What began as a stunt became an outrageous spectacle—and a secret. He could not ever admit the truth and risk the wrath of crowds of New Yorkers. Helen loved the show. Even Groote displayed a sense of humor. The crate he had sent from St. Andrew's House, guarded round the clock, contained a box of cigars.

"Mr. Romanov?"

Yurev glanced up from the vase of flowers at which he had been staring, startled by the smile of the man behind the desk.

"Please go up, sir," the man said. "The elevators are just that way."

Yurev moved quickly down the marble corridor, stopping at the elevators to remove his overcoat and adjust his tie. This appointment had been arranged for over two weeks, and the timing was bad. His sudden mantle of notability was awkward, and he wore it uncomfortably. The last thing he wanted was for Lou Hoover to be ill at ease, suspicious of a man who'd apparently orchestrated a circus act for his own notoriety. He wanted her trust. Riding alone in the elevator, he felt he had the credibility of a carnival barker.

"Good afternoon. I'm Margaret Wicks, Mr. Hoover's private secretary. Please sit down, Mr. Romanov. I'm so glad to meet you." She was a young woman in her thirties, Yurev guessed, with a firm handshake. They were in the same room of suite 31-A where he and Lou Hoover had talked in 1933. The furniture was arranged differently now, the sofa was gone, and the single painting on the wall was a portrait of Benjamin Franklin. The room had a more masculine quality, too, almost austere, and smelled of cigars.

"We read about your acquisition this morning," Margaret Wicks said. "You must be very proud."

Yurev returned her smile and felt himself go flat inside. "Yes, well, a little embarrassed by all the hoopla." He tried to read her expression but couldn't penetrate her smile. "It's really only a rock, you know. Just a large rock."

"Is it really the third largest diamond in the world?"

"In its present state, yes. The finished stone, depending on how it's cut, will be very much smaller."

She nodded. "Fascinating." She folded her hands together as if to indicate a change of subject. "So, Mr. Romanov, how can we help you?" She leaned slightly forward. "You aren't here to give samples to the Chief?"

"The Chief?"

"I'm sorry. Mr. Hoover. We're very informal around here. I'm one of four assistants in the office, and Chief is what Mr. Hoover is most comfortable with." She shrugged. "We're just little Indians, the rest of us, trying to keep up. He writes every day, holidays, weekends . . . the energy of a twenty-year-old."

"I would have thought a former president would tend to slow his pace," Yurev said. He was relaxing. Margaret Wicks' disarming manner took the edge off his nervousness.

"Obviously you don't know Herbert Clark Hoover. Action's in his soul.

President Truman has asked him to head a civilian relief organization in Europe—like he did in the first war. You may have read about it. As a matter of fact, he's in California now planning it, though I don't know why. He calls us every day to find this or that or send him some paper from the library."

"They're not here . . . in New York?"

"Here?" Her expression became quizzical. "Why, no. I thought you knew. He hasn't been in the city since Christmas. I'm terribly sorry if there's been a misunderstanding. All of Mr. Hoover's appointments are screened by one of the assistants when it's someone with whom he's not acquainted. Didn't we explain that?

"Is Mrs. Hoover in California, too?" Yurev knew about the screening procedure, they'd explained it when he had made the appointment. But it wasn't Hoover he wanted to see.

Mrs. Hoover?"

"Yes. You see we met once before. Several years ago . . . in this very room, as a matter of fact. I should have mentioned it, but I didn't think it mattered. Yes, it's Mrs. Hoover—Lou Hoover—who I had hoped to see. It's about some drawings she brought back from China. We had discussed—" Yurev stopped when he saw Margaret Wicks' face flush. She was suddenly uncomfortable, her eyes darting around the room. "Miss Wicks?"

She looked at him quickly, her generous smile failing her. "You've only recently returned to New York, isn't that right?"

"Yes . . ." Yurev felt the look of pain in her eyes. ". . . Africa. Is there something—"

"I'm sorry, Mr. Romanov, but . . ." She paused, sitting up in her chair, looking him straight in the face. ". . . Mrs. Hoover died two years ago."

Yurev knew before she said it. For a moment he was too stunned to react.

"Oh, I'm so sorry. If I'd just known—"

"No, no." Yurev raised his hand. "I . . ." His mouth was suddenly dry. "When . . . ?"

"January 7, 1944. A heart attack." She bit her lip. "She'd just returned from a movie and—"

Yurev nodded to keep her from going on. He grasped at the date, trying to remember what he was doing, as if it made a difference to know. His mind swirled with pictures of the savanna and of Lou Hoover, sitting on a print sofa, watched over by a portrait of Benjamin Franklin.

"She was a lovely, gracious person," Margaret Wicks said, filling the pause. She had collected herself. "I only knew her a few months but . . ." She shrugged, unable to complete the thought, then added, "She was president of the Girls Scouts, did you know that?"

Yurev looked at her stupidly. "No."

"Twice. Mrs. Hoover was as energetic as the Chief. She—"

"Buried in New York?"

"Palo Alto. She loved California."

Yurev nodded. "When I was here before," he began slowly, "we talked about China. About the Hoovers' travels in China. She was going to allow me to see some charcoal drawings that they'd brought back. It's very important to me that I see them."

"Drawings?"

"In charcoal. Actually more like rubbings." He measured the air with his hands. "About this size. Tibetan texts."

"She collected porcelain from China, quite a valuable assortment. And some semiprecious stones, but artwork . . . I couldn't say."

"Not art," Yurev said. "These were paper tracings. Stored with her other papers from China at Palo Alto—at their home at San Juan Hill. She said I'd have to go there to see them."

"I see." Miss Wicks glanced around the room. "Was there something in writing?"

"No. We talked in this room. She agreed to let me—"

"All of Lou Henry Hoover's personal papers have been embargoed," she said. "At Mr. Hoover's instructions."

"Embargoed?"

"Closed. They are at Stanford University—the Hoover Tower. Mrs. Hoover, you may know, spoke her mind. Especially in her correspondences to family and friends. To avoid embarrassment to anyone who survived her, Mr. Hoover had her personal papers collected and stored out of public view at the university." Margaret Wicks raised her head slightly. "If these drawings are among her papers, then I'm afraid—"

"How long?" Yurev said.

She stirred uneasily in her chair. "Twenty years. The papers may not be viewed until 1964. That provision was very firmly set, extending even to the children. I'm sorry, but that was Mr. Hoover's wish."

Yurev cleared his throat to speak but there was nothing more to say.

Five months later Yurev cut the diamond that bore his name. In the intervening period he had become a shadowy figure, shunning publicity and forbidding interviews. When he set the date for cutting, New York was not invited to watch.

Regardless, a radio station dispatched a truck to the offices of DeHaan, Spahr and Romanov, prepared to broadcast "live happenings on the spot." It was the day the name Romanov, both the man and the stone, became a footnote in the history of diamonds.

The Romanov Diamond was an event once again, and its cutting became an historic moment. The *Daily News* and the New York *Times* published artist's sketches of the uncut diamond, illustrating the three kerf marks where the stone would be cleaved. In Boston a psychic predicted that the diamond would split sideways when struck and disintegrate. A diamond expert quoted in the *Times*, after analyzing the marks, said the stone would probably not split at all, that instead the blade would break.

No one who actually witnessed the steel blade bite stone ever forgot it. Alexander Romanov created a worldwide reputation in an instant. With a single blow, he destroyed the largest diamond in existence. When blade bit stone, the 746-carat Romanov Diamond shattered like an ice cube.

◆ MILLER

◆ TWENTY-NINE

CHICAGO

December 22, 1951

"I ALWAYS BELIEVED THAT love conquered all," Abagail Abbaye Kane said, "and I certainly never dreamed a ruptured appendix could temporarily botch up the job." Her silver-gray gown glistened in the light of the parlor in contrast to her red hair, cut short in opposition to the style of the day. At forty-six, she was still unpredictable and outspoken, and with every right. But this was not her night. She glanced at Miller. He was elegant and tall, his gray eyes filled with embarrassment as he stood at Laura's side, focus of attention.

"To Mr. and Mrs. Matthew Miller Kane," Abby announced to the gathering, raising her champagne glass and bringing everybody to their feet. "May the incision of August be the only scar between them." She turned to Miller and Laura and, in a slightly softer voice, added, "May it be between them often." Miller gave his mother a private look as Laura's father laughed and Franklin, Abby's younger brother, said "Hear, hear."

The ceremony had been brief, held at home and attended by none of the crowd who made it a point to be seen at such functions. Laura's sister was maid of honor, and Franklin, of course, was best man.

"I think I should be the first in the family to kiss this delicious girl," Franklin said, shaking Miller's hand. Franklin was fifteen years older than Miller but his relationship to his nephew was more like big brother. Since Kenneth's death Franklin had taken it on himself to stand in as the adult male in Miller's life. In his eyes Miller was an Abbaye—a Kane didn't live who could measure up—and that was that.

"She reminds me a little of Alice," Franklin went on. "You remember Aunt Alice?"

Miller nodded to Laura. "Don't let him start. Aunt Alice was his second wife. The dancer. She lasted longest. Aunt Carolyn was the first of his string but I don't remember her at all. Aunts Beverly and Diane were numbers three and four. Beverly was the painter, I think. She's very popular in bus stations and motor hotels."

Franklin kissed Laura's hand. "Never mind the insensitive clod, my dear. It's my fatal weakness to love and appreciate the artistry and beauty in women."

"Women being the critical word, I understand," Laura said. She was tall, like Abby, and as Franklin straightened up their eyes were level. Her smile was wonderful. "I've been waiting for the day that I could call you uncle, you know. All those stories. Now I can hear them in person from the famous Uncle Franklin, gadget genius and playboy of the Western hemisphere."

He glanced at his nephew. "Revealing the disgusting truth, are we?"

"Just relating the legend."

"Leave it to a boy to get it wrong," Franklin said. "*Diane* was the painter. Beverly was the singer."

Laura smiled. "Maybe if you'd married them in order—Alice, Beverly, Carolyn, Diane . . ."

"Yes, well, I'm interviewing Elizabeths and Elaines presently. Miller, I like this girl. Where did you find such a gem?"

"Considering the competition in this family, first thing was to jump ahead in the alphabet."

Franklin held up his glass in acknowledgment as Abby gestured to him from across the room. "Ah, duty calls." He nudged Miller's shoulder. "Try to keep your pants on till after dessert, nephew. Your mother is trying to impress the guests."

Miller squeezed Laura's hand. "I think he likes you. I'm absolutely positive he's in love."

"How do you know when he's not?"

"He buys something."

Laura nodded. "So can I assume that I've passed the final test of family approval?"

"Well, actually, not the final test. That comes later," Miller said.

She swirled her drink, looking at him from over the rim.

"Don't worry," Miller whispered. "I'm sure you'll pass."

Laura sighed. "Let's just hope you do."

The main course was an enormous turkey. Franklin carved, rattling on like a patriarch, regaling his captive audience with stories of his favorite, and famous, failures. A boy entrepreneur, he had invested every penny of his inheritance in dozens of ill-fated technological experiments over the years—amphibious cars, disposable paper clothing, synthetic fuel, even portable toilets. Young men with radical ideas but no money were the dreamers who attracted Franklin. He championed their visions the way Abby championed her causes. And at forty-four Franklin was a wealthy man because he risked it all to be counted with the dreamers. The failures he shared were legend but so were the successes. He shared the patent on a self-sharpening drillhead that all but revolutionized tunnel boring. He helped launch the first American manufacturer of plastic buttons when bone was king. In Texas he found an electrical engineer whose idea to build transistor components out of ionized glass started a new industry. His most recent acquisition was a New Jersey company that manufactured, in Franklin's words, "the most revolutionary product since ink"— ball-point pens.

Laura seemed to enjoy Franklin's outrageous stories as much as Miller enjoyed prodding him to tell them, Abby thought. The new Mrs. Kane was witty and articulate and possessed a sharp mind of her own. That she was also a beautiful girl with rich full lips and long sensuous legs was more appreciated by Franklin.

The match almost hadn't happened. The wedding had been originally set for August, three months after Miller's graduation from the University of Michigan. He had spent three weeks after graduation at officer candidate school in Alabama and nine weeks more at a Texas flight training base. He had returned home just three days before the ceremony, an Air Force second lieutenant, proud of his silver wings and his blue uniform. But when on his first night home he turned pale and sweaty, it clearly was not due to wedding jitters.

Miller spent a week in the hospital, Laura with him every day. To the disgust of everyone who visited him, he delighted in showing off the once troublesome appendix that he kept in a vial at his bedside table. "This is for mother," he would say. "She'll be the only newspaper publisher in Chicago with a piece of her son's intestine as a paperweight." Franklin, not to be outdone, bid to have the appendage bronzed for the mirror in his car.

After Miller's release from the hospital he spent two months at a muggy

Louisiana advanced flight school learning jets and seven weeks at yet another jet training command, a desolate California base populated more by sagebrush than people, flying F-86s, the backbone of the Tactical Air Command.

Miller would be a good pilot, of that Abby had no doubt. Born to a family of constant talkers, Miller was a listener. His capacity for recalling details, even as a boy, was stunning. He forgot nothing. Keenly competitive, his stubbornness to excel affected everything he did, a trait true to the Abbaye line. But flying was his first love. He soloed when he was seventeen, secretly taught by an Illinois cropduster in a contraption that belonged in a museum. Until then, Kenneth had been the pilot of the family.

Kenneth Matthew Kane, decorated war hero, posthumously honored, and Miller's inspiration. When Kenneth was killed in an RAF fighter over the English Channel in 1941, Miller was not yet ten. His memories of his father were few but he clung to them. His most prized possession was a faded photograph of Kenny Kane, smile flashing, kneeling beside the cockpit of his Hurricane where the name "Abagail" was painted. Sons emulated their fathers, Franklin had told Abby. She knew that, and it scared her.

The sky was full of snow as the guests gathered below the columns of the front porch. Miller and Laura dashed through the traditional bombardment of rice to the waiting car.

Franklin swung open the passenger door for Laura. He'd driven Miller's car to the front drive himself, letting it run to build up what little warmth was possible in the 1947 Ford.

Franklin climbed out from behind the wheel as Miller, waving a last goodbye toward the house, hurried through the headlight beams to the driver's door.

"Your bags are in the trunk, and the tank's full." Franklin pulled his coat collar up to keep the snow off his neck. "I'll give you one last chance to take my Cad. I'll remove this heap of yours to some quiet spot and do the right thing."

Miller smiled. "Thanks anyway. Tell mother again for us that it was great. And thank you, Franklin." Miller held out his hand.

Franklin shook it quickly then pushed him into the car. "Make a man of the boy," he said, ducking down to see Laura. "God knows I haven't managed it."

Laura nodded from the depths of her heavy coat. "I'll try."

Miller's uncle stepped back, crunching snow. "Go, you two. I hate teary farewells."

Miller shifted into gear and with a honk and a wave at the small crowd on the porch aimed the car into the night. Laura snuggled against him.

The cottage they'd reserved was on the lake. The fireplace filled with wood. A note on the table said, "No phone. No electricity. Keep your own fire going. Enjoy. Abby."

Miller started a fire that cast flickering shadows over all the walls. They poured champagne for each other, drinking from cocoa mugs in front of the fireplace. The sheets on the bed were freshly ironed, covered by an enormous heavy quilt. They undressed each other, working slowly, covering awkward moments with laughter. Their first time together was frenzied. The second, slower, less tiring. Then they lay together, legs entwined, Laura's face on Miller's chest. The bed was a shambles.

"It wasn't what I thought it would be," Laura said. She stared at the fire, absently stroking Miller's hand. "It was better."

Miller touched her breast. "They're bigger than I thought."

"So are you." She raised up and kissed him. "I love you, Matthew Miller Kane. Forget everything I ever said about Tyrone Power . . ." Laura reached for his military ID chain on the bedpost, brought it back, studying the medallion that hung between the dog tags. "What's this?"

Miller glanced at the *dorje*. "A charm . . ."

"A charm? You wear a *charm* around your neck?"

He laughed. "Well, not exactly a charm. More a good luck piece. My mother brought it back from the Himalayas. She gave it to me when I was ten. They say it was made for Alexander the Great."

Laura raised her eyebrows. "Boy king to boy airman." She turned it over between her fingers, frowned at the relief of the *dorje*. "What's the wolf supposed to mean?"

"Not wolf," Miller said quietly. "Devil dog. It's a symbol of strength, to ward off evil. In the mountains it was to protect against Tibetan mastiffs. Devil dogs. That's why it's caught in the chain."

"Does it work?"

"I haven't been attacked by one devil dog since I started wearing it."

Laura studied it a moment, then placed it back on the bedpost, stretching over Miller. "The only thing you need protection from is me." She looked down at him. "It's almost dawn. Are you hungry?"

"Food is the last thing on my mind." He cupped her breast in his hand and teased her with his tongue.

Laura arched her back at his touch.

"Okay?"

"Very okay." She reached for him, found him already hard. "You don't need luck, you know. Just practice." She stared down at him. "Lots and lots of practice."

Franklin woke with the most urgent need to find a bathroom. His eyelids fluttered open, and he found himself face down and fully clothed on the bed in Abby's guest room. The time was a few minutes after six if the wristwatch in front of his face could be trusted. He vaguely remembered showing off its water-resistant claim to some nubile friend of Laura's by plunging his arm into Abby's aquarium tank. Blame the devil in his Scotch. The same devil that now allowed his mouth to taste like he'd eaten his socks.

He rolled on his side, closing his eyes to keep his eyeballs from twisting out of his head from the spinning room. The bathroom was . . . that way. Slipping off the bed, he groped with one eye open to the little room and its little bowl. He then shuffled to the sink and splashed water on his face.

"Hair of the dog s'what you need," he said to the slow-eyed face in the mirror. He blinked at his reflection, trying to focus on the weaving head.

He made his way slowly along the dim hallway at the top of the stairs, steadying himself as he went. The floor under his feet was freezing, and he was halfway down the stairway before he realized that he wasn't wearing shoes. He sat down heavily on the stair, at a loss as to what he'd come all this way in arctic cold to do. When he saw the glow of light from under the library door he remembered the liquor cabinet.

He pushed through the double doors into a room brilliant with light, or so it seemed. The fireplace crackled with the last embers of a dying log. Abby was in one of the stuffed, high-backed chairs, her legs folded beneath her scarlet robe. She looked startled to see him.

"God, what . . ." Franklin held his hand up against the light, squinting through his fingers. "Are you signaling to ships at sea in here?" He held onto the handle of the door.

"Franklin? What are you doing up?" And without waiting for an answer told him to "go back to sleep."

"That room . . . that room you are so proud to stuff guests into . . . is ninety-two degrees below zero." Franklin weaved, his eyes slowly adjusting to the light. He glanced at the fire. "Nice and cozy in here, though. What're you doing up at this uncivilized hour . . ."

He saw her eyes dart to the chair opposite hers and realized she wasn't alone. He couldn't see who it was. The chair faced away from him.

"Oh . . . I didn't see"—now he was embarrassed—"sorry, Ab." He shuffled around to leave.

"No, Franklin, don't go. I want you to meet someone."

Franklin turned back as the visitor stood up from his chair. He was tall, less than fifty, and dressed in a suit. Something was familiar about him, but he didn't recognize him from the wedding party.

Abby stood too. She was obviously nervous.

"This is . . . ," she glanced at the man, ". . . someone I knew a long time ago, Franklin." She wrung her hands together. "And I don't know exactly how to do this."

"This?" Franklin tried to follow but the devil had pickled his brain.

"Are you sober enough to think? Shall I get some coffee?"

Franklin moved to the nearest chair and sat down without waiting for an invitation. The thought of coffee made his stomach weak. "God, no." He focused on Abby. "What's going on?"

"It's about Miller," she said. "I—"

"Miller?" Franklin was suddenly alert, imagining the worst. "God, they didn't have an accident? I told him to take the Cadillac, I told him not to drive—"

"No, no. Miller's all right, for chrissake. I'm talking about us." She nodded to the man, who had yet to speak a word.

And Yurev stepped forward. "I'm Alexander Romanov," he said. "Once when I knew Abby I was Yurev Romanovna. Introductions are not among your sister's strong points, Mr. Abbaye. As a matter of fact, she's been very good at keeping family secrets."

"Yurev?" Franklin dredged the name from some unsaturated cell in his brain. "Yurey . . . from the Himalayas?"

"The same. I hope you can handle surprises, Franklin. Abby has a big one for you." Yurev looked at her. "But nothing compared to the shock it will be to Miller . . . whenever she decides to tell him."

"He doesn't have to know," Abby said angrily. "He doesn't *need* to know. I only told you because"—she groped for some explanation—"because it seemed right, after all this time that—"

"Will somebody tell me? What doesn't Miller need to know?" Franklin broke in.

"Matthew Miller Kane is my son," Yurev said quietly. "Conceived on a rock in the middle of a river in Nepal. Marrying Mr. Kane was, well, a convenience."

Franklin turned his dumbfounded look on Abby. "Kenny wasn't . . . ?"

"No."

Franklin suddenly realized what it was that was familiar about Romanov. The eyes and the shape of the nose. The long lean frame. It was Miller to a T. "Jesus," he said, and stared at Yurev. "Jesus Almighty."

◆ THIRTY

KOREA
June 1952

IT WAS CALLED LAND of Morning Calm.

The league of tribes that first settled became known as Choson. It was not an empire but an agricultural nation-state in the gentle valleys between the rivers Amnok-kang and Chongchon-gang. Eventually absorbed by the Koryo Empire, Choson adopted Buddhism and became tied to the fate of the rest of the peninsula. For a thousand years, Land of Morning Calm was a resting place for passing armies. Korean, Chinese, Manchu, Japanese and Russian soldiers bathed in the clear blue waters of Amnok-kang before moving on to distant combat. Now the land between the rivers was once again host to war, though the opposing armies did not fight a single battle on its soil. The battlefield was in the sky. Amnok-kang became known by its Chinese name—the Yalu River. And Land of Morning Calm, its skies streaked with the exhaust of turbojet engines, became known as MIG Alley.

"Bingo."

Chappy's twangy voice broke the cockpit silence. It was the first sound from Miller's radio in fifteen minutes. Time over target had expired, and Miller had not seen a MIG. It had been like this for a week. From the Chongchon River north to the Yalu, nothing. Not even the usual armada of planes cruising at fifty thousand feet, where they were safely out of range of Sabres. Just empty sky. The MIGs had deserted MIG Alley.

Miller glanced at his fuel gauge. The needle hung at sixteen hundred fifty pounds. They had been patrolling the Yalu at forty-five thousand feet, slightly higher than usual, conserving fuel, looking for action. Miller depressed the microphone button on the throttle. "Bingo plus, Lead." The first pilot in a flight down to fifteen hundred pounds of fuel announced it by calling "bingo," meaning time to turn for base.

"Head 'em home," Chappy said. "Left turn, vector one-five-five. Descend to four-zero."

Captain Charles "Chappy" Dillon was a lanky, light-haired Texan from Mule Shoe, Texas. He had punched more cows, he had often said, than mares had fleas. His capacity for whiskey taxed the meaning of excessive, even by Miller's Uncle Franklin's standards, and his sexual exploits were legendary from Seoul to Tokyo. "If drinkin' and screwin' are weaknesses then you're lookin' at a humble man," he would say in a deadpan drawl. But in the cockpit of a fighter, Chappy Dillon became a different man. He had been a navigator on a B-17 in World War II. Sent home after his twenty-five missions, he qualified as a P-51 pilot, returned to England and shot down nineteen Me-109s in the last seven months of the war. His instincts as a pursuit pilot were uncanny; he usually knew before the fact what maneuver the pilot in his sights would attempt. And he demanded absolute obedience of the other pilots in his flight, especially his wingman —which for five months Miller had been.

Squinting over his measure of whiskey in a leaky Quonset hut euphemistically known as the Officers' Lounge, Dillon had said, "Just so you'll know, I look at people with two last names as mighty suspicious." That was February 4, and the rain had been pounding the tin roof for hours. Five days earlier Second Lt. Matthew Miller Kane had reported to Fifth Air Force in Tokyo from Nellis Air Force Base at Las Vegas. His orders were cut immediately, and he was sent to the Fifty-first Fighter Interceptor Wing, Suwon. The Fifty-first had sent him to the Sixteenth Squadron. The Sixteenth sent him to Dillon. "He didn't stay with me, is what he didn't do that got him cracked up," Dillon was saying about his last wingman. "You gotta stay with me, see. That's what a wingman does. Your job, your *only* job, is to cover my ass. I don't take to a lot of radio talkin' in Red Dog flight. You call my breaks and otherwise keep your eyeballs peeled. And, Son, don't never, ever, lose me."

In five months, after sixty-one missions, Dillon never lost Lt. Miller Kane. Hanging on the tail of an F-86 that was maneuvering for position or spiraling out of a jam at six hundred miles an hour was not only frightening, it was theoretically impossible. Seeing was everything. As they were vastly outnumbered, Sabrejets flew in pairs; two planes to an element, four planes in a flight. In combat a wingman who lost sight of his leader put himself and his leader at great risk. In pairs, F-86s were deadly combinations. Alone, a Sabre, slower and less maneuverable, invited attack by gangs of MIGs.

Flying Chappy's wing, Miller had been promoted to first lieutenant and had downed one MIG. Dillon's count was four. Five was the magic number, and every Sabre pilot in Korea aimed for it. Five confirmed MIG kills got you designated a jet ace.

The North Korean Air Force's MIG-15 was a superior fighter, faster than the Sabre, its maximum ceiling higher, and it handled better in high-speed turns. But in the hands of poorly trained pilots the MIG could be relatively easy prey in one-on-one combat. The enemy had two tactical advantages to counterbalance the weakness. First, in trouble, they could run for sanctuary across the Yalu River. Second, the sheer number of planes they put in the air was staggering. Often trains of twenty or thirty MIGs—"gaggles"—would attack flights of four or eight Sabres. Officially the standing order against those odds was to run for it. Most did. Some, however, had acedom on their minds. Chappy Dillon was one of them.

Chappy's Sabrejet rolled on its wing, a glint of sun sliding down the length of the silver fuselage as the flight leader banked away from the sun. Miller followed, easing the control column to his left, pushing slight left rudder, keeping Chappy at his eleven o'clock position. The horizon tilted sideways, a line of blue above and bumpy gray below. Red Dogs Three and Four a mile and a half behind rolled with them, following an invisible arc in the sky.

From forty thousand feet Korea was a wrinkled elephant hide, a vista of unending humps and cracks. Ruddy streams and tiny rivers snaked through red, broken terrain in search of the sea. It was a familiar landscape by now, one Miller had become indifferent to. The only war he knew, or needed to know, was here in the rarefied air between the Chongchon and the Yalu. Jet combat was battle measured in seconds, at once terrifying and exhilarating. It was like a matador taking on a wounded bull without picadors in an arena sixty miles square and eight miles deep. An F-86 pilot, like the matador, had only one purpose in the arena. Sabre interceptors did not bomb bridges or attack railways or participate in ground support. Interceptors intercepted. It was the purest form of war. The individual enemy did not have a face. Just a tailpipe.

"I got a glint." Chappy's voice cracked through Miller's headset. "Three o'clock low. I lost it. Help me, Two."

Miller did not see the aircraft immediately. He searched the sky above and on both flanks. One of the Chinese pilots' favorite games was to offer bait, a couple of MIGs at twenty or twenty-five thousand feet while the rest waited above contrail altitude to come in.

"Two? See anything?"

Miller rolled up slightly on his left wing to look below. "Negative, Lead." He rolled to the opposite side, looking for silver specks above the broken pattern of the earth. Then he saw them. Two MIGs moving southeast, at about fifteen thousand feet, still carrying drop tanks, probably just launched from Antung across the Yalu. "Lead, I have two bandits at five o'clock low and crossing. Vector one-four-zero. Loaded."

Chappy's reply was short. "Go."

He dove straight for them, and Miller followed. The Sabres had the angle, coming in high at seven o'clock and closing fast from a mile and a half. The image of the second MIG slid through Miller's gunsight pipper at eight thousand feet. He touched his chest where the devil dog good luck piece hung under his flight suit. This was going to be a piece of cake—

The MIGs suddenly nosed up, dropping their tanks, and started a climbing turn to the right, leaving a white spray in their wakes from the separated fuel pods. The lead MIG broke hard left and headed straight down, his wingman right. Chappy stayed on the lead, cutting inside the turn, his guns pouring tracers across the sky ahead and below the aircraft's path. Miller hung in behind Chappy, popping his speed brakes quickly, then retracting them to maintain distance and observe. The MIG flew right through Chappy's field of fire. Armor-piercing incendiary ammunition flashed on impact as it peppered the plane's port wing and fuselage just below the tail. The MIG's exhaust turned black with smoke, then belched a plume of fire twenty feet long as bits of turbine blades blew out when the engine ruptured.

"Got him."

The MIG rolled on its back like a dead fish, spinning down. The canopy blew, and a moment later the pilot ejected. Chappy continued after the plane, and Miller stayed with him. He was going to record the crash with his gun cameras, Miller thought, proof of his fifth kill.

"Dog Two, check six o'clock. Bandit closing." Red Dog Three, trailing the action at three miles, called the warning. Miller looked back. The MIG wingman who had separated from his leader had looped behind him. Thirty-seven millimeter tracer rounds burned past Miller's canopy like flaming golf balls.

"Break right."

Miller stomped hard right rudder and slapped the control stick against his thigh, pushing the throttle forward to the stop with his left hand. He felt the thud of cannon fire in his left wing. The F-86 bucked, flipped on the right wing, then charged with power, stood on its nose and screamed toward the ground as Miller jammed the stick forward. The altimeter wound backward like a crazy minute hand. Gravitational force pressed him back in his seat. His helmet suddenly weighed fifty pounds. At eight thousand feet he rolled out of the dive, banked hard left, right and left again. The MIG followed but overshot. The pilot tried to slow, deploying his speed-brake panels to keep Miller from recovering. But Miller had already throttled back. He cut outside, then inside, turning into the MIG coming in from astern. The tracers had scared hell out of him. He'd never been that close before. He had reacted instinctively, diving for the mountains, but now he was angry. His Sabre had been hit. The left wing spar panel had several holes, the plane was sluggish in responding. The fire warning light glowed red on his instrument panel. He smelled smoke.

The MIG was twelve hundred feet ahead, maneuvering to shake Miller off. Miller hung on the MIG's tail, slipping in and out of jetwash as they scissored across the sky, the gunsight pipper sliding back and forth without settling on the target. He fired several bursts without connecting. Then the Korean pilot made his mistake. He tried to climb.

The MIG, still heavy with fuel and in the dense air at low altitude, quickly lost its advantage. Miller was low on fuel—twelve hundred pounds —and hit, but he had the MIG in his sights. Holding the pipper squarely centered on the MIG's mid-section, Miller squeezed the trigger. Flashes danced across the fuselage as armor-piercing .50-caliber rounds chewed the MIG's tail. Black smoke poured from its exhaust. The MIG slewed to the right, Miller stayed on him, let loose another burst that shot away part of the tail. Closing at five hundred feet, he fired a long burst. Pieces of the plane blew back in the jetwash, peppering the Sabre's windscreen, but the MIG kept flying, smoking badly, half its tail missing, but it wouldn't go down.

"Finish him." Chappy's voice startled Miller. He glanced back. Chappy had moved behind him at five o'clock.

"Finish him and get out, Two. He's headed for the river."

With all the maneuvering, the MIG was now headed north. The Yalu was ahead, a silver ribbon, the Manchurian border. American pilots were forbidden to cross the river and enter Chinese territory. Miller couldn't follow much longer. His fuel indicated he was already down to a thousand pounds. The MIG was going to reach sanctuary before his engine blew. A damaged Mig counted for nothing in the sweepstakes. If he didn't knock it down his troubles were for nothing.

Miller slid behind the limping MIG. They had slowed to four hundred and fifty miles an hour. The trail of dense smoke poured from the MIG's exhaust, at times engulfing Miller's plane. He was very close, less than one hundred feet, but at this distance he couldn't miss. He fired a long stream of tracers that disappeared into the blackness from the exhaust. A flame shot back from the MIG, a huge orange plume so bright that Miller squinted away from it. Pieces of the exploding engine pinged across the Sabre's wings. When he saw the MIG's speed brakes suddenly extend, Miller jerked back on the stick to avoid ramming it.

The Korean pilot ejected at the same moment. The canopy swept past Miller's cockpit. In the split second before collision, he knew the pilot had planned the sequence, popped his brakes and punched out, expecting the Sabre to crash into the doomed MIG. And it almost worked. Miller missed the MIG. He didn't miss the pilot. The jolt of impact knocked Miller forward, banging his helmet into the instrument panel. When he looked up, his outer canopy was streaked red.

"Jesus, Dog Two—you hit him, you hit the bastard . . ."

The steel ejection seat had done the most damage, crushing the nose of the Sabre with the force of a wrecking ball, shattering the fiberglass intake. Continuing over the nose, careening sideways into the canopy windscreen, the crumpled seat had cracked the bulletproof plexiglass. Seat straps, buckles and stringy sinew that didn't explode on impact were sucked through the intake port. Control panel emergency warnings lighted as the jet's power generator failed. The engine gave a low broken whine as turbines splintered, then snapped, spewing metal bits in a pink cloud of vapor. At that moment Miller's plane became a missile. Shock and an instant of sickening realization froze his hand to the stick. The jet slid on its side, tipping on its wing, the jagged edges of broken fiberglass whistling in the screeching wind. The spiraling Sabre brought Miller to his senses. He jammed the maimed nose down to recover from the spin. Emergency procedure, he remembered, was to head for the sea. All he could see through the smear on his windscreen were the gray wrinkles of Korean mountains. Whistling air filled the cockpit. The collision with the seat had dented the seam between the canopy and windscreen, just above the left forward side, causing a tiny breach. The rush of air was freezing.

"Flame out." Miller regained his voice. He worked the engine restart, his eyes moving across the instrument panel for some sign that the plane was still alive, but the engine rpm needle lay dead in its gauge. "Flame out." His mouth was dry. He could hardly hear himself for his pulse beating in his head. "Leader . . . I'm going down."

"Restart, Two. Hit your restart."

Miller gulped for air inside his mask. "Negative restart."

"Make for the sea. Turn right. Flatten out."

Miller eased back on the stick, aiming for the blurred horizon where water touched sky. The Yellow Sea was sanctuary. The navy controlled the sea and the sky over it. MIGs did not fly over water. An American pilot in trouble could ditch and wait for an air rescue helicopter to fish him out. He knew the drill. Everyone knew the drill. But the sea was seventy miles away. He glanced out of the cockpit. Below was North Korea. Rescue on the mainland was not attempted above the thirty-eighth parallel.

"Try restart again." Chappy's voice was calm. He was flying just off Miller's starboard wing, air brakes extended. "C'mon, kid. Snap out of it. You don't wanna go down in this neighborhood."

Miller's altimeter wound down through eight thousand feet. "No good. Intake is fouled. Power's gone." He checked his airspeed—280 miles per hour and dropping. He needed fifteen minutes, maybe sixteen to reach the sea. At his speed and rate of descent the Sabre had only about eight minutes of time in the air. It meant he was not going to ditch in the sea. "Can't make water."

"What's your fuel?"

The gauge showed almost empty. Not that it mattered. His engine was junk. "Hundred fifty pounds. I took some hits. Must've got a line."

"Purge your remaining fuel. I'm gonna try something."

Miller glanced across at Chappy. "Say again, Leader."

"Shut everything down. I'm going to stick my nose up your tailpipe and shove you to sea. Purge your tank, I don't want to take a bath in jet fuel."

The wrinkles below were turning green and taking on distinctive characteristics. "Negative, Leader. We're too low." The altimeter needle wound back past seventy-five hundred feet. The fuel indicator was on "empty."

Chappy waved him off. "Blow your canopy if this doesn't work." He gave him a thumbs-up sign. "Hold on."

The F-86 was a swept-wing, single-engine jet fighter, weighing ten thousand pounds empty. It was not a large plane but neither was it a glider. Miller was technically flying because the Sabre had momentum and a cutting edge, but he was also dropping like a five-ton rock. What

Chappy was proposing no one had ever tried before. Sabrejets were not designed to push the equivalent dead weight of four Buicks at critical altitude.

"Maintain trim." Miller felt a bump as Chappy nosed his Sabre against the exhaust manifold. He felt pressure from the stick to climb, and he trimmed it back. He heard, felt Chappy throttle forward. The airspeed indicator moved to 305. The stick was very tight.

"Ease up, Leader," Miller said. "Don't press it too far. Three hundred is rich enough for me." What was amazing, he thought, was that it worked at all.

"Best I can do," Chappy said. "I'm using climb power."

"Don't sneeze."

"Just steer straight, Junior. Not much of a view back here."

They were at seventy-three hundred feet, stuck together like mating beetles, covering six miles every minute. It would take twelve minutes to reach the sea.

The second hand on Miller's watch seemed to move in slow motion. After three minutes he could see the coastline. The cockpit was freezing from the narrow stream of outside air through the dent in the windscreen. Even with gloves his hands were cold and stiff, and he had lowered his goggles to keep his eyes from watering. But seeing the coast was a sign of hope that numbed the chill in his spine. This crazy scheme might actually work.

"Yellow Sea dead ahead," Miller said.

Chappy's thumb must have been on the mike. "Switch to TAC 4. Let them know you're coming."

"Switching now. Stand by."

TAC 4 was the VHF emergency guard frequency monitored by navy sea-rescue ships. Miller had never trusted helicopters, ungainly beasts that defied the laws of simple physics. But now he couldn't wait to get into one. "Mayday. Mayday. This is Red Dog Two at zero-seven-three. Vector two-one-two from tango X-ray. Mayday."

There was an immediate response. "Red Dog flight, this is Cyclops." The voice was dry with a southern accent. "What's your status?"

"Critical altitude after flameout. No restart."

"Roger, Red Dog. Are you equipped with dye marker?"

"Affirmative."

"Give me a count."

Miller counted as slowly as he could so Cyclops could take an RDF reading to fix his position on radar. "One, two, three, four, five . . . five, four, three, two, one."

"We have you, Red Dog. Can you confirm with an identifying turn to right?"

Keeping the Sabre in level flight was difficult enough. Turning was out of the question.

"Negative. Negative on turn."

"Understand, Red Dog. Cancel ID turn. Will you abandon or ditch?"

Flopping a plane on water was not something he had practiced in flight school. "Abandon," he said.

"Roger, Red Dog. We will be waiting. Good luck."

Miller switched his radio back to the normal tactical frequency. "Red Leader?"

"Go."

"I'm set for recovery." Miller was thinking about the water, about stripping out of the parachute and inflating the vest jacket. Going over the sea-drill checklist in his head. Disperse dye marker, remove helmet and side arm . . .

"Dog Two, I'm below critical . . . eight hundred pounds," Chappy said slowly over the radio. The confidence in his voice that had been contagious a few minutes ago was gone. "This exercise is gulping fuel, I can't stay with you."

Miller closed his eyes, nodded to himself. He pressed the mike button. "Roger, Leader."

"Sorry, Kane . . . pulling out . . . now."

The jet nosed down as soon as Chappy was away. Miller trimmed up quickly to keep as much glide profile as possible and watched as Red Dog Leader scorched the sky above him, making a roundhouse turn to the south, waggling his wings.

So much for Cyclops. Without Chappy pushing, Miller's airspeed dropped from three hundred to two hundred in seconds. The altimeter was winding backward again. The F-86 had a glide ratio of approximately ten to one—for every hundred feet of glide the plane would drop ten. He had about four minutes to glide eleven miles before reaching minimum bail-out altitude. It also put him short of the sea by thirty miles.

To hell with the sea. Miller shoved hard left rudder, turning the plane, pointing it east. Continuing toward the sea was useless; there was nothing except lowlands and populated areas. He'd be picked up as soon as he touched the ground. East were the mountains, or what passed for mountains in Korea. They were not densely populated—goats and farmers mostly. His chances of getting back were improved, he figured, if he could make it to the mountains. All the major military supply routes were in the foothills. In the sector nearest him ridges reached to between twenty-five hundred and three thousand feet. The plane couldn't reach the mountains but he could get close. That's all he needed—a chance. If he traveled at night, rationing himself, he might get back to friendly territory in less than a week. It wasn't impossible, he told himself. Just over a hundred and fifty miles. Maybe ten days. He remembered his mother's Himalayan trek. She'd survived the jungle, heat, crazy dogs and fanatic monks on a sixteen-thousand-foot-high glacier. He'd heard the story a thousand times. If she could survive all that he could handle a few days in these ridges. Survival was in his blood.

The altimeter slid through four thousand feet. The terrain below was distinct now. Trees and irrigation ditches were real shapes. The ground didn't look like a map anymore.

Miller cinched his seat-belt straps tight. The abandon-aircraft procedure was relatively simple—raise emergency lever from below armrest, rotate handle, head down, jettison canopy, head back, feet and elbows in, eject pilot. But depending on an off-the-rack parachute was worrisome.

Three thousand feet.

The plane began shaking, keeping Miller busy with the stick. The plane's airspeed was down to 140 miles per hour, and the controls were getting very sluggish. The vibration was normal at this altitude. Thermal radiation from the ground was making the air turbulent. Normal. Just drop the nose, advance the throttle and climb. The thermal didn't exist that was a match for the J-47 turbojet engine. Unless, of course, it had torqued itself into scrap metal.

The vibration became severe at two thousand feet. The cockpit shook and rattled with such violence that the control panel gauges became unreadable. Miller clamped his jaw shut to keep from cracking teeth. He reached for the emergency lever and cranked it upright. It was time to go.

He set his heels back tight into the foot stirrups built into the seat assembly and rotated the handle to its armed position. The ejection sequence involved two pulls on the handle trigger. One jettisoned the canopy. The second discharged a twenty-millimeter explosive canister beneath the frame that rocketed seat and pilot thirty feet straight up in less than a second. The seat was equipped with two ejection levers, one under each armrest, in the event a pilot were wounded and unable to use one or the other of his hands. It was also impossible to eject with the canopy in place—a mechanical rocker arm that detonated the canister did not snap shut until the canopy was gone from its mounts. Also, a pilot blasted out of the cockpit might lose consciousness, particularly if he was wounded, so the seat was designed to release all straps holding the pilot two seconds after ejection. As seat and pilot separated in the slipstream the last line connecting the seat assembly to the pilot's lanyard pulled the rip cord, deploying the parachute. Everything was automatic once he squeezed the trigger. Just close your eyes, take a deep breath and go.

Miller rotated the handle, felt the trigger slide into position. The plane was buffeting so heavily that he could not make out more than a blurred view of the ground. He bent his head down, a precaution against the forward canopy striking him as it left, touched his good luck piece and squeezed the trigger.

He heard metal scrape metal, saw the canopy move from the corner of his eye, felt a cold blast of wind fill the cockpit. He slammed his helmet back against the seat rest, pulled his elbows tight against his sides, squeezed again.

Nothing happened.

Miller opened his eyes wide and looked to his right. The canopy was not gone. It had moved back about four inches, and stopped. The MIG's ejection seat had done more damage than was apparent from inside the cockpit. The canopy slide was normally a straight grooved track with locking arms to hold it secure. When the locking arms were released, the canopy slid back along the track. Jettisoning became a simple matter of releasing the canopy, letting it slide backward, and the slipstream handled the rest, ripping it off the aircraft. Simple and automatic. The first foolproof step in getting the hell out. Nothing to think about.

Miller thought about it now. The dent that created the jet of air was more than a dent. Miller could see it now. The slide was so bashed that even though the locking arms released, the canopy slid back only a few inches, then jammed into the mashed track. It meant the seat-ejection system would not fire. It meant the line from the separating seat to the lanyard would not be pulled automatically, deploying his parachute, because he was still attached to the seat. Which was still attached to the airplane. It meant he wasn't going anywhere. Except down.

He used his elbow and upper arm, banging against the plexiglass, trying to dislodge the canopy. The control stick was barely controlling anything. The Sabre was very near stall speed. Damn soon it would stop gliding. He guessed he was between fourteen and twelve hundred feet. Four tons of metal dropped very quickly from that altitude.

The jet nosed over slightly and began a lazy turn to the right. The shuddering stopped. Miller could see the control panel again. The altimeter was moving fast. Eleven hundred feet. The control surfaces were useless now; the plane was just weight, obeying gravity. Miller lunged from one side to the other, slamming his shoulder and helmet against the canopy. The sun slid past, bright in the clear blue sky, then a blur of dirty green, then the sun again. Faster.

One thousand feet.

He was falling at 180 feet per second. It was a computation that came to him suddenly, even clearly, in the midst of terror, as if his brain had been holding back, waiting to release that tidbit of data, oblivious to the adrenal flow surging everywhere else in his straining body. It was a computation distilled from the fact that falling bodies reach a terminal velocity of 120 miles an hour, and then fall no faster. Miller even remembered the precise moment he learned the fact, while sitting in the third row of his high school physics lab waiting to time a steel ball bearing dropping through a beaker of mercury. At the time it seemed a strange way to prove the point.

Miller lunged again, and the beaker exploded. The seat ejected the instant the canopy broke free. His helmet shattered as it crashed against the trailing edge of the fleeing canopy. He had almost no sensation of moving. The sweat on his face burned away in the blast of wind that accompanied his catapult out of the cockpit. He felt only a searing pain in the back of his head; time lost all sequence. The world had turned inside out. He felt as if he were drowning, sinking away from the surface, gasping for air. He saw his foot—just his foot—trailing behind him, shoeless. Beyond his foot was the sun, a white-orange disc hovering above the azure water. When he looked up, he was looking down into the gray depth. Miller saw his plane then, churning like a dying shark, headed toward the rocky bottom. Its nose was crumpled and its silvery body was streaked red from the mouth of the intake manifold to its belly.

The Sabrejet exploded against a low rolling ridge of scrub pines and dull rocks. It struck the ground upside down, breaking its back, disintegrating the wings. Miller's parachute opened a moment later, and he drifted above the wreckage, beyond the smoke. Passing out once, he revived in time to prepare to land, mustering the strength to hit on his feet, knees slightly bent.

The jolt sent a shock through his body that burst in his brain. Running a few steps, he chased the parachute before collapsing in the spindly grass on the side of a hill. He was aware that his crash helmet was missing, and that somehow he'd lost one of his boots. But he was alive. He didn't remember leaving the plane. He didn't remember anything except bashing himself against the canopy, then feeling the wind in his face.

He rolled on his back to pull himself up, but a bolt of pain pinned his head to the ground. His eyes watered from the intensity of it. He had hit something coming out of the cockpit. He closed his eyes. Must have been the canopy. He tried to lie still. He'd get up in a minute. He thought about Laura. What were they going to tell her? First Lieutenant Matthew Miller Kane was missing in action? Was he shot down? No, the stupid asshole tried to eat an enemy ejection seat. He felt for the devil dog charm. Well, his good luck piece had come through for him, he was alive, and when he got up he was going to walk away from this like it was a bad dream. Like Abby had done. He thought about his mother standing at the edge of a gorge, red hair blown back by driving wind and rain, the charm dangling from around her neck. This stuff was all in the family.

Miller opened his eyes. His head throbbed with the sudden light, extinguishing the glacial valley. He blinked several times and decided that even if his head split at the seams he had to get moving.

Making it to his knees after several attempts was dizzying work. Trying to ignore the pounding in his temples, he got both feet beneath him. One step, another, that's all he had to do. Left foot. Right foot. Forget your head. Left foot. Hold on. Right foot. No problem. Be in Seoul for breakfast.

Miller took another dazed step, walking downhill, straining against the harness he was still attached to, talking to himself, and stumbled when the parachute lines refused to give more slack. He fell backward hard, taking the wind out of him, banging his bruised skull.

Ah, rest. Good idea.

The blue sky flashed white hot as his eyes closed. In the moment of pain, pain stopped. Day became midnight. And midnight was nothing.

◆ THIRTY-ONE

MILLER OPENED HIS EYES to a woman with jet-black hair standing above him. Behind her his parachute billowed against the limbs of a tree. She was dressed in a coarsely woven skirt and faded blouse that hung below her waist. She looked about forty, and she stared at him without speaking.

"On-ju." Miller slurred the word for friend or friendly, he couldn't remember exactly. The pain in his head struck back as he tried to move. He hadn't the strength to pull himself up, and he felt suddenly ridiculous in front of this Korean peasant woman, lying on his back in a yellow life vest, still harnessed to his parachute, his pistol still strapped across his chest.

"American pilot." He nodded at the sky, and a thunderbolt cracked through his brain. He just managed to roll on his side before he vomited.

He must have passed out because when he opened his eyes again the woman was holding his pistol. She was standing in the same spot, her arms at her sides. The pistol was in her right hand, pointed toward the ground, caught in the folds of her skirt. She still said nothing and did not move. She just kept staring at him.

"Help me." Miller forced the words out. It didn't matter what language. She understood. Begging was universal. He pleaded again but she made no response.

"Look, goddammit, if you're going to shoot me then get it over with. But for chrissakes do *something.*"

Her attention shifted to the sound of an engine. Somewhere near, a truck strained up a grade, and soon he was surrounded by civilians and a handful of excited soldiers with stars on their caps. Their uniforms were a mishmash of different issues, some olive, some khaki, and their rifles were long-barreled, obsolete, probably Japanese. Three soldiers tried to make him stand but Miller kept falling down so they settled for propping him against a rock. They cut the lines to the parachute and tore off his harness and life vest, keeping their rifles trained on their prisoner. No one approached him. Miller figured they didn't often run across pilots, and no one was willing to take responsibility for shooting him. That was all right with Miller.

A horseman, Chinese or Korean, Miller could not tell, rode up then. He was old—easily sixty—and an officer. The soldiers all snapped to attention as he approached. It seemed he'd been captured by a band of civil guardsmen, Miller thought, not knowing if that was bad or good. The officer rode a brown mare and circled Miller twice before coming to a halt and dismounting. The man was smartly dressed, his uniform was clean and he wore no weapon but, surprising to Miller, there was a sword and scabbard on his horse.

The officer walked straight to Miller, pointed toward the smoke from Miller's wreckage. Then he went to his horse and returned with the sword, touching it to Miller's stomach. Miller sweated. For five minutes he tried not to faint while the officer held the point to his belly and talked in his face. The crowd of civilians had grown, and it seemed this speech was apparently more for their benefit than Miller's. He'd become, he guessed, a war trophy.

Finally more soldiers arrived, quickly surrounding Miller and the old swordsman. The new arrivals were real soldiers, and they carried real weapons, automatic rifles with curved magazines. One, an officer, approached the scene, and after a quick exchange the first officer went back to his horse, waving to the crowd of civilians.

The second officer looked at Miller without expression, nodded toward the smoke, spoke slowly. "That is your plane?" Miller guessed he was Chinese, in charge.

"Was," Miller said. "But you can have it." Not a clever thing to say to one's captor, but he felt he was going to pass out any second and didn't care.

"Where is your sidearm?"

Miller glanced toward the crowd. He did not see the Korean woman. He decided not to answer.

"I would have shot you if you had your sidearm."

"Sorry." Miller's head was coming apart. Focusing was a problem.

The Chinese looked toward his men, and two of the huskier ones responded by taking Miller under the shoulders and dragging him up the hill, where a military truck waited. One dropped the tailgate while the other held Miller up, then heaved him into the back of the truck, and Miller promptly threw up on the hot metal bed. When he opened his eyes, his head was near the swinging tailgate.

Miller stared out from the truck, still dazed. Beyond the tree he saw the black-haired woman. She was standing where she had been before, staring at him. In the distance, clear in the afternoon sun, were the Korean mountains. Another five miles and he'd have made it. Five miles. The Chinese stepped in front of him, cutting off his view.

"I inspected your plane." The Chinese reached down and pulled Miller's head up by the hair.

"How did you make it bleed?"

Miller didn't understand the question. His head was exploding inside. Then he saw the shark in his mind.

The Chinese let Miller's face drop back. The soldier set a canvas bag on the bed of the truck, and flipping it sideways emptied its contents.

Miller could barely see, the pain was crushing. A misshapen melon rolled toward him, bumping awkwardly over its uneven features. The rotten melon rolled against his shoulder.

"All did not burn," the Chinese said. Miller pushed weakly at the fruit. Skin stuck to his fingers. Blinking back the pain, he refocused his vision on a severed head. Pivoting awkwardly on the uneven bed of the truck, with remnants of flight goggles still visible, the charred skull of the MIG pilot turned its savage grin on Miller.

Miller screamed as the tailgate slammed shut, forcing out the light.

In the darkness of absolute terror, his prison term began.

◆ THIRTY-TWO

CHICAGO

"YES, CLAUDE, I UNDERSTAND that, but when are you going to find out?"

Abby paced in front of the window of her office in the *Chicago Democrat*. Below, Lake Michigan shimmered in the sunlight of the warm June afternoon. "Claude, I don't care what time it is in Geneva. You're the International Red Cross, for chrissakes. There must be some way you can get confirmation"—Abby turned to glance at Laura, who sat in a corner of the sofa beside Abby's desk, face expressionless.

"Well, when are the sons of bitches going to release the names?" Abby said into the receiver, turning back to the window. She shook her head. "Claude, we've been friends for twenty years. You've known Miller his whole life. Could *you* be patient if he were your son?"

The door to Abby's office opened, and Franklin entered. He looked at Abby. "Ab, what's—?"

Abby waved him off. "Claude, Franklin's just come in. When you find out something, anything, you call me. You have the numbers? Okay. Day or night. Thank you." Abby moved to her desk and hung up the phone.

"Claude? Claude Reynier?" Franklin was frowning. "What's—?"

"Miller got shot down three days ago," Abby said.

"Oh, my God—"

"The Air Force contacted Laura this morning. Officially he's listed missing but they think he's been captured. A parachute was sighted by another pilot . . ."

Franklin sank into the sofa beside Laura. He took her hand, glanced back at Abby. "Was he wounded?"

"I don't know, nobody seems to. The Air Force will only say that Miller was over enemy-occupied territory when his plane was lost."

"Enemy territory? Ab, the only territory left in that goddamn war still occupied by the enemy is North Korea. Look, I know those bastards at the Pentagon, I'll get—"

"No." Abby ran her fingers through her red hair. "Laura called me as soon as she heard. We've been on the telephone all day. It's not a military thing any longer. It's political. If Miller is a prisoner, the Air Force or the Pentagon can't help him."

"Reynier," Franklin remembered. "The International Red Cross inspects prisoner of war camps. Claude can find out about Miller."

"I don't think so," Laura now put in. She looked at Abby. "Not from what I heard of the conversation."

Abby nodded. "According to Claude there are more than three thousand American prisoners held by the North Koreans. The IRC only has the names of a hundred and ten of them."

"Hundred ten?"

"North Korea, it seems, didn't sign the Geneva Convention."

"So?"

"*So*, the bastards aren't bound legally to obey it. What it means is that it's going to be a long time before we hear if Miller . . ." Abby looked at Laura. "I mean, when we hear something."

"It won't be the same," Laura said.

"The same?"

"His father didn't come back from his war," Laura said. "Miller will. He promised me that." Her hand rested on the bulge in her maternity dress. "Miller will come home. He'll come back to meet his child. He has to . . ."

◆ THIRTY-THREE

CAMP V, NORTH KOREA

MILLER WOKE UP TO the tromping of boots outside his cell. He pushed himself upright to a sitting position in a corner. He had been in this unlighted sweltering cell for five days without food, had no recollection of coming here. His prison was a cubicle eight feet to a side with a bulbless fixture dangling from the center of the ceiling. His bed was the cement floor. He urinated into a trough against the wall and while away the hours by swatting flies off his face. A small rusty water pipe that passed through his cell kept him alive. He had to stand on his toes to reach it and lick the condensation.

Before being put in this place he had been trucked from one interrogation center to another. For three days he had been held in a cave with two South Korean soldiers awaiting sentencing as spies. Miller assured them, as best he could since they didn't understand much English, that it was a bluff, they were all prisoners of war, each wearing his uniform. POWs were protected, Miller told them. No one could try them as spies.

The two soldiers were shot the morning of the fourth day. His interrogators promised that the same summary execution awaited him unless he confessed to his "war crimes." Confess and be saved was the refrain. His captors worked on him in shifts, and Miller recited the same information—name and rank, branch of service, date of birth and service number.

The beatings had begun the third day after he had watched the Koreans' execution. His head was usually covered with a wet burlap sack and his hands tied behind him. He could see shapes through the coarse weave of burlap but could not breathe. The session ended only when he passed out. Waking in the darkness of this cell, ankles shackled together, his mind was keen to every sound around him. From time to time he heard voices through the brick walls but they were too indistinct to identify as either Korean or English.

For some reason they singled out feet for beatings. His first two days in the cell he slept, or tried, unable to get up even to his knees. For the rest of the time he could only wait, sharing his cell with flies and stifling heat. The only sound, other than the buzzing insects, was the light clinking of the medallion against his dog tags on the chain around his neck. The medallion became a reminder of who he was—not Lieutenant Kane, USAF—but Miller Kane, son of Abagail, who had taken the worst the Himalayan snow hills had to give; the only white woman in the world to have climbed the Kali Gandaki gorge in winter. Miller kept telling himself he could do no less.

Tromping boots woke him. The door scraped across the cement floor. Miller shielded his face as the guards entered, commanded him to stand. They filled the doorway with their weapons, silhouetted against the light. Miller somehow got to his knees. The guards wrenched him to his feet and pushed him into the dimly lit corridor. Shuffling barefoot in his ankle chains, he climbed cement steps to the next level and another corridor. Walking was its own torture, as intended, and Miller tried to balance himself on his heels.

A rifle butt punched Miller's shoulder blade, a signal to stop. One of the guards blindfolded his eyes and bound his hands behind him, then prodded him up stairs.

"Good morning, Lieutenant."

Miller flinched from the light when the blindfold was removed. Sunlight streamed through a bank of large windows. He was standing in the center of a very large room, a deserted factory or warehouse by the look of it. Behind a wooden table sat a uniformed North Korean officer, shirt crisply ironed, smoking a cigarette.

"I am Major Ding." The officer was perusing several pages in a yellowed file in front of him. He set his cigarette carefully on the edge of the table beside a pitcher of water. "Welcome to Camp Five, Lieutenant Kane. We are pleased to have you here."

Major Ding was not a particularly tall man. The cuffs of his military shirt sleeves came nearly to the first joints of his thumbs. He looked to be around thirty, though Miller had trouble approximating ages of Asiatics—they seemed to him to look younger than they were. Ding's hair was black and short-cut. The middle and index fingers of his right hand were stained yellow from the nicotine of his cigarettes. His cheeks were smooth. His English was rather formal, as if he had learned it from a book, and his voice was thin. Now he said something in Korean, and a guard untied Miller's hands. Another guard dragged a wooden chair across the cement floor, putting it down hard beside Miller. The noise echoed in the vast chamber.

"Please sit down, Lieutenant."

Miller gripped the back of the chair. He hadn't sat in a chair in weeks. His chains clanked between his bare feet as he lowered himself to the seat.

"This war is at an end for you, Lieutenant," Ding said, retrieving his cigarette from the edge of the table. "We are at peace, you and I."

Miller stared at the pitcher of water. He couldn't take his eyes off it. The metal pitcher looked cold. Rivulets of condensation had made a puddle around its base.

"Lieutenant?"

Miller looked up into the major's face.

"Did you understand what I said?"

Miller made a noise, his tongue seemed to fill his dry mouth.

"Some water?" Ding motioned to the pitcher.

Miller watched as the major poured water into a tin cup. Ice rattled in the pitcher.

"We are at peace, Lieutenant," Ding said again. He stood and walked around the desk with the cup.

Miller nodded. He could smell the water.

"If that is so then we must have a pact of trust. I will do something for you"—Ding held up the cup—"and you will do something for me."

Miller's hand shook as he raised it toward the cup.

"As your demonstration of trust you will admit to your previous crimes, crimes committed before you embraced the peaceful goals of the Democratic People's Republic."

Miller dropped his hand. "Can't . . ." He closed his eyes tight. The ice clinked together in the cup.

"But you can, Lieutenant. Of course you can. It is simply a formality. All prisoners must make a confession. It is a condition before your release to the American compound. You have been stubborn, Lieutenant. It is not my rule. All prisoners must confess."

Miller shook his head. In his mind's eye he saw the cockpit of his Sabre.

"For your convenience, we have prepared the text of your confession," Ding said, ignoring the head-shake. "You may read it and make whatever changes you deem necessary for your own particular case. If you wish you may draft your own confession. It is the first step toward your rehabilitation."

Miller could hear the whine of the turbine blades gaining velocity.

"Lieutenant, we—"

Miller's tongue flicked over his chapped lips. "Circuit breakers on." His right hand moved to an invisible cockpit panel.

"Circuit breakers?"

"Windshield deicer lever up." Miller stared past Ding, hands roving the empty air. "Hydraulic pressure gauge selector switch normal."

"Lieutenant—"

"Rudder trim switch on." Miller touched the seat of his interrogation chair. "Ejection seat safety pin out."

"*Stop.*"

"IFF control board check. Boogie at twelve o'clock." Miller raised his right fist to eye level, thumb extended up, aimed directly at Ding. "Target sighted . . . pipper grid zeroed—"

"*Silence.*"

Miller jammed his thumb down. "Target . . . evaporated."

Major Ding kicked Miller's chair, sending him sprawling backward so that his head cracked against the cement floor . . .

Miller could not stand for three days. His victory, if that's what it had been, had not impressed anyone. Instead of a dark cell, the solitary incandescent bulb in the ceiling was turned on and never went out. Once a day a slat opened in the door, and a wooden bowl of rice soup slid through. Later it opened again, and Miller pushed it back, empty. The ritual was always in silence, but it was confirmation that life existed outside his cell. He had no way of knowing if it was day or night. He kept track of time with the arrival of his rice bowl, saving a single grain of rice from his once-a-day meals, storing them in the cotton lining he'd ripped from his pocket.

The bowl of rice soup became the focus of his day. It was enough to keep him alive but never enough to forget the hunger. For hours he would sit, propped in a corner of his cell, and think about Laura, not allowing himself to think about the interrogations ahead or the beatings. Anticipating pain was the short road to cracking up. Instead he thought about Laura, reliving their nights together in the cabin. He masturbated but the energy spent began to have its effect. The sexual release made him hungrier, and weaker, and after eleven days he'd rubbed himself raw. So he took to singing to himself . . . the drinking song from *The Student Prince* was his favorite.

He worked out a daily routine. The soup started his day, and he made it last as long as possible, counting each grain of rice with his tongue before grinding them to pulp and swallowing. Occasionally he found a bit of meat or gristle in the bowl, and the discovery was like a celebration. He could spend an hour with such a morsel, stripping it down bit by bit, creating extravagant dinners in his mind.

Personal hygiene was next on the agenda. Using the lining from his other pants pocket like a mitten, he washed his teeth, wetting the cloth with his saliva. On account of the heat he had stopped wearing his shirt and trousers. He tore the sleeve of his shirt to use as a swatter against the invasion of flies. The other sleeve he lay over the water pipe to soak condensation. He would wring water into his bowl, then use the sleeve to wash himself, concentrating on his toes. His weight loss was severe. The day he had taken off from Suwon with Chappy he had been one eighty-five. He guessed he'd lost at least twenty pounds.

But most of all Miller worried about misplaced time. Pieces of his days passed and he had no recollection. He could walk for what seemed like minutes only to discover that his rice bowl was full of soup just inside his door and that he had walked twelve hours straight, around and around his cell.

Hours and hours of nothing to do, day after day. It was a punishment that left no physical scars or bruises, no sores to be nursed and watched as they healed. Nothing to denote the passage of time. There were days he would have welcome a beating just to see another human face. Every day was the same . . . every hour, every minute. To fight it Miller divided his day into activities. And turd-watching came first.

Once a day the narrow trough against the wall ran with water, washing out the trough and carrying away his daily production—a single hard turd ball. And with the wash from upstream came others floating by his cell, presumably one per prisoner. Like his own, hard lumps, nine in all. Which to him meant there were nine other prisoners in this hellhole, or more, downstream of his cell. The excrement became his friends. Every day at turd wash time, an hour after delivery of his rice soup, Miller was on his stomach beside the trough. When nine lumps had passed he figured nine lives were accounted for, if not well, at least well enough. Surviving counted for everything.

After the wash Miller exercised, walking four hundred ninety-five times around his brick box. One, two, three, four, five, turn. One, two, three, four, five, turn. Four hundred ninety-five times. He walked in short choppy steps, dragging his chain, moving without thinking except to count. He had calculated the distance to be three miles.

The exercise was valuable not only for the physical activity but because it wore him out, exhausting him. It was his way of turning the tables on his captors, of attacking the tedium of isolation. He filled the hours of humid silence and oppressive loneliness by retreating into a limbo state somewhere between sleep and consciousness, brought on by walking himself to exhaustion.

He also created a new existence in his mind where animated fantasy replaced torpid reality. At first he relived childhood experiences, casting back to memories of his father and periods of his adolescence when his sexuality awakened a new curiosity. He could sustain the limbo state for hours but the sessions were unsatisfying. They had no goal. He had to find some activity he could stretch long term. The answer came to him during the daily watch. He was on his stomach, wondering where the turd wash ended, imagining a river of turds from POW camps all over Korea, bobbing together through the winding streams, headed for the sea.

Now Miller began the three-mile walk with a new sense of excitement. He was going to make his own way up the formidable Kali Gandaki River gorge. And of course he knew what it was like because he'd heard the story from his mother a thousand times—the tropical lowlands, the dizzying heights of treacherous rope bridges, the barren isolation of the high hills in winter. He knew the route and the dangers—and the goal. He was going to Tramar-Dri to face the devil dogs, then through the Valley of Weeping Winds and down the glacier to the faded red *door-chorten*, standing alone on the ridge above the Dara Khola. That was his goal— to find an ancient, eroding Buddhist shrine. And dig up the Pearls of Light.

He walked with measured purpose. One, two, three, four, five . . . turn. His chain scraped along behind him, but without weight. He wasn't in a prison cell. He was on his way to recover the pieces of Shelkagari that his mother had left behind. Sweat glistened on his skin and stung his eyes as he walked. One, two, three, four, five . . . turn. The laughter that echoed from his cell was only a shadow of madness.

◆ THIRTY-FOUR

NEW YORK

"GODDAMN BUREAUCRATS." ABBY SLID into the rear seat beside Laura and slammed the taxi door after her. "Asshole communist morons!"

Laura noticed the cab driver's eyes flick toward the rearview mirror. "Roosevelt Hotel, please," she said with a demure smile, fanning herself with the narrow brochure an embassy attendant had passed to her. The August heat was stifling, brought to oven temperature by the city's enormous buildings.

A heat that only inflamed Abby further. " 'Hysterical,' he said." She turned to Laura. "Was I hysterical?"

Laura clutched the hand strap as the cab turned past the Chrysler Building. "I wouldn't say hysterical." She held her purse to keep it from sliding off her lap or what passed for the lap of a woman nearly eight months pregnant. "Maybe it was because you called his ambassador an idiot—"

"He *is* an idiot. How can he deny that the Czech Red Cross is in touch with the North Koreans? Christ, even the Chinese don't deny that."

The appointment with the Czechoslovakian consul had lasted less than ten minutes and hadn't gone well.

"Franklin said not to expect too much," Laura said, feeling she had to comfort Abby. "It was a long shot, after all."

Abby stared out her window.

They had been in New York for three days. Claude Reynier of the International Red Cross had called four days ago from Geneva to tell

275

Abby that the IRC was quietly working on an exchange of sick and wounded prisoners. If she could meet him in New York he might have a list of names. Abby was on the next plane from Chicago, along with Laura and Franklin.

The list did not include Miller. Laura didn't know if that was a good sign or not. The list of wounded was admittedly incomplete, naming Americans the North Koreans were tired of caring for, but at least it was a list of men who were alive. The only complete list of POWs was in the hands of the Koreans. No one kept a list of the dead. The names of captive pilots were particularly guarded, except for a few fliers who had been tried as war criminals by Chinese military courts. But Miller was not among those either. Franklin had been to the Polish Embassy—he knew a vice consul there—but without any luck. He'd been told to try the Czechs.

"If one more person tells me to be patient," Abby said to no one, "I'm going to slug the bastard."

The cab waited in traffic interminably for the red light to change on Fifth Avenue. The back of Laura's dress stuck to the seat. It was like waiting for a forest fire to end. Laura touched Abby's hand. "You need a cold drink."

"What I need," she said, "is a goddamn tire iron." She leaned forward to catch the attention of the driver. "And if you miss this light, cabbie, I'm going to pay your fare in Norwegian krones."

The taxi slid to a stop in front of the Roosevelt Hotel without having caught another light. Laura bought a newspaper in the lobby concession, and they rode the elevator together in silence, still flushed from the heat.

Franklin greeted them at the door of the suite with a drink in his hand. "Come in. What did the Czechs say?"

Abby pulled off her hat. "Nothing."

"As expected," Franklin said. "Well, screw the Czechs. Miller is *alive*."

"What?"

He motioned to the foyer. "We have a visitor."

Helen Romanov got up from her chair as Franklin entered the main room with Abby and Laura. She was dressed in a summer suit with a white pleated skirt. A glass of lemonade had soaked through the napkin on the small table by the sofa.

"Helen," Franklin said, "this is my sister, Abagail Kane. And this is Laura, Miller's wife. Abby, Laura, I'd like you to meet Helen Romanov. She has terrific news."

Abby reacted first. "Romanov? You're . . ."

"Yes." Helen smiled self-consciously. "I'm sorry, showing up unannounced like this, I know it's awkward. We've been trying to reach you and only found out this morning that you were in New York."

"Sit down, everybody, sit." Franklin guided Laura to the sofa. "Can I get drinks around? This is something to celebrate."

Laura waved him off. She was still stunned by the news. "Are you with the Red Cross? Do you know something about my husband?"

"Red Cross?" Helen looked at Franklin with an expression of surprise that edged on annoyance. "She doesn't know?"

He cleared his throat. "Well . . . no."

"*No?*" Helen looked from Franklin to Abby, astonished. She turned to Laura. "I'm sorry. No, I'm not with the Red Cross. My husband is . . . a friend of the family. He very much wants to help . . . to find out about Miller. He's been in London, The Hague and Zurich asking questions. He found a Soviet minister of trade there who wasn't put off by the offer of a bribe to make inquiries among his Chinese friends. Last night he called from Bern. Your husband is alive, Mrs. Kane. He's in a prison camp in a place called No Name Valley . . . on the Yalu River. He wasn't wounded or injured when his plane crashed, according to the Soviet minister. The camp where he's being held is an interrogation center. A special camp for American pilots. For some reason he's been segregated from other prisoners. The minister didn't know why, or wouldn't say."

Laura hoped for more, but at least Miller was alive. She hadn't realized anyone else was working to get information about Miller. She didn't know Helen Romanov or her husband, but she was grateful to them. She also detected an uneasiness in Mrs. Romanov's manner, as if there were more to tell, something left out. Laura moistened her lips, half-afraid to press for more. The August heat had suddenly reached inside the Roosevelt and dried out her mouth. "Was . . . was there something else?"

Helen Romanov glanced at Abby before answering. "Yes, Mrs. Kane . . . I would say there is. I certainly would say that."

"Yes?"

Helen stood up. "Mr. Abbaye, would you mind seeing me to the lobby?"

Franklin was almost too slow to understand, then came quickly to his feet.

"Oh, of course. You're absolutely right." He turned to Abby. "She's absolutely right," he said firmly.

Laura watched as Franklin escorted Helen Romanov to the door. "Franklin . . .?"

"It's all right," Abby said. She stood, facing Helen. "Thank you for coming. And, please, thank your husband. We're more grateful than we can say . . ."

For a long moment the two women stared at one another, then Helen nodded and turned to leave.

"No, wait," Abby said. She walked Helen to the foyer, out of Laura's sight. "I—I have to explain all this to Laura, but . . . but I want you to, I want to thank you . . ."

Helen said nothing.

"I never forgot Yurey. I want you to understand that. I—I did love him. For the short time we spent together I—"

"I understand," Helen said quietly.

"No, you don't, not really. I've had this guilt with me for twenty years. I don't think I could explain it to Yurey . . . but I want you to know. I would never have left him in India. They sent me back because I was sick. Otherwise I wouldn't have left . . ." Abby's eyes were wet. "It's important to me that *you* understand. You were with him all those years . . . I can't imagine what it was like in Africa, but . . . I don't know if I could have stuck it out. I don't think—" She took a breath. "What I'm trying to say is . . . I guess it worked out like it should have. I mean, I'm glad he has you. I—"

Helen touched Abby's hand. "I thank *you* for saying that."

"Miller is just like him," Abby said, tears now on her cheeks. "He's tall and strong . . . Yurey is there, in his son."

"I would like to meet your son," Helen said. "When he comes home. And he will, if he's half as courageous as his mother . . ."

Laura stood as Abby returned to the room.

"Abby, what's—"

"Please, sit down, Laura. I've something to tell you." Abby found a chair near the sofa. Her hands were in motion, rubbing over each other as if she was washing them.

"Miller?" Laura's voice was tense.

"You've hear the Himalayan story, the search for a diamond?"

Laura frowned. "Shelkagari? Of course, Miller's told me so many times it's as if he were there, but what does—"

"Yurey Romanov, the man in Switzerland, was the man I came back with from the snow hills."

"I still don't—"

"Yurev Romanovna . . . Alexander Romanov, is Miller's father." Abby took a breath and let it out slowly. "And what I'm about to tell you now is the story Miller never heard."

Laura stared past Laura to the drapery across the room. A broad-bladed fan turned lazily overhead, quiet witness to a secret unfolding.

"So"—Laura adjusted herself on the sofa, trying to find a comfortable position for the weight on her stomach—"when Miller gets out he'll not just meet his child for the first time, but also his real father. Won't that be interesting?" She looked at Abby. "Or do you want me to lie to him, too?"

"You have a right to be angry," Abby said. "A perfect right—"

"Me!"

"Laura, I'm not going to apologize to you for my life. I only want you to see—"

"We're not talking about *your* life. God, Miller is in a prison camp somewhere in Korea because he patterned his life after his father, who it turns out *wasn't* his father."

"That's not true. Laura, you don't understand, you don't know how it was. When I came back from India it was like the world had turned upside down. My father was ruined in a few months. The stock market crash finished him. He was already overextended, and when he lost his railroad interest it was the end. He was never strong, not like Franklin or me. Shooting himself was probably the bravest thing he ever did. We inherited a financial nightmare. Then when I found out I was pregnant . . . well, everything was going to hell in a hurry, but I was going to have my baby. It was *my* child. The world could fall apart but I wasn't going to let it take my child with it."

Laura did understand that . . . nothing was stronger than the bond she felt for the life in her belly.

"Kenny Kane was like a gift from God," Abby said. "We practically grew up together but I hadn't seen him in years. Then one day he was there, running a little newspaper he'd inherited and hating every minute. When he asked me to marry him . . . well, it wasn't what you'd call a great romance. He wanted to get out from under the newspaper so he could get on with his real love—airplanes. I needed a husband, or rather I needed a name for my child. I told him about the baby, and he didn't care. Kenny Kane *was* Miller's father. That was the irony of our so-called marriage of convenience. Kenny loved Miller as if he were his own flesh and blood. I think he even loved me. Miller . . . well, he was devoted to

Kenny, worshiped him. *That's* why I never told Miller. Especially after Kenny was killed. It would have been a pointless and cruel thing to do." She looked at Laura. "Would you have done so differently?"

Laura was silent for a moment. Finally she said, "I can't answer that."

"Can't?"

"Did you try to find his real father?"

"No, I didn't . . . I wanted to but I didn't." She had told herself Yurey was dead. The last time she saw him he was sick, delirious with malaria in a frontier hospital. The further she was from India the easier it was to believe he wasn't alive. And she had paid for that rationalization with guilt for twenty years. Abby looked at Laura. "I know, right now, in 1952, that sounds cold. But in 1929, pregnant, trying to hold on . . . I guess I was just trying to survive. If he was alive, which I told myself he wasn't, he was twelve thousand miles away. It was like another lifetime ago. Can you possibly accept any of that?"

"I'm trying to, Abby. When did you find out he wasn't dead?"

"After the war. I was in Detroit trying to steal an editor away from the *Free Press*, bring him back to the *Democrat*. It was a Sunday morning at breakfast in the Fremont Hotel. I opened up the morning paper and bang, there was his picture. Alexander Romanov, 'The Russian Hammer,' the cutline said. He'd just smashed some great big diamond to bits. It was a shock, sure, and it also scared me . . . I was afraid that someday he might come across something, like I'd just done, that would lead him to me . . . and Miller, and then what? Would Miller turn on me? Would Yurey try to take Miller away from me? They look so much alike it's uncanny . . . what if they met? . . . It took your marriage for me to get up enough courage to call him. It was a *very* awkward conversation, as you can imagine."

"You told him he was a father . . . on the telephone?"

"No, I'm not that bad. I told him I had to see him, that he had to come to Chicago."

"And he came, just like that? After twenty years?"

"Of course not. I had to invent a reason."

Laura waited to hear it.

"I used the one thing that I knew he would come a thousand miles or ten thousand miles to know," Abby said. "I told him I had the key to finding Shelkagari."

◆ THIRTY-FIVE

CAMP V
September

"You will die unless you confess. Admit your crimes and live."

Miller hung between two guards before Major Ding. The thugs with leather gloves and short bamboo sticks had beaten his feet so badly that he could no longer stand alone.

"Do you wish to die, Prisoner Ten?"

Ding had stopped using name and rank. Miller was now a number or an animal, depending on the major's mood. Dog was his favorite, followed by filthy turtle. Turtle dung was, it seemed, the worst thing that a Korean could call you.

"You were an agent of the American insect campaign. Confess."

"Not true . . . no insects . . . " Miller mumbled at the floor, unable to raise his head.

Germ warfare was the subject of this latest round of interrogations. If Miller had been strong enough he might have laughed. Ding was accusing him of dropping bombs filled with insects—fleas and mosquitoes. All of them infected with disease meant to kill off great portions of the North Korean population. It was the first Miller had heard of the bacteriological warfare he was supposed to be engaged in.

"You dropped mosquitoes infected with typhoid. You're an assassin—"

"No . . ."

Ding grasped Miller by the hair. "Liar."

The session ended as usual, a backhand across the face. Next came his appointment with the beaters.

The guards dragged him away, but instead of beating they dumped him back into his cell. Miller curled into a ball, touching the soles of his blistered feet. One of his toes was swollen and inflamed. The nail was missing, ripped off by a shot from a bamboo stick. It must have happened yesterday, Miller didn't remember.

The water rolled into the trough through the turd wash hole, and Miller just managed to pull himself over to the edge. He'd missed several days' watching because he was usually entertaining the beaters. He watched now as seven turds floated by. The water eased to a trickle, then stopped.

Seven? Should have been nine. Did it mean that they were beating everyone or just a few at a time? Were his fellow prisoners being interrogated or were they sick or dead? Those turds had been his bond with other faceless prisoners for three months. Two missing was like losing two children. He even felt responsible.

The cell door screeched open, startling him. He crawled to the corner. They forgot it was beating time, he thought, they've come to correct the oversight. But it wasn't a guard who came into his cell. It was a civilian, at least someone dressed in slacks and a white shirt open at the collar. And he wasn't Korean or Chinese. Unless he'd had his face fixed.

"Lieutenant Kane?"

Miller pulled up his knees. He didn't answer. The man moved aside while a guard brought in a small wooden folding chair, something a grade school child might use, and placed it just inside the door.

"You are Lieutenant Kane, aren't you?"

He was British or Australian, from the accent. The man smiled, eyebrows raised. He was carrying a small briefcase.

Miller nodded. "Lieutenant Miller Kane. United States Air Force." He swallowed, trying to bring moisture into his mouth.

"Ah, good." The man sat down, making a table for his briefcase with his knees. "Lieutenant, my name is Desmond Smithwaithe, special correspondent to the London *Daily Worker*. I am"—he made a face, waving a hand in front of his nose—"the stench of this place." He turned, ordering the guard to open the door as wide as possible to admit fresh air. It was almost a comical scene, watching the guards struggling with the door while Smithwaithe sat in the child's chair protecting his nostrils with a handkerchief. The exercise concluded with the heavy door wedged against the concrete floor, admitting dozens of flies attracted by Smithwaithe's cologne.

"Now . . ." Smithwaithe gazed down at Miller. "Lieutenant Kane, I'd like to ask you a few questions about your treatment and these serious accusations brought by the People's Democratic Republic." He produced a small note pad from his briefcase.

Miller could hardly believe what was happening. The idiot wanted an interview.

"About your treatment . . ."

"You're not serious."

"I'm serious. How are you being treated? And the food?"

"Food? I've lost thirty pounds eating it."

"Most American do. Americans are overweight, as a rule. You should be grateful your body has been allowed to shed its unhealthy fat."

"Oh, well, since you put it that way. By the way, where's Moe and Curly?"

"And your confinement," Smithwaithe continued, "is protection against the elements?" He glanced around the brick cell. "No exposure to rain or burning sun?"

"Don't forget sleet," Miller said. "I don't get any sleet in here either. Course, the wind's the real killer, comes whipping across the plain like a goddamn williwaw—"

"Unresponsive, disparaging." Smithwaithe wrote as he spoke. He looked up from his pad. "Confinement seems adequate."

"For a shit-hole."

"You're a prisoner of war, Lieutenant. You can hardly expect us to provide you luxury accommodations."

"Are you going to put in there about the beatings?" Stupid question, he knew.

"I understand you're uncooperative and hostile. Prisoners are subject to certain punishments if they are—"

"Get out," Miller said. He tried to push himself up, using the wall for support.

Smithwaithe called for the guard, and one was suddenly in the cell, his foot on Miller's chest.

"I can have you bound up if necessary," Smithwaithe said from his chair. "Unless you decide to be more civil."

Miller couldn't breathe. "Get him . . . off . . ."

Smithwaithe snapped a command, and the guard removed his foot, went back to his post just outside the cell door.

"Now. About your part in the germ warfare against the People's Democratic Republic—"

"That's bullshit and you know it."

"I've seen firsthand your warplanes dropping germ bombs. Thousands of mosquitoes and fleas were released, all of them diseased—"

"You're an expert on diseased fleas too?"

"Typhoid epidemics are spread from your bombs."

Miller almost laughed but it would have hurt too much. "I'm sorry to disappoint you, Smithy, but I didn't drop bombs. I flew a Sabrejet, an F-86 D, which doesn't even have bomb racks. I was an interceptor pilot, we just blew up MIGs."

Smithwaithe was quiet. So was his pen.

"And—you're going to love this, old boy—mosquitoes and fleas don't carry typhus. Typhus is water-borne . . . you could explain that to whichever asshole is writing your stuff. You drink it or swallow it, you don't get bit by it." Miller licked his chapped lips. "The only way you're going to get typhoid epidemics from fleas or mosquitoes is for people to eat the goddamn things."

Smithwaithe slapped his note pad shut, got to his feet. "This interview is ended."

Miller looked up at him. "Now there's a disappointment."

"You're a filthy—"

"Darwin was wrong, Smithwaithe. Evolution can still produce subnormal intellect in primates. And it seems God found them jobs at the London *Daily Worker.*"

The appointment Miller had missed with the bamboo sticks was rescheduled.

◆ THIRTY-SIX

"C'MON, PAL, C'MON." MILLER lay on his belly, his eyes just above the stream of water that slid out from the wash hole. _"C'mon."_

It had been six weeks since the Smithwaithe interview. That day had been his last contact with another person. It was also the day his world began shrinking. Seven turds had decreased to five after a week.

Miller couldn't sleep. Watching became his life. Those hard lumps were a validation of survival. He could remain strong as long as he knew others were holding up with him. But the bond was slipping away. He was losing his friends.

Five dropped to three. Then two. By late October, one.

But today even that simple friend wouldn't come. The trough water was empty. The stream of water eroded to a trickle. Miller's eyes stung. "You sonofabitch, I told you to hang on. I _told_ you . . ." Tears blinded him. "All right, you bastards—when are you coming for me? _C'mon,_ then . . ."

He hit the door with his fist. "Turtle shit sonsofbitches you haven't got the balls of a slug—" He pounded at the door, throwing himself against it. Reason had deserted him, only rage was left. His chain banged against his shins, the shackles cutting into his ankles. He worked himself to exhaustion, finally sliding down against the wall.

No one came. He was, at last, absolutely alone.

* * *

The necklace in his mind's eye was magnificent.

He had lost all sense of time. Without the daily count he reverted further into himself, pushing his mind backward in time to the stories of his youth. There he found Alexander's necklace, and sanity in darkness.

With the devil dog medallion tight in his fist, ignoring the reality of chains and rice cakes, Miller let his mind take him to the balcony of a monastery high on the cliffs of a barren medieval place. He visualized the towering monastery, the mosaic-tiled courtyard, the dark wrinkled face of the Old One and, finally, the necklace, using all the power his imagination could summon up. In his mind the necklace was magnificent—made of gold lotus petals, each containing a wine-colored ruby. Except the six center petals. In these were the six diamonds of legend, the Six Little Sisters, the jewels of the lotus. Pieces of Shelkagari.

Miller relived the fantasy of discovering the necklace again and again, safe from the torments of his conscious existence. His dream was wonderful, without pain. He held the grand necklace in his hands, sitting on a mat in the sunshine of crisp morning, and drank tea with the Old One, god in a scarlet robe. But the dream always ended in confusion and terror. His nightmare was waking up from the dream. Always he was falling, holding the necklace, and falling backward from darkness to light. And always there was the Old One standing above him on the wall, watching, his expression neither surprised nor sad. The only sound was Miller's scream.

"Help me . . ."

"I will help you, Lieutenant. I am here to help you."

Miller woke in his own sweat, propped against the corner of the cell. The fantasy evaporated the moment he opened his eyes. Reality returned in the blurred image of a Chinese uniform. Miller blinked, adjusting his eyes, focusing on the face above him.

The Chinese knelt beside him. "They say one should not interrupt another's nightmare . . . or risk making it his own."

His English was perfect, Miller noticed that first. He was young, about Miller's age, and when he smiled his smile did not seem a weapon. He was wearing the uniform of a lieutenant in the regular Chinese Army. His boots were polished to such high luster that Miller could see the reflection of his shackles.

Miller glanced quickly around his cell, afraid he'd come awake in the middle of an interrogation.

"I'm not an interrogator," the Chinese said. "I am Lieutenant Nung Sam of the Army of the People's Republic of China."

Miller stared up at him. "What do you want?"

"You are being transferred in my care to another compound."

"Transferred?"

"Your interrogation by Korean authorities is ended. Their efforts were without success—"

"Bastards . . ."

A nod of sad agreement. "These Koreans," he said in the voice of a conspirator, "they are not the most subtle race."

Miller leaned his head against the brick wall. "I'm not signing anything, I'm not confessing to anything. Not to you, not to anyone."

Nung Sam shrugged, slid a small canvas bag across the concrete floor to Miller's side. "I have things for you—toothbrush, brushing cream, mirror, soap, shaving razor, change of clothes." He opened the bag so Miller could see. "An American khaki uniform with the appropriate service insignia. Also socks, shoes—"

"Who's it from?"

"A gift from the People's Republic."

Miller turned away, dragging his shackles on the floor as he drew his knees up. "Keep it."

"It's for you."

"You guys just don't quit, do you?"

"There is nothing to sign, Lieutenant Kane. You are in Chinese hands now." He glanced around the tiny cell. "Mukden is a much better place than this. I cannot say that you will like it, but at least the prison there is not a dungeon."

Miller looked up sharply. "Mukden? Mukden's in China . . ."

"Actually it is the capital of Manchuria."

"I'm not going to goddamn China," Miller said, rushing over the words. His first thought was that the fighting had expanded across the Yalu, that Truman had declared war on the Chinese communists. "What do you mean, I'm in Chinese hands? I'm a prisoner of war of North Korea, not—"

"They have given you to us."

"Given? Are we at war?"

Nung Sam stared at him.

"The United States and China. Are we—"

"No, fortunately not."

"Then—"

"You are going to Mukden because that is where your trial will be.

"Trial?"

"You are an American pilot charged with making war against the People's Republic, a neutral state. You are not to be considered a prisoner of war. You will be considered a foreign aggressor. You will be tried by a People's Military Court. I have been appointed to be your official counsel and interpreter."

"Charged with what?"

"War crimes."

"*What* war crimes?"

"Specifically, I do not know. You will be formerly charged before the court. Can you stand? I prefer that you bathe before we leave. It is a long ride to Mukden."

"Leave . . . now?"

Nung Sam looked surprised. "Yes, now."

Miller glanced at the wash hole. "Is that what happened to the others? Did they go to Mukden for trials?"

"Others?"

"The other prisoners. There were nine prisoners here besides me."

Nung Sam shook his head. "There were no others."

"Oh, c'mon. There were nine other prisoners here. They were here for months, just like me. Then they went away . . . one by one."

"You saw other prisoners?" Nung Sam looked honestly surprised.

"They never let us see each other," Miller said, "but they were here. The bastards thought I didn't know but I knew." He pointed out the trough where he had counted turds. "Right there. That's how I knew. Nine lumps of shit floated down that trough every day. Nine turds . . . nine prisoners. They thought I didn't know but I knew . . ."

Nung Sam stared at the trough and the wash hole.

"Just tell me what happened to them. Ding didn't kill them, did he? Were they sent to Mukden too?"

"This place" . . . Lieutenant Nung Sam glanced at the wash hole as if confirming something to himself. When he looked back at Miller he spoke with an almost gentle voice. "There is only one cell in this place," he said. He glanced at the walls. "This cell."

"That's a *lie.* I'm Prisoner Ten. Why would they call me Prisoner Ten if—" Miller stopped, looked at the wash hole where for months he had clung to a vision. "I *saw* them, nine turds. They"—he pointed to the trickle of water in the trough—"right there. They . . . every day. Weeks, months. I saw them." Miller looked at the Chinese. "Goddammit, I *saw* them."

Nung Sam's face was drawn. "Koreans, they are cruel but not stupid."

"No." Miller shook his head, refusing to believe. "No. Ten of us. There were *ten* of us. Jesus God, tell me where they are."

"I am sorry, Lieutenant," Nung Sam said. "No other prisoners are in this place. There never were. There was only you."

Miller stared at the Chinese, his mind numbed. Then Prisoner Ten began to cry.

◆ THIRTY-SEVEN

CHICAGO

"OH, GOD . . ." LAURA'S FACE and neck were slick with perspiration, a tiny pool gathered in the indention of her neck.

Abby dabbed a damp cloth over her forehead, pushing back strands of tangled hair. "It's all right, you're going to be all right."

The labor room was a small brightly lit place next to the delivery room. Laura had been prepped for surgery but she wasn't prepared for such pain. Who was? Abby thought.

The next contraction surged through her body.

"It'll be just a minute," Abby said nervously. She held Laura's hand and looked back through the open door. "Nurse—for chrissakes—"

The nurse arrived, took Laura's wrist in her hand, casually glancing up at the clock. "Well, Mrs. Kane, are we ready to have our baby?"

"*We're* about to have it *now*," Abby said. "Are you people paid by the hour? Where's the doctor?"

"Everything looks fine," the nurse said. She turned to Laura. "I think we're about ready. Is the father here?"

"No."

Laura cried out again, and Abby told the nurse, "Can you get moving? I'd like the doctor to be at least in the same room with her."

"In good time, Mrs. Kane. We're just having a baby here. A normal delivery." The nurse smiled and muttered, "Grandmothers are the worst."

It was the first time Abby had been called that. She wished she had a gun.

An attendant arrived dressed in white, his face covered with a mask. "We're ready." He unlocked the gurney brake and wheeled Laura into the delivery room.

"The waiting room is just that way," the nurse said with a nod. She was tying on her mask.

"I know where—"

"Give us twenty minutes."

Abby paced the waiting room. When Franklin arrived she let loose her anxiety on him. "Where the hell have you been?"

"Is it over?"

"No!" She glanced down the corridor again. "Dr. Kildare and his practiced staff are on the case . . . *still.*"

"Laura's all right?"

"Of course she's all right. She's only having a baby, you know."

Franklin unslung the small leather case that hung from a narrow strap over his shoulder. "There's some news." He looked solemn.

"Franklin, we're *making* news today. I haven't—what the hell is that thing?"

"Portable radio." He fiddled with the dial, sliding through broadcast stations. "Here it is." He turned the volume knob. Better the radio give her the bad news. He wished she never had to hear it.

". . . by the Red Chinese. The military court will try another American pilot for war crimes against the state. The pilot, Air Force Lieutenant Matthew M. Kane, will stand trial in Mukden, the capital of Chinese Manchuria. First news of the trial was broadcast this morning over Radio Peking by Desmond Smithwaithe, special war correspondent for the London *Daily Worker.* Lieutenant Kane, according to the broadcast, is expected to be charged with murder. This marks the first time an American has been tried by the Chinese military court for anything other than biological warfare. In other news—"

Franklin switched the radio off.

"Murder?" Abby stared at her brother. *"Murder?"*

A nurse hurried down the corridor. "Mrs. Kane . . ."

Abby turned, glassy eyed.

"It's a boy, Mrs. Kane. A beautiful nine-pound boy."

Abby nodded, sat down beside Franklin, who took her hand.

"You'll be able to see your daughter-in-law in just a few minutes. Would you like to tell her yourself?"

Abby glanced up at the nurse. "Yes. Yes . . . I'd better do that myself . . ."

◆ THIRTY-EIGHT

MUKDEN PRISON
Chinese Manchuria

A tiny bell began the trial.

"The prisoner will state his name."

The courtroom was the prison assembly hall, a drab, concrete chamber with unpainted walls. The court consisted of ten officers of the People's Republic Army and a chairman who did not wear a uniform. They sat on a platform behind a long table. The court outnumbered the spectators. Rows of empty wooden benches filled the rest of the hall, arranged with a central aisle. At the other end of the room two guards and a prison warden stood against the wall. In the last row of empty benches sat a civilian with a notebook. Desmond Smithwaithe.

The Chairman waited a moment then, speaking louder, said, "The prisoner will state his name for the court."

Miller returned the stare from the chairman without blinking. He stood with the aid of a chair. His feet were still swollen from the beatings at Camp V, and he wore Chinese slippers because shoes would not fit.

"You must answer," Nung Sam whispered nervously. "It is the procedure."

"The prisoner," Miller said, "does not recognize this court. The Chinese government has no jurisdiction to try me."

"You cannot say that." Nung Sam was almost white.

"My feet are killing me," Miller said. He sat down.

For several minutes there was activity in the courtroom. Two guards were summoned and took up positions at the bench immediately behind Miller.

The little bell rang again. Order prevailed once more.

"The prisoner will stand," said the chairman.

Miller dragged himself to his feet.

"The prisoner will state his name."

Miller put his weight on the chair, trying to take as much pressure off his feet as he could. The slippers were no help on the concrete floor. "This isn't a goddamn court, and you're no—"

The blow to his kidney came from behind, something very hard, swung with vicious force, and gravity did the rest. Miller fell, the chair tumbling sideways, scraping across concrete as he crumpled, his right side suddenly paralyzed. The guards pulled him to his feet. Miller's breath was gone. He gasped for air. His side was on fire.

"The prisoner will state his name."

"Answer," Nung Sam pleaded.

Miller raised his head to see the chairman. "Lieutenant . . . Matthew Miller . . . Kane . . ."

"The prisoner will be seated."

Miller heard the scrap of the chair as it was retrieved. The guards shoved him hard into the wooden seat, rekindling the fire in his side.

"The prisoner, Lieutenant Matthew Miller Kane, is charged with crimes against the People's Republic," the chairman began slowly. He was reading from a paper that he held in his hand. "The prisoner is charged with aggression against the peace-keeping forces of the People's Republic, with wanton destruction of people's property and with the merciless and deliberate assassination of a people's comrade." The chairman looked down at Miller. "Does the prisoner understand the charges?"

Miller tried to straighten in the chair, but the effort made him gasp. His mouth tasted of bile. He couldn't see clearly.

"You must answer," Nung Sam urged.

"I'm going . . . to be sick," Miller said. He leaned forward, holding his side.

Nung Sam spoke quickly in Chinese. Miller was aware of footsteps. He was sweating, the hair at the back of his neck was wet. A glass appeared in front of him and he reached but couldn't find it. The room was spinning, getting darker. Miller fell off the chair, protecting his damaged side. He heard the bell again, a fading sound, ringing in the back of his mind. As he drifted into unconsciousness, he thought of dozens of sheep, climbing a narrow trail in the mountains with tiny bells around their necks sounding off together. He remembered that he should wear a hat. No one goes into the hills without a hat.

* * *

The clanking of keys woke him, and he opened his eyes as a warder admitted Nung Sam into the cell. Yellowed sunlight cast an image of the small-barred window high on the flaking cell wall.

Miller dropped his feet slowly to the floor from the wood-slat bunk. It had taken two days before he could stand up straight. A doctor had examined him and given him pills but no water. He passed blood the first day. A bruised kidney didn't show so they put the bandage on the outside, a consideration of the benevolent People's Republic. His trial, however, had continued without him.

"It's over?"

Nung Sam nodded.

"You don't have to look so glum. They said guilty, right? You don't expect me to be surprised."

"Tomorrow will be the formal reading of conviction," Nung Sam said. "You will be brought to the court. You must show respect."

"For those kangaroos?" Miller winced when he tried to laugh. "So after conviction, what?"

"You will be returned to your cell, and there wait for sentencing."

"Which means nothing changes. I get the same treatment as a prisoner of war or a convicted war criminal. Was Smithwaithe there for the whole thing? The reporter for the London *Daily Worker*. Sat in the back. Short little bastard . . ."

"The British correspondent? Yes, he was there. He wrote notes . . . You will behave tomorrow?"

"We'll see, depends on what I have for breakfast."

"You must be serious, do not antagonize the court."

"How many times have you done this . . . whatever it is you do. You're certainly not a defense attorney. Did you tell them it was bullshit, that assassination stuff? I didn't murder anybody. I told you, the pilot ejected straight into my plane. It was an accident."

"An accident? How can you say accident when you were trying to kill him when he was in his plane?"

"My job was to shoot down MIGs. He was the enemy. He would have shot me if he had the chance, which he did. Hitting him was . . ." Miller remembered the collision, the canopy streaked with blood. He shook his head as if to wipe it away. "It was a freak. It just happened. I wasn't *trying* to hit him. Did you tell them that?"

"The military court is not required to hear from the accused."

"What?"

"Evidence was presented. Evidence that could not be refuted. I was not allowed to comment. You must not interrupt the court tomorrow. Do not tickle the dragon's tail."

"Don't *what?*"

"Use good judgment. 'Do not tickle the tail of the dragon for the other end has teeth.' Tomorrow you listen to the formal reading of the conviction. You may not comment."

"And let Smithwaithe tell everyone that Miller Kane just stood and took their lies? Not on your life."

Nung Sam sighed, he turned to the cell door. "I must go."

"Wait. What about sentencing? What's the penalty for . . . assassination? And the rest?"

"The military court decides sentencing at another time." Nung Sam knocked at the door for the warder. He glanced at Miller. "None of the Americans tried by the tribunal have been sentenced. I have heard that they will never be sentenced—at the request of our negotiators in Panmunjon. Until they are sentenced they fall under the category of military prisoners. They may still be released, or exchanged. Prisoners sentenced are turned over to the People's Ministry of Special Security. The People's Ministry carries out all sentencing immediately. I do not think you want that to happen. Prisoners sent to the People's Ministry are not seen again."

Miller frowned. "If no one's been sentenced, how do you know they aren't seen again?"

"I said the American prisoners have not been sentenced. Korean captives have been tried and sentenced."

"To what?"

"They were hanged."

A tiny bell started it off.

"The prisoner will stand."

The warder had come early in the morning with a change of clothes. Miller was to wear the green quilted prison suit instead of his khaki uniform. He'd resisted but the warder insisted, making the point with a pair of guards to help him if necessary.

He had been marched from his cell wearing ankle shackles. He didn't understand until he entered the assembly hall. The place was packed. Every bench space was taken. A dozen photographers crouched below the red banner at the tribunal's platform. A large red star five feet across hung by wires from the ceiling above the platform. As he was led in he searched the crowd for Smithwaithe but didn't find him. But he knew he was here, somewhere. Smithwaithe wouldn't have missed this.

"The prisoner will state his name."

"Matthew Miller Kane, First Lieutenant, United States Air Force. Service number four-two-two-four-two-five-one."

Several photographers snapped their cameras, momentarily blinding him with their flashbulbs.

"The prisoner, Lieutenant Matthew Miller Kane, has been tried by the People's Military Court," the chairman said. "The People's—"

"I want to say something."

The chairman glanced down at him. "The prisoner may not speak."

"The prisoner didn't even get to attend his own trial. I have a right to speak."

"Do not do this," Nung Sam said behind him.

"The prisoner will be silent."

"I won't. This trial is a joke, you don't have any authority to try me."

The chairman nodded and guards moved toward Miller. "The prisoner will be taken away if he interrupts again."

"A joke," Miller said defiantly. "This whole charade."

The guards thrust his arms high behind his back, lifting him to his toes. Miller gasped, pain bolted through his conflicting bones, sucking his breath away. The chairman studied Miller for several moments. Then he motioned to the guards. "Remove the prisoner."

They took him to a cell without a bunk. It was one of the cells on the outside wall of the prison, and it was cold. Miller remembered that it was November. It was November when his mother had come back from the snow hills twenty-three years ago.

He sat against the wall, pulling up his knees. Nung Sam would be pissed but that was too bad. Besides, Nung Sam was part of it. The war couldn't last much longer. He just had to wait it out . . .

Miller spent an hour figuring his back pay and what he'd do with it. Let's see, if he was released in six months he'd have accumulated nine thousand seven hundred dollars, assuming the hazardous duty supplement included his time as a prisoner of war. In eight months he'd have over eleven thousand dollars. He thought about Laura and the baby who, until now, he had not allowed into his thoughts. His son, or daughter, would be about two months old now. In their last letters Miller and Laura had worked through the alphabet to the J's, searching for a name. James or

Jennifer had been the last. James Kenneth Kane had a strong, masculine ring. He repeated it over in his mind—James Kenneth Kane—trying to put a tiny face to it, remembering pictures of himself as an infant. Miller gave it up when he realized his heritage . . . Kane children, it seemed, did not favor their fathers.

A warder came for him and with three guards led him to a small room with a wood floor and no windows. The room was warm. On hand were Nung Sam, and sitting in a chair against the wall, Desmond Smithwaithe.

"What's he doing here?"

Nung Sam said, "I am to read to you the verdict of the court."

"Fine, but throw this creep out."

"You have a filthy mouth, Kane," Smithwaithe said. "I am here as an observer . . . to record your reaction to your punishment."

"Punishment?" Miller turned to Nung Sam.

The Chinese answered by reading from the paper before him. "The prisoner, Matthew Miller Kane, has been found guilty of all charges as indicted by the People's Military Court." Nung Sam looked up for the first time. "Now I am to read to you the formal sentencing of the court."

"Sentencing? What are you talking about? You said Americans weren't sentenced."

"Surprise, old boy," Smithwaithe said. "You really are a bloody fool."

"The prisoner, Matthew Miller Kane, for aggression against the peace-keeping forces of the People's Republic: the sentence is five years' confinement as a reactionary criminal against the state. For wanton destruction of people's property the sentence is five years' confinement as a reactionary criminal against the state. For the deliberate assassination of a people's comrade the sentence is capital punishment, with twenty years' suspension of execution, confinement with forced labor. The prisoner, Matthew Miller Kane, will be released to the People's Ministry of Special Security for execution of sentence immediately." Nung Sam set the paper aside. He looked up at Miller without speaking.

"You have to be crazy," Miller said. "Capital punishment?"

"With twenty years' suspension of sentence."

"What the hell does that mean?"

"It means you will serve twenty years at hard labor to think about your crimes," Smithwaithe said. "Then you will be hanged." He stood up, tucking his notebook into his jacket pocket. "You will be forgotten, Matthew . . . Miller . . . Kane. Hanged and forgotten. Actually," Smithwaithe added, "I have forgotten you already."

Smithwaithe had moved close, tickling the dragon's tail. His lips were still pursed when Miller crunched his jaw, hit him just below the chin and slightly off center, sending him careening into the chair and toppling over it as his notebook skittered across the floor.

The guards were on Miller in a second, but Smithwaithe lay on the floor sputtering blood, kicking his stubby legs.

"Forget that," Miller said, and to Nung Sam: "I guess you'll just have to hang me twice."

◆ THIRTY-NINE

TSAO LAN TSE PRISON, CHINA

FOR A BRUTAL PLACE, the prison had a poetic name. Tsao Lan Tse meant Meadows of Green Dew, after a Buddhist monastery that had once stood on the same spot for centuries and in the mountains beyond the old imperial Winter Palace it commanded a view of a small valley. But then it was razed to erect this bloodspot. The prison was built of red bricks, many from the heaps left over from the monastery. A small, twisted road led to the place, although there were few visitors. Officially the prison was Detention Center Five of the Peking Bureau of Public Security. Actually it was run by the People's Ministry of Special Security to hold counter-revolutionaries and political prisoners. The guards were Sepos—security police. No one ever escaped from Green Dew Meadows, or tried. Remoteness, and the Sepos, who carried Russian Kalashnikov machine guns strapped over their shoulders, guaranteed that.

Miller arrived at Tsao Lan Tse in the back of an old Studebaker truck with two other prisoners, all chained together. After stripping in an unheated room he was issued his prison uniform, a gray cotton jersey and pants, quilted in Chinese fashion. The buttonless jersey hung to the middle of his thigh and came with a gray cotton belt, similar to a judo vest except it did not open. Prisoners did not wear underwear. He was also given a black quilted jacket with buttons to the neck, a canvas hat with ear flaps and canvas boots with rubber soles.

Everyone, Miller noted, wore the same outfits, only the colors were different. Sepos wore yellow-green; warders, blue.

Miller's cell was number eight in a line of sixteen. It was slightly larger than the cells he had known, about ten feet wide by ten deep. A metal bunk folded down from the brick wall, held by a chain at each end. High on the wall was a thick glass window fronted by wooden bars. Nothing else. Home, until death by hanging.

◆ FORTY

CHICAGO
October 1957

"MAKE A WISH, SWEETHEART, then blow out all the candles with one big puff."

Benjamin Miller Kane scowled at his mother with the short forbearance of a five-year-old. "Mom, I *know* . . ."

Laura waved the match dead after lighting the last candle. "Uncle Franklin bet a quarter that you couldn't get every one."

The boy looked across the table. "Did you, Uncle Franklin?"

"A quarter?" Franklin gave him a frown. He looked ridiculous in the party hat and colorful paper bib over his tuxedo. "No, of course not. I'm sure it was a dollar, one for each candle."

Laura had made the cake, a three-tiered affair with pink Mickey Mouse ears and a happy birthday smile in blue frosting. It had been her second effort. The first had been devoured with ice cream by sixteen kindergarten classmates earlier in the day.

Ben closed his eyes tight, wishing and inhaling all at once, puffing up his chest with exaggerated dramatics, then let loose with a whoosh, opening his eyes wide and extinguishing five tiny flames.

Abby led the applause.

The boy beamed with pride, looked at Franklin.

"All right, all right, boy, you'll get your fiver. I'm good for it. But let's have some cake. I'm dying for an ear . . . that big one on the right."

Afterward, in the living room, the women had coffee while Franklin nursed a Scotch without ice. Warmed by crackling flames from the fireplace, Ben lay asleep on the sofa, worn out by the day, one leg draped over a cushion. He clutched a Howdy Doody hand puppet under one arm.

"He wished for his father to come home," Laura said, staring into the fire. She held her coffee cup in front of her, elbows resting on the arms of the sofa chair. "He asked me today if it was all right to wish it for his birthday." Her cup rattled in the saucer. "I'm sorry . . . it's just that on Ben's birthday I remember the most." She set the coffee down. "They aren't doing anything, you know. The State Department . . . they've forgotten Miller."

"Not forgotten," Abby said. "Not with the pressure we keep putting on them. I'm sure they'd like to forget but we can't give up—"

"I'm not giving up, it's just the endless double talk . . . 'We're doing our best, Mrs. Kane.' 'We expect to hear something soon, Mrs. Kane.' 'We'll call you when we know something definite, Mrs. Kane.' Lord . . . five *years* of it."

"It's been five years for all of us," Franklin said, and downed the rest of his drink. "We *all* want Miller home."

"I know, I know . . . I'm sorry, Franklin, you've done as much as anyone."

"Yurey called during the party," Abby said. "To wish Ben a happy birthday. He also said he's working with another contact, in Hong Kong this time."

"Another Russian? The Chinese don't seem to be on the best of terms with them lately. I think it's a dead end, looking for help from the Russians," Laura said.

Abby shook her head. "No, a Chinese. Something to do with the trade ministry."

"Trade ministry?" Laura closed her eyes in deep frustration. "Miller's in a prison, for godsakes."

"Everything helps, Laura." Franklin turned in his chair. "Have you forgotten it was Yurey who found *which* prison Miller was in? He missed Frederich's wedding going to Prague for that information."

Laura nodded. "God . . ." She got up from her chair. "I'm not fit company tonight. I'm sorry." She walked to the sofa, leaned down to get her son.

"Let me." Franklin tried to push himself up from his seat. The Scotch made it difficult.

"I have him." Laura started for the stairs, Benjamin in her arms, then turned back. "I know I sounded selfish. I just . . . when I think of Miller and what it must be like I—" Benjamin stirred in her arms, pulling the puppet under his chin. He was awake for a moment, then asleep again. "We love you both, very much," Laura managed to say. "Without you, we'd . . ."

Abby watched her move up the stairs.

"She'll be okay," Franklin said, pouring himself another drink. "It's that time of year, she'll be okay."

"I hope so . . ." Abby looked at her brother. "Helen's dying."

Franklin's glass stopped short of his lips. "What?"

"Yurey hasn't told the boys yet. Alex is at Princeton, and Frederich is in Amsterdam on a buying trip. It's cancer."

"Oh, Jesus." Franklin set his drink down. "We'll send her to Mayo." He struggled to his feet. "I never trusted New York doctors—"

"She's already been."

"Is she in a hospital?"

"It isn't time for that yet. Anyway, she wants to spend as much time as she can with her grandson. Warren is still a child."

"How much time . . ."

"Yurey doesn't know. A few months, a year." She shook her head. "It takes its own time. I'm going to New York to be with her."

Franklin gave her a look. "With . . . Helen?"

"She *is* my friend, Franklin."

"Of course she is, but . . ." Franklin paced a moment, then returned to his Scotch. "Is that a good idea, Abby? I mean, you're not exactly a close relative. Yurey has the two boys to help him. *His* family. You're not part of that. Is this something for them to face with an outsider?"

"How can you say that? My God, Franklin, after everything Yurey has done for us. We wouldn't know anything about Miller if it weren't for him."

"Yurey's been looking for his son. What he's done he's done to help his son, not you or Laura. I'm not being cynical, Abby, you know that, but that's the truth. Besides, Laura needs you here. Laura and Benjamin, *they're* your family."

Abby looked away from him. "I've made reservations on a flight for the day after tomorrow. I'll explain to Laura. *She'll* understand."

"Yes, but will Helen?"

"Oh, for godsakes."

"Hey, this is Franklin you're talking to. You're still in love with the man, Abby. You can tell Laura whatever you want, but don't try to fool me—"

"I—"

"You've already made one mistake about Yurey. Don't make another. You're not going to New York to give Helen support. You're going for Yurey."

"You're drunk, Franklin. That . . . that stuff has pickled your senses—"

"Right. I'm a lush, and I talk too much, but alcohol hasn't made me blind. You don't have to admit it to me but you'd better know what you're doing. For Helen's sake, and your own."

Abby turned away, staring into the fire. "Oh, God." She buried her face in her hands.

Franklin knelt beside her, stroking her hair. "It's all right," he said. "It's all right." But he didn't know.

New York
April 1958

" 'Alexander Yurev Romanov, pictured at right at a grinding wheel, is the foremost diamond dealer in the United States.' " Helen glanced up from the page of the National Geographic magazine. "What on earth possessed you to wear *that* suit?"

Yurev leaned forward from his chair beside the hospital bed. "What's wrong with it?"

"It's brown. You look terrible in brown. Didn't I say to wear the gray?"

Yurev managed a smile. "But it's what all the best diamond dealers are wearing these days."

Helen stared at the photograph, shaking her head. "It makes you look like something from the Crimean War. And when was the last time you sat behind a grinder?"

"That was the photographer's idea," Yurev said. "I was supposed to pretend that I actually knew something about the subject. The article was about diamonds, after all."

"I see they didn't forget about your greatest feat." Helen ran her finger over the page until she found the paragraph. " 'Known in the trade as Alexander the Great for his innovative designs, Romanov once shattered the largest diamond ever brought to America."

"But they didn't even mention my greatest achievement."

Helen eyed him. "Which stone was that?"

Yurev took her hand in his. "It wasn't a stone. It was a flower."

Helen made a face, trying to hide a smile. "Oh, for God's sake, stop that. You look ridiculous."

"Shall I get my brown suit?" Yurev made a move as if to leave, but Helen's grip on his hand held him.

"Stay put, Mr. National Geographic Magazine. I have—ahh—" She winced, shutting her eyes, pressing her head into the pillow.

"Helen . . ." Yurev was on his feet.

"No, no . . . it's okay." She held his hand tight until the pain passed. "It's okay."

"Let me get—"

"No. It's all right, I promise. The pills just make me sleepy. Sit down."

"The pills are *for* the pain. I don't want—"

"Are you a doctor now, too?"

"Take the pills."

"Will you please sit? If it gets too much I'll let you know."

Yurev sat down. He held her slender fingers between his hands. "Another pain and I'm calling the nurse."

"All right, maybe just one pill."

He poured a glass of water from the pitcher on the nightstand, held it to her lips as she swallowed a bright green capsule. "Enough?"

A nod. "You're a terrific nanny."

He kissed her hand. "You've taken care of me for over twenty years."

"Twenty-four."

"Not a bum one in the lot."

"The worst were the best." Helen touched his hand. "Remember shoveling sand in the river? And the old sieve? Busted more than it worked." She stared at the ceiling as if seeing into the past. "You know, I loved Africa best. The savanna and the breeze at sunset. That great big golden moon rising out of the plain. It *was* lovely, wasn't it?"

"I'm sure it still is. We'll go back."

"We fired the house."

Yurev's throat burned. "We'll build another."

"Yes . . . Don't you think Warren would like it there—all that open country? You could show him the rhinos like you did with Frederich and Alex."

"He would. I'm sure he would."

"It was a lovely place, wasn't it, Yurey?"

Yurev caressed her arm. "Yes, the best."

After she was asleep Yurev called the nurse. He told her about the pain and the pill and got her promise to tell the doctor. Then he slid wearily into his heavy tweed overcoat and left the hospital. He walked seven blocks to his brownstone and made tea in an empty kitchen. It had been his ritual these last five weeks. Upstairs he undressed, brushed his teeth, busying his mind with the routine before sleep. Then he sat on the edge of the bed, surrounded by the silence of darkness, and let the tears come.

Helen died in May.

◆ FORTY-ONE

WORLD EVENTS DID NOT trouble the inmates at Tsao Lan Tse. News did not penetrate the walls of the prison, with one exception. Joseph Stalin's death during Miller's second year marked a period of collective mourning inside Meadows of Green Dew. The People's Ministry of Special Security decreed that every prisoner would give up a day's ration in the observance. The Great Leap Forward paused, as if to honor a chief benefactor before a great feast, and eleven prisoners died of starvation as thanks.

There was an exchange of news at Tsao Lan Tse, notwithstanding the rules for isolation and silent contemplation for righting self-wrongs. As a designated Severe Criminal of the State, Miller was placed in a detention cell segregated from the rest of the prison population. The unconfessed criminal was the leper of the colony, and Miller enjoyed all the privileges that went with it. He labored three years to learn the language of his wardens and another two to understand its inconsistencies. His news consisted of overheard exchanges between guards, mostly gossip or threats against the cook. Through the years his life became a well-ordered drill. Tuesdays were wash days. Fridays were for trimming fingernails and toenails. Every third Sunday he received a haircut. At Detention Center Five nothing was wasted. Nails and hair were collected once a month and sent to a glue factory.

Miller's measure of time—his measure of everything—became the Chinese way. He adopted the cyclic animal calendar. He had been captured in the Year of the Dragon. He was tried and sentenced to Tsao Lan

Tse in the Year of the Snake. With years of practice he had learned patience and precision. He woke up at the same time. He worked. He slept. In seven of the last ten years he had made one acquaintance. His Sepo guard, Howe, was a stout Chinese from Tangshan. They weren't friends, but in spite of the regulations against communicating they sometimes talked.

It was in the Year of the Hare, Miller's eleventh Chinese year in prison, that Howe marched Miller outside the prison compound. They stood in a driving rain as Howe explained what was expected of his prisoner. It was the east wall; the prison was falling apart.

"It won't work." Miller squinted up through rain at the gaping hole in the prison wall. He was standing in the soft earth below the wall, his sandals squashed deep in mud. It was the first time he had been allowed outside the prison. Considering what they wanted him to do he'd rather be back in his cell. At least it was dry there, and nothing threatened to fall on him.

He turned to Howe and in Chinese repeated, "It won't work."

Howe's expression was sympathetic but his instructions were clear. "You must labor with the others."

Miller wiped the rain from his face and stared up at the five-story scaffold. It was an enormous, cumbersome structure built of bamboo that stretched across the breach in the prison's outer wall like an unfortunate Tinker Toy experiment. A hundred men labored on the scaffold, relieved in shifts every second hour, to repair the rift.

Stepping out of his sandals, Miller started up the bamboo ladder. He was to be a cement hauler because of his size and strength, pulling buckets of mortar at the top of the scaffold from the mixers on the ground. The laborers, all prisoners, were supervised by Sepos. It was an exciting exercise in socialism at work, Miller's study officer had told him. It would be a great lesson in the Great Leap Forward. For Miller it was a lesson in futility but he kept it to himself. He climbed to his assigned place and hauled buckets, hoping the scaffold held until he could get off the goddamn thing.

The Meadows of Green Dew monastery had overlooked a large pond from its gently sloping hill, but as a result of the destruction of the monastery the construction of the larger prison involved appropriating some of the pond. A levy was built, tons of earth moved and the east wall and its buildings raised where, for centuries, water had been. But the depth and strength of the wall's foundation were miscalculated. The mistake went unnoticed or ignored for fifteen years in spite of cracks and water seepage inside the prison. It took a guard out for a stroll around the pond to remark on the swaybacked appearance of the wall before it was agreed that inch by inch the east wall was sinking.

Still, nothing was done except to fill the ever-widening cracks with mortar, which increased the weight and stress on an already overburdened bedplate. No prisoner dared question it. The sagging portion of the towering red brick wall became known as Buddha's Belly, an ironic twist considering the history of the place.

On a gray morning in April, after five days of steady rain, the belly of the Buddha erupted, spewing out like a ruptured hernia. Seventeen inmates in the east compound died, crushed to death by the collapsing walls of their cells. Miller did not hear of the disaster for three days, related through his study officer during their monthly session. Within a week the scaffolding had been erected, and repair work began. When Miller was called to duty, half the wall had been "mended" from the edge of the pond to the thirty-foot mark. "Be happy in your work and hasten your reformation" became the slogan of the day.

Miller's arms and legs ached in his happiness. He was on his third two-hour tour, raising buckets, dumping mortar into a trough for the brick workers, then lowering buckets. The rain had not let up, and his clothes had not dried since his last tour. He was at the forty-foot mark, barefoot on the latticed scaffold, when he felt the first tremor.

The bamboo poles sang with vibration beneath his feet. The mortar trough overturned, spilling the gritty cement over the heads of workers below. The next tremor sent Miller scrambling for support.

Earthquake. On the ground, men were running for cover, slipping in the mud. Miller hugged a bamboo pole fifty feet above the ground and watched the wall move away from him, then realized that the only thing shaking was the scaffold. A bamboo support snapped with a sharp report. Miller's pole shuddered once more. The whole structure began to creak and splinter, slipping further away from the wall until gravity reasserted itself, and the scaffold started its long, slow slide toward the pond.

Instinct told him to hold onto the bamboo pole, but as the acceleration of the fall increased, centrifugal force pushed him to the end of the wet pole as if it were greased. Twenty feet from the water Miller lost his grip and catapulted upside down into the air. He hit the water with his left shoulder. The impact hammered out what breath his lungs still held, and his world turned dark in the murky water.

He rose to the surface dazed and gasping for air, his arms treading water. For several seconds he could not see but he could hear. The water was alive with screams of agony as men splashed everywhere, panicked.

A drowning Chinese appeared, hands grasping for Miller's face. Miller paddled away, then without thinking circled behind the gasping head and grabbed a handful of black hair. Swimming with a scissor kick, he pulled the Chinese to the shallows of the pond, where other hands dragged the choking figure onto muddy ground. Miller went back again into the deep pond, and again, finding bodies, pulled them to shore. It was like hauling buckets. Up and down or out and in, it made no difference. It was his job. He didn't count the buckets or the bodies because it wasn't his job to count. He was only a cog in the wheel of the state.

Pain charged through him like an electric jolt as shock was finally overcome by realization. He was paddling in the shallows when two Sepos waded in and dragged him from the water. That was when he felt the pain in his shoulder, a pain like fire. Voices filled his tiny world, but he'd suddenly lost his comprehension of Chinese. He didn't remember the scaffold or the prison. He was just a man in the rain, staring blankly away as a rubber-soled sandal drifted past on the water.

Miller drifted too. He closed his eyes. The pain had not gone, had instead become a dull throbbing. Lying on his side, clutching his shoulder, his mind filled with images of the trail and the *door-chorten* on a mountaintop. He was slowly sliding into his dream, his escape from pain and monotony. In the Year of the Goat he'd perfected his fantasy escape from the realities of Detention Center Five. He knew the details of Abby's search for Shelkagari so well he had made the search his own in his dream. He'd made the trek up Kali Gandaki a thousand times. He'd found the necklace Yurev had buried at the *door-chorten,* and held it in his hands —pieces of Shelkagari. He'd done it alone, in his exercise against insanity, making his dream more real than the nightmare of existence.

Miller felt himself drifting and didn't resist. He welcomed the darkness like the smile of an old friend. Shelkagari waited.

◆ FORTY-TWO

MILLER WOKE UP IN a new place, a room with two full-sized windows and window shades. The walls were covered in a small-print wallpaper, and there were things in the room—a plain chest of drawers, a mirror, a lamp, a small ceiling fan, a chair. His biggest surprise was the bed. A *bed*. A mattress, not wooden slats. With sheets and a pillow. God, it had been—

"Comrade Kane?"

The stab of pain seemed to pin Miller to the bed when he tried to look behind him searching for the voice. His left arm was in a sling but the pain came from his collar.

A Chinese came into view, and immediately Miller was on guard. He was not anyone Miller recognized, and he wore a uniform different from the ones in the prison. It was brown, and all the buttons matched. It also was clean. Miller could even detect the smell of starch.

"I am Hsing," the man said in Chinese. He was carrying a folder, and as he pulled the chair closer Miller saw his own name written on the cover. "Do you mind if we speak Mandarin? I am not well spoken in English."

Miller nodded. He had not spoken English, except in his dreams, since he came to this place. Also, no one here had ever used Miller's given name. He was Prisoner of Isolation Cell Eight when he was anybody. As far as he knew he was the only Severe Criminal of the State in the southwest compound. Just him and his Sepo guard Howe.

"Are you feeling better? You broke your collarbone in the accident. I hope it is not too uncomfortable."

Miller quickly reviewed what he remembered of the aftermath of the

311

scaffold collapse. He'd probably broken the bone when he hit the water. He didn't know why he hadn't felt the pain earlier unless he was flying on pure adrenalin. "It's all right." He wanted to add that whatever had happened, it certainly couldn't be considered an accident. Reckless incompetence, no accident. He held back, though. For slandering the state the penalty was one week at half-rations.

"You've been unconscious or asleep for three days. A few times you were awake . . . I mean, you opened your eyes but I don't think you were actually conscious. Do you remember it?"

"No."

"Are you hungry? Thirsty?"

Miller was starving, but he shook his head. Hsing wanted something, and Miller was going to find out what before they took anything away from him. He'd played this game before.

"Nothing at all?"

"What do you want?"

"Just looking in on you."

Nobody ever—*ever*—just looked in on a prisoner in this place. Concern was not a hallmark of Tsao Lan Tse. Miller stared at him. "Why?"

"Why? Do you question me?"

That's better, Miller thought. Hsing was just breaking the ice. They should be getting down to business now, whatever it was.

"You are a reactionary, a dangerous person to the state," Hsing said. He was glancing through the pages in front of him.

Miller was a little disappointed. The file didn't look very thick . . . not much to show for ten years. Still, one didn't do a lot in Isolation Corridor.

"You have been uncooperative, hostile to your study officer. A rotten egg."

Miller couldn't help but smile. To be called *huai-tan*, rotten egg, was considered a severe insult in China. Before he'd learned Chinese he had called his first study officer a motherfucker, but the man didn't understand. He even thought Miller was praising his family. Until he got a new study officer Miller had delighted in referring to the fellow as Motherfucker Chen.

"What makes me curious," Hsing went on, "is your reactionary past. It does not seem consistent with your actions during the Incident of the East Wall."

Incident of the East Wall, was, obviously, the scaffold disaster. If you weren't alert, half of what these people said never made sense. Miller only nodded.

"You rescued nine who might have drowned in the water," Hsing said. "Do you remember?"

Might have? "I remember."

"Why did you do that? Why did you swim out to bring them to shore? You had a broken collarbone. It must have been painful. You had no obligation yet you risked yourself. Why?"

Hsing seemed genuinely interested in the answer. Too bad, Miller thought. It was a predictable reaction from someone with the People's Ministry of Special Security. Miller had always found it interesting that every government agency was the People's something, as if it meant they cared. It hadn't even occurred to Hsing to call them men, those Chinese in the pond. He'd just said nine, not nine lives. The Great Leap Forward might as well have been referring to fish.

"I just did it," Miller said.

"They were strangers to you. You could not possibly have known them."

"Look, I used to be a lifeguard, okay? Where I come from we don't let people drown if we can help it. It upsets the tourists, all that screaming and choking." Miller surprised himself. It was the most he'd said in years.

"You joke. I am being serious, and you joke."

"What do you want me to say? Tell me, and I'll say it." That was the way it worked in this prison if you wanted to eat or sleep.

"I want your own words," Hsing said. "You were thinking of reward?"

"Reward?"

"A consideration from the state. A favorable consideration of your case."

"Oh, sure. That was my first thought out there with a lung full of water and a busted shoulder. I just did it. Forget it, next time I'll know better."

The Chinese was quiet for some time, then said, "It was admirable, what you did. The People's Republic wishes to thank you. Four of those you saved were Sepos."

"Sepos?"

"Yes. You didn't know?"

Miller shook his head. "My mistake. Chinese all look alike." It was a lie but he was angry about the reward remark.

"Have you heard of Chairman Mao's special amnesty declaration?"

"Who would I hear it from?"

"Would it interest you to know of it?"

"Only if it applies to falsely accused American prisoners—"

Hsing closed the folder.

"All right, all *right.*" Miller raised his hand to keep the Chinese from leaving. "I'm interested."

"Wise of you. I am Hsing Kai-Hu, Second Administrative Assistant for the Standing Committee of the National People's Congress considering amnesty to convicted criminals under detention."

Miller said nothing.

"The amnesties apply to many categories, among them criminals condemned to capital punishment. They range from reduction of sentence to full pardon. Your case came to the attention of the Peking Bureau. It has been discussed at the highest levels in China. Because of the circumstances of your crime, your nationality, but also because of the letters. Letters to Chairman Mao, letters to the Central Committee, letters to members of the National People's Congress—in ten years dozens and dozens of letters." Hsing shook his head. "But words from outsiders cannot undo a crime."

Miller winced as he sat up from the pillow. "Letters from who?" It was forbidden for a Severe Criminal of the State to be told anything about the world outside his prison.

"I cannot say."

"My wife? State Department?"

Hsing twisted uneasily in his chair, avoiding Miller's stare. "Private parties." He opened the folder, busying himself searching for a page. "We will not speak further of letters. I was sent for another purpose."

Miller lay back on the pillow. Images of Laura flooded back to him. Laura at twenty-one, when he knew her.

"In view of your actions during the Incident of the East Wall," Hsing said, returning to control, "I was sent to look into your case." He patted Miller's file. "After reading this my mind was made up, but then . . . I decided that I should see you anyway." Hsing wrinkled his brow. "It is all very inconsistent. Why do you taunt your study officers with slanderous insults against the state but risk your own life to save others on the path of reformation?"

Miller had no good answer to that one.

"One mandatory condition exists for all remissions. The prisoner must truly have reformed himself from his evil past to a virtuous present. You do not seem to fit that condition. Also, the prisoner must write and sign a cognition."

Cognitions were just another way of admitting guilt by apologizing for having done wrong by the state. A good cognition, if written well and profusely, counted toward salvation. Several such cognitions boded well for leniency. Most prisoners, of course, were illiterate.

"I won't confess to anything."

Hsing blinked, confused for a moment. Laura was in Miller's head. When he spoke, the words were in English.

"I won't confess to a lie," Miller said, reverting to Chinese. "I was convicted by a court that had no authority to try me." It had been eight years since he had tried to convince anyone of *that*. He had quit because obviously nobody was listening.

"The state does not lie and cannot make a mistake."

Hsing was beginning to sound like a study officer.

"I'm not a war criminal and you know it. Shoot me or beat me or goddamn eat me but you'll never get me to sign a confession. Not after all this time . . ."

"I am not here to take your cognition," Hsing said.

"Then what?" Miller's shoulder began to throb. He wanted to go back to his cell. Isolation Corridor was home to him. This room, the stark cleanliness of it, was making him sick. "What the hell do you want from me? I'm sorry about the pond, I should have left them alone. I won't do it again. Just let me go back to my cell."

Hsing closed the file, said nothing.

"What are you going to do? What does it mean, this sudden interest from the Standing Committee of the National People's Congress? Where the hell do I fit into it?"

"Where, indeed." Hsing got to his feet, sliding the folder under his arm. "I think it makes you an embarrassment," he said quietly, mostly to himself.

And Miller finally understood. He was a Severe Criminal with compassion . . . an enemy of the people who apparently honored life more than the state. That was his real crime, and it made him more dangerous than a war criminal.

◆ FORTY-THREE

CHICAGO
July 1963

LAURA GRABBED THE PHONE on the first ring. It was Franklin, in San Francisco.

"Pack a bag," he said.

Laura's mouth was too dry to get a word out.

"Laura? Are you there?"

"Yes . . . is it real?"

"We're going to Hong Kong. Yurey just called. He'll be waiting for us. It's set."

"When?"

"Thursday."

"Oh, Jesus."

"Pack a bag. All of you. I've already booked you on the seven-twelve from O'Hare. Three seats on TWA. Salt Lake to Frisco. Flight number —are you writing this down?"

Laura scratched frantically through the drawer below the telephone for a pen, wrote the information across the face of a canceled check.

"Have you got it?"

"Yes."

"Where's Abby?"

"At the office."

"Tell her to get packed. One bag. We're not hanging around."

"God, Franklin, I can't believe it. It's really—"

"Sweetheart, cry later. Pack now. The connecting flight from Hawaii leaves in seventeen hours."

"I will. I will. Thank you, Franklin. God—" Laura heard the line go dead, then hung up herself. She closed her eyes, then remembered Abby. She was dialing when Benjamin opened the front door. He was in swimming trunks with a towel around his neck.

"Hi, Mom. Is it okay if"—he stopped short—"Mom?"

Laura hung up the phone. "Ben, go upstairs and get dressed. We're going on a trip."

"Are you crying, Mom?"

"I"—Laura felt her cheeks, wiped them with her fingertips. "It's all right. You and Grandma and I are going on a trip."

"Now?"

"Yes." She smiled. "We're going to Hong Kong with Uncle Franklin." The tears were back, she felt them warm against her cheeks, streaming down her face.

"We're going to get your father," she said.

◆ FORTY-FOUR

CHINA

MILLER WOKE IN DARKNESS.

He'd been to Kali Gandaki again, past the gorge to the hilltop of the *door-chorten*. Digging in the dry soil had finally given up the goat bag. The necklace was inside, like always. But his hand stung from the digging, stung enough to wake him from the dream.

He toweled off his shoulders and lay back on his bunk. He was nude, the summer heat too stifling at night to wear the cotton uniform. Besides, it gave his clothes a chance to dry. With one shower a week to wash himself and his prison clothes, the less time he spent dressed meant less soap used. Prisoners who conserved soap were awarded good conduct merits that could be redeemed for increased food rations in winter. Miller had been the champion soap saver for six years running.

"Light, Prisoner Eight."

Miller dropped his feet off the bunk, a hand up against the glare of light as Howe switched on the overhead bulb. It was the beginning of the morning routine—lights on, door open, latrine, back to cell, work party. But this morning the light was too early. It was too early by hours, Miller knew instinctively. His body clock was so attuned that he could remind Howe to wind his watch when he'd been late for Lights On.

The door swung open but instead of Howe, Hsing stood there, the Second Administrative Assistant to the People's Something. Miller squared his shoulders, repeating the drill but in a surprised voice: "Prisoner Eight."

Hsing's immediate reaction was to gasp. "Where are your clothes?" He turned his head, averted his eyes. The Chinese, Miller had learned, were great prudes.

"Dress yourself," Hsing ordered.

Miller pulled on his pants, reached for his shirt. "What is it?"

"You are not to speak unless spoken to," Hsing said as he stepped into the cell. "You are to"—his eyes widened with astonishment as he turned slowly, taking in the walls of Prisoner Eight's home.

Every inch of Miller's cell had been painted. Landscapes overlapped one another in montages of mountains and valleys, forests and glaciers, jungles and rocky crevices. Every scene had been colored and shaded to catch a particular light of day; some were bright, others subdued with shadows. There were villages of thatch-roofed houses, a variety of rope bridges, rivers, barren plains, and, overlooking it all, a range of peaks of near silver shaded with gray rising to the ceiling. The centerpiece drawing, the largest and most detailed, was on the north wall. It showed a structure in red, built of stone, sitting alone on a mountain. In the center of its base was a doorway but no door. In all the drawings, there was not a single human being.

Hsing turned, stunned by the impact.

"What is . . . this?"

Miller glanced over his shoulder at Kali Gandaki gorge. He looked at Hsing as if he were an intruder. "This is where I live."

Miller's mural had started on the first anniversary of his imprisonment in Tsao Lan Tse, a few months after he'd inherited his job as shit-drum cleaner from a released prisoner. It was the only work detail at the prison delegated to one inmate. Since it was forbidden that Severe Criminals of the State mix with other prisoners, Miller was the perfect candidate for the job. Also, as it was considered by the Chinese the most disgusting and demeaning work, Miller, the war criminal, was the only logical candidate.

As it turned out, Miller couldn't have been happier with his assignment. No one bothered him. Guards avoided him, and so he was less frequently subjected to their abuse. The job also gave him access to water and several varieties of disinfectants. The problem of lice, for example, which had plagued prisoners and guards alike, ended for Miller when he took the job. With so many chemicals he began experimenting with scents, developing one he dubbed "Toi-lot SuperChief," which disinfected but didn't make your eyes water. It was during this experimental period that he discovered he had the perfect ingredients for making dye. With the supplies at hand he could make any color, although blues and browns were trickiest.

Painting his cell came to him after one of his trips to Kali Gandaki. After two years in prison it wasn't enough to slip into a trance and fly away from his cell. Somehow the fantasy had to be made more real.

Smuggling dye past the guards was no major problem. Nobody searched too closely the shit-drum cleaner. The problem turned out to be the dye itself. It was too runny; the coarse, porous bricks of his cell absorbed the dye. No matter how many times he repainted a brick the problem persisted. The answer had to be a new surface; he had to cover the cell walls with an adhesive, like plaster, that would fill in the pores, dry and take his special paint.

Miller worked for months with mixtures of different proportions of dirt and clay. When it was mud it covered the bricks, but once the water evaporated it cracked and crumbled like a dry sand castle. Dirt was dirt, and nothing Miller tried could make it plaster. He had one more idea. The medium required a great amount of "Toi-lot SuperChief," but on his first attempt it worked perfectly. It bonded to the bricks like cement and dried without serious cracking, hard as a rock. And the beauty of it was that Miller had an inexhaustible supply, tons of the stuff. Turds.

Miller didn't know the scientific explanation, but for some reason prisoners on a diet of primarily rice and wo'tou—rough cornbread— produced excrement with the properties of glue and concrete. By adding his special disinfectant solution and beating the combination into a paste, Miller had invented a plaster that adhered but didn't offend.

Applying a bit at a time, Miller managed to plaster his entire cell in seven months. The stuff was marvelous to paint on and had an added benefit in that it discouraged insects, particularly centipedes. Flies, of course, were not put off by anything.

Miller's big worry had been that one day someone would enter his cell and find out his secret. But no one visited the shit-drum cleaner. The study officer, who was required to meet with prisoners once a month, made a habit of having Miller come to him. By this time, Howe was his Sepo guard, the only person actually to look inside the cell. Once Miller provided Howe with his formulated anti-lice disinfectant, his lips were sealed.

Year after year, Miller's mural grew until it filled the cell. He painted over scenes, adding bits and items as his trips took on more importance in his solitary existence. Fantasy became reality, and prison became the dream.

"Who has done this?" Hsing snapped.

"I have."

"You?" He looked at the *door-chorten*. "But . . . how?"

"Excrement," Miller said. "Turds," he said in English.

Hsing stared at him.

"A long time ago you people tried to make me crazy with a turd trick." Miller nodded at his work. "Well, these turds have kept me sane."

The Chinese shook his head, gestured to the door. "Out, out."

"What are you going to do?"

"You must go, now."

"Look . . ." Miller moistened his lips. "You don't have to tell anyone. It didn't cost the state a penny—"

"You must go, you are leaving."

"Leaving?"

"Yes," Hsing said quickly. "You are going today."

"Leaving Tsao Lan Tse Prison?" The thought struck terror in Miller. Hsing looked up into the American's face. "Leaving China."

Miller sat with Hsing in the rear of the dark sedan that in less than forty minutes arrived onto the tarmac of an airport where a large jet aircraft with markings Miller didn't recognize stood waiting, engines running. It was a passenger plane, the first commercial jet Miller had ever seen. All the seats were empty.

Once in the air, Hsing handed him a small suitcase. "You are to wear these clothes." He pointed to the lavatory. "Change in there."

"Where are we going?"

Miller remembered Major Ding threatening to turn him over to the Soviets. It had happened almost eleven years ago but the threat seemed real to him now. "You're not dumping me on the Russians?"

"No talking. Go change."

The suitcase contained clean underwear, socks, a white button shirt, gray trousers with an elastic waistband, black shoes and a light raincoat. No labels.

When they landed, another car waited on the runway. The sky was still dark, crowded with stars, but the eastern horizon was growing purple. A soldier with a machine gun strapped over his shoulder stood beside the car holding the door. A Chinese soldier. Miller climbed into the back with his suitcase. This time Hsing did not follow.

"The driver will take you to a place," he said, leaning down. "You are not to speak to the driver. When he stops you will be met by an officer of the army. Follow him and do exactly what he says. Do you understand?"

Miller stared up at him. "No. I don't understand any of this. Where am I?"

"Do you understand the instructions?"

"Yeah, sure, but—"

"Then goodbye, Mr. Kane." Hsing held out his hand.

Miller took it. He hadn't shaken hands with another person in so long that it seemed foreign.

"Good luck," Hsing said. He slammed the door and signaled to the driver.

Miller watched through the back window as Hsing climbed quickly up the ramp into the plane. Then the sedan turned a corner around an empty hangar, and the plane was gone from sight.

Miller didn't recognize the rank insignia, but the red stars on his lapels identified him as Chinese Army. The officer had been waiting, leaning against a gray brick building smoking a cigarette. It was the middle of a train freight yard. When the car stopped, the officer flicked his cigarette away and motioned to Miller.

"This way."

Miller followed, the empty suitcase in his right hand. There were signs everywhere, but although Miller had learned to speak the language he couldn't read it.

"Where are we?" He didn't expect an answer.

"Shumchun."

"Shumchun? Where is—"

"No talking."

For a man shorter than Miller, the officer walked very fast, until Miller realized that he was used to taking short steps, that years of pacing his cell had conditioned him to an abbreviated stride. They stepped over tracks and waited for a locomotive to pass, then finally found a gritty sidewalk that led between two buildings. Miller lengthened his stride. As he drew abreast of the Chinese, Miller saw the bridge.

"Bridge of Lo Wu," the officer said. He nodded beyond the river across the bridge, "Kwangtung."

Miller could see burning to the south the lights of the massive city where it lay crowded among the hills of the Kowloon mountain ridge. To come on the largest city in the world after spending a third of his life in a ten-foot-square cell was a shock to the system. Miller stopped, staring at the glow of the British crown colony on the South China Sea.

Hong Kong.

Dawn's light shone silver on the river as Miller walked past the last Communist Chinese checkpoint on the bridge. Below, ferries loaded with cargoes of boxcars and train engines chugged through the rising mist of morning.

Halfway across the bridge Miller saw the colonial policeman behind the red-and-white swing barrier that marked British territory. Standing toward the middle of the barrier were two figures, a man and a boy.

Miller quickened his pace. The useless suitcase was suddenly heavy in his hand. The barrier tilted up as he approached. He did not recognize either of the figures when he was close enough to see their faces.

"Miller Kane?"

The man spoke, not the policeman. And in English.

"Yes." Miller set down the suitcase. The sun was visible now, dancing on the glass of the guard-station windows.

The man took a deep breath. "I'd like you to meet your son, Benjamin Miller Kane."

The boy put out his hand, as rehearsed. "H-hello."

Miller took it. He could barely breathe. His throat burned.

"Would you like me to get Mom . . . and Grandma?"

Miller was still holding his hand. He could not speak.

"They're right over there in that little house." Ben withdrew his hand to point to the guard station. "Shall I?"

Miller nodded, watched the boy hurry past the barrier.

Miller turned to the man. He glanced at the ground. He suddenly didn't know what to do with his hands. "I'm sorry, sir, I don't think I know you . . ."

Yurev had to force himself to speak. He had debated with himself whether to tell Miller when he first met him, or wait, make it more gradual, at an easier, better time. But there had been too much waiting, and when was a better time? His son deserved to know what others already knew, and if it went badly for the father, what was that compared to what his son had endured?

"My name is Alexander Romanov," Yurev said. "I am your father."

◆ FORTY-FIVE

CHICAGO

THE WORLD HAD NOT changed for Miller, it had mutated.

The world players were all new to him. "Uncle Joe" Stalin was dead, and a warty little man named Khrushchev now headed the Soviet Union. The president of the United States was a young Roman Catholic Pulitzer Prize winner and son of a Massachusetts millionaire. In Cuba the bearded son of a farm laborer had liberated his island from one form of oppression to deliver it into another. It was high irony to Miller that he had traveled ten thousand miles supposedly to fight communism, only to return and find it established ninety miles from Key West. He had missed General Eisenhower's presidency as well as the addition of two states to the Union. People were talking about civil rights, school prayer and a rule called Miranda. Cars were supercharged, detergent was superclean, stores had super sales and a Super Power meant more than gasoline. Even cigarettes were "new and improved" with filtered tips in crushproof boxes.

Maestro Toscanini was dead and so were Sibelius and Prokofiev. Radio belonged to children, and the beat that pounded across the airwaves had the musical subtlety of a gang rape. Television was the most pervasive change from his former life. It had been transformed from a small round screen with an inferior picture to three times the size, plus living color. Jack Benny had made the transition from radio, Perry Mason from the printed page and The Untouchables, so far as Miller could see, from lower primates.

The Dodgers were no longer in Brooklyn, and Rocky Marciano, the "greatest heavyweight," had fought and retired during Miller's absence. Bogart and Cooper were dead, and Flynn and Gable and Mario Lanza too.

Miller's Sabrejet was a relic of history. Jet flight had become commonplace in a society that accepted underground silos of transcontinental missiles bearing hydrogen bombs. Submarines now ran on nuclear power, and war was as near as a button. Space was the new frontier, and astronauts were the new heroes. Sputnik represented ancient technology when Miller first heard of it. Men had looked into the heavens, circling the earth in their spacecraft, while he had cleaned shit cans in China.

This America was bigger and faster, louder and richer, than the one he had left. It had moved on while he had marked time. Everything had moved on. His homecoming was not what he'd expected because so much was different, so much he didn't recognize. Abby had called it a miracle that he'd finally come home. But Miller had not really come home—the home he knew was only a memory. He had simply, like Lazarus, come back.

"Miller?"

Laura's voice was a whisper in the darkness. Miller was aware of movement near him. Howe never entered the cell without first turning on the light. He was caught in the twilight between two worlds, unsure which was real. "I've nothing to say . . ."

"Miller? It's all right, darling. It's Laura." He felt her touch his bare knee with her fingertips. "There's a small lamp here, I'm going to turn it on."

Miller turned his head away as the light came on. He was sitting against the wall in the corner of the bedroom, naked, his knees drawn up in front of his nude body. He'd found himself like this dozens of times after waking up from a dream. In the seven weeks he had been back, his dreams were all of China, of his cell. He knew it was weird to think that he could miss such a place, but his cell was a familiar world where he had controlled everything. Being free was frightening—it was too real.

"Darling?" Laura moved in front of the lamp, shielding him. Her nightgown was transparent in the light that highlighted the tiny hairs on the edge of her skin. She kneeled down beside him, placing her hand on his knee. "Are you all right?"

Miller nodded. He'd been trained to respond to questions.

"You were speaking Chinese. Did you have a bad dream?" She tried to keep her voice calm.

"Not a bad dream," he said. Which was true. He'd just been sitting in the cell.

"You're perspiring, shall I get you a towel?"

"I'm okay."

"Won't you come back to bed? It's all right, I promise you it is." Her hand stroked his hair. He wasn't used to people touching him. "It's four-thirty in the morning, darling. Wouldn't you like to sleep?"

Miller's body clock was haywire. He still woke at exactly the same time every morning, before the sun. Six hours of sleep, that's what he was used to. He couldn't break the cycle.

He touched her arm. "I'm all right, Laura." He tried to smile.

Laura stood, held her hands out to him. "Come."

He followed her to the bed, lay on his back without covering himself. A light breeze from Lake Michigan disturbed the curtains at the window, cooling his chest. He felt cold.

"The doctors said I shouldn't pressure you with questions," Laura said. "They said when you're ready to talk you will." She lay on her side, not quite touching him, leaning on her elbow to see his face in the dim light. "But I want you to talk to me now, Miller. I need to know what you're thinking. I want to try to understand."

Up to now, that he was alive was all Laura needed to know. Which was fortunate. Miller still officially belonged to the Air Force. She had waited patiently while he stayed four weeks in Bethesda Naval Medical Center Hospital to be checked, interviewed and debriefed. His debriefers treated him as if he should have known some great Chinese secrets, when all he knew was how to survive. The doctors had found him to be reasonably healthy for a thirty-three-year-old male, considering where he'd been for the last eleven years. They found he had healed from two broken ribs, a broken collarbone and a ruptured eardrum. He had a small stomach ulcer, and one of his kidneys was permanently damaged. His eyesight was less than perfect, and a dentist had extracted six unhappy teeth. Otherwise, they told him, he was fine. He would never fly again as an Air Force pilot but he was fine. If anyone deserved to ask questions, it was Laura.

Miller looked at her now. "What do you want to know?"

"I want to know everything that you haven't told me yet. Did they try to brainwash you? I've heard stories about what they did to prisoners . . . did they hurt you?"

"I don't have scars that show," Miller said. "I wasn't brainwashed,

either, whatever that means. They treated me pretty bad at the beginning
—that was the North Koreans—but the Chinese treated me like a prisoner."

"They beat you, didn't they?"

"It was a long time ago, Laura. Some of that time I don't even remember."

"The papers said you refused to talk during your trial. Unbreakable
Kane, they called you."

Miller remembered the chairman of the tribunal and the guards. "I said
a few things, but nothing that did me any good. It wasn't really anything
to be proud of."

"Was it terrible, prison?" Laura made a face. "Oh, God, what a dumb
question. I'm sorry, darling, I—"

"Actually I was treated better at Tsao Lan Tse than anywhere else. I
can't recommend the food, but at least nobody beat on me."

"You were alone?" Laura touched him, absently caressing his chest
with her fingertips. "The whole time, alone in a cell?"

Miller's debriefers had been very curious about that too. No one ever
said it, but Miller had the impression that they didn't think a man could
stay sane after so long a time alone in solitary. Which was probably why
they didn't object when he asked to resign his commission. He couldn't
fly, so what was the point? Besides, what did the Air Force need with a
guy who'd never heard of an F-4 Phantom or Sidewinder missiles?

"I didn't have a cellmate," Miller said, "but I saw guards every day and
once a month I saw the study officer."

"Study officer?"

"A Chinese from the ministry. They came around to tell me how bad
I was for being an American and to explain the good life in the People's
Republic."

"What did you do when you were alone?"

Miller had not told the debriefers or the doctors about his Kali Gandaki
trips or about the mural in his cell. They would have thought him nuts.

"I slept mostly."

"Did you think of me?"

It was a logical question for a man's wife to ask. Miller told his first lie.
"Every day."

"How did you . . ." Laura searched for a way to ask. "I mean, did
you—"

"There weren't any women, and there weren't any men," Miller said.
The psychologists were especially interested in that too. No one ever asked

him about his job as shit-can cleaner. "Yes, I did for a while. Later, I didn't need it."

"Did you think of me when you did it? Oh God, another stupid question."

"I didn't think of anyone in particular. It was just a release."

"You didn't think about women at all?"

"From my trial in 1952 until you walked out of that guard house on the bridge, I never saw a woman. Not one. If you don't see a woman, even an ugly one, I guess your imagination fades. And your memory. I might have *tried* to think about being with you, but I didn't. I had to stay in control. Sexual fantasies only make you a little more crazy, and I couldn't let that happen."

Laura was quiet for several moments. Her fingers continued to caress his chest. "When you saw me on the bridge, was it a disappointment? I mean, after so long. Other POWs from Korea, after they were home, said their wives weren't as attractive as they remembered them. There were a lot of divorces. Was I different to you? The truth now, I want to know."

She was right, of course. But Miller had forgotten what she looked like altogether, attractiveness notwithstanding. Time had bleached her features until his memory of her was more a feeling than an image.

"You weren't a disappointment, Laura. I promise you that."

"I'm thirty-one years old. I was twenty when you left. I must have looked different to you."

"Not different, more mature. A little older, sure, but no crone. You're a beautiful woman, Laura."

"I wasn't fishing for that."

"It's true."

"Am I still desirable? Tell me the truth."

"What kind of a question is that?"

"We've made love three times since you've been back." She seemed embarrassed to admit it. "San Francisco, Maryland and here. I just wondered if . . . if you'd lost interest, like in prison."

Miller reached for her, but she pulled back.

"Something is the matter," Laura said. "I have a damn good body for a thirty-one-year-old woman, and I've been throwing it at you every chance I've had—without results. If you haven't lost interest, then what is it that keeps you so . . . distant?"

"I . . . ." He was at a loss.

"You're not in a Chinese prison anymore, Miller. You're home with your wife and son, only you don't seem to know it. Something is holding you away from us, and I won't let it destroy what we have. Whatever it is that drives you into the dark corner of our bedroom is going to stop. I'm here to share those burdens, to break them down, and that's what I intend to do. You're not the only one who knows how to masturbate, by the way. That's something else that's going to end. Your job is to start satisfying my needs and, believe me, it's been eleven dry years. But first you have to start leveling with me." Laura sat up on her knees. "Now would be a good time to begin." She gave him a look. "Just what the hell is your problem?"

Miller blinked. Nobody at Bethesda had tried this approach to rehabilitation. Laura had stripped away everything, down to the wound. He was stunned by her sudden aggressiveness. It left him nowhere to hide.

He stared at her for some time. "I'm glad you're not Chinese," he said. "Your subtle technique would revolutionize interrogations." He even smiled when he said it. He hadn't smiled, and meant it, in years. He felt as if a load had been lifted from him. She was right.

"I've lived inside myself for so long it's tough to realize I don't have to anymore." Miller looked up at her. "I'd forgotten where home was."

"Well, it isn't a cell. You'll never have that again. Not ever. Your home is in this house."

"No." Miller reached for her, and this time she didn't pull away. "Home is here." He raised the nightgown, pulling it over her head, letting it drop off the bed, and kissed her breast, and then the other. "And here." He put his arms around her, and she melted against him. "I love you, Laura Kane. I'm sorry . . ."

"Don't." She touched a finger to his lips. "Don't you dare apologize. Just tell me again."

Miller pressed her back onto the bed. "I love you, Laura Townes Kane." He kissed her, caressing the soft lines of her body with his calloused hands, then his mouth, his fingers gliding over her legs with gentle strokes. She parted her thighs to his touch, arching her back in need of him.

Her voice was husky when she spoke. "Yes . . . please . . ."

The times before, in San Francisco and after, had been mechanical release, obligatory, without passion. He had performed sex, not lovemaking, and felt no guilt in the emptiness afterward. This was different. Laura had melted the years that separated them, and her need became his. Her body was warm and soft and vulnerable, and he was her caretaker, a responsibility he had not wanted or felt up to before.

Laura panted with short breaths as Miller kissed her. She was so beautiful, her hair splayed out dark against the white sheets, her face flushed, a sheen of perspiration glowing in the light of the small lamp. They had even finished together, like an eruption, in the midst of a bed in shambles.

"Don't move," Laura said. "It's lovely to have you there."

Miller wiped a strand of hair back from her forehead. "We need to talk some more—"

"Oh, I don't know, this beats talk."

"I need to tell you what happened to me. You wanted to know. Now I think I'm ready."

"About China and prison?"

"I have to do something. I have to go somewhere. It's very important to me, and it's been on my mind for, . . . " he shrugged, "a long time."

"Go where? Not more debriefing, I hope."

"No." He rolled onto his side, disengaging from her.

"Oh, Miller—"

"Sorry, I want your full attention." He found an edge of rumpled bedsheet and pulled it up over her waist. She was too distracting. He propped himself on his elbow so he could look directly at her. "First I need to explain what kept me sane while I was in prison."

"Obviously it wasn't the constant thought of me." Laura took his free hand, interlacing their fingers, and kissed it. "But I forgive you."

"I went into the high hills," he said, ignoring her, "beyond the gorge of Kali Gandaki." The words came out more solemnly theatrical than he'd intended, but he wanted to break the afterspell of their lovemaking, if only this once. He had to make her understand what drove him to survive, what still drove him.

Laura wrinkled her nose. "Went to the high hills? You mean like Abby and Yurev?"

"Like Abby and my father," Miller corrected her. He had met his real father and his real son at a time when his senses had been dulled to what was true. Those things that had been sensible to him for eleven years were his own curious blends of truth and reality. But when he left China that world vanished. The difference had been so overwhelming that he had learned to accept anything if it were declared real and true, like a view of earth from space or a child he'd never known or a father he'd never met. It was accepting on blind faith, something the Chinese had tried to make him do and failed.

"I created a world of escape, and I lived in it for almost nine years," Miller told her.

"A dream, are you saying?"

"No, not a dream. More a trance, or an hallucination . . ." Miller remembered the vivid colors, the dank smell of jungle foliage, the little brown people with such trusting sad smiles—things and senses he had never really known but had manufactured in his mind.

"I'm not sure what to call it, except that it was an existence. It became something real to me. Like . . . going to a movie but being in it instead of just watching. It started as a way to fill the hours. The North Koreans kept me in a hole for almost three months. That was my first solitary confinement. It gets very boring, alone day after day. I tried things to pass the time, but I decided I needed some long-term goal. It just came to me one day—daydreaming this adventure that I'd heard about from my mother and been fascinated with since I was a kid—I'm talking about finding the lost stones of Alexander the Great."

As he talked Laura absently drew small circles with her fingers on the back of his hand. She looked up at him now. "Shelkagari? You told me a little about it once, and I asked Abby—"

"I decided to find it, at least look for it."

"In your head, you mean."

"It was *real* to me, Laura. That's what I'm trying to explain. Living in a cell became the bad dream, the nightmare. The snow hills were reality. I know it sounds crazy but you've got to understand—going on, staying alive, that's how it started. I went into the hills to keep from going nuts." He told her about the cell then, about the mural that gave shape and substance to the fantasy. He told her about traveling to the red monastery in the cliffs, Tramar-Dri, in the Valley of Weeping Winds; about the glacier and the gorge; about the monument on the hill; and about the goat bag and the pieces of Shelkagari inside it.

Laura was silent, her eyes staring at nothing. Her fingers ceased their movement while her mind tried to grasp Miller's notion of sanity.

"What you're saying . . . what you're saying is that you're still having those . . . illusions? You're still fantasizing about going there? Escaping there? That's where you are when you're sitting in the dark against the wall?"

"I'm not crazy, Laura. I've lived nine years with it."

"Miller—my fingers."

He glanced down where he held her hand in his. He was squeezing her fingers in his fist. He quickly released his grip, touching her hand to his face. "I'm sorry, Laura. I didn't realize—"

"I know. You feel you have to go there, don't you? To put your ghosts to rest. To satisfy this, this nightmare."

"It isn't a nightmare, Laura."

"It is for me." There were tears in her eyes. "Because you're going to do it alone. Isn't that what you mean?"

He didn't answer.

"You're going to leave, and I'm going to wait. *Again.*"

"I won't be long, I know exactly where I'm going. I've done it a thousand times—"

"I hate it, but if it will bring you back whole . . . tell me what you want me to do."

Miller put his arms around her, pulled her close to him. "There's nothing you have to do. I love you, Laura, I won't hurt you again. You and Benjamin are my life now. I know that. I won't hurt you ever again. . . ."

As he spoke Miller was already leaving her . . . he saw the high hills, majestic and powerful. He was going at last to face his fantasy in person. To end the dream. Which was to return, finally, to reality. In his mind he saw the *door-chorten,* standing alone on a hilltop, a faded red streak against a turbulent sky. Waiting for him.

It wasn't Shelkagari he was after. It was his sanity, his life.

◆ FORTY-SIX

NEW YORK
October

MILLER SAT OPPOSITE FREDERICH and Melissa Romanov at the dinner
table. Yurev was at the head of the table, patriarch for this evening,
flanked by his two oldest sons—Miller and Frederich—who were meeting
for the first time. Frederich was Miller's half-brother, oldest son of Yurev
and Helen Romanov, and both men had been awkward meeting each
other. Frederich had coincidentally just returned that morning from a
London buying trip, the same day Miller had arrived from Chicago to see
his new-found real father, Yurev. Frederich was three years younger than
Miller, with fine sandy hair and wearing steel-rimmed glasses. He didn't
talk much but that wasn't his fault. Melissa was the conversationalist in
that family and just now was pressing Miller about *how it was. . . .*

Melissa and Frederich—she called him Freddy—lived in Connecticut
but kept an apartment in the city on Fifty-seventh Street. The firm, now
Romanov, Inc., after the deaths of DeHaan and Spahr, also leased a flat
in London near Harrod's that was used by them on their buying trips to
DeBeers. Melissa was the fourth and youngest daughter of a well-known
Virginia horse-breeder who also owned a vineyard in southern Germany.
She was a perky brunette with facial makeup that would have flattered an
Egyptian pharaoh. Her son Warren was a gifted five-year-old who appar-
ently spent most of his time with his nanny, a woman named Brigette.
Melissa loved to travel, especially to Europe, particularly to Paris. Having
exhausted the subject of her own life Melissa had begun on Miller's.

"At least now it's all behind you," Frederich said while Melissa refilled her glass. Frederich complemented the union with Melissa. Quiet and studious and comfortable in the role of listener, he had little choice with his wife. He apparently had inherited Yurev's patience if not his drive. "What are your plans, now that you've retired from the Air Force?"

The president of the United States had asked him the same question. It was when Miller was at the Bethesda Naval Hospital, having lunch, sitting in bed in his pajamas with a tray across his lap, and in walked a man dressed in a dark pinstriped suit. At first Miller had taken him to be one of the never-ending visitors from the psychiatry staff. The president, it seemed, had been in for a routine checkup of his back. He welcomed Miller home, and they chatted for about ten minutes before a Secret Service agent appeared to take the president away. Laura had missed the whole event—she'd gone to the bathroom—but didn't really care. She had only one man on her mind.

"Resigned, not retired," Miller told Frederich. He hadn't corrected the president.

Frederich nodded. "Piloting still?"

"No." His glance touched Yurev. "I've sort of lost interest. Anyway, it's all changed since I flew Sabrejets. Everyone wants to be an astronaut these days."

"Don't you?"

"Not with my medical history."

"You shouldn't have to do anything," Melissa said, then added brightly, "Maybe you could teach Chinese. Papa Romanov says you learned Chinese in prison. How did you learn it? Did they give you lessons? It must have been impossible. I mean, all those erratic little marks. It would have driven me utterly insane."

"I learned Mandarin," Miller said. "There isn't any language called Chinese. It was the one thing I picked up in prison. To speak it, I mean. I never learned to read it."

"Oh, say something in Chinese." It was as if she'd been told he could play the piano.

"Huai-tan Tsao Lan Tse Huntung."

"My." She glanced at Frederich. "That sounds *exactly* like Chinese, doesn't it, Freddy? What does it mean?"

"Literally it means the Meadow of Green Dew belongs to rotten eggs."

"Oh. Well, inscrutably Chinese, I'm sure. Is it a saying, an epigraph, something like that?"

Miller looked at her and said in all seriousness, "Yes, exactly. Something like that."

* * *

After Frederich and Melissa had left, Yurev and Miller decided to go for a walk in the cool night air. They were almost the same height, and the measure of their strides was equal. Walking was one of the things Miller often did, for the exercise as well as the exhilaration of not having to turn ninety degrees every seven steps.

"I hope you weren't too bothered at dinner. Melissa can be like that when she finds someone who interests her."

"I never sat beside a queen of the Nile before."

Yurev laughed. "The look, yes. Strange, but apparently very fashionable. Inspired by a Mary Quant, British designer. Melissa entertains all sorts of avant-garde types in London."

"The British, leaders of fashion?" Miller shook his head. "Things have changed. Is your other son married?"

"Alex?" Yurev exhaled a long visible breath. "No. He's a lawyer in Philadelphia, corporate accounts. Since his mother died we haven't been close."

"I'm sorry."

"Nothing to be sorry about. Alex has his own life, and I don't interfere. He shares an apartment with an architect, and they come to the city from time to time for the shows. I was never much interested in Broadway, playacting. I guess I get enough of that in day-to-day life."

"You live alone?"

"I sleep alone," Yurev said as if the distinction were important. "The rest of the time I'm surrounded by people. Actually I prefer being alone. I read and walk in the evenings. It's nice to have some quiet at the end of a day. To think."

They turned at the corner of Fifth Avenue, heading toward the blaze of lights from Rockefeller Center. They walked silently in step until they reached St. Patrick's Cathedral.

"Did the Chinese tell you why you were leaving?" Yurev had stopped to button his jacket. "I'm sorry to ask after the grilling you've had tonight. But I just wondered."

"They just said come and not to ask any questions. I thought they were turning me over to the Russians. It was almost scarier than the trial, not knowing. I didn't realize what was happening until I got to the bridge. Who did you talk to?"

"Intermediaries. I never spoke to a representative of the People's Re-

public until the week before, and even that wasn't an official meeting."
The traffic light changed, and Yurev stepped off the curb.

On the other side of the street Miller said, "Who was it, did he give
you a name?"

"A Mr. Hsing. I don't know if that was his real name or not. He told
me that you were a lucky man, that your lucky charm finally worked—
made it possible for you to cheat the court. I wasn't sure what he was
talking about."

Miller touched his chest, felt the medallion beneath his tie. "You
should have been. It belonged to you once—the *dorje*. It was the one
thing they let me keep in prison. They thought it had religious significance."

"All that time?"

"I didn't always wear it. Most of the time it hung on the wall in my
cell. They're very superstitious. The warders thought if they took it away
they would have bad luck. In a way, I think they were almost afraid of
me. It turned out *I* was the inscrutable one."

They walked around the plaza, then started back up Fifth Avenue. The
slight breeze that had been at their backs was now in their faces. It was
colder, and Miller's nose began to run.

"I'm going after the diamonds," Miller said abruptly, wiping a handkerchief over his nose.

"What?"

"The necklace of Alexander, the Pearls of Light."

Yurev stopped. "You're going to Nepal?" Suddenly he looked pale.

"I came here to find out if you want to go with me. Abby said I should
ask you."

"*You're* going to the hills? But why?"

"It's a lot of explanation, but it comes down to something I have to
do—"

"Have to?" Yurev shook his head. "The necklace is better left where
it is, buried. It belongs in the hills. That's why I—"

"I'm going," Miller cut him off. "You can come with me or not. As
I said, I'm only here because Abby made me promise to ask you."

"Miller, you don't even know where it is, or what it's like in the hills.
You've never been there, you're not prepared for such a—"

"No. I've been there a thousand times. I grew up hearing that story.
And it kept me sane for eleven years, reliving it. I conditioned myself to
live in another world, in those hills. Prison was just a place where I ate
and slept. I know the Kali Gandaki gorge, I know the whaleback bridge,

I know the *door-chorten."* He looked at Yurev. "I know *all* of it. I've seen the trail, I've lived in those hills"—he tapped a finger to his head—"here."

"And the dream didn't stop when you left China." Yurev's voice was understanding, as if he knew.

"It's like an obsession, I admit," Miller said. "I'm afraid to sleep. It's driving a wedge between Laura and me. I can't explain it to her. She tries to understand but"—he shrugged. "I have to go, I have to get the necklace—make the dream *real.* If I don't I *will* go nuts."

A cab pulled up beside the curb and discharged a woman wearing a large hat who fumbled in her purse for the fare as she tried to keep her hat from blowing away, and Yurev was suddenly reminded of Abby on the humpback, grabbing for her *chuba* in the wind, then tumbling after it . . .

"I have my own obsession about the high hills," Yurev said after they'd walked a little further. "My own dream."

"Shelkagari." Miller nodded, wiped his nose again. "I know."

"Abby asked you to see me about this? Why?"

"You buried the necklace. I figure she thought that you should be there when it's recovered—"

"I don't *want* it recovered," Yurev said, his breath visible in the light of the street as he glanced at Miller. "That's why it's still in the hills. I could have gone back for it anytime in the last thirty years if I'd wanted it. The necklace isn't important. Shelkagari *is.* That's why—"

"It's important to *me."* Miller reached the corner. He turned to Yurev. "Well, do you want to come or not?"

"What about Shelkagari?"

"Shelkagari?" Miller made a face. "Goddammit, who's talking about Shelkagari? I'm only interested in the necklace. I told you why. It has nothing to do with your mythical stone."

"If you believe that you're a fool."

Miller's eyes turned dark. The leather of his new gloves creaked, stretching over the broad knuckles as his hands became fists.

"Shelkagari is not a myth," Yurev said. "We can find it, you and I. The secret to finding Shelkagari has been locked away for almost twenty years. In a few months I'll have it. We can—"

"Months?"

"Lou Hoover's papers will be released in February. It's there, Ayrub Ravi's manuscript."

"I don't care about Ayrub Ravi. I know about the carvings in the monastery floor, okay? And I don't care. That's your obsession, and Abby's. *Not* mine."

"Miller, I've waited twenty years for this. We can go together. In a few months—"

"I'm not waiting a few months, goddammit. That's what I've been doing in the goddamn shithole all this time, waiting. I'm not waiting anymore. In two weeks I'll be there."

"Two weeks?"

"I'm leaving San Francisco for Bangkok on the twenty-fifth. By the thirty-first I'll be in Kathmandu."

"No—"

"In a few months I'll be home with my wife and son, sleeping right through every night. I don't care about your fabulous Shelkagari stone. I just want peace. You told me that Alex has his own life and that you don't interfere. Do the same for me, okay? I'm sorry, but I can't wait, and I won't. If you come, it'll have to be on my terms."

"Miller . . ."

Are you coming or not?" Miller had stopped again, at the corner of Fifty-first and Fifth. Perspiration lined his forehead in spite of the cold.

Yurev avoided his son's eyes. "I can't, Miller. It would be for nothing."

"Fine. So it's settled?"

Yurev lied with a nod. The dream that had driven Miller was not Yurev's. Miller's obsession could end on a hill in a shallow hole beneath a *chorten*. Yurev's only began there. Nothing was settled, only postponed. . . .

◆ FORTY-SEVEN

JALJALA PASS
Kingdom of Nepal

HE HAD REACHED THE high hills. Lum was behind him, ahead was Dara Khola gorge. In less than an hour's walk he figured he would be at the rope bridge where Barbaree had left Abby and Yurev to die. This was the day he had waited eleven years for.

Jaljala Pass was a broad, open plateau bordered by fir and birch trees, the highest elevation so far on the trail, eleven thousand feet. From west to east was a panorama of towering peaks. Nearest were Putha Hiunchuli, Churen and Gurja, but in the misty distance were Dhaulagiri, Annapurna and Annapurna South, white brooding monsters crested silver in the morning light.

It had taken eight days to reach this spot from Kathmandu, the capital. He'd spent five days by airplane just to reach Nepal. The longest leg of the journey was the first, San Francisco to Honolulu; the shortest was a quick flight from the capital to Pokhara, little more than a scenic settlement with a runway.

Miller's trek began from Pokhara once he found a guide. He'd interviewed several prospects and settled on Jakot, a man who claimed to know the territory behind and below Dhaulagiri and one of the few who would go there so late in the season. Jakot spoke English and was familiar with the several hill dialects of the region. He was also the laziest human being Miller had ever met, a fact learned only after the first day on the trail. He was Buddhist, ethnically a Tamang, which usually meant a hard worker. But not Jakot. Jakot complained . . . about the weather and the trail, about his feet and the burden he carried on his back, about daylight and about the sun and at night about the lack of it. He even complained about the view. Nothing in Jakot's existence escaped his censure—except sleep. For sleep Jakot had no complaint, and he addressed it as often as possible.

"Jakot." Miller kicked the tent pole. "We're going." He returned to the fire and poured more tea. Miller's habit of early rising had confused the Nepalese from the first day. Jakot had never known a sahib to rise ahead of the sun. Another subject worthy of complaint.

A head poked out from the tent. "Ai, it is too cold, Miller sahib. We wait for the sun, I'm suggesting." He particularly didn't like climbing, a maddening attitude from a guide in the middle of the Himalayas.

Jakot joined Miller at the fire, squatting in the hill fashion, jabbering to himself about the cold. He had small ears and a thin neck and the darting eyes of a thief.

"How far to the bridge?" Miller said.

Jakot replied, chewing around the *tsampa*, "Not far." He pointed. "That way. Trail going up and down hills. Not far. Two kilometers by the wings of an eagle. Better walking when sun is higher, Miller sahib. Some resting after drinking tea, I'm suggesting."

"We'll go now," Miller said. "You strike the tent." He poured his tea into the fire. "I don't want to waste any more time."

Jakot sighed into his steaming cup of tea. "Ai, today I will die from walking."

The bridge spanned a narrow gap between granite cliffs, just as Abby had described it to him. Miller stood at the wooden anchor posts that held the rope suspension bridge, staring into the river below. Jack Barbaree had caught the goatskin bag from Yurev standing on this precise spot. He imagined Abby, his mother, stranded in the center of the bridge and Barbaree with his knife hacking at the rope fibers. He sensed what it must have been like, even the rain. Miller ran his hand over one of the anchor posts . . . the ropes would have been changed after all this time but not the posts.

"These posts." Miller slapped the solid wood with his palm. "Hundreds of years, they've been here. Wouldn't you think?"

Jakot shrugged. "Some long time, yes."

Miller opened his jackknife, choosing the smaller, sturdier blade. "We'll leave our mark," he said. "In a hundred years people will wonder who this MK was who came this way." He gouged the letters in the hard wood.

Jakot was on his feet. "Bad luck, cutting on wood."

"No, good luck," Miller said, "it's all good luck from now on." He looked across the gorge. "How long to the monument?"

"Maybe four hours, maybe not." Jakot shook his head, his attention still absorbed by the defiled post.

"By noon then?" Miller pointed to the sky. "When the sun is there?"

Jakot looked up. "Maybe yes. But tea first, then walking."

"I'm not thirsty." Miller started across the bridge, moving as if he'd done it all his life. He was only hours away from the prize that Yurev had left behind. "C'mon, Kancha. We're almost home."

The *door-chorten* appeared like a vision, a dark solitary silhouette against the white background of Dhaulagiri. Miller was a mile away, trudging over the top of a smaller hill when he saw it, its cone-shaped top rising from the uncluttered ridgeline like a cathedral steeple.

Miller climbed without taking his eyes off the shape, as if to look away would make it disappear. The *chorten* loomed larger as he approached, until he stood in its shadow, panting, staring up at the faded red monument, its edges eroded by time. And *this* was no vision. Miller dropped his pack. He removed his hat and touched one of the circular reliefs in the wall at the base of the monument, letting his finger roam across the gritty surface. He was here, not in a cell. This was no dream, no hallucination, there was nothing to imagine. He could touch it, feel it. This was reality, not paint on shit.

Miller retrieved the folding shovel from his pack, moving quickly into the sheltered passageway, past the charcoal remnants of a campfire. He attacked the ground, digging on his knees into the loose soil along the wall. It took only a few minutes to find the place. An edge of the manuscript, rolled like a newspaper, yielded to Miller's shovel. He tossed the shovel aside and carefully teased the bundle of Tavernier's pages out of the dirt, lifting it by the ends.

The necklace slid into his hand.

"God . . ." Miller almost dropped it. The chain was solid gold, connecting twelve sculpted lotus petals, also gold, each containing a stone the size of a walnut. Six of the stones were rubies. The other six, three on each side of the center drop, were black. Miller pulled himself up and carried the necklace into the light. With his knife he scratched the black beetlenut from one of the stones. Exposed directly to the sun, the diamond turned brilliant in his hand, spinning colors from its ancient facets that had not been touched by sunlight in two thousand years.

Miller just stared at the necklace, aware of its cold weight in his hands. A dream had brought him to this moment. He had done what he'd come to do. He'd found the necklace. The Pearls of Light were his. It was done. He'd survived.

On his knees now, he held the necklace in his fist, raised to the cloudless sky, and called out in Chinese, "I beat you rotten eggs . . ." Grief and misery, contained so long in those wasted, joyless years, rose inside him until he could not hold back. For the first time in more than eleven years, he wept, unable to control himself, his body shuddering with the anguish of release. His journey, at last, was over.

◆ FORTY-EIGHT

IT WAS DARK, THE *door-chorten* at the top of the ridge invisible in the night. The Nepalese, Jakot, had made camp below the hill where firewood was more accessible. He refused to use the monument for shelter since it was a Buddhist holy shrine.

"Tramar-Dri," Miller was saying. "I want to go there. You take me." The monastery had been on his mind since afternoon. His own nightmare was behind him now, but with that release, with the necklace and manuscript tucked away inside his pack, he felt a continuing surge of energy. There was, after all, Yurev's obsession—Shelkagari. He'd spent the evening reading Yurev's few notes about the mother stone of the Pearls of Light. If he could get to the monastery and record the text carved into the balcony floor, well, then he would have accomplished what even Yurev couldn't do, and in his present mood such an additional triumph very much appealed to him.

"Where is this place?" Jakot said.

"Tramar-Dri," Miller said. "The monastery. You have heard of it." It never occurred to him that a hill guide would not have known of the place; it had been there for a thousand years.

"Tramar-Dri *gumpa?*" Jakot shook his head.

"Jakot, how can you not have heard of Tramar-Dri?" Miller pointed into the night. "Beyond Dhaulagiri. The Valley of Sorrowful Winds. Above the Kali Gandaki gorge."

"Further than the great Dhaulagiri Himal? Miller sahib, you not truly wanting to see a *gumpa* in such a place, I'm suggesting. I know a holy *gumpa* at Bagshi on Dara Khola. A most beautifous *gumpa*—"

"I don't want to see another monastery, I want to see Tramar-Dri."

"But I do not know this place."

"What about a village named Benithog? Have you heard of *that?*"

Jakot's face brightened. "Oh, a very high village in the snow hills above Kali Gandaki. A place where a most enormous piece of rock has fallen itself across the gorge."

"Take me there."

"To Benithog?"

"You do know how to get there?"

"I have not visited there but I have heard of it . . . a village of great smallness, but there is no *gumpa* at Benithog. Also the coldness is most disagreeing. Peoples coming down from those hill places in these months, not going up."

Miller nodded. It was exactly as it had been for Abby and Yurev. "Yeah, I know. You just get me to the village. I'll lead *you* to the *gumpa.*"

"Miller sahib, there *is* a gumpa."

Miller stood at the edge of the cliff, the frigid wind in his face, staring across the colossal stone that made a bridge over the Kali Gandaki gorge. It had taken them three days to reach Benithog.

Miller turned as Jakot climbed through the rockpile of bolders that led up to the granite slab. Behind him a group of villagers followed at a respectable distance.

Jakot pointed into the saddleback of strewn rocks that led into the Valley of Weeping Winds. "That way, Miller sahib." He moved to the edge of the cliff and glanced down then retreated several paces to a sturdy rock to sit on. "But only emptiness is there."

"What?"

"All holy ones going away many long times ago. Gumpa filled with emptiness now."

"Abandoned?"

"Most positively, sahib."

Miller looked toward the valley. "Gone? How can they be gone?"

"The old one . . ." Jakot pointed to one of the elderly villagers, a toothless little man with white hair. "That one saying holy ones leaving gumpa, going into hills, making new gumpa. Some many years ago. Whole village having much sadness when holy ones going."

"How many years?"

Jakot shrugged. "Not counting very good, these peoples. Much great ignorance among hill peoples."

Miller crouched down beside his guide, nodding at the village leader. "Ask him . . . why did they leave?"

Other villagers entered the conversation with Jakot, shaking their heads and pointing fingers toward the valley.

"Benithog peoples saying Most Holy One dying most horridly many years ago. Falling off gumpa, squashing on rocks. New Most Holy One saying leave gumpa, going to other places. Old gumpa all empty. Bad lucks at old gumpa now."

"I don't believe in luck. Any kind of luck." Miller stood up. He stared into the saddleback, squinting against the wind. "We're going up."

"But sahib, Jakot is believing," the little Nepalese said. "Bad lucks for Miller sahib, going to—"

Miller cut him off with a look. "Get the packs."

Tramar-Dri was a ghost town. Thirty-four years of neglect had changed it dramatically from the palace that Miller had envisioned. The red-painted walls of the cliff monastery were faded and chipped. Sand and dirt, blown by dust devils from the valley over the intervening years, covered the once well-swept stairway in drifts. Spindly plants grew from cracks in the walls, and broken sticks and paper were all that remained of the prayer flags. The twin stupas that had once flanked the entry stairway to the monastery lay in heaps of rubble. And something had been carved on the wall beside the stairs.

"What does it say?"

"Mantra," Jakot said. "It saying, 'Hail the jewel of the lotus.' "

Miller climbed the stairways to the main level, scuffling through the buildup of dirt that covered the mezzanine's stone floor. Every room was empty. The patio where Yurev and Abby had first waited to speak to the *unze* was littered with animal dung; the beautiful blue-tiled fountain that Miller's mother had described was a pit of dried mud.

"Dogs, Miller sahib." Jakot stepped carefully over the droppings. "Wild dogs have been in this place."

Miller ignored him, moving into the passage that led to the private quarters of the high lama. He found what he expected had been the book room. It had been stripped bare; even the wall paintings were obliterated.

"They sat here," Miller said, standing in the center of the small chamber. "The altar was there. Yurev and Abby on pillows, here . . . Barbaree and Kancha, there . . ."

"Pillows?" Jakot glanced around the empty room.

"The balcony is through there." Miller lowered his head to get through the small door, and a low whistle of wind greeted him as he stepped onto the lama's balcony into warm sunlight. Like everywhere else in the vacant monastery, a layer of dust and wind-blown sand concealed the balcony's stone-block floor.

"This has to be cleaned off," Miller said, and removed his pack. "This whole floor . . . we have to clean it off."

Jakot was standing beside the low rampart, staring over the wall. His yellow face was pale. "Most Holy One . . . he was falling from here."

Miller moved to one of the corners, kneeling down to find the edges of the first block. "We'll draw every block square by square and number them by rows. We have to get them exactly right—"

"No, Miller sahib. We must leave this place. There is very much bad lucks here."

"Goddammit, Jakot, do what I tell you. We have to clean this floor. We're going to map it, copy every block onto paper. Hand me my pack."

"It is forbidden, Miller sahib." Jakot pointed.

Below, at the bottom of the wall, was a small *chorten* among the piles of rocks. It was, Miller realized, the spot where he'd been told the high lama had died.

"The Most Holy One," Jakot said. "We cannot stay here. This is a holy place." He moved back to the door.

"I'm not leaving," Miller said, and brushed his hand over the stone block. "Not until I have—"

"Please, sahib. Be coming away."

"We're not hurting anything, for chrissakes."

Jakot slipped through the door.

"Jakot? Come back here." Miller stood up. "Jakot? Jakot!"

Miller retrieved his pack, setting it beside the first block in the corner. "All right, I don't need your help, damn you." He unbuckled the straps and took out pad and pencil. He scraped the square block with the edge of his shovel, carefully loosening the caked dirt, then vigorously rubbed it with his hand until only one stone was visible.

"I can do this—"

The stone was clean, unmarked.

What the hell . . . ?

Miller moved to the next block, repeating the process. The stone was the same as the first, smooth. He moved to a block on the next row. Clean.

He shoved his pack to the center of the balcony, quickly brushing away the dirt and sand from another stone block, pouring water over it and wiping it dry with the sleeve of his shirt, and stared unbelieving at the smooth, flat surface. His throat was dry, his lips caked with dust. "You bastards . . ." A whisper against the drone of wind.

The balcony floor had been cleaned. A last housekeeping chore before abandoning the monastery. Every stone block had been methodically, efficiently erased. Hubris had its own reward.

Hail the jewel of the lotus.

◆ FORTY-NINE

O'HARE AIRORT, CHICAGO
November

"MILLER." LAURA THREW HER arms around him. "God, I missed you."
She hugged him, clinging tightly.

"I've missed you, too." He had to say it, but avoided kissing her. He
breathed deeply to clear a crushing headache while his eyes played tricks
in the bright sunlight. He thought he saw Howe, his Sepo guard, but it
was only a limousine driver in a short-brimmed cap.

"You're home, that's all that matters, finally home."

Miller had sent the telegram from Manila saying he would be delayed
for two days. He had spent the time at a Philippine university, having
Tavernier's manuscript translated from French. He had read and reread
every word of the twelve-page translation, and he kept coming back to the
same passage that was a warning delivered long before there were Caesars
in Rome. Tavernier had called it a "prayer of harm," and while he had
discounted it as hill superstition the verse had clearly frightened the
Frenchman. And now it frightened Miller too. Fact and fantasy had
merged for him in the high hills. Shelkagari was real, Miller believed that.
And the verse was a warning, a prophesy across time. And now Miller
believed that too. . . .

"Where's my father?" Miller squinted against the wind, across the sea
of faces. "He was supposed to be here."

"Tomorrow," Laura said. "A shipment of stones came in for sorting or
grading—whatever they come in for. He'll be here tomorrow. How are
you feeling? You look so tired."

Miller's head was worse. "I haven't slept since—how do we get out of here? I just want to get out."

"Oh, of course. This way, darling."

Miller saw his reflection in a glass door as they entered the terminal. His stubble of beard gave his wind-burned face a weathered look. A mountain rose behind him in the reflection, a huge mountain white and shimmering against the blue sky, and he spun around, but saw only the tail of an airplane . . .

Laura looked back too, following his gaze, her lips still parted with a smile. "Forget something?"

"No . . ." His tie was strangling him; the inside of his collar was wet and cold against his neck. He nodded toward the glass-enclosed terminal. "I need my bag."

They waited in line while luggage was unloaded from carts in the baggage area. Miller rubbed his temples, massaging the pain.

"Did anything happen while I was gone?"

"Happen?" Laura glanced up at him. "No, nothing." She took his arm, held it close to her. "The package came last week. I haven't opened it. I thought you'd want that honor." She smiled brightly at him, sensing something was wrong, not knowing what it was. . . .

Miller had mailed the necklace from Kathmandu by registered mail, the same way Yurev had received diamonds from London. It seemed an appropriate way to steal the most valuable necklace in the world. The stones had finally left the subcontinent in a cardboard box—after 2,300 years. They had his fingerprints on them . . .

"Miller, are you all right? Your face is white."

"I have to talk to Yurev, I have to—"

A short man wearing a croupier's green eye-shade pushed by him through the waiting passengers. For a moment Miller stared after him, bobbing his head to keep him in sight as the man weaved through the crowd and claimed a battered cornet case from the bin of luggage. When he came back to leave Miller saw his face.

"Jakot?" Miller straightened, blinking, his eyes on that face. "Jakot?" He let go of Laura's hand, pushing aside another traveler. "*Jakot!*"

"Miller?" Laura's voice rose with the last syllable.

Miller bumped through the throng of people, hearing only the throbbing inside his head, and reached the man as he stopped to light a cigarette.

Miller grabbed him by the shoulder, twisting him around. "What are you doing here?"

The half-lit cigarette dropped to the floor. The musician stared back at Miller. "Hey, man . . ."

"How did you get here?"

"T, W and A. What's your gig, man?" His eyes were blue, not brown.

"You're not Jakot." Miller was panting. His eyes stung with sweat.

"No, dad . . . ain't Jack, ain't Jill. Never heard of the cat, Jay Cot?" He studied Miller's face. "Man, you look sick, and that's no jive."

Laura arrived at Miller's side. "Miller? What's the matter?" She took his arm.

He only stared at her.

She looked at the musician. "Please, help me get my husband to a taxi, he's not feeling well."

"I look like a porter, lady?"

"Ten dollars," she said quickly.

He looked at Miller. "He *got* something?"

Laura produced a bill from her purse. "Here. Please."

The musician's little shoulders shrugged beneath his large coat. "Fred C. Dobbs never turned down a paying gig." He took Miller's other arm. "Watch out for burros, man."

"It was gone," Miller said, speaking to no one. He held Laura for support as they walked out of the terminal.

"It's all right, darling." She guided him toward the Yellow Cab where the musician held the door at the curb. "We'll be home soon—"

"They erased it . . . ground it down to nothing." Miller's face was beaded with sweat. "In Benithog . . . they knew. They knew someone was coming—"

"Miller, please, get in the cab."

"The dogs had been there, waiting for me. It was my turn."

"Miller, please—*get in the cab.*"

Laura slammed the door behind her, shoving herself across the rear seat beside him. When she gave the driver directions he didn't look back. His attention was consumed by the radio. Only then did she hear the announcement.

". . . motorcade in downtown Dallas. Repeating, the president has been shot. President John F. Kennedy has been shot. We don't have—give me that . . . The president has been taken to Parkland Memorial Hospital in Dallas, Texas. An unconfirmed report says that the president and Texas governor John Connally have been wounded by gunmen while in a motorcade in downtown Dallas. This station will update further reports as they come to us . . ."

"Oh, my God!" Laura turned to Miller, her mouth open, but he was staring outside, at the sky.

"For he will suffer the violence of the divine faces," Miller said. "He died for our sins . . . the punishment of kings."

"Jesus, Miller, what's—"

"The blue dogs couldn't guide me . . . the words were gone." When Miller looked back at Laura his eyes were filled with pain. In his fist he held the *chaka*, the devil dog medallion. "It was my turn to fail."

Laura couldn't speak. She just stared at the man beside her, caught in his nightmare.

"Hail the jewel of the lotus," Miller said softly. His eyes were closed now, shutting himself inside.

◆ FIFTY

"YOUR SON'S CASE, AS I mentioned, is classic POW trauma," the doctor said. "Schizotypal depression, noncommunicative, hallucination brought on by an inner conflict of encompassing guilt. Obviously it had been building up inside him for some time. News of the assassination was probably the final straw."

Dr. Stewart's office was a bleak room painted white. Double windows, straining sunlight through venetian blinds, admitted a view of Chicago's gritty winter. In the distance Yurev could see the city's skyline, a dark broken line against the overcast.

"How long will he go on like this?"

"Oh . . ." Dr. Stewart waved his hand in the air.

"Damn it, how *long?* Weeks, months, years—what?"

"I can't give you an answer to that, Mr. Romanov. We're playing by his rules. He's retreated to a safe place in his mind, and he'll stay there until *he* decides to leave."

Yurev stared at the distant skyline. In New York, Miller had been obsessed with finding the necklace. But he'd done that. It was supposed to put an end to his nightmares.

"What does President Kennedy's death have to do with Miller's problem? Miller was nowhere near Dallas."

"If we knew the answer to that, Mr. Romanov, we'd be much further along. He's withdrawn inside himself for protection, just as he must have done in his captivity. He does speak, as I told you, now and again, but it's an Asian dialect. Chinese, we expected, but it turns out not to be.

353

We're still working on that." The doctor opened a file folder. "There is this, however. Miller reads it constantly." He pushed the contents of the file across the desk. "We don't know what it means, or if it means anything."

Yurev glanced through the pages. He recognized it immediately as a translation of Tavernier's manuscript. The dog-eared pages contained scribbled pencil notes in the margins.

"There are passages underlined and highlighted," the doctor said. "But one in particular was heavily marked with brackets and notes. We have no idea what it means."

Yurev found the passage. He'd seen it before—thirty-four years ago.

> *Hear ye all, mighty potentates, covet not Shelkagari. For he who embraces the Mountain of Light, shall he inherit the Island of Jewels, yea also suffer the violence of the divine faces. Until heir of the third princely son loosen the hounds of azure, shall only the Divine One possess the Miraculous Gift.*

"Do you recognize it, Mr. Romanov?"

"Ushas' promise," Yurev muttered to himself.

"I'm sorry?"

"It's a sort of mantra." Yurev's mouth was suddenly dry.

"Mantra?"

"An ancient verse, a prayer . . . more or less." Yurev remembered sitting on the balcony with Abby at Tramar-Dri as if it were yesterday. His other life. "From the high hills—"

"Hindu?" The doctor looked puzzled.

"Tibetan, from Sanskrit," Yurev said, but his attention was on the pages. Miller had repeatedly written words in the margins and circled them, interconnected by looping arrows—"potentates" . . . "suffer violence" . . . "third son." The backs of the pages were filled with Miller's scribblings, most of them indecipherable. On one page the names Hoover and Kennedy were scribbled.

"Was Miller especially interested in Tibetan folklore?" Dr. Stewart had found a pipe. He spoke around the stem in his mouth as he tried to light it.

Yurev held the typescript open to the verse. "Miller reads this?"

"Oh, yes. Continuously. It's his primary diversion. He doesn't write anymore—writing instruments are not allowed to our patients—but he pours over that manuscript. He just sits, sometimes staring at a single page for hours. He also seems to find solace in that medallion he wears around his neck. Normally we don't—"

"You let him wear it?"

"Well, he can't hurt himself with it . . . Miller isn't at all self-abusive or violent. That's the normal profile of a case like this. I've written dozens of papers on classic cases like your son's. Former POWs don't want to fight anyone—quite the contrary, they want to be left alone. You might say Miller is hiding, waiting for some event to occur that will signal him to come out again."

"What event?"

"Well, that's why he's here, to find out. Or so we hope."

"He's an idiot. He doesn't know the first thing about Miller." Yurev was pacing before the fireplace in Abby's study.

"Yurev, please, sit down." Abby was seated on the couch with the translation of Tavernier's manuscript in her lap. Yurev had told her to read it, which she did. He said it was the key to Miller's illness, which she did not accept.

"The man actually believes Miller's condition is a direct result of his time in prison. POW trauma, he calls it." Yurev stopped to stare at Abby. "That's nonsense."

"Dr. Stewart is not an idiot, he's the preeminent psychiatrist in the field, and we're lucky to get him. He's made a career studying cases like Miller. Hundreds."

"Miller isn't someone's case. He's our son, and I'll be damned before I give him up to a man whose primary interest is writing profiles on classic mental patients. He's got it all backward, Abby. The cause and effect, it's upside down. It's Shelkagari, not his time as a prisoner of war, that's taken over Miller. When I tried to explain that—the verse, how it fits with Shelkagari—he just gave me an idiotic smile."

Abby glanced at the open manuscript. "What the hell did you expect? You want him—and me—to accept that Miller believes this, this legend? And that stuff about Hoover and Kennedy? Don't get sore, Yurey, but I don't buy it either. Ten years in a Chinese Communist prison, for godsakes. If that's not reason to go a little nuts then nothing is."

"And every minute he was there his mind was on Shelkagari, whether he admitted it to himself or not."

Abby threw up her hands. "Yurey, how can you—"

"The potentates," Yurev said, stabbing his finger at the manuscript. "The verse, it's a warning to kings and potentates—leave Shelkagari alone, or be punished—"

"Miller doesn't think he's a king. At least, not yet."

"Not Miller—*Hoover.*" Yurev's face was flushed. "You haven't been listening. Miller believes the verse was talking about Hoover . . . and Kennedy. They were both potentates in his eyes, presidents of the United States. Hoover's punishment was the Depression. Kennedy paid with his life—"

"Paid for what? It doesn't make sense. Hoover didn't have anything to do with Shelkagari. Kennedy—hell—I'm sure he never even heard of the goddamn thing. How could he have?"

"The necklace is a *part* of Shelkagari . . . the little sisters," Yurev said as if she should have remembered. "Hoover and Kennedy didn't have to know about it." He sank into the chair opposite Abby. "*We* took the necklace. You and I. Do you remember when we were there, at Tramar-Dri, the date? It was late October 1929."

"I was going to forget that, right?"

"Was it a coincidence that the stock market crashed at just that time? We took the necklace, we had it. Then for thirty years it lay buried in the mountains until Miller came along and dug it up. The day he came back Kennedy was assassinated. The potentates paid through their surrogates—you and me . . . and Miller."

"That's the craziest thing I've ever heard."

"I didn't say it was true. I said it's what Miller *believes.*" He motioned to the manuscript. "Look at his scribblings. It's all in there. Miller thinks he's failed because he didn't uncover the final clue to Shelkagari. He thinks that's what he was supposed to do, find a clue. All he did was recover the necklace."

"Failed?"

"Abby, I know what Miller is thinking. He's the third son *in* the verse. That's what he believes. And what he believes is what counts."

"You understand this?" She held up the manuscript to him. "You know what this means—hounds of azure and third princely sons?"

Yurev shook his head. "Not completely, no. It has to do with the *chhatra*—the medallion. It means something, I just don't know what yet. The answer is in Ayrub Ravi's script—"

"Which has been ground to dust—"

"If I can produce the script for Miller—"

"How—divine revelation? I don't give a damn about the legend or the necklace or that goddamn huge stone. All I care about is Miller—getting him well."

"So do I, Abby."

"Then get off this." She threw the manuscript to the floor. "Himalayan voodoo is not going to help my son. I trust him to Dr. Stewart, not the ravings of some eleventh-century monk."

Yurev picked up the manuscript, folded it and slid it into his jacket pocket. "I'm going to California in April, it's a trip I've been planning for twenty years. You're welcome to come if you like—"

"California? A vacation is not one of my high priorities just now."

"Not a vacation, Abby. I'm going to Palo Alto. Hoover made a tracing of that floor in 1901. He gave it to his wife as a gift. I think it still exists . . ."

"Oh, Jesus God . . ."

"The tracing of Ayrub Ravi's script is in storage there, where it's been since 1944. Lou Hoover's papers will finally be made available to the public in April. I'm going to find the script and bring it here." If Miller had only waited they could have shared the moment together.

"And prove what, for godsakes?"

"I don't know yet. An answer, I hope." He got up to leave. "Maybe an end to the suffering."

Abby's eyes were full of tears. "It's only a myth, Yurev. Just a myth." Her voice was low, choked with sadness. "You're a fool to think it's anything more."

Yurev bent down to her, wiping the tears away with his thumbs. He kissed her gently on the mouth. "Maybe," he said quietly. "Maybe."

◆ FIFTY-ONE

PALO ALTO, CALIFORNIA
April 1964

STANFORD UNIVERSITY, HOME TO the Hoover Institute, official repository for President Herbert Hoover's War Library, was an enormous compilation of documents relating to European governments during World War I and a collection of papers from his forty years in public service. Room 212-B, illogically located on the third floor of Hoover Tower, was reserved for miscellaneous filings. Known affectionately as the "garbage room," it contained anything that did not relate directly to the primary library or the Presidential Documents Section. It was also the designated repository of Lou Hoover's private collection of papers, correspondence and other assorted collectibles accumulated over forty-three years of marriage. Among them lay a secret smudged in charcoal on tissue-thin parchment.

Yurev stood patiently outside the door to Room 212-B. His guide, a young assistant curator named Carl, produced a large ring of assorted keys. Yurev was being allowed into this room but only with a staff member who would supervise his search.

"It's one of these," Carl said, searching through the keys. Yurev waited, staring at the perfect part in the young man's hair.

"I've never been in here myself," Carl said, "so I can't vouch for exactly what we'll find."

Yurev nodded because his throat was too dry to speak. His palms were moist, and he hid them locked together behind his back. He had taken half a lifetime to reach this threshold, and the anticipation was almost too much.

Carl continued to fumble through the keys. "You understand that Mrs. Hoover's collection was not recorded in any specific inventory, so it may be a job for us to locate anything in particular."

Yurev nodded again. "Yes." He wanted to rip the ring from Carl's hands and find the goddamn key himself.

"The collection is only of incidental interest to scholars, you see. Of course, there was the twenty-year nonaccess rule but—" Carl had finally discovered the brass key and held it up cheerfully for Yurev's inspection. He inserted the key, snapping the lock back, and opened the door, flipping on the light switch as he entered.

Banks of fluorescent lights flickered to life across a vast ceiling. The room was windowless and huge. Yurev stared into a sea of file cabinets and cardboard boxes, some reaching to the ceiling. Tables held piles of books and bulging file folders earmarked with green catalog streamers. Two narrow aisles disappeared into the stacks of documents. The air reeked of yellowed paper. Tons of it.

Carl turned to Yurev. "What are we looking for, again?"

"Drawings," Yurev said. "A Devanagari Sanskrit text in charcoal on tracing paper."

Carl swallowed. "You're sure you *want* to look for them . . . in this?"

Yurev stared across the room for several moments, then with a sigh took off his jacket. "Can we prop the door open? Circulate the air?"

"We can."

"How do we do this?" Yurev said. He began rolling up his sleeves. "You're the expert, Carl."

The graduate student shook his head. "A shovel wouldn't hurt." He glanced at Yurev. "You really, *really* want to find drawings on tracing paper?"

"Really."

Carl took a deep breath, letting it out in a low whistle. "Okay, Mr. Romanov. If they're here, we'll find them. I don't know when, but we'll find them. It'll be like searching for an anthill on a mountain, but I'm game if you are."

Yurev nodded. Another mountain.

No one had ever requested material from Mrs. Hoover's collection, and with the public ban on her papers there had been no reason for the expense of an itemized inventory. The catalogs of files that did exist were often incomplete or worse; labeled cabinets or boxes had been combined and refiled. Some had not been opened, and therefore not indexed, since the day they were stored. It took a week just to inventory the hundreds of cabinet indexes. Every box and cabinet had to be searched individually.

After two weeks Yurev had to return to New York to inspect a diamond shipment from DeBeers and was not back in Room 212-B until the middle of May. With Carl's academic schedule, Yurev had access to the collection for only a few hours a day, some days not at all. The intervening time he spent on the phone directing Frederich with business in New York, checking on Miller with Abby and Laura in Chicago and mapping out the next section of the collection to be attacked.

The inventory went incredibly slowly, approximately one file cabinet per day. Every cabinet was locked, and every day a new key had to be requested. The Institute would not budge from its policy . . . in all historical sections, particularly areas containing private family papers, only one cabinet could be opened at any one time in any given room.

By October Yurev had inspected ninety-six file cabinets and all the cardboard boxes. Only twelve had contained anything of Lou Hoover's. There were one hundred and thirteen cabinets left.

"I have a feeling, Mr. Romanov, that we're going to get lucky today." Carl greeted Yurev with a grin and his usual rejoinder. It was Tuesday evening, just after Carl's 9:00 P.M. class. After eight months they had become a familiar pair at the Institute—the old man and his scribe. Since the beginning, Yurev had paid Carl ten dollars for each session in the "sweat chamber," Carl's name for Room 212-B since the summer. By now Carl would have come whether he was paid or not. Yurev's dedication and perseverance were contagious. He was going to find that goddamn tracing if it took until Christmas.

"We've got number 17479 tonight," Carl said, reading the file cabinet identification from his key. "Nineteen twenty-four." He flashed his smile. "Was that a good year for you, Mr. Romanov?"

It was the year he had married Celeste, in his former life. He was fifty-six years old, but Celeste, for all time, could not age in his memory.

File cabinet number 17479 turned out to be a gem in the collection. Half of one drawer was filled with Girl Scout correspondences from the period Lou Hoover had headed that organization. One of the letters, misfiled, was a 1937 note from a San Francisco antique dealer who had written to bid on two pieces of Blue China in her K'ang-hsi Dynasty collection. A carbon copy of her response was attached to the note, thanking him for his interest but politely rejecting his offer. "My Asian collectibles," she replied, "the china, semiprecious stones and all the other knickknacks I've accumulated are more valuable to me than gold for the memories they possess. And I won't part with my memories."

"Carl, put that down." Yurev shoved the yellowed pages into his hands. "Read this."

Carl read. When he glanced up, he was beaming. "She didn't throw away anything!"

"At least not through 1937."

"That's great." Carl climbed to his feet. "I told you, didn't I? I told you we'd turn up something. Wait a minute. Let me go downstairs and make a copy. We want to keep this." He gave Yurev a thumbs-up sign.

The letter seemed to be a sign. After so many months of frustrated searching it was like an omen of hope. To Yurev it was proof that Lou Hoover had not discarded the tracings. They were here, somewhere. He was getting closer.

Yurev slid the Girl Scout correspondences back into the folder and made a quick note of its contents on the catalog ledger. The hours, the days, the months he'd spent here, ruining his back and his eyes, were beginning to pay off. He looked down the rows of cabinets still locked and untouched. In one of them, maybe the next one, he would find Ayrub Ravi's message—

"Mr. Romanov?"

Yurev turned back to see Carl standing beside the open door, the letter in his hand by his side. He'd lost his beaming grin.

"Carl, what's—"

"I just heard, Mr. Romanov." Carl's face was drained of color. "At the desk downstairs . . . they just got the news—"

"What news?"

"It's Mr. Hoover." Carl licked his lips. "He died tonight, in New York . . . an hour ago."

"Hoover died?"

"We have to leave, Mr. Romanov. The Institute is closing."

"Closing?" Yurev's mouth went dry. "For how long . . . did they say?"

"I don't know. A few days, I guess. I don't know."

"But . . ." Yurev nodded at the files behind him. "We're almost done. Can we come back tomorrow? It's right here, close. The drawings aren't twenty feet away from where I'm standing . . ."

Carl put the letter on top of the file cabinet. "Then a few days won't make any difference. If the drawings are here they aren't going any-where."

Yurev nodded. "You're right, I'm sorry, it'll be all right." He got his jacket. "It will be all right."

But it was not all right. Herbert Clark Hoover stipulated in his will the founding of a Hoover Presidential Library in West Branch, Ohio, his hometown. The Hoover Institute would remain at Stanford although all family papers would reside in perpetuity at the new West Branch site. As he was a public figure most of his life the former president granted scholars and students of government access to read and study his public and private papers. That freedom of access, however, did not extend to the private papers of his family. To avoid embarrassment to persons who might survive him, Hoover ordered that all private correspondence, and other communications of his wife, be closed to public scrutiny again, for a period of time commencing at his death. The period was to be twenty years—the files to be closed and sealed until 1984.

Yurev would never return to Room 212-B. He would never find Ayrub Ravi's text. It was not, his turn.

◆ FIFTY-TWO

CHICAGO
January, 1985

THE SILVER NOSE OF the 747 gleamed against the night as it slid into the pools of light beside the jet port. Laura, standing at the passenger lounge window, could see directly into the cockpit.

"Not reassuring, is it?" Franklin said, at her side. "Such a small brain for such a large beast."

Laura glanced at him. Slim was no longer a description that fit Franklin. Twenty years ago, when he was fifty, he looked forty. Now his classification was plain "old." They were all older now, not particularly wiser, just more practiced. Age had been much on Laura's mind these last several weeks. She was fifty-six, the "middle years," according to Franklin. But standing here, waiting for this plane, she felt strangely younger, as if the years had been turned back. Tonight, she felt, marked a new beginning. She had sensed Miller's anticipation even in his silence. Yurev was coming, this time to stay. She thought of Benjamin, wishing he could be here and knowing he wouldn't. For now, it was enough that Yurev was coming. Coming home.

"There he is," Franklin said, raising his hand.

Yurev was the last of the first-class passengers to deplane. Laura recognized his tall profile above the heads of the other passengers. Time had been kind to Yurev. His hair was silver gray and full, and his suit fit him without old-man sags. For a man a year older than the president of the United States, Yurev Romanov carried himself with a strength and dignity that denied his age.

"Yurev, over here."

He kissed Laura's cheek. "Hello, Laura, thanks for coming."

Franklin pumped his hand. "Well, you don't *look* like a man who just chucked it all. How does it feel to be among the ranks of the retired?"

"Frightening."

"You'll get over it. Couple games of shuffleboard under your belt, you'll be fine."

Laura took Yurev's arm. "Never mind him, it's wonderful to have you here at last . . . home." She started to say that she was sure Miller would be glad to see him, but it wasn't necessary. Yurev knew better than anyone what his son thought.

Yurev squeezed her hand. "Where's Abby?"

"What, you don't smell the aroma of musk in the air?" Franklin said.

"Franklin, you promised to behave yourself." Laura took Yurev's ticket folder, pointing toward the baggage area. "Here. Get the luggage. I want to talk to Yurev without waiting for a punchline." Her face softened. "Please, Franklin?"

"Righto." Franklin gave Yurev a wink. "Won't be a minute." He turned and lumbered off, corporate executive become baggage boy.

"He's awfully happy you're here," Laura said, watching after him. "Airports make him terribly nervous. It was all I could do to keep him out of the bar." She looked at Yurev. "We're none of us too fond of airplanes."

Yurev nodded.

"So . . ." Laura's face brightened. "It really is good to see you. Abby's been like a demon, making things ready. She very much wants you to feel at home."

"I didn't want her going to any trouble. It's not like I haven't been here before—"

"But you always left. Now you're staying."

"Where *is* Abby? I guess I thought she'd meet me."

Laura shrugged. "I have my instructions. We're to take you to the Hyatt. Your old suite."

"The Hyatt?" Yurev made a face. "What in the world—"

"Your *last* hotel stay in Chicago. It's to be a farewell celebration, Abby said."

"Nothing melodramatic about Abby, is there?"

Laura smiled. "I don't think it has anything to do with melodrama."

*   *   *

The Hyatt Regency, or the Mayfair, had been Yurev's residence for his visits over the twenty years he had been coming to Chicago. Abby had called him silly and stubborn not to stay at Abbaye Mansion, but Yurev had insisted otherwise. It was a strange set of principles, she had repeatedly told him, that he wouldn't marry her but that he would sleep with her, except never at the mansion. With retirement, Yurev had finally given in. He would not discuss marriage, and Abby had long since dropped the subject, but living with Abby, including her in his everyday life, had become his last obsession.

He sat now beside the phone in the living room, idly glancing through a magazine that he could not bring himself to concentrate on. In the lobby Laura had told him to change for dinner and wait for Abby's call, then she and Franklin had left, Franklin smiling like a loon.

"Mr. Romanov, I presume?"

Abby's voice startled him. She'd entered from the adjoining suite. The door was ajar, and he saw the glow of candlelight in the room behind her.

He got quickly to his feet. "Abby, what is all this—?"

"Welcome to Chicago," she said. *"Home* now."

She looked wonderful. She wore a crimson gown that nearly matched her hair. She was slim, as always, with a waist women her age only dreamed of. Yurev went to her, held her. "I don't know what you're up to, but I am not complaining."

"Not bad for a ditsy old broad, eh?" She took his hand. "Come, I want to talk before dinner."

Her suite was awash in candlelight. The drapes had been pulled, revealing a panorama of Chicago's wintry nightlights and a glistening sheen of moonbeam across the shorefront. They sat together on the large sofa.

"Is it all finished with Romanov Diamonds?" Abby's eyes were intent.

"Yes. Warren runs it now, it's all behind me."

"I think it's rotten, what Warren's done. Using the necklace that way—"

"Abby—"

"I'm just telling you what I think."

"I know what you think, and I appreciate it, but I'm not part of it anymore. Whatever is ahead for the business is Warren's responsibility. It's his ship now."

Abby stared at the nightscape. "God, what grandchildren we've sired."

"How *is* Benjamin?"

"I couldn't tell you. Franklin sees him, of course, but he doesn't call

Laura, that I know of. He just sits in Connecticut and architects." She glanced back at Yurev. "I could wring his damn neck."

"They aren't children anymore, Abby. We can't make them what we'd like."

"I know, I know . . ." She rubbed her hands together, changing moods. "Look, the hell with them. This is our night. I don't want you thinking about anyone but me."

Yurev nodded. "That won't be hard."

"We're staying in tonight. Dinner's being delivered. So it's just us."

"Good."

"I've ordered everything. I hope you're hungry."

"Very."

"And not too tired."

Yurev kissed her. "Not yet."

"I'm glad you're here, Yurev," Abby said, touching his face. "You're a stubborn old man, but I love you. I don't care how that sounds. I have no regrets."

"It sounds fine," Yurev said. He pulled her to him. "No regrets."

◆ FIFTY-THREE

LONDON
January 1985

"MR. ROMANOV, NICE TO see you, sir." Willem in a black suit and tie greeted Warren at the Charterhouse Street entrance.

Warren handed him his dripping umbrella. The sky had been gray all day, drizzling rain and sleet, but the downpour had only begun when Warren left the Dorchester. He'd stepped into a swirling puddle at the curb, soaking his right foot and pant leg as he entered the taxi. "Rain, rain . . . doesn't it ever just snow?" He slid out of his wet overcoat and wiped his forehead with a handkerchief. In a mirror he straightened his red tie. He was dry except for his shoes. "Look at that." Warren stamped his feet. "Ruined. Two hundred dollar Guccis . . . ruined."

"Sorry, sir," Willem said without looking sorrowful.

As many times as Warren had been here he'd never known Willem's last name, the official greeter to the DeBeers inner sanctum. He was a large black man with a pleasant face and enormous hands. He didn't carry a gun—this was England, after all—but whatever his special talent Willem was more than an ordinary doorman. His speech, crisp and cordial, was hard on the vowels in a way that made Warren figure him to be South African. He had the whitest teeth Warren had ever seen, on the infrequent occasions that he smiled.

Willem took Warren's coat. "If you'll wait a moment, sir, I'll announce your arrival."

Warren took a seat on a padded bench below a portrait of the Syndicate's founding chairman. Always before, he ate here, but an apologetic secretary had called this morning, rescheduling the "sight" for two o'clock. Until today the routine had been the same for ten years, since his first trip to London with Yurev. Walter Doyle, managing director of the London operation, would meet them at eleven sharp and escort them to the office of Sir Arthur Groote, a man Yurev had known for forty years. Groote had been with the Syndicate almost fifty years. Now he was chairman of the directors, the most powerful man in the DeBeers' multilayered hierarchy. After a sherry Groote would entertain them at lunch in the private dining room, whence they would proceed to the chairman's viewing room, where Yurev received his packet of diamonds. An audience with royalty couldn't have been more structured or mannered.

"I'm sorry, sir." Willem was back. "Mr. Doyle has been detained. I'm to deliver you upstairs."

Warren got to his feet, damp socks cold at the instep. "Detained? He's not out, is he?"

"I couldn't say, sir."

This was a first, Doyle not meeting him. This was a special day for Warren, an historic day, and already it was getting fouled up. Warren Romanov had arrived at Charterhouse Street not simply unaccompanied by his grandfather, but as president of Romanov, Inc., on the retirement of Yurev two months earlier. Doyle certainly knew about it, Warren thought. In anticipation, Walter or even Groote himself had probably planned some quiet celebration. Buoyed by the expectation Warren nodded, the trauma of London weather forgotten. "Lead on."

He followed the guard across the expansive reception hall to the elevator. He enjoyed the sound of his footsteps on the marble floor, it was the music of power echoing against the highly varnished paneled walls of the Syndicate's world headquarters. Everything was properly British here. The building, if not the people who worked in it, radiated a certain majestic elegance that begat a curious, almost comical, seriousness. At this rarefied level of business the British took on a solemn reverence for historic etiquette. Warren played the game because it was expected. Still, he rather liked the grand foolery—they treated him like royalty even if what he'd come to do was collect a box of stones. The difference was that, now, they were Warren's stones.

For forty years Yurev Romanov had been the guiding force behind Romanov, Inc. Now, with Warren at the helm, things would change. His grandfather had enjoyed an enviable reputation throughout the industry based on his innovative and simple jewelry designs. He was well respected for his fairness and integrity, affectionately known as Alexander the Great in the trade. Frederich, Warren's father, was neither brilliant nor innovative when it came to the business of diamonds. He had found contentment in Yurev's shadow.

But Warren was of a new generation. Competitive edge was a tenet of the new economics, and Warren had learned it well. What the diamond business was about was selling diamonds. He had studied the Syndicate's strategy in introducing the engagement ring to the world, and learned. The way to sell diamonds was by promotion, and Warren possessed a gift for masterminding promotional campaigns that made Romanov stones among the most visible diamonds in the world. But there was more to do.

Yurev had constructed a magnificent ship in Romanov, Inc. Warren's duty, as he interpreted it, was to streamline the vessel and make her attack. The Koh-i-noor campaign was his first victory. . . .

"Here, sir."

Willem escorted Warren into a second-floor viewing room. The office-sized room was appointed with Queen Anne furnishings and illuminated by a tall window in the northern wall. In the center of a desk covered with black velvet lay a plain white cardboard box—Romanov's packet of diamonds. A man who had been standing at the window turned as Warren entered.

"Ah, good afternoon, Mr. Romanov. Good to see you, sir." The man had the smile of a grocer, cheerful and empty. He was tall and thin—and decidedly not Walter Doyle.

"Who are you?"

"Northlake, sir. Bryan G."

"Where's Walter Doyle?"

"Occupied, I'm afraid." The smile reappeared. "It is indeed an honor to meet you, Mr. Romanov. Please . . ." He gestured toward the chair in front of the desk.

"Occupied?" Warren didn't move, stunned by the realization that Northlake was simply an employee and without a title. "What do you mean . . . Doyle's not coming?"

"*Mr.* Doyle, sir?" Northlake seemed amused by the notion. "Oh, no, sir. Not for a sight." He nodded at the cardboard box between them. "I believe it's all in order. A handsome collection, if you don't mind my saying. "Two million, one. Dollars, of course."

"*Two* million?" Warren shook his head. He understood now. Somebody had screwed up. This guy was waiting for somebody else. They'd probably gotten confused because Yurev was not here to represent the company. A two-million-dollar packet was too small. "Look, there's been a mistake. I'm Warren Romanov of Romanov, Inc., in New York."

Northlake looked suddenly pale. "Mistake?" He swallowed and, nervously trying to keep his composure, reached for the packet.

It wasn't Northlake's fault, Warren figured. Somebody else screwed up. He wondered where Doyle was. He'd never heard of anything like this happening before, and on *this* special day . . . Warren almost smiled. He'd caused DeBeers an embarrassment. Now *there* was a first.

"Romanov, Incorporated," came a weak voice. "New York City."

Warren glanced at Northlake as he read from the label on the box.

"Special code, seven seven aught five." Northlake blinked, staring up at Warren. "That *is* correct, isn't it, sir?"

Warren took the box. The name and identifying code were written in bold script along with the value of the packet. Something was very wrong here—the changed appointment, the canceled lunch, the reduced allotment. The Syndicate only took such action when a client violated a rule. It was a lesson—a warning—about power, and who had it. The Syndicate had the power. They never accused a client of anything. They were too polite for that. Romanov was being punished for a misdeed. Suddenly Warren knew what it was.

"The silly—"

"Sir?"

Eight hundred diamonds rattled inside the box as Warren tossed it to the table. He gave Northlake a studied look. "I want to see Groote. Now."

Northlake's eyes became round. "Sir Arthur?"

"Now," Warren said. "Tell him Warren Romanov got the message."

"I'm sorry, but that's quite impossible."

"It's possible," Warren said, containing his rage in a subdued voice. He had not seen this coming, and he should have. Groote, in his way, was making his point very clear. Warren glanced at Northlake. "He'll see me. He's waiting for me now."

The Syndicate was displeased, Warren realized, and Koh-i-noor was the reason.

It is a curious trick of nature that the only two crystalline forms of carbon should be so widely divergent in their distribution on the planet. One form is graphite, a plentiful resource. The other is diamond.

Until the late nineteenth century diamonds, as gems, were the rarest of stones, valuable for their scarcity and found only in India. That changed forever when diamonds were discovered in Brazil in 1730, and within eighty years, while India was still mining diamonds measured by the handful, Brazil was producing 300,000 carats every year—some 2,100 ounces. But Brazil was only the vanguard. In 1866 Erasmus Jacobs, a farmer's son, picked up a sparkling stone along a river bank. That fifteen year old's find began a stampede, creating the greatest concentration of commercial enterprises ever known—diamonds had been discovered in South Africa. Afterward they were mined in twenty countries, with South Africa, the Soviet Union and Zaire the largest producers.

Ninety percent of all diamonds mined were sold through the Syndicate, a monopoly undisturbed for eighty years presiding over fifteen tons of diamonds every year.

The oldest and most famous Indian stone was traced from ancient India and had been owned by kings and potentates—Koh-i-noor, the "Mountain of Light." And its fame derived from the folklore that every shah, king or raj who ever possessed the Koh-i-noor has come to an untimely end. Only a woman was spared retribution from whatever hex hung over the ancient stone. When it was presented as a gift to Queen Victoria she found its shape disappointing and had it recut—reduced from 186 carats to 108—to its eventual brilliant oval shape. A superstitious lady and aware of the Koh-i-noor's so-called curse, Victoria bequeathed the stone to Prince Albert's wife and since that time Koh-i-noor had not been worn or touched by a British king, coming to rest in the Tower of London along with the crown jewels, centerpiece in the Queen Mother's crown, safe and secure behind bulletproof glass.

Until Warren Romanov's campaign. His sudden preoccupation with the Koh-i-noor derived from an event as accidental as Erasmus Jacobs finding the first South African diamond. But Warren didn't find a rock, he saw a computer image made possible by microinterferometry—passing light through a diamond facet in order to illuminate its atomic surface and taking a color photo. Like snowflakes and fingerprints, no two diamonds, he knew, were alike. As a service to the British government the Syndicate offered to make photographs, each called a mini-burst, of the entire collection of the crown jewels. Selected mini-bursts in the collection were featured in dozens of publications. The National Geographic Society Magazine displayed a full-page reproduction of a view through the Koh-i-noor—right opposite a photo of Alexander Romanov.

By mere chance some thirty years later Warren Romanov sat in front of GemStone, his company's latest high-tech acquisition, a new state-of-the-art computer that held in memory an exact mapping of the particularly defined characteristics of 20,000 mini-bursts registered with the International Diamond Index. Placing a mini-burst photograph on Gem-Stone's copying glass, the computer could read the image, mapping details, and scan its inventory for an image match. If no match was found, the new image was given a registration number and added to memory. If a match was found GemStone displayed both images side by side on a screen for comparison, with data further identifying the matched stone. With this method diamond dealers could protect themselves against registering stolen or lost diamonds, and the client was provided with peace of mind.

On this night Warren had been mapping mini-bursts of clients' diamonds into GemStone. He had saved the six stones of the Pearls of Light for last because they belonged to the company. With the first stone from the necklace, the computer indicated a match. Warren thought he'd made a mistake, but the second stone found a match. And the third. All six found a match. The same match:

IDI REG NO: 0095832

DENSITY: 3.5243
REFRAC IDX: 2.416
TYPE: HEXOCTAHEDRON
MACLES: NONE
CHEM: N (.0000036%)
SPECTRA: 461 NANOMETERS

GemStone had one blind spot in identifying diamonds, and Warren had just found it. Stones with common parentage—split or cut from the same source—were a problem for the computer since the diamonds would exhibit exactly the same characteristics. What Warren had discovered, to his amazement, was a diamond that shared the same parentage as the Pearls of Light. The absolute proof glowed on the screen before him— six separate verifications. Warren's mouth was dry as he turned through the pages of the registration directory . . . the diamond listed as IDI number 0095832 was registered to the British government. It was Koh-i-noor.

Warren's campaign enjoyed great success, beginning with brochures rendering the mystical story of the Koh-i-noor diamond in words and pictures and the discovered connection with the Pearls of Light, the necklace wrought by Alexander the Great for his Persian queen Roxanne. To every place that sold Romanov diamonds went a Koh-i-noor display; replications of the majestic 100-carat diamond solitaire and the fabulous ancient necklace—"Together Again."

When the British Exchequer issued a statement in London that there was no conclusive evidence connecting the Koh-i-noor and the stones of the necklace, no one expected the storm of controversy it would arouse —or the sale of Romanov diamonds. While experts debated the issue of diamond parentage, diamond business soared.

The new company motto became "Diamonds Only A Woman Can Wear—by Romanov," in this fashion emphasizing the legend of the great stone. Romanov Diamonds introduced a new line of necklaces, based on the original, and rings and earrings called "Koh-i-noor Pearls," small diamonds set in gold. The Pearls of Light, billed as "The six little sisters to Koh-i-noor," toured twenty-seven American cities, ending as an invited special exhibition in the Metropolitan Museum. Warren became the center of media attention.

But there were critics, most vocal of whom was the British government, though through unofficial channels. A great and historical diamond of the crown jewels should not be subject to such debasement. Warren ignored the complaints except for one outburst in response to a British reporter who characterized Warren's campaign as vulgar and arrogant in the face of finer British sensibilities. Warren's reply was swift: "The Pearls are still magnificent stones. Koh-i-noor was magnificent, too, until you people hacked away forty percent of it."

Warren had long forgotten the incident by the time he arrived in London. Others had not forgotten. Sir Arthur Groote was one.

"Warren, my boy. How good to see you."

Walter Doyle was pouring tea from a cart when Warren entered the chairman's private club room.

The room smelled faintly of varnish and pipe smoke. Leather sofas and chairs were arranged around a large Persian rug. Within easy reach of any seat were antique tables where a guest might set his teacup. Oil paintings of African wildlife decorated teakwood walls, a reminder that the chairman of the Syndicate was, in his time, a hunter. Warren imagined the directors meeting here, under the subdued light of the crystal chandelier, deciding how best to teach a young American a lesson.

"Come, come," Doyle said, motioning with a lazy gesture as if summoning a bellboy. "We're just having tea. Join us." Walter Doyle looked robustly healthy for a man in his mid-seventies. He wore a dark suit with a powder-blue silk shirt and matching tie.

The thick Kirman rug swallowed the sound of Warren's footsteps as he walked across it. Arthur Groote sat puffing a pipe in one of the large overstuffed chairs. He seemed almost oblivious to Warren's presence, reading instead from a folder in his lap.

"There's been some kind of mixup about the packet," Warren said coolly, not sure which of the men he should address. He looked at Doyle because only Walter was looking at him.

"Is there?" Doyle's hairy eyebrows lifted. "Well, then, you'd best sit down and let's see what's to be done." He handed Warren a cup and nodded to the empty chair between himself and Groote.

"The allotment is short by a third," Warren began. "The market may be slow but it's not that slow."

"I should think we're in a better position to judge that, old boy," Doyle said with a fixed smile. "Margins are slimmer recently. We're making some adjustments. All of our subscribers saw a bit thinner packets this time."

"Thirty-three percent thinner?"

"Well . . ." Doyle fluttered his hand as if to indicate a wobbling economy. "The consensus of the board was that certain adjustments *were* in order."

"Adjustments?" Warren turned to Groote, the chairman, ignoring Doyle. "You're cutting back my supply, my company's lifeblood. I want to know why. I *demand* to know."

Sir Arthur Groote removed the pipe from his mouth, glanced up, his watery eyes measuring Warren. "Demand?"

"I want to hear you say it," Warren said. "It's the campaign, isn't it?"

"Actually," Sir Arthur said, "we're not enthusiastic about your promotional strategy, that's true. And you've heard our mild objection to it before, which you've ignored. It is an uncomfortable position for us, Warren. The Koh-i-noor is a national British treasure. We'd rather not see it the focus of an advertising campaign. We find the controversy . . . embarrassing."

"Embarrassing? But this has nothing to do with the Syndicate. The British government has blown this thing completely out—"

"As I recall," Sir Arthur said, "you discovered the match on the IDI machine quite accidentally."

"So?"

"The photographic images of the British Royal Crown Jewels provided to IDI were supplied by us. We underwrote the original photo session some years ago. So, you see, we are indirectly responsible for your matching the stones and, consequently, for your campaign." Sir Arthur exhaled a tired sigh. "At least that is the way certain parties in authority view the situation."

"That's absurd."

"Of course it is, Warren, but that's hardly the point."

"You're getting pressure from the government. I'm to be punished to get them off your backs."

"It is the business environment that concerns us most. We are a British company doing business in the heart of England. It is a small island. It makes for a very crowded community. When a minister gets a cold, people cough. As Walter mentioned, certain adjustments have been made."

"You and my grandfather have been friends for *forty* years. We have a contract—"

"That we do. Have you ever read the contract between Alexander Romanov and ourselves?" By which he meant the Syndicate, as if it was a living, breathing thing.

"Of course I've read it."

"Oh, excellent." Sir Arthur touched the folder in his lap. "I remember the day I sat across from Alexander on his veranda in Africa discussing this document. He knew exactly what I'd come to offer him." A gentle smile. "Your grandfather could be a cunning old dog. I'd misjudged him then. I'll try not to make the same mistake with you."

"You already have, sir. That contract grants us certain privileges," Warren said, trying to regain control of the conversation. "They are privileges, Sir Arthur, that the Syndicate is violating in reducing the size of our allotment. You can't do it—"

"Perhaps you haven't read it recently," Groote said. He handed the folder over to Warren. "The arrangement is changed. Our agreement was with your grandfather so long as the company remained under his control and management." Sir Arthur nodded at the folder. "I believe you'll find that on the first page."

Warren's empty stomach knotted.

"Our contract was with him personally—not Romanov, Incorporated. It's been a special association, dealing with your grandfather, but those days have come to a close. He has retired from the business. You represent the company now, Warren. And we have no special agreement with you."

"The Romanov company will continue to be one of our most valued clients," Doyle said, taking it up. "Only now, it will be on a more equal footing with our other clients."

"This is outrageous, you can't—" But Warren now realized that they could. They had.

Doyle avoided Warren's stare, looking instead behind him as someone entered the room. "We do understand your disappointment, Warren. Even so, we have every confidence that Romanov Diamonds will continue to prosper . . . with whatever promotional tactics you may undertake in the future."

A nervous Northlake appeared beside Doyle's chair and handed him the packet of diamonds. The managing director set the white cardboard box on the table before Warren. "Do please finish your tea before you leave, Warren." His smile was as polite as his words. "Young Northlake here will see you out."

Warren looked unhappily but no longer belligerently at the old man.

Sir Arthur Groote's lined face indicated nothing. His old eyes held Warren's for several moments. "Good luck."

◆ FIFTY-FOUR

CONNECTICUT

Spring

SUSAN CALLED.

Benjamin was at the creek below the house repairing the rock dam when he heard the phone. He ran up the slope to the wooden deck in his rubber boots.

"Hello, Benjamin Kane," he panted into the receiver.

"Hiya, big guy. Long time no see." The throaty, sensuous telephone voice was unmistakably Susan's. He was surprised to hear from her. It had been six months.

"Susan . . . hello."

"You sound out of breath. Am I interrupting something?"

Benjamin wiped his face on the shoulder of his sleeveless sweatshirt and saw his reflection in the sliding glass door. His hair was matted with sweat, his face dotted with mud splashed from the creekbed. "No, not interrupting. I've been down at the creek. The big oak came down last week, fell across the dam. A cutting service was here yesterday. I was just fixing—"

"The big oak? Not the one with our swing?"

"The same. It just fell in the storm last week. DOA." Benjamin found a towel on the bench beside the telephone and wiped at the mud splotches. It hadn't been *their* swing in two years. The separation had been her idea. Susan had not wanted a divorce. She couldn't afford it. Benjamin paid for her New York apartment, though he'd never seen it. He'd thought there was still a chance for them and he had clung to that hope, but time was his enemy. Since the separation he'd seen her four times. He heard she'd gone to Rio last January for the Mardi Gras. Susan loved crowds.

"I was just calling to see how you were, Benji."

"I'm fine." No one ever called him that except Susan.

"I'm surprised you're not slaving away in your den," she said, "design-ing the ultimate Piggly Wiggly." Nothing Susan said was ever intended to hurt, it just never occurred to her to think first. She was in show business.

"As a matter of fact, I just got confirmation on a project in Ohio. Half a million square feet . . . I sent a check last week, Susan. Didn't you get it?"

"Don't get horsey," she said sweetly. "Can't I call to see how you're doing? I do miss you from time to time. We aren't enemies, you know."

True. It had been an amiable parting as separations went. Susan wasn't adulterous, and Benjamin didn't beat her. They never fought, which was identified as the real source of their troubles by their married friends. They'd been married eight years, and eight years had simply been enough for her. Susan had been a dancer when they met, a chorus girl in an off-Broadway musical. She had done some television, fill-ins on soaps, and commercials. Lately she was hosting an early morning aerobics class for a cable network—thirty minutes of stretch-and-pull before the business news. It paid almost nothing, but the exposure was good. Besides, Susan had magnificent legs.

"Yes, I miss you, too," Benjamin said, "from time to time."

"I even miss the old homestead sometimes, you know, listening to the grass grow . . . did you ever fix the radiator in the bedroom? That clinking noise?"

"Last winter."

"Well . . . that's good."

They had picked out the house five years ago. It was a perfect architect's residence, she had said at the time—Frank Lloyd Wright without the cantilevers. On two acres that saddled a small wooded ridge, the house was isolated in the middle of a Connecticut farming community by trees and a winding drive. The city, meaning New York, was only thirty miles away. Susan's love affair with the house lasted six months, long enough to realize that thirty miles might as well have been three thousand to her friends without cars. The Connecticut house became her gulag.

"Ben, the reason I called, I . . . I wanted to see how you were doing."

"We did that already, Susan. I'm fine."

"I don't mean that. You know I don't. I was just wondering if, you know . . . are you seeing anyone?"

"No."

"No one? Really?"

"Really."

"Would you like to?"

"Is that an offer?"

Susan laughed, and Benjamin closed his eyes at the sound, imagining her smile. "I could come up there," she said. "If it's all right."

He started to ask where her Rio companion was but decided against it. He wanted to see her. "Why don't I come to the city. My Uncle Franklin is in town. I'm supposed to see him tomorrow for lunch. I could stay in the city tonight . . . we could have dinner. That place on—"

"No, no. I'd rather drive up there. I'd like to see the old place. Do you mind?"

"No. Here would be fine. We could have dinner at Gino's in Ridgefield. I'll call and—"

"Ben, I'm not negotiating for a date, and I'm not hungry. I just want to see you. Be with you for a while. Tonight. If that's acceptable, all you have to do is say come. If not, just—"

"Come."

"I'm being selfish, Ben. I know that."

"You're right. Come anyway."

"Really? I'll leave tomorrow. You know I will."

"Yes, I know." He looked at his watch. "It's four-thirty. If you hurry, you'll miss the traffic."

"Okay. I'm leaving, ten minutes. Give me an hour and a half. A little after six. Okay?"

"You remember how to get here?"

"Vaguely." She laughed again, and Benjamin felt weak.

Benjamin walked to the railing and for several minutes stared at the glitter of sun in the rippling water of the creek. The last time he saw her she had just returned from California. They had met for lunch at the restaurant in Rockefeller Center. She was tan and beautiful against the background of swirling ice skaters. And brokenhearted. The audition for a part in a miniseries was a bust. She had called Benjamin because she needed consoling. If he did anything well, it was listen. He was Benjamin the priest, devoted listener. When it was over, Susan left, her old self again. He always paid the check and always drove home alone.

Benjamin straightened up from the railing, stretching the kinks in his spine. To his reflection in the glass door he said, "What an idiot."

Benjamin heard the Volvo crunch down the drive and went to the front door, unsure whether to wait or go to her. He decided to go when she turned sideways in the seat, sliding her legs out of the car.

"Well, here I am."

She wore a light yellow summer dress that seemed touched by gold in the late afternoon sun. Her hair was longer, full of curls, and fell in folds around her shoulders. Benjamin's mouth was dry.

"Yes, here you are." He stood on the walk, two feet away, with absolutely no plan.

"I am completely without scruples, coming here like this. I thought a dozen times to turn around and go back. It's terribly unfair. I'm ashamed and embarrassed. But . . . I came anyway. I—are you going to stand there and let me go on making a fool of myself?"

He reached for her hand. Her fragrance rode a tiny breeze that electrified his senses.

"It's all right to kiss me, Ben. I've had all my shots."

She fit against him perfectly, soft and pliable. He tasted her lips, received her tongue.

She pulled away, looked up at him. "Well . . ." She moistened her lips, took a breath. "Well."

Benjamin's arm hung down around her waist. "I made dinner. Chinese vegetables." He shrugged off her look. "I had to do something until you got here. Lie and tell me you're hungry."

"Okay, I'm starved."

For a moment he just stared at her. "You look great, Susan. You really do."

She touched his face. "You're very sweet," She smoothed her dress, gliding her hands down her hips. "Are you sure you haven't been seeing *anybody?*"

"Does it show?"

Her answer was a smile.

They ate by candlelight and talked about nothing—the weather, Susan's new job, Benjamin's new project.

"You want some coffee?"

"Coffee? Before dessert?"

The deck lights had come on automatically with the darkness. The living room was unlit except for the glow from outside through the sliding glass doors. Susan was standing in silhouette against the light, her face in shadow. She'd kicked off her shoes. Now she turned toward him, her figure beneath the dress dark against the outside illumination. She put her hands on her hips and widened her stance. The lower buttons of her dress were unfastened. "What do you think?"

"I thought you wanted to talk."

"Come here, Ben."

He moved to her, closing his arms around her waist. He kissed her neck, undoing the remaining buttons. When the light summer dress fell open, he slid his hand up to cup her breast. "I guess this takes us beyond the chitchat threshold." He kissed her neck again, pressing her body against the glass with his own.

Susan sighed, closing her eyes. "Thank God . . ."

Susan leaned on her elbow and looked into Benjamin's face. The bed was a tangle of sheets. They'd left their clothes downstairs, where they'd fallen. She snuggled against his chest. "This is nice, isn't it?"

"We could do it on a more permanent basis if—"

She stiffened in his arms. "Ben."

"All right, all right." He ran his fingers down her back. "If it's just sex you're interested in, Susan, you don't *have* to drive into the wilds of Connecticut for service."

"No, but I'm thirty-two, an awkward age, attractive to the opposite ends of the libido range—boys who think they're endowed with the Washington Monument, and the tinged-with-gray set who aren't sure anymore but want to be. I already know your potential, big guy."

"Thanks."

"I *told* you my motives were selfish. You could have told me not to come."

"I happen to love you. What am I going to do, say no?"

The answer was obvious, and she was damn glad . . . grateful even . . . that he hadn't. For several minutes they were silent, arms and legs intertwined, bound together by different needs.

"Does your mother still hate me?"

"Did you get a Christmas card last year?"

"I wish your family had liked me. I liked them. I did, really. Especially your grandmother. I like Abby. I respect her. I wish she had liked me. How's your father?"

"The same." Benjamin rolled on his side. "What if I called you? We could spend a weekend together—"

"Let's don't start making plans, Ben. I like it like this—spontaneous. Don't you ever see anyone? I mean, architecting is nice, but you can't sip wine with a set of blueprints."

"I don't *want* to see someone else. If you'd spend less time in Rio being spontaneous with whatever flavor of the month—"

"Ben, don't. It's been so lovely. Please?" She found his hand and placed it over her breast. "We've gotten onto the wrong subject." She began caressing his chest. "Let's talk about something else."

"We *have* to talk. How long are we going to live like this? Are you ever going to come back?"

"I'm here now." She adjusted herself to him, massaging another part. Her hands were warmer now. "Relax, Benji. You were in such a good mood before."

"I guess my spontaneity quotient has peaked."

"You think so?" She leaned over him, her hair falling on his chest. She teased him with her tongue. When she looked up again, she was smiling. "Now, *that's* better." Her fingers continued a gentle caress. "You were saying, about peaking?"

He arched his back to her touch.

"I knew we could change the subject if we tried hard enough." Her long bare leg slid between his thighs. "You can't get this kind of service from a blueprint . . ."

Susan, of course, had won again. He closed his eyes and reached into darkness for her.

He woke up clutching a pillow. He rolled on his side, reaching out beside him. "Susan . . ." His hand found another pillow. He sat up. "Susan?" He was alone in the bed.

He untangled himself from the bed sheets, hurrying to the window. "Susan . . ." He drew up the blinds, squinting against the bright morning light.

The drive was empty.

◆ FIFTY-FIVE

DESMOND DOWNS
Western Australia

WARREN STOOD AT THE edge of the giant pit staring into the wide, dish-shaped excavation. Earth-moving equipment covered with gray tarpaulin at the bottom of the mine was parked in neat rows. A dust devil, swirling between two empty trucks, was the only movement in the Argyle Joint Venture Diamond Mine.

"Sad, ay?" Elmo Gann tossed a pebble down the sloping wall. He was a square-built, rugged man in his forties with a face as brown and weathered as the rocks that surrounded this desolate place.

"Nine months ago five hundred mates was workin' that hole." Gann cocked his hat back on his head. A black-and-white dog sat obediently at his feet, staring at the stick in his hand. "Just me and Billie come here now. Ay, girl? Come here for a bit of throw and fetch. Bloody expensive playground."

There were a dozen other mines in the area as idle as this one. When diamond deposits were discovered in the north of Western Australia in the early 1980s the stampede to file claims was like the gold rush days. Corporations were formed, fueled by investors anxious to get rich. Many went quickly out of business; some due to bad management, others because they dug for diamonds where there weren't any. Surviving companies discovered that the early indications of enormously rich deposits were misleading. Instead of excavating extremely high-grade ore of two carats per ton, as estimated, the mines were averaging less than .4 per ton, and the percentage of gemstone-quality stones was lower than expected.

But to the Syndicate diamonds were diamonds. As the world's primary diamond trader, the Syndicate controlled the pipeline that fed the retail gemstone market. With unchallenged control it also had the power to enforce its rules on its clients. The message to Australia's diamond corporations was, join the Syndicate family or be frozen out.

When word leaked that the Syndicate was offering to buy at eighty percent less than the existing market value, Australians were outraged. Also the Syndicate was a major contributor to South Africa's policy of apartheid, a policy anathema to the Australian government, which forbade the sale of Australian diamonds to the Syndicate until racial segregation in South Africa was discontinued. The ban ended negotiations and investor interest. With the only world buyer of raw diamonds denied to them, the corporations had no place to sell their product. Corporations worth millions on paper were suddenly worthless. Diamond mining in Australia stopped almost overnight. . . .

Elmo Gann stared across his dusty diamond pit. He was president and board director of the Argyle Joint Venture Diamond Mine and its only employee except for a part-time secretary. Of three million shares outstanding, Gann owned two million. One other person held the rest. Warren Romanov.

"How long would it take to get this place producing again?" Warren broke the silence first.

Gann shook his head. "If I were you I'd be looking for a gun to take back to the States. I mean, to do in the bloke who sold you this," Gann said. "Shares were at twenty-nine, thirty American dollars this time last year."

"I bought them at eight and a quarter cents." Warren glanced back at the pit. "Best eighty-three thousand dollars I ever spent. Now you said you turned about six hundred tons a day . . ." Warren closed one eye, figuring. "Eighteen thousand tons a month. That about right?"

"Nearer sixteen. We shut down weekends for maintenance and repairs."

"Ratio of what—bort to fancies?"

"Hardly any colored stones. Mostly whites. Ratio, I guess, five to one."

"About twenty percent then—gem quality."

"Roughly. Why?"

"Fifteen hundred carats a month."

"Eight thousand carats a month—"

"I'm not counting the industrial grade . . . just gem quality."

"Fifteen hundred . . ." Gann nodded. "That's about it. Not that it matters. I couldn't sell the equipment without a stockholders' meeting, but since we *are* the stockholders"—he withdrew an envelope from his jacket—"contractor from Perth offered me five hundred thousand for the lot. Trucks, haulers, cranes, pumps—"

"Just five hundred thousand?"

"That's Australian, Mr. Romanov. In U.S. dollars it's nearer three hundred sixty thousand. I need your agreement to sell."

"The debt is what, two million six?"

Gann gloomily held out the signed offer. "You want to look this over? I doubt we'll get another."

Warren wiped his neck with a handkerchief, found a bench and sat down. "I want to be the chairman of the board of directors."

"Huh?"

"We represent all the stockholders, Mr. Gann. I want to have a stock-holders' meeting."

"Now?"

"Can we take a vote? As a stockholder with thirty percent interest in Argyle Joint Venture Diamond Mine, I nominate myself to the board. Now I'd like a board vote on the new chairman."

"There isn't any bloody board—"

"Vote, please. Will you step down as chairman for me, Mr. Gann?"

"We call it director, not chairman."

"Director then. Agreed?"

"If you're so anxious, then righto. You can call yourself whatever you like, Mr. Romanov." He nodded at the pit. "It's still only a hole in the ground. Now, this is a good offer from a Mr. Duncan. He's willing to pay cash for—"

"I don't want to sell. We're not going to liquidate. I want to get this mine back in production."

"What?"

"I'll put up a million dollar bond against twenty-four percent of your outstanding shares. You remain majority stockholder and president of the company. I'll refinance seventy percent of the debt through my bank in New York to be paid out of net earnings over the next fifteen months. You'll pledge your holdings as security against the rest through the Bank of Australia in Melbourne with a similar payback schedule. That should satisfy creditors. For the first year of operation, or until we've established a retail pipeline, you'll receive a floating salary tied to the average yield of salable stones produced each month. Say, six percent of net sales. Bond money will go toward purchase of a better water separation unit, workmen housing and more trucks. I want shift supervisors who know what they're doing and a seven-day production week . . . So, Mr. Gann, how soon can we get this mine operational again?"

"Ah . . ." Gann cleared his throat, his eyes on Warren as if there was danger of contagious disease. "A million dollar bond—for water separation and—"

"Is two months too soon?" Warren said. "For full production?"

"Mr. Romanov, it isn't the operation. I mean, twenty new water separators and a thousand workers won't solve the problem. We've got no place to sell. No buyers. The government banned all sales to the Syndicate. We can't spend without income, and stockpiling stones is just another way to commit suicide. There's no place we can get rid of the bleeding rocks—"

"I'll buy them," Warren said. "My company, Romanov, Inc. I'll buy everything you can dig out of the ground. We cut diamonds as well as retail them."

"But the IGs? You can't sell industrial grades as jewelry, even to Americans."

"Let me worry about the bort. At its peak this mine produced less than eighty thousand carats in a year. That's nothing, Gann. South African mines do that in one day. Marketing industrials won't be a problem."

"But . . . the Syndicate. They won't let you sell these stones. They have rules about—"

"I'm quitting the Syndicate," Warren said. "They've pissed on my shoes for the last time. They can't threaten me, not if I have my own diamond mine. Don't worry about the bort. We'll stick the Soviets with it. They need IGs and don't care where they get them."

"You only interested in the gemstones? That's why you're doing this?"

"Right."

Gann shook his head. "But why this mine? There are others. Why Argyle?"

"Because I did my homework," Warren said. "You're very small, and your stock was easy to get. Your gem-yield is good, half to one and a half carats on average weight, and the monthly volume is right. That's important because I need a steady flow of roughs. Also, you were one of the few operations in Australia that wasn't approached by the Syndicate, which means they probably didn't think you were worth the trouble. The Syndicate has hurt both of us, Mr. Gann. I'm never going to let that happen again." He glanced into the pit. "Sir Arthur Groote slapped my hands but he didn't cut them off. That was his mistake." Warren looked back at

Gann, stood up and smiled. "So . . . did I risk eighty-three grand for nothing or do we have a partnership?"

Elmo Gann stared at Warren, then wiped his hand on his pants and held it out. "Mr. Romanov, you may be daft as a bloody wombat—but I'm game."

They shook hands in the late afternoon sun, laughing. Billie sat patiently with the stick between her teeth, ready for another run.

◆ FIFTY-SIX

NEW YORK

Summer

WARREN WORE A DARK pinstriped suit and a red tie—his trademark. On his little finger he wore a signet ring set with the first diamond from the Australian mine, his badge of honor in defiance of the Syndicate. He had cut and mounted it himself. If there had been any doubts about Romanov Diamonds' ability to play hardball in the marketplace, Warren had overcome them with his coup against the giant. For a hundred years the Syndicate's monopoly of diamond trading had been invincible. Now there were two players. Goliath had not been slain, but he had been put on notice.

"This is better than Koh-i-noor, Ben," Warren said, stabbing the ice in his drink with a plastic swizzle stick. Benjamin and Franklin Abbaye sat across the table, a captive audience. "It's a hundred times better . . . the next logical step for Romanov Diamonds. Just think of it"—he made a grand gesture—"Shelkagari, the mother stone. It's beautiful, the *perfect* campaign."

The midtown restaurant's lunch crowd was long since gone. The main dining room was a sea of empty tables. A couple, seated near the bank of windows overlooking Fifty-second Street, held hands across the white tablecloth. Outside, Manhattan shimmered in August's latest heat wave.

Benjamin tried not to look restless. His cousin had set up this special meeting, even asking his Uncle Franklin to fly in from Chicago. Warren had called it "family business" as if they were all Sicilians.

"So, what do you think, Ben?" Warren leaned forward on the table.

"You're in pretty good shape. How about an expense-paid vacation for a few days of mountain climbing?"

Benjamin glanced at Franklin. His uncle remained unusually quiet, smoking his imported cigar. His gray beard was silver in the filtered sunlight. "You knew about this nutty idea?" Benjamin said.

Franklin nodded. "For the most part. Actually, we wanted to see what you thought." Franklin tapped his cigar against a glass ashtray.

"We?"

"Your mother, Abby . . . me." Franklin shrugged. "And Yurev."

"What *I* think? Since when?"

"Since always." Franklin looked at Warren. "Your cousin hasn't been home five times in"—he glanced at Benjamin—"what, ten years? He has this irritating habit of avoiding people who care about him."

Benjamin's face tightened. "We're not here to discuss *my* shortcomings, Uncle Frank. So just drop it." Franklin had no right mentioning Chicago, especially in front of Warren. Besides, he hadn't run away from Chicago. He'd escaped.

"How about it, Ben?" Warren said. "Say yes and you'll have a hell of a story to tell your grandchildren."

Benjamin's mind flashed to an image of Susan. She was in California again, auditioning for a miniseries.

"Ben?"

Susan's image faded. Benjamin looked at Warren. "You want me to go with you into the Himalayas? Seriously?"

"That's right."

"You're nuts, Warren."

"No, no. I'm a genius, don't you read the papers? I'm 'The Man Who Defied the Syndicate—and Survived.' "

"When you make Architectural Digest I'll be impressed."

"Look, it's two weeks out of your wonderful life. Three at the most. We fly to Hawaii, Calcutta, Nepal. We go up the mountain, we come back."

"And that stunt's going to sell diamonds?"

"It is."

Benjamin shrugged. "It doesn't make sense. Shelkagari is a myth. Why go if you know you're not going to find anything . . . or even look?"

"*Going* is what matters. Very existential. It'll stir up controversy, and controversy begets headlines. We'll have people arguing about Shelkagari for years. Is it the mother stone of Koh-i-noor and the Pearls of Light? Is it a myth or is it real? This will generate such attention to Romanov Diamonds—"

"Warren, *I'm* an architect, and I don't have any clients in Asia."

"Two weeks, for godsakes," Warren said, working to keep his smile alive. "I'm not asking you to give up designing your damn parking garages. What's a couple of weeks? I *need* you for this. It won't work without you, Ben."

Warren was still hungry. The success of the Koh-i-noor business had introduced him to the world. His defiance of the Syndicate was heady. Now he needed an encore. A big one. He had, he felt, found it in Shelkagari. "Quest for Shelkagari" was sure to generate global attention. His plan was to mount an expedition into the greatest mountains of the world in search of the biggest diamond of all time—parent of Koh-i-noor and the Pearls of Light. It would work because it was both mystical and romantic. The story of Shelkagari would especially appeal to women. Unlike Koh-i-noor, the legend of Shelkagari was founded in hope and enchanted love. His campaign would begin with the retelling of the ancient myth—Ushas, beautiful goddess of dawn, and her beloved boy-prince. Warren would show Ushas, consumed with grief, transforming her martyred prince into the eternal diamond—the great Shelkagari.

Facsimiles of Shelkagari would dwarf the Koh-i-noor. Shelkagari was nearly three hundred times larger. Romanov would offer Eternal Stones made of Australian diamonds—hardest on earth—as "the crystalline embodiment of everlasting affection." His line of diamonds was to be called The Promise of Ushas.

"Quest" would give the campaign Warren's stamp of personal commitment. He would search for Shelkagari just as his grandfather, Alexander Romanov, founder of Romanov Diamonds, had searched for it nearly fifty years earlier. The heirs of the original adventurers would renew the search. It was for the third generation to find Shelkagari.

"I hate it." Benjamin stirred uncomfortably in his chair.

"Hate it?"

"The whole idea. Yurev and Abby didn't go through hell so that someday their grandchildren could exploit what they did. You don't even believe Shelkagari exists." He turned to Franklin. "I can't believe Abby agreed to this."

"She hasn't agreed to anything, yet." Franklin patted his jacket for a lighter. "Neither has Yurev, for that matter. That's why we're meeting today. All this is still in the development stage. Warren *wants* it to happen, but it's really up to you."

"You mean if I agree . . ." Benjamin shook his head. "You put it on *my* head?"

"You're the one who has to go, not them." Franklin found the lighter, held it under a new cigar. "Whatever *you* decide, they'll stand by it. They feel that way about you, always have." Flame jumped at the cigar, crackling the tobacco. "Ben, what you need to do is give this a few days, mull it over. Don't make up your mind right now, it doesn't have to be decided today. Just think about it."

"There isn't any reason to dismiss it out of hand," Warren said.

"Maybe just a dozen."

"Ben . . ." Franklin touched his arm.

"All right." Benjamin held his palms up. "All right, I'll think about it."

Warren nodded, a quick smile for Franklin. "That's all I want." He gave Benjamin a serious look. "I'll promise you one thing—this *could* be the experience of your lifetime. You'd be a part of history—"

"Sure," Ben said and thought of Susan. Would Warren's special diamonds appeal to her . . . something to wear at Mardi Gras?

◆ FIFTY-SEVEN

"WRITE, IF YOU EVER learn how," Franklin called across the terminal. He was at the boarding tunnel, plastic glass raised in farewell.

Benjamin waved, holding the railing for support. He'd barely delivered his uncle to the gate in time. He waved again as Franklin took the arm of the boarding hostess and walked her down the rampart to the plane.

Benjamin forced himself to stand erect in front of the plate-glass window as the 747 lumbered away from the dock and disappeared into darkness, lights flashing. Concentrating on appearing sober, Benjamin made his way out of JFK into staggering humidity and managed to find a taxi. Inside he lay his head back against the seat. He was getting too old for this. Uncle Frank was seventy-two but he could match, drink for drink, two men half his age. It had been crazy for Benjamin to think he could keep up. It always was.

The JFK send-off had become a tradition. On his last night in the city Franklin took his nephew to dinner at a small restaurant near the Shubert Theater. The challenge afterward was to hit as many bars between Forty-fourth Street and the airport as they could—luggage in tow—before Franklin's flight. The all-time record was seventeen, set the day after Benjamin received his architectural license. The tradition had started as a sort of a rite of passage when Benjamin was in college. The only ground rule was that seriousness on any level was taboo. They could talk about women or sports or travel but not business and never family. Uncle Frank was, despite his age, Benjamin's best friend.

It was 3 A.M. when Benjamin returned to Connecticut. He had fallen asleep in the cab by the time it reached the midtown garage where he'd parked his car. He bought black coffee from a vending machine, knowing it had no effect on alcohol in the blood but determined not to spend the night in the city. The drive home was a chore, keeping his eyes open, but he managed. He was asleep the moment he fell into bed.

The doorbell woke him.

A Connecticut State Trooper waited on the porch, the lights of his car revolving in the drive.

"Benjamin Kane?"

Benjamin squinted against the bright light of midmorning. He held his robe together at the waist. "Yes." His mouth felt hairy.

"I was sent out to check on you, sir. Mrs. Kane has been trying to reach you for several hours. It's an emergency call."

"Susan?" Benjamin blinked. The telephone rang in the living room.

The trooper glanced past Benjamin. "Is everything all right here, Mr. Kane?"

"Susan's been calling for hours?" Benjamin ran a hand through his hair. His head was still fuzzy. "Is Susan okay?"

The trooper's gaze was still focused inside the house. "Has your phone been out of order?"

Benjamin shook his head and immediately felt dizzy. "No, I . . . I've been asleep."

The phone kept ringing.

"Mr. Kane. You don't look so good." He helped Benjamin to a chair. "Shall I get that, sir?"

Benjamin waved him on.

"This is the Kane residence, Trooper Dale Greene speaking."

Benjamin felt incredibly foolish—sitting in his own house, barefoot and in a robe, having his phone answered by a state trooper. This was the last time—the absolute last time—that he would allow himself to drink so much.

"Yes, ma'am, he's right here. He's been asleep. He seems to have been drinking."

"Is that Susan? Is she okay?" Benjamin got to his feet.

Trooper Greene listened for several seconds more. "This is Mrs. *Laura* Kane, sir."

"My mother?"

"You'd better sit down, Mr. Kane. This isn't good news."

Benjamin took the phone. "Hello?"

"Oh, Ben . . . we've been calling and calling . . . we—have you seen the television news?"

"No. What's—"

"It's Franklin," she said with more control. "His plane. There was an accident. It was circling Chicago, coming in to land and . . . it hit another plane . . . the airline called us . . . Abby's gone to . . ."

"Mother, is someone there with you?"

"I've been calling and calling—"

"Mother—" Benjamin doubled his hand into a fist. For several moments he couldn't speak. The Connecticut house was silent except for his mother's breathing. "Mother . . . is anyone else there with you?"

"Else?" A pause. "Yurey went with Abby, if that's what you mean . . . They're all dead, Ben. Everyone."

Benjamin held the telephone close to his mouth. He squeezed his eyes shut.

"Come home, Ben. I think you should come home."

◆ FIFTY-EIGHT

CHICAGO

THE AFTERNOON SKY THREATENED rain as Benjamin arrived at Abbaye
Mansion. A breeze from the lake tempered the late August heat. He stood
on the cobblestone walk with his bag, pausing to absorb the time passed.
He had not been home in eight years—not since he married Susan—and
he took the moment to reacquaint himself.

On close inspection the bright green lawn inside the horseshoe drive
was flecked with brownish grass, evidence of the hot, extended summer.
Strangely, Benjamin remembered a winter's morning, when he was seven,
rushing across this same ground, in snowball combat with his Uncle Frank
buried inside a herringbone coat. Nothing had significantly changed, yet
the place was different. It was like revisiting a former playground, quiet
with memories, where playthings had become small and inert with time,
as if the place had changed, not the visitor.

Abbaye Mansion had been one of the first colonial-style homes built
when railroad was king and Chicago was a long buggy ride to the south.
But the city had since swallowed the estate whole, a tired monument on
Rosewood Lane. A rock wall encircled the grounds now and, once inside
the gate, the mansion burst into view like a white pillared fortress.

Abby had been born in this house and Benjamin's parents, Laura and
Miller, married here. It was the only home Benjamin had ever known until
he went to college. For half of his childhood, Abbaye Mansion was an
enormous playhouse, open to his playmates. That changed before he was
twelve. For years Benjamin had thought the change had come when the

stone wall was built. But it had begun before the wall. It began on a bridge at dawn in a faraway place, when he met his father for the first time, a lonely, haggard figure with a suitcase who walked slowly out of the morning mist and shook his hand.

Benjamin's life was to be forever different. Abbaye Mansion ceased to be a playhouse. The wall went up and with it a silent mood of troubled tension was born inside its boundaries. Twelve-year-old Benjamin had sensed it but not understood the reason. It had its effect on him. He became afraid of the dark, had nightmares of being left in a house without doors. He dreamed of being alone in darkness and that something, or someone, was in the darkness with him—silent, watching. Eventually Abbaye Mansion became a place to fear, and that fear eventually drove him out. . . .

Benjamin stared up at the white pillars. He hated coming here, to bury the one relative he felt closest to, the one person who enjoyed life without apologizing for it. After eight years the ambivalent emotions of his childhood came back to him. He was afraid to step inside the wide foyer and experience it all again.

Abbaye Mansion was his home, his real home. But it was also a fearful place—this was where they kept his father.

"Ben." His mother hugged him in the foyer that was crowded with flowers and wreaths. As always Laura was slim and petite and lovely even in black. "I'm sorry, Ben. I—"

Benjamin kissed her. "You look good, Mom."

Laura stepped back, offering a soft smile. "And you." She glanced behind him. "Is Susan . . ."

"No."

She nodded. "It's going to be a large service, I'm afraid. Franklin knew so many people."

"Where?"

"Forest Lawn. It's a beautiful plot, near a pond. He picked it himself."

Franklin had once told Benjamin that he wanted a Viking's funeral. A burning ship with sails ablaze, set adrift in Lake Michigan. "I want to go out a spectacle," he'd said, "stuffed and mounted on the bow, hand raised in final farewell with a vestal virgin caressing my backside."

"I have your room ready," Laura said, "if you want to take your bags up."

"Where's Nan?"

"Right here."

Benjamin turned. Abby started down from the top of the stairs. At the bottom step she waited for him to come to her. She hadn't changed. Her hair was as fiery as always, like her temperament. "So, you've come to help us bury Uncle Frank. Nice of you to show up."

Abby's directness hadn't changed either. She said exactly what was on her mind.

"Nan, I'm—"

"I know, I know." Abby nodded at the flowers. "Everyone is sorry. We're *all* sorry. The old place is pretty much like you left it—mourning. Welcome home."

It was already starting. Benjamin felt the old fear rising inside him. He wet his lips, but had nothing to say.

Welcome home.

The funeral the next day was not grand. A drizzling rain and a few claps of thunder distinguished the service. A hundred people with umbrellas muddied the ground at the grave site while a minister read a passage from a wet Bible. The casket was lowered, and it was done. Not enough for Franklin, Benjamin thought. Not nearly enough.

"He's mourning in his own way." Yurev stood at the French doors. "That's what he's doing out there." He looked at Benjamin. "He always walks when he's troubled about something."

Benjamin stared through the leaded glass at the lone figure on the deserted field. He and Yurev were in the second-floor study, a room adjacent to the guest bedroom with a view of the grounds behind the mansion. Uncle Frank had called the backyard "the rear forty acres," although it was considerably less than that. Still, it was large, as large as a polo field. The stone wall that surrounded the property was a broken line in the distance, partially obscured by rows of trees that stood like soldiers inside the perimeter, lancers against the wind. Benjamin's father, dressed in a tweed coat but without a hat, was in the center of the field, strolling across the leaf-strewn ground, sometimes stopping, sometimes glancing back at the main house. If he saw Benjamin he didn't react.

"How can you know what he thinks?" Benjamin said suddenly, turning to his grandfather.

It was a stupid question, and Benjamin realized it the moment he spoke. Yurev lived here now, with Abby. "Beautiful sinners," Franklin had said, describing their marriageless state. But Yurev was here for Miller too. He sat with his Miller, talked to him, read, and Miller listened, or seemed to. Benjamin had no right to question that relationship. If anyone could know what Miller Kane felt, it was Yurev.

"I can't of course," Yurev said patiently. "It's just a feeling. Your father and I have sort of an understanding—I talk and he listens. When he gets up and walks out, I stop talking. It works quite well."

Yurev had not shrunk like most men his age. He was healthy and looked it. His hair had thinned, and he'd developed a slight paunch but otherwise he appeared younger than his seventy-odd years by a decade. His one visible concession to age was his bifocal spectacles, wire-rimmed glasses that gave his angular face a certain dignity. Benjamin had not seen his grandfather in almost two years. Seeing him now, listening to his sensitive humor, Benjamin did not detect any sign of a man obsessed by a dream.

"He knows you're here," Yurev said.

"You told him?"

"I did, yes. You should see him, Ben. I think he'd like that."

It was what he dreaded most, sitting in that room with his father. He remembered the torture of it as a boy, the silence, waiting for a look, praying for a smile.

"You're the one I want to talk to," Benjamin said. He turned slightly, removing the specter of the figure outside from his peripheral vision. "I've been talking to Warren. Actually, I've been *listening* to Warren."

Yurev nodded.

"He has this big plan."

Yurev adjusted a chair and sat down. "I take it you don't think much of this big plan of his."

"No, I don't. He's turning Romanov Diamonds into a carnival—"

"Possibly."

"You know what he wants to do? This Quest for Shelkagari? Make public the ordeal you and Nan went through for publicity . . ."

"That was a long time ago. Abby and I can't be hurt by anything Warren does."

"What about Miller Kane? It's bound to get out that he's your son . . . Abby's illegitimate child."

"Are you worried about Abby's reputation or Miller's? I think we're all beyond the embarrassment it might cause, Ben. Anyway, that doesn't concern you. All you have to decide is whether you want to go with—"

"I *don't* want to go." Benjamin was on his feet. "That stone is what's screwed this family up. Is everyone so obsessed with it that they can't see? Shelkagari isn't real. It never was. Well, *I'm* not going to let it control my life." He swung around, pointed toward the window. "I'm not going to wind up like *that.*"

For several moments Yurev said nothing. He reached for the porcelain samovar on the table beside his chair and poured hot water into a cup and added a teabag. "Well, I certainly can understand that," he said.

"You don't care, do you?" Benjamin stared at him.

Yurev sipped his tea.

"What the hell *do* you care about?"

Yurev set his cup aside. "I care about Abby and Miller. I care about your mother. I am *also* very interested in Shelkagari. Still. Yes. They're all tied together, from my point of view. They've been that way since before you were born."

"But—"

"Please. As long as we're on the subject, let's discuss what *you* care about. You left home fifteen years ago? You went to college, became an architect, settled in the East and got married. In that time how often did you visit your mother? Five or six times? You were married by a justice of the peace in New York. Do you remember how you announced the news? You sent a telegram. Laura Kane's only child gets married and sends a telegram."

"Look, if you want to make me out an uncaring s.o.b.—"

"Ben, if you want to get into personality traits we can look at selfishness, disregard for . . ." Yurev raised his shoulders and let them fall. "Of course as an old man obsessed by a fantasy my interpretation of things as they look is suspect."

"Don't do that to me," Benjamin said. "You never lived in this house, day after day, year after year, afraid of something you couldn't see. I visited my father once a week. *Visited.* We lived under the same roof, and I saw my own father by appointment only. You don't have any idea—"

"You could have tried harder to understand, Ben. You ran away—"

"Understand? My father lives in his own world, created by himself. He has nothing to say to anyone outside it—not to me, you, anybody. Matthew Miller Kane exists. How can I relate to that? He isn't my father, he's a flesh and blood extension of a nightmare. He"—Benjamin glanced up and stopped dead in midsentence.

His father stood in the doorway. The lapels of his tweed coat, turned up at the neck, hid part of his weathered face. His matted, windblown hair glistened in the artificial light. He stood there, hands deep in the pockets of his overcoat, gray eyes on his son. Then he turned and was gone as he had appeared. Without a word.

Benjamin didn't breathe. He looked at Yurev. "Why didn't you say he was there? Why didn't you say something?" He swallowed air. "God, I —" He ran to the door. "I didn't mean that." The corridor was empty. He looked back at Yurev. "God—I *didn't mean that.*"

"Well, you don't need an appointment anymore, Ben."

The room where Miller Kane lived was a storage place of mementos. The walls were crowded with framed photographs, yellowed newspaper clippings and certificates of achievement. The corner bookcase was filled with plaques and trophies of schoolday accomplishments. A small reading table contained a lamp and six books. A worn leather baseball glove hung from the back of the chair. The top of an old wooden dresser was a parking place for a dusty, badly painted model airplane.

Benjamin stood in the center of the room, overcome. He had never been allowed in this room as a boy. Always, when he met with his father, it had been in the adjacent sitting room, but never here. Never where he lived.

All of his life Benjamin had longed for his father's show of acceptance. Everything he did as a boy in one way or another was a plea for his father's recognition. A sign, even a secret look from his father . . . Instead there was only silence. Emptiness. Benjamin deeply felt a need for love from the one person who seemed to have none to give. *That* was what had made him leave. Laura and Abby could not fill that emptiness, no matter how much they tried.

Benjamin's work was his sanctuary, a world he could control. What he lacked in his life he tried to make up for with cardboard models and plastic figures. Inanimate constructions that had no opportunity to disappoint. Susan was the one flesh-and-blood relationship he had thought he had a chance with, but not surprisingly he had tried too hard, been too possessive. She had rejected him just as his father had, or so he thought.

But now . . .

Miller Kane stood in shadow, still in his overcoat. Benjamin moved slowly toward his father, fearfully, unsure, but determined not to let this opportunity slip by. He'd waited too long. . . .

He barely managed the word . . . "Dad . . ."

Miller continued to stare at him, then, taking a step, slowly held out his hand.

Benjamin took it, and felt its strength and the warmth, just as he had at the threshold of a dirty bridge in Kwangtung province. The sign he had waited so long for was here, all around him. The school books on the shelf, the plaques, the crummy little model airplane— everything in this room—was *his*. His father had made them a part of his world.

Benjamin shook his father's hand, barely able to see him.

Miller's lips formed the faintest smile. It was a beginning.

Yurev was reading by the light of a small lamp when Benjamin returned. He walked to the windows and stood silent, as his father had done, looking into the darkness outside.

Yurev set his book aside. "It's been hours. What happened?"

"It's been years," Benjamin replied. He turned to face Yurev. "He gave me back twenty years."

Yurev nodded.

Benjamin sat down. "I cried in front of him. I haven't cried since . . ." He looked at Yurev. "He gave me a manuscript to read. A three-hundred-year-old manuscript. It's about Shelkagari."

"Yes."

"He had me read a passage over and over again. About potentates and sons of sons."

Yurev leaned forward in his chair. "And what did you think?"

"I don't know. I . . . *he* believes it, that's what matters. He also gave me this." He reached into his pocket and took out the *chatra* the devil dog medallion. "You have to explain this to me. A lot of things need explaining . . . if I'm going after it . . ."

"You'll go?"

"Not for Warren, or you, or Abby." Benjamin nodded over his shoulder. "For him. I don't think I'll ever believe it, but he believes. I'll try to find it for his sake. *Understand that.*"

Yurev sat back. "Good, Ben. I do understand."

"That's what this is all about, isn't it . . . closing the circle? First you and Abby. Then my father. Now me."

Yurev held his breath. It was more than he had dared hope for.

Benjamin turned the *chatra* between his fingers, rubbing his thumb across the raised surface of the dog emblem. "Well, whatever it means, it's apparently my turn now." He looked at Yurev. "I wonder if I'm up to it."

"You won't fail, Ben. You're going to have something no one else had. Something I've waited forty years for."

"Divine guidance?"

"Close." Yurev smiled. "Very close."

Warren reached for the Princess phone on his nightstand. The dial glowed when he picked it up. "Hullo?"

"Warren?"

"Yes . . ."

"It's Ben Kane. Are you awake?"

Warren snapped on the reading light over his bed, flinching from the brightness. The clock radio read 2:30 A.M. "Do you know what time it is?"

"I'll go."

Warren sat up, suddenly awake. "You'll go?"

"There's one condition."

"One? Name it."

"I won't be part of a charade. We're going to look for Shelkagari."

Warren smiled. "That's the spirit, Ben."

"No, I mean it. We're *really* going to look for it."

"Where are you?"

"Chicago. We buried Franklin today."

"Oh, right. I'm really sorry about—"

"Agreed?"

"You've been talking to Yurev, haven't you?"

"Doesn't matter who I've been talking to. Do you agree?"

"Ben, you want to look for real . . . we'll look."

"That's all I wanted to hear. Go back to sleep."

Warren couldn't sleep. He made several phone calls, waking people all over Manhattan. It was on.

His last call was long distance. To London. "Get your passport in order," Warren said, "I'll be calling for you within the next sixty days." He nodded. "Yes, the trip *is* on. Ben Kane changed his mind. He *wants* to hunt for the stone."

Warren smiled. Benjamin's sincerity was the perfect final touch.

◆ FIFTY-NINE

WEST BRANCH, IOWA

THE HERBERT HOOVER PRESIDENTIAL Library was less than Benjamin had expected. Instead of a towering monument faced with glass and doric columns he found a stone-gray building surrounded by a hundred and seventy acres of graceful park land landscaped and dutifully maintained. Benjamin parked in the visitors' lot and stretched his back the moment he was out of the car. The trip was less than two hundred miles, but Benjamin hadn't spent four hours behind the wheel of a car in years.

"They're buried up there." Yurev came around the car. He nodded toward a gentle rise beyond the main building where an American flag fluttered lazily in the light wind. "Hoover chose the spot himself."

As Franklin had, Benjamin remembered. He continued to work on his spine, relieved that Hoover wasn't from the Dakotas. Benjamin's education about the Stone of Light had begun and ended with Herbert Hoover. Like the other principals involved, Hoover's role, and his wife's, had been woven into the fabric of the Shelkagari legend. They were as much a part as Tavernier or Ayrub Ravi. And they never knew it.

"Mr. Romanov, nice to meet you at last. Mr. Kane. Please, come in, sit down."

Byron Ford, the director of the presidential library, was a tall lean man in his fifties. He wore round, wire-rimmed spectacles, and his hair, once yellow-blond, had not quite made the transition to senior white. His office was comfortable with the aroma of hickory pipe tobacco. He waited now for his guests to be seated on a wide divan before taking his place in a

403

brocade chair before a low coffee table. Benjamin liked that. He hated sitting in an office in front of someone's desk, it reminded him of bankers and lawyers—used car salesmen without the smile.

"Well, sir, I feel as if I'm finally meeting a longtime pen pal," Ford began. "We've been corresponding for what, five years, has it been?"

"I think so, yes," Yurev said. "I'm glad finally to be here."

Ford looked at Benjamin. "Mr. Kane, you're the grandson I've heard mentioned. Good to meet you."

Benjamin nodded. "Thank you."

"Now, I know you're probably anxious to see the Lou Hoover collection. We have set up a room for you to work in but nothing may leave that room."

"What about copies?" Benjamin said.

"Photocopying is permitted. The nearest machines are in the archivist's office—"

"We won't be needing photocopies," Yurev said. "The drawings we're looking for are on tracing paper." He looked around. "Laid out, about a quarter the size of this room. We'll make a copy of the text by hand. We're only interested in the text."

"As you know, the collection has only recently been released to us. Mrs. Hoover's personal papers had been restricted, as per instructions in the president's will. When it was moved from Stanford to West Branch in 1968 everything was stored in a local bank vault. Consequently I'm afraid, we haven't yet catalogued or inventoried the collection."

Benjamin knew the story of Yurev at Stanford and the months he spent searching through tons of file cabinets. As he had plowed through the mountain of papers in California, Yurev and his assistant had inventoried as they went, but it was all for nothing. Since the Herbert Hoover Presidential Library was a federal repository, subject to the federal bureaucracy, only a federally approved inventory was valid, which meant it all had to be done again.

"We're aware of that," Yurev said. "Ben and I will be here until we find what we're looking for. We've made arrangements in Iowa City for a place to stay."

"Ah, good. If there's anything I can do to help, let me know. I'd like to have you take a short tour of the facility if you've the time. We're very proud of it."

Yurev hesitated, then nodded. "Yes, of course."

The Herbert Hoover Presidential Library was actually a library, an archive and a museum all in one. Its main attraction to tourists was, naturally, the museum. The lobby was a representation of Hoover's life in photos, sketches and memorabilia arranged chronologically on the walls. There were pictures of the original Hoover home in West Branch, of Herbert as a boy, a student and sitting on a camel in Australia on his first job as a geologist.

With the lobby as hub, rooms and alcoves displayed vignettes of his life. One display was a recreation of his Oval Office with the first telephone used by a president on his desk. Another, called the Walnut Library, was a colorful room with bookcases filled with elegantly bound books and selected pieces of Lou Hoover's famous blue-and-white china collection. The room's centerpiece was a magnificent antique dining table set for twelve with matching chairs.

Herbert Hoover had always been a mystery to Benjamin. All the pictures he remembered were of a pudgy, severe-looking man in high starched-collared shirts. Seeing him here, a tall young man with conservative mustache, made Bert Hoover come alive for him. The China pictures with his young bride, posed before a dusty stone wall in the midst of a city under siege, were the most interesting. Here was Hoover the enigma, adventurer and peace-loving Quaker.

Benjamin turned to Yurev. "I didn't know—" He looked into the startled face of an elderly woman in a black hat. "Oh . . . excuse me." He moved out of the tour line and found Yurev sitting in a chair beside the Walnut Library, head bowed.

"Yurev? You tired? You want to rest?"

His grandfather shook his head slowly.

"Are you all right?"

Yurev raised his head. His eyes were filled with tears.

"Yurev—*hey?*" Benjamin dropped to one knee. "What is it? Are you okay? Jesus, say something." He grabbed the knot of Yurev's tie, loosening it.

Yurev pushed his hands away, motioned with his head, indicating the Walnut Room. "The rug . . . look at the rug."

"Rug? Are you all right?"

"All right . . ." He shook his head with measured slowness. "For over forty years I've been waiting . . ." He looked up at Benjamin. "Forty years. She never mentioned a rug—"

"I'm getting a doctor."

Yurev caught his sleeve. "No . . . look at the rug, Ben. Under the table. *Look at it.*"

Benjamin looked. It was a large hand-woven rug with dark reds, browns and blues on a sandy-colored background, approximately twelve feet square. It was divided into blocks. Each block contained separate designs. The sign identifying the items in the room called it: TIBETAN TAPESTRY, UNKNOWN ORIGIN.

"Oh, Jesus."

"I've been looking, waiting, for forty years, Ben—*in the wrong place*. Lou Hoover used the tracings as a pattern to have a *rug* made." Tears were rolling down Yurev's cheeks. "Forty years." He looked into Benjamin's face. "It doesn't change, it doesn't ever change . . ."

◆ SIXTY

BENJAMIN FOUND THE BUZZER marked S. Granville and pressed the button. Professionally Susan used Granville, her maiden name. Apparently she used it socially as well. He had never seen her apartment. He pressed the buzzer again.

"Mark?" The metal speaker didn't do her voice justice; it was tinny and flat, without that sensuous texture.

"No, it's Ben."

"Ben?"

"Ben, Susan . . . your husband."

There was a long pause then. "Just a minute."

He waited on the stoop, trying not to wonder who Mark was. The security door buzzed, unlatching the lock, and Benjamin entered. She was in apartment two, on the first floor. She opened the door before he could knock.

"Ben, hello. This is a surprise." She was wearing a sleeveless smock, loose, with a rope belt at the waist. She was barefoot. "What are you doing in town?"

"Just tying up some loose ends. I'm on my way to Chicago. I thought I'd stop by."

The apartment was cozy with a kitchen that looked out on a small patio. Open stairs with a landing led to a bedroom loft. Sunlight from sliding glass doors to the patio illuminated the living room. A young man wearing white denims sat in the corner of the section sofa.

"Ben, I'd like you to meet Philip Garner. Philip produces the aerobic show."

Philip raised up halfway to shake Benjamin's hand. "Hiya." He was chewing gum. "You're the architect."

It wasn't a question, just an acknowledgment. Also, Benjamin noted, it was architect, not husband.

"We were just going over some routines for the show," Susan said. Her cheerfulness had a slightly forced edge to it. "Drink, Ben?"

"Thanks, no. I just wanted to stop by. I'm catching a plane at four."

She sat on the sofa, folding her bare legs beneath her. "I'm so sorry about Franklin, Ben. If I could have made it to the funeral—"

"I know."

She turned to Philip. "Ben's uncle was killed on that plane last month. The one that crashed in Chicago."

"Yeah? I saw it on TV." He sipped his drink, apparently very much at home here.

"Susan"—Benjamin gestured toward the patio—"I just need to speak to you for a minute."

She got up from the sofa. "Sure." She smiled at Philip. "Family conference, Phil. You don't mind?"

"Nooo."

The patio was about ten feet square, colored blocks. Susan closed the sliding door behind her. "You could have called, Ben."

"I should have, sorry."

"It's embarrassing. Phil's my boss."

He took an envelope out of his jacket. "I opened an account for you at Chase. Susan Granville. There's a card you have to sign in here." He handed her the envelope. "Fifteen thousand. Twelve months of apartment rent."

Susan frowned. "Checking account?"

"I can't do it any longer, Susan."

"Do what?"

He nodded at Garner behind the glass watching television. "This."

"What have you heard? Phil is just a friend, Ben. We work together. We—"

"I'm not accusing you of anything, Susan. This has nothing to do with your friend, Phil. We don't have a marriage anymore. I just want to end the charade—"

"Ben—"

"Just listen, please. I saw Isaac Stroud yesterday. He'll call you in a few days. You can have your own lawyer if you want but it's really not necessary."

"Ben, do you *want* a divorce?"

"Yes." Finally. He felt strangely free.

She sat on a small concrete bench. "Well, then, it's come to this, has it?" A soft smile brightened her face. "I guess I can't complain, can I?"

He remained silent.

"Okay. Whatever you say, Ben. I don't want anything. I mean, the house. I have a car . . . paid for by you." She glanced at the envelope. "I would like the money, though."

"It's already been transferred to Chase."

She looked at him. "It hasn't been *all* bad, has it, Ben?"

"It never was."

She stood up, kissed him.

"I'd better go."

"Yes, I suppose so." She looked in on Philip. "If you were wondering about Phil—"

"I wasn't."

And, he was delighted to discover, he really wasn't.

"This is where you're going," Yurev said, stabbing his finger at the map. "The Kingdom of Lo—the true Back of the Beyond."

The sectional satellite map from the Library of Congress was spread over the desk in Abby's study. She and Yurev and Benjamin poured over it like schoolchildren; Abby had the magnifying glass. The Kingdom of Lo—marked as Mustang on the map—was a remote principality beyond the Himalayan ranges. It was shaped like a thumb in northern Nepal, jutting into Tibet. Swirling contour lines on the map denoted massive mountains and passes that Benjamin could only imagine.

"Here's Benithog," Abby said. She marked the spot. "The humpback bridge is here. Up this way . . . this way—there." She made another X. "Valley of Weeping Winds. That's the monastery in the red cliffs." She looked at Benjamin. "Where Jack Barbaree killed the high lama."

"Our traveling monk, Ayrub Ravi, came this way from India, across the foothills, up the Kali Gandaki gorge and on to Mustang." Yurev traced the route with his pencil, heavily circling a tiny valley among the jumble of contours. "Lo Mantang. The feudal capital of a medieval civilization. That's where Shelkagari is, Ben." He set the pencil aside. "Somewhere."

Ayrub Ravi's message, carved in stone on the balcony of the monastery and winding up as a rug in the Hoover Museum, was a roadmap in Sanskrit. It described his trek, following a star, to Lo Mantang. It described the places he had been and what he had seen, but as for the final resting place of his special prize, there was only cryptic Sanskrit. Yurev and Benjamin had analyzed Ravi's text for weeks, filling a notebook with guesses. Their efforts at interpreting a message nine hundred years old, written by a Buddhist monk on the run, were less than rewarding. Ravi's final clue was both a warning and an answer and impossible to decipher.

Abby turned to the translation. Half of it they understood, the warning. It was relatively simple: Leave Shelkagari alone. The rest was a mystery. They'd been reading it to each other over and over, trying to unlock its secret. Abby paced in front of the desk, reading again.

"Until the heir of the third princely son loosens the hounds of azure —shall only the Divine One possess the Miraculous Gift."

The Divine One might have been the king of Lo, but it also was used in referring to Buddha or high holy ones—lamas. Did Ravi give the stone to a priest? To the king of Lo? Would he trust it to the care of another person, even a holy one? Then there was the enigma of the hounds of azure—the blue dogs. In Ravi's time domesticated dogs were trained to protect temples from intruders, a fact that Abby and Yurev well understood. The *chatra* that had hung from the Pearls of Light represented a devil dog clutching a stone in its jaws. Was Ravi saying that blue dogs —devil dogs—protected Shelkagari, ultimate symbol of the jewel of the lotus? They had gone at it a hundred different ways without a definitive solution.

"It's tied to this," Yurev said. He dangled the *chatra* above the map. "It means *something.*"

"Watch out for wild Tibetan dogs." Benjamin stretched his back. "That may be *all* it means. It's just a charm, after all, like thousands of charms in that part of the world. It doesn't *have* to mean anything more than that." He looked wearily at Yurev.

"Warren's kicking off this campaign of his in San Francisco in two weeks. He's arranged a press affair at the Fairmont Hotel to celebrate our departure on the magnificent 'Quest.' So if we're going to solve this, we have until then to figure out what unleashing a pack of wild dogs means, if anything."

"We may not," Abby said.

"Exactly. Which leaves us with what?"

"We know Shelkagari is in Lo Mantang," Yurev said. He gave Benjamin a look. "We *know* that."

"If there is such a thing."

Abby stared at her grandson a moment, then, adjusting her glasses, began pacing again. "All right, let's try this once more." She read: " 'Until the heir of the third princely son loosens the hounds of azure . . .' "

The ballroom of the Fairmont Hotel was packed. Banners emblazoned "QUEST FOR SHELKAGARI" hung from the ceiling.

Benjamin had purposely arrived late to avoid as much of this as possible.

"Ben, it's about time you showed up." Warren was wearing a tuxedo and a red tie. "I've been waiting for you. I want you with me when I make the announcement. Come on, there's someone I want you to meet."

Warren led him by the arm, delivering him to a window balcony. A woman in a blue dress was standing alone, staring at the lights of Chinatown. "Diana?"

She turned. "Oh . . ."

"Diana, I want you to meet my cousin Ben. Ben, meet Diana Mayhew."

"Mr. Kane." Her handshake was cool and firm. She seemed vaguely familiar.

"No, no, it's Ben," Warren said. "Diana's British—"

"Australian," she said quickly. Her deep blue eyes stayed on Warren a moment, then moved to Benjamin. She had red hair. "Actually my father was British, I guess that makes me British by default, in some eyes."

Benjamin nodded. "That accounts for the accent."

"Does it? I thought you blokes had the accents."

Her dry, cool manner had an edge of nervousness. He wondered if she was one of the press. He hoped not.

"I love this lady," Warren said. "You will too." He patted Benjamin's shoulder. "Look, entertain Diana, will you? I'll be back."

Benjamin watched him slide into the crowd. When he turned back Diana was staring at him.

"You're taller than I expected," she said. "A little younger, too."

"Expected?"

"Warren told me about you, said you weren't especially enthralled with this notion of his when he first brought it up."

"I could do without the theatrics."

Diana smiled for the first time. She wore a diamond necklace and matching earrings, but they seemed to make her uncomfortable. She wasn't one of Warren's jet-set crowd, not hiding out on this balcony.

"Have you been here before . . . San Francisco?"

"Never been to the States before," she said. Her gaze had drifted back to the lights. "Flew directly from London."

"You're in the diamond business?"

"Diamond business?" She gave him a sharp look. "Heavens, no. Is that what you think?"

"No, I—"

"I'm the announcement."

"What?"

"Warren's surprise. You're going to find out soon enough anyway. I'm" —she glanced nervously into the ballroom—"I'm going with you. To the Himalayas. I'm the surprise addition to the trip up the mountain. It's to be you, Warren and me after the stone. The three of us. I just wasn't expecting all this—"

"*You* are going?"

"Just like the first trek, two men and a woman—the heirs of the original adventurers, as Warren likes to put it. Well, John Barbaree was along on that first trek, too, you know." Diana Mayhew looked Benjamin in the eye. "He was my grandfather."

It took a moment to register before Benjamin understood. Warren had covered every angle. He was taking a *woman* with him into the high hills. A goddess had created Shelkagari, why not a woman along to find it, the granddaughter of Jack Barbaree—named Diana.

"Surprise," she said.

◆ SIXTY-ONE

KATHMANDU

FOUR DAYS WAITING FOR their gear and a snafu with the air freight service had added unnecessary drama. The hiring of a Nepalese guide and a cook were featured on American television networks. Warren had forbidden interviews with Diana (to protect and insure her mysteriousness).

Benjamin avoided reporters. In the wait for the equipment to arrive he walked to a small village in the nearby hills. The temples and shrines of these people were intricately designed, architecture inspired by emotional dedication.

"Mr. Kane, I presume."

Benjamin sat on the edge of a stone walkway, watching a band of rhesus monkeys scampering for food on the steps of a shrine. He had returned to Kathmandu from the west on a visit to Swayambhu, the valley's most holy Buddhist temple.

"You seem pensive," Diana Mayhew said. She was wearing slacks and a khaki shirt. Her hair, almost golden in the afternoon sunlight, was tied back. A canvas art bag hung from her shoulder. She nodded at the walkway. "May I?"

He dusted a spot with his hand.

"What are you doing here?"

He pointed at the massive dome of the Swayambhu temple. "To see that. What are you doing out? I thought Warren kept you on a short leash—"

"Nobody has me on a leash," Diana said in a flash of temper. She set her bag down. "Actually I got out to do a bit of sketching. I didn't expect this city to be such a treasure trove of subjects. The people, the sights, the landscapes . . ."

Diana was an artist, that much Benjamin knew from the biographical information Warren allowed to be known about her. A fine arts graduate of Melbourne University. She had done some acting in college and spent a short time with a modeling agency but was considered too big to make it a career. That's all Benjamin knew. In the ten days since leaving San Francisco Benjamin had had very little contact with Diana Mayhew. Warren had kept her inaccessible to the public, which by extension made her inaccessible to him. It would change once they got into the hills out of reach of a microphone. In the meantime Diana was the draw, the silent, mysterious element of this group. And she handled it very well.

A monkey approached, chattering, and touched one of Benjamin's boots, pulling at the shoestring. After a few moments two others joined him.

"Don't scare them off," Diana whispered as she pulled a pad from her bag and began sketching. Rhesus monkeys appeared on the page, poured from her charcoal.

"You're good," Benjamin said.

Her eyes flicked from monkey to pad, in quick concentration. "They aren't that difficult. The eyes, there's the trick."

A larger monkey, leader of the band, screeched across the walkway, dispersing Diana's subjects. Her fingers continued over the drawing, filling in details.

Benjamin was fascinated by her talent. "Is it as effortless as it looks?"

"Wildlife is my specialty. I grew up drawing animals in the Outback. I learned it from an aborigine, charcoal because we couldn't afford chalk. Later on I did watercolors. When I was ten I was selling drawings to tattoo parlors in Kalgoorlie."

"Tattoo parlors?"

"It's how we made our money, Mr. Kane. We weren't a rich bunch like your lot. My mother and pops got married in a five-minute ceremony on a loading platform of the Trans-Australian Railway. Trains used to come by once a week. Still do. He was a miner, and she was a camp cook. He died when I was eleven."

"How did you wind up in London?"

Her fingers stopped a moment. "Scholarship, you could say."

"Do you like it there?"

"London is the center of the world to a girl from the desert fringe of Western Australia."

"That's where you met Warren, in London?"

She hesitated, then held the pad up for him to see. "How's that, then?"

"The aborigine taught you very well."

Diana shrugged. "Not bad, coming from a family of miners. W.A. isn't known for its artists."

Jack Barbaree had arrived in Western Australia on a tramp steamer in 1930. The sketchy biographical data said he had tried his luck at gold prospecting and like most others, he didn't find it. Benjamin's awareness of Barbaree had come from Yurev or Abby, and it didn't add to a flattering picture.

"What was your grandfather like? I know you were young when he died but do you have any . . . feeling for him?"

Diana slid the pad back into her bag. "It's getting late," she said. "We'd better head for the hotel."

"What's the matter?"

"Nothing." She stood up.

"I was just asking because—"

"I know what you and your family think of my grandfather." Diana's expression was dark. "He wasn't a monster, you know. He was a kind and gentle man from what I remember, which isn't much."

"I didn't mean anything by it, Diana. I was curious."

"I don't discuss him. Warren said I didn't have to talk about my grandfather, and I won't, especially to you." She slung the bag over her shoulder. "Anything else, Mr. Kane?"

It was a long silent walk back to the hotel.

◆ SIXTY-TWO

THE MIDDAY SUN BORE down on the waiting DC-3, engines running. Four people stood beside the plane's open fuselage door, blinking against the swirling dust from the prop wash.

"All right, cheese everybody."

Warren grinned at the cameraman from the center of the group, one arm over Benjamin's shoulder and the other around Diana. Warren wore safari khakis and an Australian bush hat—blood red—with a thin red strap that hung below his chin.

The photographers satisfied, waving their arms against the dust, Benjamin helped Diana into the plane. Warren was last to enter, saluting his audience before the cargo door slammed shut.

"It begins, Ben," Warren said, bending down over Benjamin's seat to shout above the noise of the engines.

The charter plane rolled on the steamy runway forever, grudgingly lifting off the tarmac, barely gliding above the trees. Benjamin watched the capital slide away below, swallowed by the lush valley as the plane banked and gained altitude. Mukjom was less than a hundred miles away, a small trading village and police outpost with the shortest, northernmost runway in the entire kingdom. To approach it at this time of year a pilot had to fly the Slot, a narrow north-south corridor between and below the Dhaulagiri and Annapurna peaks—following the Kali Gandaki gorge.

A landscape of rich green patchwork gave way to faded olive wrinkles as the plane climbed above the foothills. After twenty minutes the starboard wing dipped, banking in a slow turn, and Benjamin saw Annapurna's jagged twin peaks, white and forbidding, seemingly near enough to touch. Straight below was the gorge, a black, rugged crack in the earth. Benjamin strained to keep it in view, pressing his cheek against the plexiglass as the plane eased out of the turn. For several minutes Benjamin stared, mesmerized, into the dark, winding chasm. It was a breathtaking sight, haunted by ghosts.

"Five minutes . . ."

The pilot's voice was startling, booming from a thicket of static through the speaker.

"Passengers, cinch your seat belts. We're descending now. The approach gets a little rough with these winds."

The buffeting began as the angle steepened, and Benjamin grasped the armrests of his seat, squeezing them tighter as the airplane bounced beneath him, bucking from side to side in the turbulence. Outside his window the entire surface of the wing vibrated. The cargo bay was a hollow chamber, reverberating with the screaming noise of the engines. Benjamin glanced across the aisle. Serchen, the little wrinkled cook, who had never been on a plane, held the kit bag in his lap with a death grip.

Benjamin stared past the wing, waiting. They would be passing Benithog, the village at the mouth of the Valley of Weeping Winds, and Benjamin waited to see the sight he had only heard about. The uneven face of the gorge was very near. Its craggy walls were ugly and dark, no more than fifty feet below the plane. When it came Benjamin saw it for only a moment—an incredible chunk of rock slid beneath the plane. He was astounded by the size, much bigger than even he had imagined. An enormous slab of granite, smoothed by the winds of eons and as big as the Chrysler Building, lay wedged across the gorge. The humpback.

Benjamin tried to imagine Yurev and Abby, in their twenties, crawling on their bellies across the scarred rock. He had heard again and again the story of Yurev grabbing Abby's hair in the wind and sliding to the edge, but he had to see the humpback to understand the terror. The Kali Gandaki River was a thin, crooked ribbon two miles below. Benjamin couldn't wipe the sweat off his hands.

"Did you see what we just came through? Did you *see* it?"

Warren sat on the edge of a wooden cart that had been brought to unload cargo from the plane. The wind was brisk, and he blew into his cupped hands for warmth.

"The wing couldn't have been more than twenty feet away from that canyon wall!" He looked at Benjamin. "Did you *see* that?"

"I saw."

Benjamin had just returned from walking Diana to the tiny flat-roofed building that served as air terminal for the village. Her only comment since leaving the plane had been a request to find the rest room. Benjamin didn't lose the rubbery feeling in his legs until he returned to get Warren. Mukjom didn't have a paved tarmac like at Kathmandu. Its runway was a flat clearing populated by wary chickens bordering the gorge.

Benjamin offered a hand to Warren. "You all right?"

Warren pushed his hand away, hopped down from the cart. "I'm cold, is all."

"Well, we're at twelve thousand feet elevation," the pilot said from the cargo door. He jumped to the ground, sending a bony rooster scurrying. "Thin air is cold air, especially in these mountains. I told you to wear something warm, Mr. Romanov."

Warren blew into his hands, looking toward the terminal. "Where's our guide? He was supposed to meet us."

"Probably still beating the bush for porters," the pilot said. "Won't be many'll want to go across the plateau this time of year." He glanced at the gray range of peaks in the distance. "I hear it's cold as a bitch up there. If you change your mind I'll be going back in about fifteen minutes."

The pilot, an American from Idaho named Candy, had been flying a charter service for ten years in Nepal. Benjamin was surprised to find so many westerners living in this isolated country. Many of them operated hotels or small restaurants in the capital, catering to the tourists. Candy was the only pilot in Nepal who flew into Mukjom. It was one of his regular stops, ferrying the shift change to the frontier police station once a month.

"No, we're not going back yet," Warren said impatiently. "You just be here waiting for us in ten days."

"I'll be here."

The guide's name was Thak.

"No can do, Warren sahib. No Mukjom peoples wanting to go walking along to Lo Mantang."

They were seated on mats before a small table, Diana and Benjamin flanking Warren at one end, Thak alone at the other.

"Tell them we'll pay double the going rate," Warren said.

"Mukjom peoples not caring for more monies, Warren sahib." Failing in his first task for the American expedition leader was humiliating but it wasn't his fault. The Nepalese regulation about expeditions into the high hills distinguished between the two kinds of people who lived in the kingdom—hill people and valley people. Hill people lived a more rugged existence, many never venturing to the lowland. By comparison valley people were urban city dwellers. As trekking became more popular with tourists the government was forced to decree that only hill people could hire on as load-bearers. Valley people died in the high hills. Falling off mountains carrying overloaded packs was common. And so the regulation.

Lo Mantang was a long hard trek across the Tibetan Plateau, which was a dangerous place no matter what season it happened to be. There were bandits—*khampas*—in the Kingdom of Lo, the Red-Faced Devils, so-called because of the ochre dye they smeared on their faces against the bitter cold. There were vicious dogs that traveled in murderous packs in the Kingdom of Lo. And, finally, there was the wind. The Kingdom of Lo was also known as Land of the Fearless Wind. More than the bands of *khampas* or marauding dogs, hill people feared the winds that sweep across the plains of the forbidden kingdom. It was believed that Churels haunted the winds of Lo—women who walked on backward feet and whispered songs of hell. Churels could make you crazy.

"We don't need porters," Benjamin said. "We can carry what we need ourselves. One pack animal can manage the food."

"Do you know how much gear I've had flown up here?"

"Yes, too much."

When Warren protested, Benjamin said, "The question is, do you want to go on or go back . . . and explain to all those reporters that you couldn't find anyone to carry your air mattress. Do what you like—go, stay—but I'm in Mukjom now, and I *am* going on."

Warren looked at Diana. "What do *you* want to do?"

Diana shrugged. "I rather like rice. And I can't imagine how to explain it if we return to Kathmandu. He's right about that, you know."

"You don't mind?" Warren looked surprised.

"Oh, I bloody well mind, all right." She folded her arms across her chest. "I don't fancy lugging about a kit bag for five days, but I don't see we have a choice. Do you? And, Mr. Kane, you can't go alone and you bloody well know it." She turned to Thak, who had been listening in awe. "Mr. Thak, can you get us an animal and have it packed and ready to leave for the morning?"

Thak had never been called mister in his life. His head bobbed several times. "Oh, quite assuredly, yes, miss memsahib, can do."

"Please do, then." Diana climbed to her feet. "Gentlemen, that's how we do things in Australia, we just do it. Carping at the fire isn't going to get us off this bloody cold mountain." She bent down and retrieved her mat. "Tomorrow, then."

◆ SIXTY-THREE

WARREN WAS ANGRY THAT nearly seven hundred of the nine hundred pounds of equipment and food he had brought along had to be left behind.

Each of the sahibs carried a pack that contained less than thirty pounds, mostly food. But even thirty pounds could be a burden, Benjamin learned, when the carrier was unaccustomed to bending at the waist and walking over uneven terrain.

Thak had hired a yak to carry the rest of the equipment, about one hundred and fifty pounds. Actually there were two yaks in Mukjom, a cow and a bull, but the owner would not part with the cow. She provided milk for four families and was temperamentally unsuitable as a beast of burden. The bull, called Solo, was only slightly more suitable.

Solo was a giant black shaggy beast, five feet tall at the shoulder with a long flowing coat that nearly swept the ground. His nose had been fitted with a ring of juniper wood tied to a rope which a yak handler used to guide the animal. Serchen, the wrinkled little Nepalese, barely recovered from his airplane ride, was to be yak-boy as well as cook on this trek. He had handled *dzos*, a crossbreed between yak and cow. The little man said *dzos* were tamer than yaks but that he could make friends with this bull. Benjamin didn't believe it. Solo did not have a friendly hair on his hide. From the first moment the gear was tied to his massive back the infuriated bull kicked up its hind legs like a bronco, flailing its head from side to side, gouging at the packs with its horns, after which all of the load lay on the ground. The second and third loading of Solo's packs produced the same

421

result. Undaunted, Serchen tried again, cinching the harness ropes even tighter around the brute, all the while singing to the angry bull as if to a child. The barefoot cook, who might easily have been trampled or gored, danced in and out of danger, touching the horns, caressing the head of the beast between its eyes, chanting a monotonous tune. On the fourth attempt, the yak gave up, too tired to fight the inevitable. With a smile revealing brown teeth, Serchen gave a slight bow to the sahibs and held the rope to the yak's nose ring tight in his tiny fist. *"Saathi,"* he said. Friends.

The first day was filled with unhappy adjustments to the terrain and the pace. Trekking in the highlands, Benjamin discovered, was a torturously slow ordeal. From Mukjom, Thak followed a path that led deep into the Kali Gandaki gorge. The short green grass of the upper plateau disappeared as they made their way along the narrow trail that hugged the side of the cliff, entering a parched, barren world of towering ochre rock. It was like edging into the Grand Canyon with its hues of red, brown and yellow. The Kali Gandaki was little more than a stream on a bone-white riverbed. Ahead, the gorge stretched to the horizon like a deep, winding groove in a sandpile under a blue, crystal-clear sky.

They reached the bottom of the gorge after three hours, walking single file, Warren following Thak, Benjamin behind Diana, and Serchen with Solo at the rear.

"What desolation." Warren stared through his binoculars at the gorge ahead, his red bush hat pushed back on his head, the band stained dark with sweat. They'd stopped to rest among the rocks beside the stream. The yak stood in the shallows up to its belly, drinking the icy water. "It makes Western Australia look like a picnic ground. Want to take a look?" He glanced at Diana, lowering the binoculars, ready to lift the strap that held them around his neck.

Diana shook her head. She held a sketch pad on her knees, her pencil making bold strokes, filling in an angle of cliff with shade. The arms and neck of her khaki shirt were moist with perspiration.

"That's good," Warren offered, leaning down toward her. "You did that just now?"

Diana gave him a pointed look. "I'm an artist—remember?"

"Oh, right." Warren toweled himself with a kerchief, glancing back at the cliffs. "God, it's hot. Why is it so hot? Yesterday it was cold."

"We're below the plateau, out of the wind," Benjamin said. "It's the heat retained in the walls of the canyon that makes it hot." He sat against a sun-bleached rock, fanning his face with his hat.

"I guess it pays to be an architect."

Benjamin shrugged. "The sun's rays are stronger because of the altitude. It heats the cliff walls and the rocks down here." He nodded at the opposite wall. "Makes a natural oven. And the source of my knowledge isn't a book but Serchen."

"Warren sahib, we please be moving now." Thak gestured for everyone to get up. "Solo not feeling so good in warm climates. Bad for yak having too much warmness."

Warren climbed to his feet, motioning to Diana and Benjamin. "You heard the man. We don't want to inconvenience the yak."

They walked for four more hours, making camp at a bend in the gorge. Along the way they'd passed a village high on the ridge of a cliff. Surrounded on three sides by painted, windowless stone walls, the village had the look of a huge white box or, more likely, a fortress. The side without a wall faced the gorge, a perfect lookout point. People had gathered to watch the tiny caravan pass. They did not wave. The houses visible from the floor of the canyon were three stories high and apparently flat-roofed. It was a reminder to Benjamin that he was moving into a different world, and it excited him. Into the world of his father's, and Yurev's and Abby's, past. The thatched slanted roof houses of Kathmandu with its outgoing, friendly Nepalese Hindus were behind him. He was entering a fiercely spartan land of Tibetan Buddhists whose Mongolian ancestry included Kublai Khan and a rich warrior heritage, including severe distrust of foreigners.

With the setting sun, the temperature plummeted. By nightfall the dry, warm breeze that had pushed at their backs all afternoon, turned cold. Benjamin and Thak pitched the nylon tents while Warren and Diana went looking for firewood. Serchen's first meal, a rice dish, was supplemented by canned peaches and baked beans from Warren's stock of food.

"We came, we looked, so far we've conquered nothing." Diana rubbed her hands together, pushing her fingers deeper into her gloves. She pulled the parka tight around her neck against the chill. "I must say this all sounded less risky in London in the summer."

Serchen's fire crackled, emitting low heat and flame, casting flickering shadows across the rocky cliff. Diana and Benjamin sat across the fire from Warren, who stared into the fire as if he could see the glowing future.

Benjamin edged closer to the fire. His back was stiff and he forced himself to stand, punishing his sore joints. "There's one thing you keep forgetting, Warren. Ignore, I should say."

"What's that, Ben?"

"That we *are* looking for Shelkagari."

"Are we?" Warren smiled at Diana. "He's right. I keep forgetting that.

By dusk the next day they reached the village of Torjok. It had been a long, hard day, even hotter than before. Thak had led them along the slopes of snow-capped mountains that rose like gray icebergs ten thousand feet above. The trail had deteriorated from a hard footpath to a series of sandy parallel ruts made by herds of goats. It was all hill walking, climbing up the shoulder of one in loose slippery dirt and sliding down another. By staying to the western ranges Thak avoided the deep eroded canyons bordering the gorge which began to widen as they progressed northward.

On the ridge of a mountain Benjamin could see into the gorge—just awesome, stretching out below him toward the horizon like a grainy sepia photograph, two miles wide, winding and disappearing among the sea of hills that lay ahead. They had reached thirteen thousand feet, and patches of a sturdy, weedlike grass were the only plant life and an occasional juniper. Everything else was brown, sandy dirt, strewn with rocks and back-breaking to walk on. Thak had pointed out the village two hours before they reached it, bleached white buildings crowded together at the notch of a ridge. About that time Benjamin had felt the wind, and as the caravan approached the village the wind grew stronger, coming from above and behind. His body ached as they trudged single file into the settlement, happy finally to arrive at a resting place. Torjok was a milestone—it marked the end of hill climbing. The village stood on the edge of the great Central Asian steppes and the southern border of Mustang. From this point on he would walk in the Kingdom of Lo.

"Not speaking to any peoples, Benji-sahib." Thak's face was pale as he whispered to Benjamin. They were in the center of the village near a communal well. There were ten buildings in Torjok. Stone three-story homes, which meant at least fifty families lived here, but there was not a soul to be seen. Benjamin had been so preoccupied with thoughts of rest and food that he became aware something was wrong only by the look of fear in Thak's eyes. Warren and Diana loitered beside the well. Benjamin slipped the pack from his shoulders and hung it on the heavy timber that framed the well. He was not encouraged to find the wood splintered, apparently recently, by bullets.

"What's going on?" Warren said in a low voice. He kept his head down, pretending to inspect the well. "Where are the people?"

Benjamin rested his foot on the stone bench where Diana was slumped. "I don't know." In front of the houses were large baskets stacked with gnarled, twisted juniper branches. Each basket was at least five feet high. Benjamin tried to imagine where so much wood had come from. He hadn't seen a tree in two hours.

Serchen, leading the yak, moved to the well, tethered the animal to a post, then sat down, legs crossed, with his head bowed.

Thak walked over to Warren but spoke to Diana. "Memsahib, please turning face down. Keeping hat on head. Not speaking."

"What is going on?" Warren demanded.

"Please, Warren sahib. Be not talking. Most dangerous for you to be speaking to peoples here."

Warren glanced around. "People? Who? Where?"

"*Khampas* at this place."

"Who?"

"Tibetan bandits," Benjamin said, suddenly understanding Thak's predicament.

"But—"

"Shut up, Warren. We could be dead fast if you start anything. Nobody here is impressed with Romanov Diamonds or its boss." Warren nodded, sat on the bench alongside Diana.

To the Khampas, Chinese, like everyone else not Tibetan, were foreigners, and when they entered Tibetan territory, chasing Tibet's living god, the Dalai Lama, it was like waving a red flag in the face of an angry bull. *Khampas* took a special delight in killing Chinese, and Benjamin prayed that his light skin did not qualify him as Chinese in the minds of a *khampa* . . . because from the shadows of a nearby doorway one of them was just now emerging.

He was a large man with greasy, braided black hair wearing a khaki *chuba* and heavy boots. He carried a rifle on a sling over his shoulder, and cartridge belts crisscrossed his chest. Stuck in his belt without a sheath was a *khukuri*, an enormous curved knife half the length of a sword.

Thak went to him, smiling and bowing, talked very fast and pointed to the sahibs. After a time the *khampa* snapped a command and Thak was instantly silent. He pushed past Thak, moving toward the well.

Benjamin's feet were frozen to the ground, but it seemed the *khampa*'s interest was in Solo, and he walked by Benjamin to inspect the yak.

Serchen cowered as the soldier slapped the packs on the animal's back with the *khukuri*. The nylon tents were wrapped around their poles and secured with rope to the outside of the packs. The *khampa*'s curved knife sliced through several layers of nylon almost without a sound, then, with quick, short flicks, severed the harness ropes. Solo's burden slid off his back from both sides, crashing noisily to the ground in two heaps. Startled by the sound and the sudden loss of weight, the bull stamped its hind legs. Benjamin had seen this reaction many times in the last two days. Solo was a skittish animal, given to snorting and kicking and shaking his huge head at the slightest provocation, especially at night with the far-away howling of wild dogs. Little Serchen had been a godsend when it came to the yak. He talked to Solo on the trail, sang to him in the evenings, even slept with him. And the yak had responded to the little Nepalese like a dog to his master. When Serchen sprang to his feet, reaching out with skinny arms to calm his massive companion, it was a reenactment of faithful concern that surprised no one—except the *khampa*.

The warrior struck with abrupt swiftness, his wrist bent back and slightly turned. The knife stroke was a powerful backhand slash, a practiced, almost graceful killing blow. The blade of the *khukuri* caught Serchen just below his right jaw, slicing across his neck with such force that his head almost separated from his shoulders.

Serchen dropped where he stood. His face did not even register surprise. The yak glanced at the crumpled body with an unconcerned, slow-eyed look. Shaking its head like a dog with a tick, it scratched an ear against the post, ringing his bell. The *khampa* took even less notice. Wiping the knife clean behind his knee, he poked through the packs on the ground with a casualness of a vegetable shopper.

The *khampa* kicked something that rattled, glanced at Thak, pointing to the pack with his knife. It was one of Warren's food packs. Thak hurried over and emptied the contents, spilling cans of fruit and baked beans on the ground. The knife tip punctured a can of Del Monte fruit cocktail, and the *khampa* tested the juice with his tongue from the palm of his hand. Apparently pleased, he held the can like a coconut, letting the bleeding container aimed at his mouth pour the sticky liquid over his face.

Benjamin pushed the image of Serchen out of his mind. If the *khampa* could be persuaded to take the canned fruit they just might all survive . . . it could be an offering of peace, a gesture of friendship . . . anything to keep him from using his knife again.

The question became moot when the *khampa* raised his hand. In the time it took to drain the fruit can, nine more *khampas* appeared in the tiny square, dressed alike, some with automatic weapons. Two of them relieved the sahibs of their backpacks while the others attacked the canvas bags. The *khampa* with the knife, speaking who knew what, pointed at Benjamin with his weapon and motioned him forward.

Benjamin glanced at Warren, who only stared back, his lips blue. Diana's head was bowed, the brim of her hat quivering. Earlier on the trail she had put on her parka against the mounting cold and stuffed her hair into her hat. Luckily, Benjamin thought, she didn't look female. In the long shadows of late afternoon she appeared to be just a frightened sahib, like the rest.

Benjamin took a breath of cold air, squared his shoulders, and walked on rubber legs to stand beside Thak. Like a pair of schoolboys sentenced to face their school master, they awaited fate from the man with fruit juice on his chin.

The *khampa* spoke to Benjamin, waited.

Benjamin stared at him. "I don't know what he wants." He looked at Thak for help. "Tell him, I don't"—he felt the blade beside his ear, froze as the *khampa* tilted his head, interested in something else. The tip of the knife drew a line down Benjamin's neck, hooking the chain inside his collar. The *khampa* squinted hard when he raised the medallion dangling at the end of the chain. He stared at the devil dog *chatra*, then let it drop back on Benjamin's chest. When he spoke again his voice was much louder, as if the communication problem was a matter of volume.

Benjamin felt the *khampa*'s breath on his face. Something had changed. The *khampa* studied him in a different way, as if he were searching for something. Very slowly, Benjamin shook his head, acutely aware of the *khukuri*. "I don't understand, I don't speak your . . . words . . ." His mouth was too dry to go on. He tried to communicate with his eyes.

The *khampa* returned the stare, finally grunted, barked at Thak, then folded his arms, the knife pointed at Benjamin's chest.

Thak's translation: "Benji-sahib, this being *pombo* Angdu Pal. He is wanting to know why you coming to this place."

"We're friends," Benjamin said quickly, holding the *khampa*'s gaze. "Tell him he doesn't have anything to fear from us."

"He is knowing this already, I think, Benji-sahib."

"Tell him we're going to Lo Mantang. Tell him if there's anything we can share with him and his men we'd be happy to."

Thak relayed the message. Twenty feet away the other soldiers were busy ripping into the packs, picking over the food and clothing. One stripped the boots from Serchen's body.

"Angdu Pal is saying thank you," Thak said, "and wishing you good lucks on your journey . . . He is also saying many dangerous peoples on way to Mantang."

Benjamin had no trouble keeping a straight face. The *khampa* leader's eyes bore into him, adding malice to a smile, then snapped an order to his men and the soldiers moved off, their *chubas* loaded with booty.

It took them less than ten minutes to load the baskets of wood on Tibetan horses and lead them out of the village the same way Solo had come. Angdu Pal was last to leave. Mounted on his pony, he circled the well twice, prancing over the strewn remnants of canvas packs and their littered contents, his stare never leaving Benjamin. Stopping beside Warren, the *khampa* reached down and snatched the red bush hat from Warren's head and pulled it snugly over his own hair. He then slapped his horse's flank with the flat blade of his knife and galloped off toward the fading sun, and never looked back.

Benjamin began to shake. His wobbly legs would not support him and he dropped to his knees. Trembling fear caught hold of him, a swirling darkness that he could not hold back.

Diana was beside him, stroking his head, when he came to. She was on her knees, her face smeared with tears.

In the center of the square he could see Warren, standing with his hands at his sides, staring at the corpse of Serchen.

No one could speak.

◆ SIXTY-FOUR

"THEY'VE TAKEN EVERYTHING WORTH taking," Warren said. Butter lamps gave his face a yellowish sheen. He sat on a mat beside Benjamin in a small room warmed by a fireplace. Diana held a wooden cup of steaming tea in both her hands, and still she shivered. Warren, who had gone with Thak to the square to take inventory, stared at the fire. "They left us flashlights and toilet paper, but food, extra clothes, boots, even the medical kit—all gone. They threw away the binoculars but kept my camera. What are they going to do with a Nikon?"

The people had come out from their homes only when it was clear that the *khampas* had left. The *pombo* of Torjok was the head of the village's largest family, and after a brief conference with Thak offered his house to the strangers as a gesture of peace. He was an old man, even by hill standards, with long gray hair wrapped around his head and held in place with a thick band. His name was Tsetin, and he explained through Thak that the *khampas* had ridden into his village the day before looking for firewood. The ten baskets had been filled by villagers who had walked miles into the surrounding hills gathering juniper twigs. The soldiers had taken over one of the houses, drinking *rakshi* and using the timber in the well frame for target practice. It was unlucky that the sahibs had arrived when they did—twenty minutes later and the *khampas* would have been gone.

"What about Serchen?" Diana glanced up from her tea. "Did someone . . ."

"Thak's taking care of that," Warren said. He looked at Benjamin, who was studying Thak's map, and nodded toward the outside wall. "You know what's out there? More of the same. Between here and up there, Magars, Thak calls them . . ."

"You knew the risks," Benjamin said quietly.

"Bandits. I heard about bandits, I didn't know they were killers. And they know where we're going . . . all they have to do is wait for us."

"They know we don't have anything of use to them. You said so yourself, they took everything. I don't think that *khampa* would bother to ambush us when he could have done the job here."

"Right, Benjamin, the architect is suddenly an expert on the homicidal bandits of Central Asia."

"You want to go back?"

It wasn't a question Warren needed to consider. "Yes, I want to go back. I'm not going out there. Enough is enough. We came as far as we could. No one's going to fault us for turning back, not after this. We've done what we set out to do." He shrugged. "We'll pack up, what's left, and go home."

"You go," Benjamin said. "Thak will take you. I'll keep the yak."

"To do what?"

"I'm going on."

Diana leaned up on her knees, looking at Benjamin. "You stupid, bloody sod. Do you *want* to die? Become a martyr to this ridiculous obsession of yours? Good Lord, a man just died before our eyes. Isn't that enough?"

"I'm going to Lo Mantang."

"You're crazy if you believe that," Warren said. "Do you think you can get past those people without food? Not that you'd need much with your throat slit open."

"I know a way." Benjamin stabbed his finger at the map. "The same way Ayrub Ravi went a thousand years ago." He took his notepad from his jacket. "He left directions, remember? I have them, right here. I am going to Lo, Warren. To look for Shelkagari. *That's* why I came."

"No. What do I say when I get to Kathmandu . . . that I turned back but my cousin went on? I'm not a fool or a coward, Ben. You know that. But my objective is finished. You came on my terms, my instigation. Now—"

"No, Warren, I came on *my* terms. I gave credibility to your promotion . . . *that's* why you wanted me. Because of my link to the attempts before —my father's and Abby's and Yurev's—"

"We're leaving in the morning," Warren said, not choosing to argue. "We'll take whatever we can salvage."

"Begging your pardons, Warren sahib, but most better we be going tonight," said Thak, who had just entered.

"Tonight?"

Thak sat down before the small table. He poured himself hot tea. "Most better. Tomorrow maybe *khampas* coming back, Tsetin is telling me. Most better, going tonight. Taking yak, after eating foods, *pombo* Tsetin is saying. Be far away from Torjok when sun is coming."

"Look, we've walked for twelve hours today. Uphill. You want to go back down those hills again without rest in the dark?"

"If the alternative is waking up to find those men," Diana said, "then I'll go back on my knees and be bloody glad to do it."

"To Mukjom, then," Warren said. "We're not going any further. After what happened to Serchen—"

"Mukjom?" Thak looked confused. "Not Mukjom, sahib." He pointed north. "Lo is lying along that way."

"We're not going to Lo," Warren told him, voice rising. "We're going back. Mukjom. We're going back to the airstrip."

Thak looked at Benjamin for help. "Benji-sahib, please . . . be looking on map. *Khampas* going to Magar at cliff village. Jomolekh. Please . . . be showing Warren sahib."

Benjamin looked at the map, found where Jomolekh was marked, beside the Kali Gandaki canyon. He handed the map to Diana.

"Oh, my God . . ."

"You can't go to Mukjom." Benjamin's voice was calm. He was going to Lo. So was Warren.

"Ben. I'm still running this expedition—"

"We can't go to Mukjom," Benjamin went on, "because we've already passed Jomolekh. Yesterday. Remember the village on the edge of the gorge with the white walls? Jomolekh."

The lines in Warren's forehead deepened. "Yesterday?" He grabbed up the map from Diana.

"It means we can't go back yet," Benjamin said. "It means that our friend—the fellowing wearing your hat—is *behind* us." He would have smiled, but twisting the knife would only have spoiled the moment.

"Tsetin is saying most better to be going to Lo through the Way of the Ancients, the Valley of Winds." Thak lay the map between Warren and

Benjamin, pushing his finger along contour lines north of Torjok. "This way."

Warren looked at the map. "Valley of what?"

"Windy places, sahib. Lo is meaning wind in Tibetan speaking."

"How long to Mantang?"

"Walking three days."

"What about running into more *khampas?*"

"This way not being used. Very much cold. Very much winds. *Khampas* not liking winds so much."

Warren studied the map. "It's a longer way, isn't it? This route to Mantang?"

"One day more, but no *khampas.*"

Tsetin spoke from the other end of the table, gesturing with frail hands raised above his head.

Thak nodded. "*Pombo* Tsetin is saying very much dangers in Valley of Winds." He lowered his voice so the old man would not hear, as if he could understand. "Tsetin being Bon-po, Warren sahib. Most all peoples here being Bon-pos. Believing in magic and other strangeness. He is saying it is a terrible place . . . more bad than *khampas.* But he is a Bon-po."

Warren looked to Benjamin.

"Bon-po is the oldest religion in Central Asia," Benjamin told him. "It predates Buddhism and Hinduism. It's preoccupied with sorcery and mystical aberrations, even more than Tibetan Buddhism. What Tsetin is afraid of is the Churels—"

"Churels? More *khampas!*"

"No. Churels are women. Or rather the ghosts of women who died in childbirth, pale-skinned in death and carried on the winds. They haunt lonely roads looking for the minds of men. Something like the sirens in the *Odyssey,* they sing in the wind. Churels are a lot more to be feared than *khampas.*" Thak nodded in agreement.

"That's it? Singing ghosts?"

"Apparently it's enough, Warren."

Warren shook his head. "I'll take on a hundred of them if it means avoiding real live killers. I'm *not* a Bon-po." He turned to Thak. "If we go this way, you're sure we won't run into any *khampas?*"

"*Khampas* also not liking Churels, Warren sahib. They not going to Gumpa Te."

"Gumpa Te?"

"Bon-po holy place. Lamas all gone long times gone. No peoples going to Gumpa Te. Churels living in Gumpa Te now."

"It's an abandoned monastery," Benjamin said. "Didn't you read my notes on Ravi's text? This is the same way Ayrub Ravi went in the eleventh century, following Ahile. Don't you *read* anything but profit and loss statements? Never mind, but let me fill you in. The star, Ahile, was known in hill folklore as The Lonely One. It was the one heavenly body that didn't change position through the night. The Greek name for Ahile was Cynosura, the dog's tail, because it was the last and brightest of the string of seven stars that made up the Dog constellation. It was the North Star and its spinning appendage, the Little Dipper, that led Ayrub Ravi up the Kali Gandaki gorge into the Kingdom of Lo to Gumpa Te, and finally to Mantang. The Lonely One is the one constant in the whole enigma of Shelkagari. It can guide us just as it did Ravi—"

"The Lonely One? Singing sirens? The Valley of Winds?" Warren shook his head. "Is this real or a George Lucas nightmare?"

"Real enough."

"All right, if we're going to Lo Mantang, let's do it." Warren untangled his legs, stretching them out. "I can't wait to see this garden spot of Central Asia." He looked at Benjamin. "The *original* windy city. That should appeal to you, cousin. Sort of home away from home." To Diana, he said, "What say, my dear? I promised you adventure, didn't I? Well, it seems you're to have a bellyful of it now. *Real* adventure."

Diana's stare was hard. "I'll tell you what's real. A man died here. Remember Serchen, the helpful little man who talked to yaks? I want to know what you intend to do about him. Are we going to bury him or just ignore the body as we steal out of this village?"

"I told you, that's been taken care of."

"Taken care of?" She shook her head. "Is that all it is to you, a loose end? And you call *khampas* barbarians."

"Disposing of the dead takes three days," Benjamin said. "It's a ritual. Obviously we can't—"

"Oh, right. Do either of you care? Have either of you said a single word of regret over the death of that kind little man?"

"Don't get hysterical," Warren said. "These are his sort of people. They'll see that he gets a proper burial. They take care of their own. We can't wait around."

"There will be people to mourn for him," Benjamin said.

"And who, I wonder, is going to mourn for us? You are, both of you, bloody fools. If we go on, we still have to come back. Have you thought about that? How are you going to manage it, I'd like to know? The *khampas* will still be behind us, waiting. What are you going to do about them?"

Benjamin and Warren were silent. Only Thak had an answer.

"I think praying, memsahib," he said.

Thak led Solo, picking his way along the rocky ridge by the light of the moon. They walked for two hours before resting, then three hours more until they reached the pass that opened onto the Valley of Winds.

Benjamin had fought to exhaustion against his flapping *chuba* in the wail of wind. The last two hours he had walked without thinking, just one step and the next, keeping his head bowed and holding the yak's tail. He was aware of Warren and Diana, also with hands full of tail, trudging beside him, but only vaguely.

The wind had built in intensity as they approached the high ridge of the pass, a dark irregular shape against a billion stars. At times Benjamin had to gasp for breath just to catch the air that blew like a gale from behind. His legs and back ached from the exertion of climbing and at the same time of being pushed uphill. When Solo stopped, Benjamin waited with his eyes closed for the animal to start again. He wasn't struck by the beauty of the night or fascinated by the size and clarity of the moon. He was numb. They had walked and stumbled for hours, but it seemed a lifetime since they had begun.

"This way, Benji-sahib."

He heard Thak's high voice in the wind, but only reacted when he felt him grasp his arm. The Nepalese led him to a crevice in the cliff, an angular space out of the wind just large enough for a man to lie down. It was dark, full of loose stones and smelled of animal urine, but Benjamin praised God for it. He curled his feet inside his *chuba*, drawing his legs up, and pulled the monk hood over his face. He didn't think about Diana or Warren or if they had a place like his. He was alive and dry and at least not freezing.

He closed his eyes and felt the tension drain out of his aching muscles. He did not allow himself to imagine what was ahead. There was only now. A place to rest. And sleep. Tomorrow was tomorrow, and that's when he'd deal with it. . . .

◆ SIXTY-FIVE

THAK ROUSED EACH OF his charges at midmorning from their separate crevices, allowing them to sleep long after dawn to make up for exhaustion. In another wider crack in the rocks he served them rice, breadsticks and unheated tea for breakfast. Diana and Warren were subdued. Benjamin tried rubbing the soreness out of his legs and shoulders.

The *chuba*, Benjamin discovered, was a wondrous garment. Worn over his regular clothes, it was like an enormous robe cut for a man ten feet tall. The trick was folding the skirt and tying the belt so as to produce a pocket that encircled the waist. The double folds provided added insulation as well as huge pockets. The fabric was coarse and heavy, but made like a bulky warm mitten. Without tents or sleeping bags or fire, it was the edge for survival.

"How far to this haunted monastery?" Warren nodded toward the pass and the sky beyond. From the shelter of the cliff, slightly below the ridge of the pass, they could not see the valley that lay ahead.

"Two days, Warren sahib."

"I mean in *miles*."

"Not knowing in miles, sahib. Maybe can be seeing from top of ridge. Valley of Winds being all very much flatness."

"Climb up there?" Warren gave Benjamin a challenging look. "There's the Eagle Scout." He held out his binoculars. One of the lens was cracked. "Go ahead, Ben. Check it out for ghosts. I'll help Thak load up Secretariat here."

Benjamin hesitated.

"I'll go." Diana stood, grabbing the binoculars.

Benjamin reached for her. "Diana, don't . . ." She slipped by him.

Warren laughed as Benjamin pushed past him, following Diana.

It took fifteen minutes of laborious work to climb to the top of the ridge and stand together at a lookout point, panting in the raw wind. The pass was called Not, Thak had told Ben, which meant empty view. An appropriate name, he thought. To the south the landscape was unspectacular. Torjok was somewhere among the sea of sandy brown hills three thousand feet below. Looking back at the way they had come gave Benjamin a new appreciation for Thak's ability. The trail, only slightly wider than a yak, threaded along the edge of a canyon. That Thak had managed to lead their tiny caravan in darkness without misstepping was remarkable. But it was the view ahead that commanded Benjamin's attention, a landscape like nothing he had ever imagined.

The Valley of Winds lay at his feet, barely a ripple in the vastness of the Central Asian highlands that extended to the horizon in undulating waves of rounded, barren peaks. Directly north, in the far distance, were the high ranges of Tibet, gray against a thin blue sky. There, too, in the shadow of China, lay Mantang. But reaching the capital of Lo meant first crossing hell.

"My God, Ben . . . it's a desert." Diana held his arm against the wind and had to shout to be heard, her hair snapping around her face.

At least, Benjamin thought, they didn't have to worry about meeting up with wild dogs . . . Below him Not Pass opened into a parched yellow-and-ochre universe of wind-eroded crags like towering stalagmites; gullies and sharp rugged canyons crisscrossed the barren terrain like scars on a whale's back; as far as one could see there was not a blade of grass, not a tree or a bush, just the wail of wind on sun-scorched land, invisible, screaming chaos amid silent desolation. The Valley of Winds might have been called the Valley of Death—nothing, absolutely nothing, could possibly live there.

The day was spent in swirling wind. Bits of sandy rock bombarded the travelers like icy missiles. Benjamin walked with one hand grasping his hood in front of his face, allowing a tiny flapping slit to see out from. Thak led them into gullies whenever possible to avoid the full brunt of howling wind. They stopped three times in nine hours, short rests for water. It was not possible to eat. Solo was the only member of the caravan unaffected. The bull yak plodded along without tiring, negotiating the steep gullies with amazing agility for such a large beast. He did not even pause to relieve himself. He simply raised his tail and ejected in great heaps too heavy for even this wind to disturb.

The sandy cliffs along nearby hills were honeycombed with caves. Thak found one large enough for camp protected from the wind by the broken tip of a crag that had rolled from the top of the ridge. Without fuel for fire Thak prepared cold *tsampa.* Everyone ate in silence, too tired for conversation. Besides, there was nothing to say and no energy to speak above the screech of wind. Benjamin devoured his portion and retired to a corner for the escape of sleep.

The next day was a repeat. They rose at dawn and walked till dusk— fourteen hours in unrelenting wind, searching for a holy ruin to the rhythm of a yak bell.

Thak saw it first. Gumpa Te squatted on top of a cliff, square and weary in the quickly fading light. Wide stone steps, rounded smooth by ancient winds, ascended a steep slope to the arched entrance flanked by eroded *chortens.* Whatever had been carved into these stones had long ago been erased by time's sandblasting. Nothing remained with a defined edge.

It was nearly dark when they reached the forecourt, having climbed more than six hundred steps. From the top of the cliff the valley looked like a colorless still life from another planet. The monastery was a medley of sounds in the wind. Thak tied Solo's nose reins to the stump of a prayer flag and unloaded the packs, passing them to his sahibs. Digging out the flashlights, he led the way inside. Benjamin was amazed by the preserved state of the place. Some of the halls and larger chambers had suffered collapsed walls and ceilings, no doubt victims of the ravaging wind. Interior rooms, protected from direct attack of the blizzard sandstorm, seemed untouched. Murals burst to life in the crossbeams of their flashlights. Solid wooden doors set in heavy timbered frames were carved with the reverse swastika, sign of the Bon-po. Wood did not rot in this frigid climate, Benjamin realized.

"Here, sahibs." Thak dropped his pack, his light searching the narrow room until it found a basket filled with juniper wood. He hurried to it, pointing at the large fireplace that commanded the center of the adjacent wall. "Making fire quickly, please."

"Burn, damn it." Warren worked for precious minutes to make his lighter start, but his numb fingers could not turn the flint wheel quickly enough to spark the wick. When it finally caught, the wood would not burn. In desperation he ripped the film from one of his exposed 35-millimeter canisters, jumbled it into a ball and lit it. The film crackled and melted, producing a low blue flame, singeing a twig of juniper that turned black, and another. Finally a faint orange flame blossomed, consuming another bit of wood. The flame gained strength, spreading slowly up the tiered branches until it was a legitimate fire, crackling and spitting through the ancient wood.

"Get more wood," Warren commanded. "Break up that table."

Over their first meal in two days, cooked by Thak, Diana said, "I don't know why the hill people lived here at all. It's bloody creepy, this place is."

"Well, thank our lucky star it's here. What was it, Ben? The North Star or whatever your holy man called it?"

Benjamin sat with his legs crossed, mesmerized by the fire. "Ahile."

Warren nodded, then to Diana: "I didn't see any ghosts, though. Did you?"

"I don't like it here," she said, ignoring him. "How long, Thak? How many hours to where we're going?"

"Could being five hours walking, memsahib. Finding Aimai Khola, going out of Valley of Winds."

"Thank God."

"Am thanking very much already, memsahib."

"What's Aimai Khola? A village?" Warren asked.

"Oh, Aimai Khola being Tibetan name for Kali Gandaki. Long river. Going into hills beyond Lo land."

"Not another gorge?"

"Not so deep, Warren sahib. But winds being finished."

Warren held up his cup. "I'll drink to that."

Diana climbed to her feet. "I have to . . ." She nodded toward the room's only door. ". . . where should I go?"

"Any place you like," Warren said. "Bring back some wood while you're out."

Benjamin had piled all the batteries near the fire to conserve their power. He loaded two into a flashlight and handed it to her. "Be careful. Stay away from the outside walls. Parts of this place are a hairsbreadth away from collapsing."

She switched on the light, stepped through the door into darkness.

Warren and Benjamin lapsed into silence, into their own thoughts after she left. They both began to doze off when they heard a scream, Diana's voice echoing in a hundred passageways.

Benjamin was quickly on his feet, cramming batteries into plastic flash-lights, tossing one to Warren. Flicking on his light, he grabbed a length of wood and was out the door, following the sound of her voice that was screaming his name. He ran, jerking his light from one corridor to another, confused by the echoes. The darkness was freezing. He called to her, but his voice only reverberated with hers off ancient walls.

"There." Warren's light pointed through a crumbled doorway where another light flailed on the ceiling.

They found her huddled against a fallen beam. Six feet away a gaping hole in the wall yawned with a view of the valley five hundred feet below.

"I told you to stay away—"

She waved him silent. "A man . . . there's a man—"

She grabbed Benjamin, pressing her face against his chest. "I tripped . . . on his legs . . . oh God, get me out of here, please, get me out—"

"What man?"

She pointed her light without looking. "Over there."

Benjamin washed the opposite wall with his light while Warren shone his down from a gaping hole in the roof. And the two beams of light converged on a man sitting against what remained of a breached stone wall, exposed to the wind. His arms were tight across his chest as if he were holding a blanket. His legs were extended out in front of him, a large beam across them. He was wearing long leather boots and khaki shirt and trousers. His gaunt bearded face protruded from beneath the hood of a *chuba*. Remnants of the *chuba* were still clutched in his hands, the rest fluttered in the wind. His eyes were open, staring nowhere. The body was frozen stiff.

"Roof must have fallen on him," Warren said from the doorway. "Froze to death just sitting there." He squinted after his light. "Am I crazy or is that guy white?"

Benjamin helped Diana to her feet. "Keep your light steady, Warren." He stepped over broken rubble, moving toward the body.

"What are you *doing?*" Diana called. "Leave him alone, let's get out of here . . ."

Benjamin knelt beside the corpse. Judging from his face, the dead man was young, early thirties. Benjamin shone his light on the shirt and trousers. The fabric was a coarse-weave wool. The belt was thick leather with an old tarnished brass buckle.

"What do you think, Ben?" Warren said above the wind. "Prospector? Soldier?"

Benjamin pointed his light at the man's head, reached for the bit of *chuba* that had protected his neck and sides of his face, then yanked the hood back, exposing the right side of the head. He leaned back on his haunches, aware of his own breath. "Oh, God . . ."

"Ben?" Warren's light wavered around the body.

"I know who this is."

"You know?"

Benjamin continued to stare at the corpse. The dead man's ear was ripped, torn by dogs' teeth. Even now, it looked to be healing, frozen in time. The face was still young but the body was very old . . . some ninety years. Benjamin stood up.

"It's Barbaree," he said. *"Jack Barbaree."* He held his light on the man's face. "So he never left Nepal . . ." His mind was racing now, recalling bits of the story he'd heard from Abby and Yurev. *He simply disappeared. The British thought we killed him.* "He doubled back," Benjamin said, suddenly realizing. "He didn't go to Australia, he came here, on his way to Mantang. He followed Ayrub Ravi's directions—*he read the text from the balcony floor."*

"That's nonsense," Diana said, "my grandfather"—her eyes went to Warren—"tell him, tell him that isn't . . . isn't . . ." But she couldn't go on with it. And Warren was gaping at the body, struck silent.

Benjamin shone his light into her face and tried to control his voice. *"This* is Jack Barbaree, Diana. He's not anybody's grandfather because he's been sitting *here* for sixty years. Not in Australia. Not mining the Outback. Right here—frozen stiff. Okay . . . so who the hell are *you?"*

◆ SIXTY-SIX

DIANA SAT IN FRONT of the fire bundled in her *chuba*. Her eyes were dry.

"My real name *is* Diana Mayhew, if it matters. I met Warren in Australia, not London. The rest of my not so glorious story is true, except for Barbaree."

The hysteria was gone from her voice. She faced Benjamin, holding a cup of hot tea in her hands for warmth. Warren sat slightly away from her.

"Which explains why you didn't want to talk to anyone. A device to protect this charade, wasn't it?" Benjamin paced across the stone floor, kneading his hands as if to contain his anger.

"Yes," she answered, neither defiant nor contrite.

"Just a charade, a part for you to play."

"Warren made me an offer . . . and I took it."

"An offer? Well, I guess that follows. Warren is very good at making deals."

"So now you know," Warren said. "So what? I would have told you eventually—"

"What, that you hired an actress to play Barbaree's nonexistent granddaughter? You thought I'd agree to that?"

"Look, Ben, I *tried* to find Barbaree. Hired a private investigator. All we were able to come up with was his military record. He was an only child. His mother went under a bus a year after he was born, and his father died of mustard gas poisoning in 1917. No other family. He did six years in India attached to a British surveying regiment in Nepal, then went on his own. Nobody's seen him since he took Yurev and Abby up the Kali Gandaki. The police suspected Yurev killed him but there wasn't any proof. Anyway, nobody really cared. The British had their hands full in India at the time . . . Barbaree just got lost in the crack."

"Until you resurrected him."

"It wasn't a crime, Ben. All I wanted was to find a descendant but there wasn't any. So I invented one. I had to. 'Quest' wouldn't have worked without a Barbaree heir."

"A female heir?"

"The best possible situation for my purpose was to take a woman. When I met Diana, she was perfect. And with the name of a Greek goddess. It's her real name, too."

Benjamin could only shake his head. "How did you find her?"

"Freemantle. She was doing charcoal portraits for tourists at the America's Cup trials. Five dollars a head. We got to talking—"

"I can speak for myself, if you don't mind." Diana looked directly at Benjamin. "Talk is exactly all we did. Warren seemed to like my work. He was interested that I'd done some acting and modeling. When I said that I wanted to go to London someday, study at Sommes . . . Warren said perhaps there was a way he could help. He explained about Barbaree, and, well, I agreed to do it."

"Just like that."

She stared at him without reply.

"Diana grew up in the Outback," Warren said. "I saw that as a plus. I needed someone who could handle inconvenience. I knew this Himalayan trek wasn't going to be a picnic, although I underestimated it, no question."

"You just let him talk you into this?"

"He didn't talk me into anything," Diana said, her anger flaring. "I'm quite a big girl. I also can think for myself."

"Who thought up that story for the press?"

"My grandfather *was* British. He *did* come to Australia on a tramp steamer and spent his life looking for gold. His name happened not to be Barbaree."

"It all fit beautifully, Ben. Can't you see that . . . two men and a woman in the treacherous Back of the Beyond. Like with Abby."

Benjamin was still watching Diana. "And what did you get out of this?"

"Twenty thousand dollars and a plane ticket to London."

"Ah, the scholarship."

"*And* a career-builder," Warren added quickly. "Don't forget that. When she gets back the world will know her."

Benjamin ignored him. "I suppose it's written somewhere that you promise not to reveal this."

"Why? Who would I tell?"

"Don't you see, Ben? It works for everybody. It's our secret. Nobody gets hurt."

Benjamin turned. "Tell that to Serchen."

"That wasn't my doing. You're the one hell-bent on going to Lo Mantang."

Hell-bent . . . in a way he was right . . . "Well, stoke the fire, Warren," Benjamin said, and sat down, suddenly bone-tired. He poured himself tea and stared into the cup, too weary to drink. He felt Diana's eyes on him.

"I'm not ashamed of this," she said. "Get that straight. But for what it's worth, I'm relieved the pretense is over."

"Over?" Warren tossed a handful of branches onto the fire. "Nothing's over. Ben's not going to mess it up. Not now." And sounding less confident, "What *are* you going to do, Ben?"

"What I came to do—find Shelkagari."

"When we get back, are you going to back me up or . . ."

"Ask me again when I'm holding Shelkagari in my hands."

"Ben, I don't play games, not at this level. Not for these stakes. You know what this expedition means. It's too important—"

"When we reach Mantang, *then* we'll know how important it is."

"And in the meantime?" Diana looked up at him with quiet intensity.

Benjamin didn't answer her. He stared into the fire rather than look at her. Diana's role in this had stung him more than Warren's. He could expect this from his ambitious cousin, but he had almost convinced himself that Diana was special, that she was somehow pulled into Warren's scheme against her will. But it seemed she wasn't so different. She was a player. Like Susan . . .

◆ SIXTY-SEVEN

IT HAD TAKEN ALL morning to reach the crest of the ridge. Benjamin looked back at the Valley of Winds. Gumpa Te was still visible, a rusty square at the top of a cliff overlooking the gashed, rutted terrain. Ahead were rounded peaks floating above a blue haze.

They walked up and down gentle slopes until they reached a narrow valley strewn with rocks that Thak identified as Kali Gandaki. It was no longer the formidable gorge, miles deep, that sliced through the giant peaks of the Central Himalayan range. The river was now a stream at the bottom of a shallow ravine, and the black river was now only gray and without arrogance.

Thak pointed to the opposite side, indicating what lay beyond. "Lo Mantang."

They crossed the bubbling river by way of a rickety goat bridge made of tree trunks across large rocks protruding from the water. Benjamin climbed eagerly up the rocky trail ahead of the others, stumbling in his haste to reach the small pass between two bluffs. At the top he stood against a brisk wind, out of breath, and stared into the treeless, feudal Kingdom of Lo.

The valley, the Plain of Prayers, was a landscape of jagged contours and ravines that slithered into the rising mountains on every side, absorbed by the rugged hills and the shadows of the afternoon sun. In the center, surrounded by rough green fields of barley and irregular irrigation ditches, lay a rectangular city with walls thirty feet high and windowed towers at each corner. Between the towers were great supporting abutments, evenly spaced. Along the tops of the walls waved hundreds of long, featherlike prayer flags. It was a majestic, impregnable fortress, its great walls of sandstone golden in the sun; a medieval castle, banners flying, in a timeless universe.

Lo Mantang.

Diana climbed the last few feet behind him, breathing heavily. Like Benjamin, she stood in awe of the spectacular view.

"Ben, it's . . . magnificent."

Benjamin didn't answer. He glanced back. Warren was only halfway up the hill, Thak and Solo trailing behind. "Better wait for the others," he said. "I'm going down."

"They don't need any help," Diana said. "I'm going with you."

The fortress had been built in the shape of a square, less one quadrant. Its only entrance, a huge gateway facing north, was set in the side of the missing quadrant. Ornately carved wooden columns supported a massive lintel. The passageway through the wall was twenty feet. Walking around the walled city to find the entrance, Benjamin measured the length by his step and found it to be almost three hundred yards. Lo Mantang was not a large place—the Kane estate was twice as big—but it was palatial by any local standard.

Warren came around the wall, joining Benjamin and Diana in the small square outside the gate. Children with pigtails had gathered to inspect them. Warren looked up at the jagged stone wall, listening for a moment to the prayer flags snapping in the breeze. "So this is Shangri-La."

Thak arrived with Solo and went to the gate, where several townspeople met him. A discussion followed, Thak doing most of the talking, then they all disappeared, including the yak, inside the gate. From the top of the wall Benjamin noticed several curious faces that withdrew when he glanced at them. He had settled back to wait when one of the children stepped out of the crowd. Benjamin smiled and the boy moved closer, tentatively extending his hand.

"He wants to touch you," Diana said.

"The beard . . . they've never seen a man with whiskers before." Benjamin took the boy's hand, gently rubbing it across his jaw. "Whiskers." Another boy came forward. And another. Soon Benjamin was surrounded by children touching him, feeling his beard, the hair on his arms. Diana was also a center of attraction as brown fingers caressed her white skin, fascinated by the fine red strands of her hair—

Two figures in red *chubas* with red pointed hats abruptly stood at the gate. They wore grotesque masks and carried long ugly swords.

Thak appeared behind them and hurried to Benjamin. "Big festivities, Benji-sahib. All Mantang peoples making big celebrations." He indicated the pair at the gate. "These being holy ones of high lama."

"What do they want?"

"Wanting nothing, Benji-sahib. Welcoming." He waved that the sahibs follow him. "Coming in, please. King of Lo saying come. I fixed all up. We being guests, watching celebration."

Benjamin looked at Diana.

She stared back. *"King* of Lo?"

The ceremony was the last day of an annual three-day ritual—Chasing Out of the Demons—in which the high priest rid the city of bad spirits. Thak and his sahibs were led through empty streets and alleyways into a great square the size of a high-school gymnasium. The population of Mantang, about a thousand, was crowded around the fringe, all wearing their finest clothes—bright, gaily colored *chubas* of blues and greens and yellows. Women wore brocade capes around their shoulders with silver clasps, some with intricate designs of peacocks or other birds on the back. Most of the women wore jewelry, necklaces of sparkling coralline stones and bracelets of ivory-white conch shells. The better-off had elaborate headdresses—leather straps studded with turquoises as large as half-dollars that hung down their backs.

In the center of the square the high priest stood between two rows of seated monks who wore red *chubas* like the two at the gate. The lama was dressed in a robe of gold-and-blue brocade. He wore a black, wide-brimmed hat embroidered with a dragon standing on a human skull. The lama was the representation of Mara, god of death, Thak whispered.

The monks burned juniper wood in small offering plates while the lama chanted incantations over them. Signaling with a shriek that made Diana jump, the lama raised his hands and the two monk-swordsmen, in their Tibetan devil masks, began dancing about the square, slashing the air with their swords. The performance lasted five minutes until all at once everyone stood, caught up in the frenzy, chanting feverishly. And then they were running, and Benjamin was swept along as the crowd poured through the narrow streets toward the gate, waving prayer flags on pencil-thin sticks above their heads. They ended up outside the walls of the city led by the lama and his monks. The plates of burning offerings were dumped into a pile and ground into dust under the bare feet of, first, the high priest and his red-robed followers, then everyone else. A cry of jubilation rose from the throng as the people applauded themselves. Mantang was rid of its demons for another year.

Benjamin found Diana and Warren as the crowd filed back into the city.

"I've heard of house-cleaning," Diana said, beating the dust from her *chuba*, "but this . . ."

"Where's Thak?"

Warren nodded toward the gate. "Inside, last I saw." He withdrew a leather headdress with five turquoise stones from his pocket. "Found these. Poor grade, but nice color. I wonder if they mine these somewhere in these hills."

"Where did you get that?"

"In her hurry to crush smoldering twigs, the little woman ahead of me threw it off her head."

"Well, we'd better find Thak."

They wandered back to the square to the curious looks of townspeople intrigued by the white-skinned strangers.

Thak stood at the edge of a porch in the midst of a group of villagers. When he saw Benjamin, he hurried to meet him. "Good lucks for us. Lobos very friendly peoples."

"Lobos?"

"Peoples," Thak said, opening his arms. "Lo peoples. Lobos."

"Ah."

"King of Lo wanting to meet sahibs. Very much interested."

"The king?"

"Indeed, yes, Benji-sahib. King of Lo very wise Lobo. Speaking English—"

"*English?*"

Thak nodded, lowered his voice. "But not so good as Thak. King of Lo having teacher. Come. Be meeting Tutor." Thak led them to the porch, where a middle-aged man sat on a thick rug. He wore a blue *chuba* and a fur cap. The side of his face was badly scarred and his right eyelid had been sewn shut. His right arm ended in a stub, just above the wrist. Benjamin saw immediately that the man, whatever he called himself, and whatever he was, was no native Lobo. Even with his weathered, sun-darkened skin, he was plainly not Asian.

The man Thak called Tutor hobbled to his feet, propped a wooden crutch under a thin shoulder.

"This being Benji-sahib," Thak said in introduction. "Being looking for the great stone of Miraculous Things."

The old man gave Benjamin a frail nod. "Welcome to Lo Mantang. Tutor is what my Lobo friends call me. I teach a bit, you see." His voice was vaguely British. He held out his only hand. "My given name is Smithwaithe. Desmond Smithwaithe."

Desmond Smithwaithe. Benjamin almost froze when he heard the name. How many times had he seen that byline? "Special dispatch by Desmond Smithwaithe." He had read the newspaper articles since he was thirteen, yellowed clippings from the London *Daily Worker* that his mother had saved. The clippings were the only published accounts in the West of Miller Kane's criminal trial. He had seen his father described as a warmonger, a spy and a lying, murderous American pilot, "piteously without remorse for innocent civilian lives." A coward, Smithwaithe had written, "who had the backbone and dignity of a cowering pig." Benjamin had learned to despise the name without a face. He had always imagined a hard, bitter man with slits for eyes. Looking at him now, a fragile, broken figure, it was almost impossible to associate this old man with those arrogant, faded words on brittle pages.

"Excuse the crosswise bother," Smithwaithe was saying for his left-handed handshake. His dry, slender hand was weightless in Benjamin's grasp. "Lost the good one years ago. Hardly notice it nowadays."

"You're . . . British?" Benjamin said, hoping he was wrong but knowing at the same time that he wasn't.

"British?" Smithwaithe shook his head. "Not in an eon. Almost Chinese once but the buggers tried to have me off. Lobo now." He gestured that his guests sit. "Please."

A servant poured tea while Warren and Diana introduced themselves. Neither of them, of course, knew who the old man was. The trial had been held before either of them was born.

"How in the world did you get here?" Warren said. "I mean, do you *live* here . . . ?"

Smithwaithe smiled, his one eye gleaming. "Most assuredly. Mantang is my home. I've lived here for, I think, thirty years. I wouldn't live in another place."

"There was a Smithwaithe," Benjamin said, pausing, "a journalist . . ."

The old man gave him a look of surprise. "Surely before your time." He cocked his head. "My, my . . . a *very* long time ago. In my former life. Yes." He nodded, glancing at the sky as if seeing back in time. "Before the fall."

"Fall?"

"Ah, well . . ." Smithwaithe's gaze refocused on Diana. "I was a devout follower of what you might say were other men's dreams. As the movement changed, I was . . . expendable."

Benjamin kept silent.

"What movement?" Diana asked.

"An age ago, child."

"China, wasn't it?" Benjamin said. "What happened . . . they put you in prison?"

Smithwaithe's thin shoulders moved. "Punishment is purification. Do you ever wonder why the symbol of Great China is the dragon? I think it is because when the dragon is enraged it bites its own tail. As it happened, in my time, it bit me." He touched his face and his eye. "Here . . . and here . . . and here. They shot me. My reward for diligence was punishment. I was left in the hills. Dead, they thought. But not yet. Horsemen found me. *Khampas.* They mistook me for a Chinese. *Khampas* had a shortage of guns in those days." He held up the stub of his right hand. "But not swords."

"Jesus Christ."

He looked at Warren. "No, my young friend, Lobos save me. They are the kindest people on the earth. They took me in, nursed me, made me well again."

"Why didn't you leave?"

"I have no toes," Smithwaithe said. He swung an invisible sword with his remaining hand. "*Khampas,* they'll take a whack at anything." He shrugged. "It's not possible to walk in Lo without toes . . . the rocks, you see, and the wind, of course. I could not leave and had no one to take me. Still, it turned out to be a blessing. Where is there a place like Lo Mantang? We have no unemployment and no hunger and everyone is happy." He nodded to himself. "You see, punishment *is* purification." He cocked his head and found his teacup. "Now, then . . . this evening you will meet our king. I will arrange it. But first you must tell me, is there still an England? A queen?" He looked at Benjamin.

The old man was in his own prison, Benjamin realized. One he could never leave. But he had it backward—purification was punishment. "Yes, still," Benjamin told him.

"Ah." Smithwaithe raised his eyebrow, holding his cup near his chin. "How lovely."

◆ SIXTY-EIGHT

IN THE KINGDOM OF Lo Desmond Smithwaithe, reviler and tormentor of Miller Kane, became host to his son Benjamin. His house was adjacent to the king's palace but looked no different than the other houses in Mantang except that it was larger. Each house also contained a toilet room, a small square cubicle with a low bench and a hole. Below the hole was a shaft to the ground that could be cleaned by an outside door at ground level. Smithwaithe had explained that one way in which status and wealth of a Lobo was measured in Mantang was in the height of the shaft. As good a measure as many at home, Benjamin thought.

"The King of Lo has another question," Smithwaithe was saying. They were in the royal eating room. Nothing about it suggested palatial grandeur. It was well-lit with butter lamps, and the aroma of cooked rice and vegetables hung in the air. The King of Lo sat on a slightly raised wooden platform while everyone else sat on a mat. Two dogs lay beside the king's place while two chickens roamed the room at will, hopping around on tiptoes, inspecting each bowl.

The king's entourage included nine men in variously colored *chubas*, plus the high priest and his two favorite monks. Rather than let the king stumble through his limited range of English, Smithwaithe served as special interpreter. The routine had the king asking a question of Smithwaithe, who in turn asked it of Benjamin, who then replied to Smithwaithe, who reported back to the king. The sahibs, because they were foreigners, could not speak directly to the king, or vice-versa. Women were not received by the king in his official capacity, but Diana was allowed to attend in honor of the special circumstance. She was not, however, permitted to speak. Which infuriated her, and she proceeded to take every opportunity to break the rule whenever it was Benjamin's turn.

"The King of Lo is interested to know," Smithwaithe said, "when these astronauts fly into space, what do men see when they look back?"

Benjamin had just covered twenty different topics of royal interest, but the idea of space travel seemed of most concern to the king. Smithwaithe was fascinated as well, but at least it was not so foreign an idea to him as it was to the king. For all Benjamin knew, Lobos thought the world was flat.

"Women have been in space, too," Diana said. "And *died*. Tell him *that*."

"They see oceans and clouds and continents," Benjamin said, deciding to answer the king rather than inject Diana's understandable if out-of-place pique. "They see brilliant blues and swirling masses of white all in a sphere surrounded by the blackness of space. It's a beautiful sight."

Smithwaithe passed on the reply, using wide arm gestures like a practiced Kabuki storyteller. The king listened, nodding delightedly as Smithwaithe painted a picture in the air. Benjamin had not mentioned that men had walked on the moon. He was not sure how such news might be received. The last thing he wanted was the king to take offense at some revelation about the outside world—the world they all represented.

After a while the king clapped his hands, startling the pair of sleeping dogs beside him. There was an exchange between the king and the high priest, whereupon the lama spoke to his attending monks, who, bowing to the king, left the room.

"An honor," Smithwaithe said, impressed.

Benjamin gave him a questioning look. "What is it?"

"The King of Lo is calling for the great *molla*—the golden book of kings."

"*Molla?*"

"The history of Lo," Smithwaithe said. "It's a national treasure, the *molla*. You should be greatly honored that the king wants to read to you from it. I myself have only seen it twice."

A Lobo brought a small intricately carved bench, setting it in front of the king. Another Lobo lay a red-and-blue silk cloth over the bench. The high priest moved to it, chanting as he touched each of the four corners with his index fingers. The lama then lit the contents of an offering plate and took a seat between Smithwaithe and the king. The room filled with the acrid smell of incense while they waited. Shortly, the two monks dispatched earlier returned, carrying a solid-looking table that held a stack of thick pages. The *molla*. Each page was three feet wide by one foot long, and the monks labored with the weight of it, finally placing it beside the bench.

The lama offered another chant, touching the silk scarf that lay across the top of the book. When he finished he withdrew the scarf, revealing a lacquered board of bright red inlaid with delicate designs in gold. The king removed the cover, placing it upside down on the bench, then went through the loose pages, lifting them carefully at the edges and turning them down, as he had with the cover, one at a time.

The pages were solid gold, hammered thin. Each sheet was exquisitely illustrated at the borders in blue and red. The text had been etched into the soft metal, then inked black.

"That's *gold*," Warren said in appreciation.

The golden book of kings contained one hundred and ten pages. After several minutes the king found the place he was apparently searching for, looked directly at Benjamin, and began to read.

"In the fourth Year of the Sheep," Smithwaithe said, interpreting as the king's voice droned, "in the time of Ngorchen Dorja, ninth King of Lo, came a holy prophet from the land below the black river. The holy prophet was called Arub Rav and with him he brought a great gift. Arub Rav stayed in the great palace of Lo. At this time of Ngorchen Dorja, King of Lo, the great God House of Lo was built, temple of Maitreya, Buddha who is next to come. Arub Rav, holy prophet, left his gift to Ngorchen Dorja, King of Lo, saying . . . so long as the stone of Miraculous Things is safely kept, so shall also the great God House remain holy. Arub Rav, holy prophet, returned to his land in the fourth Year of the Sheep. He said to Ngorchen Dorja, King of Lo . . . another will one day come, as I. Wise son after the third son of a great prince will he be. To him show kindness as to me and say only, the way to enlightenment is with the Great One, possessor of the light of wisdom. Hail the jewel of the lotus . . ."

The king looked up from the page, his eyes on Benjamin. He spoke quietly.

"The king wants to know," Smithwaithe said, "are you this man . . . this wise son, as it's written in the *molla?*"

Benjamin could barely speak. His heart was beating so hard he was sure everyone could hear it. So Ayrub Ravi *did* come to Lo Mantang. Benjamin had known it—and not known it. He knew that his father believed, and Yurev did, but until now, this moment, he hadn't been sure himself. But the *molla* was proof. Ravi had come to *this* place, possibly sat on *this* very floor in front of another king. *And he had Shelkagari. The stone was here.*

Benjamin licked his dry lips and looked at Smithwaithe. "Tell him, yes. I am that man."

◆ SIXTY-NINE

WARREN HAD HOLD OF Benjamin's arm. "Just what are you trying to do?"

They were on the rampart of the south wall, away from the wind, above Smithwaithe's house. The sky was black and studded with stars. A flickering butter lamp cast a pool of light on the narrow walkway. Benjamin had climbed the wall to find refuge and think. He'd been granted free access to see or inspect anything in the kingdom. The king was keeping a promise that had been made a thousand years earlier by another king to another sahib. But it wasn't enough.

"You wouldn't understand, Warren—"

"Like hell, I wouldn't. It's here, isn't it? Shelkagari, it's here."

"Take your hand off me."

"Tell me, Ben. Ravi, he really did bring a diamond to Lo Mantang, didn't he . . . Shelkagari."

"Yes."

"Ben, do you know what this means? You've found it. The greatest diamond that ever existed. Everything I ever said I take it back. You were right. Yurev, the old goat, he knew, he's been right all along. We found Shelkagari, do you know what that means?"

Benjamin blew into his hands, said nothing.

"The God House." Warren leaned against the wall, looking back over the city. "He said it was in the God House. Which one is it?"

"It isn't here."

"What?"

"This city doesn't have a God House."

"Ben, I heard him read from the book. They built a God House. In the Year of the Sheep. A God House, temple for the Buddha who's coming." He stared into the night. "It's got to be in the palace."

Benjamin rolled his hood up against the chill. "I've been talking to Smithwaithe. Mantang is only seven hundred years old, give or take a generation."

"So?"

"Lo Mantang means Palace of Lo, literally where the king resides."

Warren looked at him, waiting.

"It means that Lo Mantang is wherever the king is. It means, Warren, that a thousand years ago *this* Lo Mantang didn't exist. Ayrub Ravi went to the palace of the ninth King of Lo"—Benjamin pointed north—"up there. They call it Lo Dzong now. It's been deserted for five hundred years."

"There's more than one Lo Mantang?"

"No, just one at a time."

"Lo Dzong? How far?"

"A day."

"A day—*one* day?" Warren smiled. "So we have another day's walk. We're veterans of the Valley of goddamn Winds. One more day is nothing."

"It isn't that simple—"

"What's the matter with you? We know where it is, we'll go get it."

"It's in China," Benjamin said.

Warren's smile disintegrated.

"Smithwaithe showed me on the map. Lo Dzong is in a disputed territory claimed by the Chinese. It's in the high hills, on a cliff at the source of the Kali Gandaki River. It's a rugged place, and there are *khampas* in the area, raiding parties into China."

Warren slapped his hand on the wall. "I knew it. It couldn't be easy. No, no . . . China. No."

Diana stepped out of the darkness into the flickering light of the butter lamp. "I say, let's go home."

Benjamin gave her a sharp look.

"Please, let's go home. Back, anyway. I'm willing to take my chances on what's behind us." She looked across the city to the north. "You can't go into China—"

"You heard?"

"Let it go, Ben. Please. A piece of rock isn't worth dying for, or getting yourself hacked half to death like Desmond Smithwaithe."

"Maybe they have guns in this place." Warren paced along the wall. "If we had a couple of good rifles—"

"Against bandits? You've already seen what they can do. What if you run into the Chinese army? Let's go, leave this place. You can keep the money, I don't care a damn about it anymore. Let's just *go.*"

"We still have a contract—"

"To hell with the bloody contract." She turned to Benjamin. "Ben, listen to me. You're not chosen for this. That son of the third son nonsense is just a myth. You don't *have* to do this. It's not real. *Goddamn it, listen to me.* If you go into China you'll die. Are you trying to outdo your father—martyrdom instead of silence? Is that what it means to be a Kane?"

He looked at her for a moment. "Should I subscribe to your test of integrity?"

"Benjamin, I—"

"I'll go myself. Lo Dzong isn't far. I should be back in a couple of days. Anyway, it's my neck, and it's why I came—it's my turn."

"Wait a minute," Warren said. "You're going alone?"

"Less visibility is less risk. One person is better than four. I won't need Thak. I'll follow the Kali Gandaki. Besides, if there's trouble, Thak can guide you out of here—"

"Warren, for godsakes, you can't let him go—"

"He's gotten this far . . . we'll wait. He's right. One person has a better chance . . ." Warren looked at Benjamin, smiled. "You go get it, Ben."

Benjamin shook his head. Warren didn't understand. But he wasn't meant to. Benjamin glanced at the stars, picking out Ahile and its six teasing sisters. Tomorrow it would be done.

◆ SEVENTY

BENJAMIN CAME AWAKE SLOWLY to the gentle prodding of Thak's hand on his shoulder. He rolled on his side, exercising his eyes. It had been his first good night's sleep in days.

"Thak . . . what time—"

"Memsahib saying getting up most urgently."

"Did she?" Benjamin got up from his sleeping mat, pushed open the window shutters and shrank away from the blinding light of day. He glanced across the room. "Warren, we should have been up long before—" Warren's mat was empty.

"Memsahib saying coming most quickly—"

"Never mind, Thak. I'll speak to Benji-sahib now." Diana stood in the doorway.

"Where's Warren?"

"Gone. He took a pony."

Benjamin balanced himself against the wall, pulling on a boot. "Gone where?" He struggled into the other boot, stamping it to fit. "Diana?"

She said nothing.

Benjamin froze. "No . . ."

"Yes."

"When?"

"Early this morning. Smithwaithe says five or six hours. He didn't take any food."

"What does he think he's doing?"

"I think he doesn't trust you, Ben. Can you ride a horse?"

"I don't know yet." He grabbed his *chuba* and map case.

"I can. It's one of the things we do well in Australia." Diana met his look. "Five hours is too much time to make up if you're no better on a horse than he is. He also took a sword. One of those ceremonial things from the palace. It will weigh him down, slow him down, which is a plus for us—"

"Forget it, I'll take Thak."

"Thak's Hindu, Benjamin. He can lead a horse, or a yak, but he can't ride one. You're stuck with me, unless you want to take a Lobo you can't understand."

"Look, Diana—"

"I thought about what you said last night . . . my test of integrity. That was rather cruel, what you said. Even gratuitous. Anyway, it occurred that I might change your mind. Besides, I *want* to help you."

"I don't want you involved in this—"

"If you think you're leaving me here—don't. I won't sit around waiting with Smithwaithe, wondering if you two loving cousins have killed each other. We'll go together." She looked at him with an ironic smile. "*You* need *me* now."

After an hour riding in the loose gravel beside the Kali Gandaki River, Benjamin's legs ached fiercely. Tibetan ponies were rugged but small animals, and his feet all but dragged on the ground as he bounced along the trail, banging his knees and ankles on outcrops of rocks as punishment for poor steering.

As the hours stretched into afternoon the terrain turned sandy. Ahead, the river cut into a high plateau that zigzagged between peaks. The narrow river valley was slowly changing into a desolate gorge as it twisted its way toward the mountains—snow-coned hilltops lying one on another to the misty horizon. With the increase in altitude as they kept up their northerly trot came an increase in the wind that blew in their faces. Fighting horse and *chuba,* in a wind that would only get stronger became a battle that Benjamin felt himself losing. He began to think less of catching Warren than of surviving the scrapes and bruises to his battered legs.

At a bend in the river Diana reined her horse over and Benjamin managed to stop, too.

"Over there," Diana said, and pointed to the sandy soil of the canyon cliff. A gleaming sword protruded from the earth, stuck fast. "He left his sword. He's getting tired, lightening his load."

"He didn't leave it," Benjamin said. "He threw it. Look how it's buried." He scanned ahead, shading his eyes. "He's getting frustrated. What time do you think it is . . . four?"

"Later." Diana moved to the water's edge, allowing her horse to drink. "I thought we'd have seen him by now. Are you all right?"

Benjamin rubbed his knee. "I feel like I've been beaten up by midgets."

"I don't think we're going to catch up with him before dark . . . Did you see it—the palace?"

"See it? Where?"

Diana pointed. "Behind that ridge. Two hours. We'll have to take one of these gullies up to the top of the gorge soon. It's getting too steep."

"Two hours?" Benjamin checked the sun. The shadows were already stretching out. "Nearly dark in two hours."

Diana reined her horse around. "He doesn't have a sword, Benjamin."

Benjamin prodded his pony on with a sore knee. "Let's hope he's too tired to throw rocks. Or worse."

Lo Dzong rose like the prow of an enormous ship from a precipice of the renewed Kali Gandaki gorge. Even in ruins, the huge walls were a formidable sight, towering above the cliffs in stairstep fashion, following the ridgeline to its peak. The palace was a city in itself, half the size of Lo Mantang, with narrow steep streets that wound past shells of houses without roofs. Wind hustled through vacant windows in the early twilight, pushing the sound toward Benjamin and Diana.

They had crossed the plateau directly south, leading their ponies on foot as the wind made riding too difficult. For half an hour Benjamin had studied the structure that rose above all others in the palace. At the top of the ridge, like a lighthouse on a craggy promontory, stood a squat, four- or five-story domed building. It was red, the color of monasteries and shrines, and featured elongated openings, not windows but wind-vents. The God House. He was sure of it. Where else would they put it?

"Warren's here, all right." Diana turned away from the wind, pointing to a trail of horse dung, still soft. "He rode his pony all the way."

"In this wind?"

"Pity the horse, not the rider."

The sound of gunfire spooked Benjamin's pony as the animal's head reared, fighting Benjamin's grasp on the reins.

The sound came again, a short burst from an automatic weapon, echoing like cannonfire across the plain. Then again. It was coming from the ruins, carried on the wind. Diana's pony broke away from her.

"Let it go," Benjamin yelled into the wind.

"We can't—"

"Before they start shooting at us . . . ." He dropped the reins of his pony and grabbed Diana's hand as another round of firing began. He headed for the gateway to Lo Dzong, the nearest cover. The yawning entrance was a hundred yards away. They ran together, fighting for breath. Every step of the way the shooting got louder. Benjamin heard the ricochets slamming off stones with a high-pitched zing. But worse than the noise of bullets was the shrieking, whining cries of tortured animals. A part of his brain tried to identify the sound while the rest made him run. Twenty yards from safety, he knew what the animals were.

Dogs.

Gasping, they fell together inside the entrance passageway. A section of wall had collapsed after centuries of exposure to wind from the gorge. The gate, still intact, had long since been blown off its hinges, creating a tiny shelter across the rubble of stones. Benjamin shoved Diana inside it and crawled in behind her. The shooting had subsided except for single shots, and the noise was different now, as if from a different weapon.

Benjamin sucked in his breath. "Not shooting . . . at us." He nodded toward the city. "Somebody is . . . shooting dogs . . ."

Diana just stared at him without expression.

Another shot rang out, a thunderous, booming report that echoed through dark empty streets. Diana huddled against him. "Do you think they saw us?"

Benjamin waited for his chest to stop heaving. "Not they—he. That's only one weapon being fired."

"One? But *khampas*—"

"*Khampas* don't shoot dogs. And they would have spotted us miles away." He took her hand. "Come on."

"Wait, what are you doing?"

"Among other things we're going to find out how Warren got hold of a gun."

They moved through moonlit streets, swept clean by a screeching wind. In the center of Lo Dzong Benjamin found the palace, a long building full of empty halls with a large courtyard protected from the wind. The walls and floor were remarkably smooth.

"Benjamin . . . is that smoke?"

Cordite. Somebody had fired a lot of ammunition. He moved to an adjacent courtyard and stepped on something soft. He did not take another step. "Move back, Diana. Don't come in here." The floor was sticky under his boot.

"What's—oh, God!"

They had found the dogs, their bodies piled at measured intervals around the perimeter of the courtyard. They had been tethered with ropes to posts and shot where they stood. Blood was everywhere, black pools in the moonlight.

A beam of light flashed in Benjamin's face. He froze.

Warren switched off the light and stepped from a doorway, a semiautomatic weapon strapped over his shoulder. "Not such good guard dogs, were they?" He held a pistol in his hand. "Welcome. I had a feeling you might show up. I just wanted to be here to make sure you understood who was still in charge of this expedition. You were beginning to get confused about that, Ben . . ."

"Where did you get those guns?"

"They're everywhere. Rifles, machine guns, pistols, ammunition"—he held up the flashlight—"flashlights. It's all Chinese, by the look of it. Used. There's even some food."

"A *khampa* raiding party cache." Benjamin fought to sound calm. "Whoever left this can't be far away."

"I wasn't going to move in," Warren said. He pointed toward the top of the ridge. "You noticed the God House?"

"Yes."

Warren smiled. "Wait until you see what's inside it."

The God House was actually outside the walls of Lo Dzong, though it was difficult to see that when looking up from the plains. A narrow walkway connected the ground floor gallery of the shrine to the rampart of the city's westernmost wall. Standing below the God House, with the stars as backdrop, it seemed to stretch into space. The wind-vents, huge slits ten feet tall and two feet wide, were framed by wooden beams as solid as the day they were cut. A small colonnade led to the entrance.

Warren stopped at the door. "You first."

Benjamin ducked his head and went in. The light of the moon spilled through the wind-vents from the north, falling across a colossal statue of the Buddha Maitreya, fifty feet tall, sitting legs crossed on a lotus-blossom base. Its giant hands were raised, holding the sacred Wheel of Life that incorporated twelve spokes, each representing a year of the cyclical Tibetan calendar. The spokes protruded through the circular wheel like the handholds of a ship's wheel. The Buddha gripped the life wheel by its opposing spokes—the Year of the Ox and the Year of the Sheep.

Buddha's head, forty feet above the base, was easily ten feet wide. Its face was sculpted in the familiar pose of peacefulness with eyes all-seeing. Handcrafted of wood, this symbol of life to come had endured a thousand years with only the slightest evidence of windburn. A wreathed garland of carved and painted wooden lotus blossoms had been attached to the figure, as if hanging from its neck. The stone floor, marked into square blocks, was chiseled with Sanskrit praises, and each wall was festooned with frescoes and woodcuts and other offerings left by fifty generations of pilgrims.

"Incredible," Benjamin said. He walked around the statue after the butter lamps had been lit, bathing the wood with a golden hue. Five galleries, one at each story with stairways between, surrounded the idol.

"All right, Ben. Where is it?"

Benjamin took out his map case, unrolled his notes. " 'Until the heir of the third princely son loosens the hounds of azure . . . ,' " Benjamin read, " 'shall only the Divine One possess the Miraculous Gift.' "

"What's that about hounds of azure?"

"The blue dogs," Benjamin said. "Tibetan mastiffs. Protectors of the jewel of the lotus."

"What does it mean?"

"I don't know," Benjamin said shortly. "I'm afraid these cryptic Sanskrit clues weren't made with your promotion in mind. I suppose if Ravi had been a sport he'd have said look in the box by the door—"

"Not funny, Ben. Not at all. Let's get to it."

Benjamin walked around the base of the statue, tapping his knuckles against the wood. ". . . Loosen the hounds . . ." He continued tapping, looking for a secret compartment but it was solid wood. He stood up, shook his head. "I need Smithwaithe, someone who reads Sanskrit. There could be more instructions—"

"You're going to carry him up here? Besides, the minute those bandits get back nobody will be left around here to read Sanskrit notes."

"You shouldn't have killed the dogs," Benjamin said. "They wouldn't have known anyone had been here."

"I suppose if you'd been here you would have mesmerized them into house pets? You should be glad I came ahead."

"Why did you?" Diana put in.

"I was getting the notion that my cousin here was beginning to forget whose show this was. I figured I had better remind him, not to mention making sure I was on hand to protect my interest in his stone. Stones are, after all, my business . . ."

"Are you sure you weren't planning on a monopoly?" Diana said, looking directly at him, and then at Ben, who she suspected shared her suspicion.

"That is, to borrow your word, a bloody stupid thing to say, Diana, especially to the man who is going to make your fortune. . . . So, let's get to it. Ben, I believe the honors are yours."

"It could be anywhere—the walls, the statue, the floor."

"Floor?" Warren stared at the chiseled blocks. "You're *supposed* to be the expert. It's time to figure it out. Do it."

"Oh—" Diana was sitting beside a wind-vent facing south. She looked quickly at Benjamin. "You'd better see this. Someone's coming."

A procession of lights moved across the plains, heading for the entrance to Lo Dzong. Riders. The beat of hooves was just now faint on the wind —horsemen with torches.

Khampas.

Warren started with the nearest butter lamp, moving around the gallery extinguishing flames.

"Warren, for godsakes, they already know we're here, thanks to you."

Diana's words had no effect as he rushed from one lamp to the next.

"I count at least thirty," Benjamin said.

"We've got to get the hell out of here—"

"How?" Benjamin spoke from the shadows as Warren snuffed the last flame. "We're on the edge of a cliff. The only way out is the way we came in."

Warren unshouldered his semiautomatic weapon, hurriedly yanking the slide back. A round slammed into the chamber with a loud snap. "With this if we have to."

"Fight against thirty of *them?*"

Warren waved the muzzle of the weapon toward Benjamin. "What do you suggest?" He crouched beside the wind-vent, studying the line of riders. "They'd kill us in a minute, we found their hideout." He stood up. "We'll load up with whatever we can carry. We've got the high ground, the firepower. Maybe they'll think we're the Chinese army come to collect what they stole. We can drive them off."

Diana looked pleadingly at Benjamin. "Lo Dzong is a big place. If we work our way back we could climb down and hide in the gorge."

"Not without some insurance," Warren said, and prodded Benjamin with the light. "You lead. I know where the grenades are."

They hurried along the walkway to the rampart, then down winding narrow alleys to the main avenue and the palace. Benjamin's light flashed over yawning, empty doorways and windows, seeming to give eerie form to the chorus of winds. In the courtyard of dead dogs Warren directed them to one of the large rooms and they stumbled inside, gasping for air.

Weapons and ammunition were stacked along the walls. Piles of clothing and boots, some bloodstained, lay in a corner; in another were blankets and food parcels. None of it had been sorted, just left. In the center of the floor a pile of juniper wood branches reached halfway to the ceiling. The room was more than a munitions warehouse. It was also dry storage for firewood, the precious commodity in this land of rocks.

"Diversion . . ." Benjamin managed to get out.

Warren found another light. "What?" His face glistened with sweat despite the cold.

"We can't fight them." Benjamin gulped air. "We're not soldiers, outnumbered anyway." He pointed at the wood pile. "Burn the wood. They'll come running to save their stuff. Look at this place, this is their treasure. What's more important to them . . . guns and ammunition or us? It should give us a chance to get out, maybe find some horses before they get around to us."

"All right, all right." Warren fumbled in his pocket for his lighter. "Here."

Benjamin sent Diana to watch for the *khampas* while he made a torch from a quilted Chinese army jersey wrapped around a detachable rifle stock. The bottom of the pile caught fire easily, the flames spreading rapidly through the twisted juniper wood, licking toward the ceiling.

"Where are the other stores?"

Warren was busy loading himself with clips of ammunition, stuffing them into the folds of his *chuba*. He pointed toward the courtyard. "Out there. The rooms around the courtyard."

"You can't carry all that."

Warren glanced up. "I'm going to try."

Benjamin left him, ran from one storeroom to the next, lighting fires, avoiding the stiff carcasses that littered the courtyard. He was lighting the last fire when Diana rushed in.

"They're at the gate—"

Benjamin jammed the torch into the woodpile. "Let's go!"

They met Warren at the colonnaded hall of the palace, the walls behind them now glowing orange from the fires.

Warren had two weapons. "AK-47s," he said, and offered one to Benjamin.

"The idea is, Warren, to escape—not start a war."

"Insurance—"

The sound of stomping horses and shouting men cut him off. The *khampas* were in the city. Benjamin grabbed Diana's hand, pulling her after him. "This way . . ."

He headed south, moving through alleys, keeping off the main avenues. The smell of smoke was heavy in the wind now, and angry voices echoed through the vacant streets. Benjamin moved at a jog, holding Diana, stopping only at corners to check intersections.

"Where are you going?" Warren pointed with his elbow. "The gate's *that* way."

Benjamin nodded at the massive south wall. "Up there. The rampart has a walkway protected by a parapet. They won't see us, we can get off the streets and follow the wall to the gate. And get rid of that stuff. You make more noise than they do."

Warren shook his head. "Not yet."

Benjamin found steps beside an abutment tower. The thick fortress walls slanted like the sides of a pyramid, causing the stairs leading to the rampart at the top of the abutment to narrow sharply.

Benjamin hadn't expected it to be a problem until they'd climbed halfway up the thirty-foot stairway. Above the level of buildings they were exposed directly to the wind. Treacherous, swirling gusts attacked their *chubas* as they inched up the smooth, wind-eroded stone stairway. Diana's hair flailed her as they gripped each other's hands, moving sideways with their backs against the cold wall. Loaded down with a score of ammunition clips and weapons in both hands, Warren's first misstep would be his last.

Benjamin crouched behind the parapet, pulled Diana up the last step, then reached down and grabbed a handful of Warren's *chuba*, yanking him forward, flopping him flat on his belly in a clatter of metal.

The south wall was the tallest around Lo Dzong. From this vantage point, Benjamin could see the whole city like a map, a ghost town of unmarked streets. The palace was ablaze. The individual fires had already consimed their origins and burned through the timbered roofs. Whipped by the wind, the fire was spreading, *khampas* were running, pulling, shoving what they'd managed to save into a central pile. Ammunition was exploding, faint bursts in the wind.

"Burn, damn you." Warren knelt beside Diana, peering over the parapet, then glanced at Benjamin.

"You go first, Warren." Benjamin nodded down the parapet toward the gate. "Stay low."

"Right," Warren said eagerly. He set himself in a duck crouch, Chinese weapons in both hands. "See you at the gate."

Benjamin turned back to Diana. "Let him get about fifteen, twenty feet ahead, then you go. I'll be right behind."

Benjamin poked his head above the parapet for a last look. Heavy smoke cast a haze over parts of the city. More buildings were burning, flames leaping from one structure to the next, pushed by the wind. The courtyard was the center of a burning ring. He could see it clearly. The bodies of the slain dogs were like dark hour-markings on a clock without hands. In the fiery light, their black coats shone blue.

Blue dogs. On a round, faceless clock.

"*Hounds of azure . . .*," Benjamin said to no one as he slid away from the parapet.

Diana tugged at his sleeve. "We'd better go."

Benjamin's mouth was dry. " '*Until the heir of the third princely son*' " —he looked at Diana—" '*loosens the hounds of azure.*' "

"Benjamin, what—"

"The blue dogs." Benjamin leaned back against the wall. "Ravi was from India. Tibet was a foreign land to him."

"Benjamin, we have to go."

"Just any dog wasn't good enough." Benjamin licked his lips, feeling his heart run. "It had to be a *Tibetan* dog. He had to get it right. *That's* why he hung the charm on the Pearls of Light. The clue was the dog . . ."

"For godsakes, Ben, what are you raving about?"

Benjamin looked back across the city, at the God House. "I know where it is." He looked at Diana. "Shelkagari. God help me, I know where Ravi hid it."

"No." Diana pushed away from him. "*No.* We're leaving—"

"Diana, I can't, not now. I know where Shelkagari is—"

"You *can't* go back, we're almost out—"

Benjamin looked up at the God House, safe above the smoke. Silent and dark against the stars beyond, it seemed to waver slightly, as though beckoning to him.

"Benjamin."

He turned back to her. "Follow Warren—"

"Please, don't . . ." Her face was now streaked with tears. "Please . . ."

"I have to," he said. "I just have to."

The rampart was narrow and uneven, causing Benjamin to bump into the sides of the parapet as he ran low to avoid being seen by *khampas.* From the abutment to the west wall the rampart's walkway was uphill for one hundred and fifty yards. He stopped once to get his breath and rub his bruised knees.

At the entrance to the causeway leading to the God House he looked back. He could not see Warren or Diana, but he could see the *khampas* fighting fires and chasing down frightened ponies. It was confusion everywhere as they tried to save their cache, and Warren and Diana, he felt, could get out. Until he spotted a single *khampa,* still mounted on his black pony, directing men with his *khukuri* knife. He was obviously the leader of this band, and on his head was a red Australian bush hat.

Angdu Pal, the *khampa* from Torjok. Serchen's killer.

Benjamin ducked below the parapet. Had he followed them across the Valley of Winds? Was Lo Dzong his territory?

Benjamin bolted across the causeway, not willing to know the answer. Shelkagari was almost his . . . as surrogate for those who had come before . . . Miller, Abby, Yurev . . .

A mournful wind surged through the vents as Benjamin entered the darkened God House. The giant Buddha's gaze was serene in the shadows of the moon, mute to its treasured secret of a millennium.

Benjamin hoisted himself onto the lotus-blossom base. Balancing against the figure's belly, he pulled himself onto the left forearm and climbed up the wrist. Then, holding the delicately carved thumb for support, he sat in Buddha's hand, thirty feet above the stone floor. The Wheel of Life hung from the wooden fingertips.

Benjamin reached out to it. The protruding spokes were large rounded cylinders of solid wood, a foot and a half long and over twelve inches in diameter. Buddha held the Year of the Ox in his left hand. Benjamin wasn't sure of the order. The last year in the cycle was the Rat, preceded by the Pig. A bar of moonlight fell obliquely across the wheel. He could see the carved symbols of the rats and pigs—each figure carved on four sides—but the next spoke was obscured by shadow. Holding Buddha's giant finger, he leaned out from the enormous hand and touched the third spoke, its smooth surface cold to his clammy palms. Working slowly down, his fingers found the carved animals. Year of the Dog.

Loosens the hounds of azure. The blue dogs of Tibet.

With a quick jolt Benjamin butted the heel of his palm against the spoke, moving it sideways in its mounting hole. The sudden movement caused him to lose his balance and his grip on the statue. He was falling, grabbed frantically for the wheel, caught it with both hands, his momentum swinging him into the partially detached spoke and knocking it free.

The Year of the Dog dropped out of its peg hole, and behind it, slipping out of its secret hollow, sliding silently past Benjamin's startled eyes, was a leather goat bag.

"No." Benjamin grabbed for it with his right hand, and the trailing leather thong caught in two of his fingers. A moment later the wooden peg hit the stone floor with a thud, bouncing and spinning against the statue base.

Benjamin swung in Buddha's shadow, hanging to the Wheel of Life with his left hand. From his right dangled the Stone of Light, banging softly against his foot. He tried to kick his legs up to catch hold of a wooden finger but his *chuba* was too bulky. The muscles in his arms ached. The goat bag was enormously heavy. Above, the massive Buddha face shone coolly in a shaft of moonlight, peacefully indifferent to pain or pleasure. There was no sound except the creaking of the wheel, strained by Benjamin's weight, and the moaning wind, teasing him in the cold air, lazily flapping his *chuba* as he dangled like an earring.

Exhausted, Benjamin let go.

The goat bag banged against his chest as he fell. Benjamin grabbed it with both hands. He struck a lotus petal in the base, snapping it off cleanly and only slightly breaking his fall. He hit the stone floor on the rebound, coming to rest on his side, his body protecting the leather pouch. For a few moments he simply lay there, numb and cold, unaware if he had broken anything, clutching the bag.

He dragged himself to a wooden support beam and sat against it with his legs splayed out. His right ankle hurt terribly. He'd slammed it against the base in the fall. He yanked at the drawstrings of the ancient pouch to see his prize. The brittle leather bag, hard and cracked with age, opened grudgingly. Inside, the stone was intact. It looked like an enormous chunk of ice, an odd, oblong shape, thick at one end and tapering away like a glass snout. Like a calf's head.

Benjamin touched the stone, the first man to see it in over a thousand years. Holding it between his legs, he slid the Stone of Miracles out of the bag. Cool to his touch, the diamond gleamed in a shaft of moonlight from a wind vent. Shelkagari's surfaces were incredibly smooth with defined edges, still sharp. He held it up, rotating it between his hands. Planes of the stone shone like mirrors then turned transparent as he changed the angle of the light. He tried to imagine how Alexander the Great, fresh from the battlefield, had received the stone. Had he marveled at its brilliance? Had he held it like this in his own hands? Benjamin set the heavy diamond aside. Exhilaration fought the pain in his leg. He had found the greatest gem in history, and crippled himself in the process. He thought of Arub Ravi, the all-suffering monk who had brought the stone to this place, and then those who had come after him—Tavernier, Yurev, Abby, Miller . . . Barbaree had come the closest, and lost the most, sitting for all time in a forgotten monastery, frozen like a slab of beef. Benjamin closed his eyes. What was next for him? He didn't know, and at this moment, he didn't care. He had found the stone that couldn't be found. He'd *done* it. The rest was not up to him—

Footsteps. Someone coming across the causeway. Running. Benjamin shoved the diamond back into the pouch, pulled himself back into the shadows.

"Benjamin—"

Diana had come through the door, searching the darkness.

"Here . . ." He propped himself on an elbow in an effort to rise, but his right leg told him no.

She rushed over to him, helping him sit up. "The *khampas* from Torjok"—she pointed back toward the walled city—"they're *here*. The one who took—"

"I know—ahh!"

"What is it?"

He nodded at the statue. "I fell." He pointed at his ankle. "I don't think it's broken but it hurts like—"

"Fell?" Diana saw the broken lotus petal. "Did you find it?"

Benjamin nodded. The goat bag was beside him. He dragged it over and pulled open the ancient leather. "Here it is . . ."

"My God . . . it's so huge . . ." Diana reached out to it, felt its smooth surface with the tips of her fingers.

Benjamin glanced up at her, suddenly angry. "What are you doing here? I told you to go."

"There were *khampas* at the gate—"

"Where's Warren?"

Footsteps on the narrow causeway answered him, followed by Warren ducking inside the door, still with his weapons. He glared at Benjamin. "You know who's out there?" He turned to point. "That murdering guy who took my hat . . ."

Benjamin didn't respond, seemed to be looking through him.

Warren frowned at Diana. "What's the matter with him?"

"He fell"—she nodded toward the statue—"from that."

"We got to the gate," Warren said, "they left sentries—what's that?" He was staring at the leather bag. Then, slowly, he sank to his knees. He opened the pouch, began running his hands over the ancient stone. "My God, it's real, it's . . ."

Benjamin reached for Diana. "Help me up." He leaned against her for support. "It's the ankle, broken maybe, or sprained."

"They're coming this way," Warren said, still caressing the stone. "They didn't see me but they're coming to check out this light house." He looked up into the domed ceiling. "There's a parapet up there. I saw it from the wall. I could shoot from up there." He got to his feet. "I've at least got enough firepower here to make them think twice about coming across that causeway. If they come they're going to pay for it." He looked at Benjamin, waiting for an argument.

There was none. He waved Warren on and nodded to Diana. "You too, Diana. Give her a weapon."

"What are *you* going to do?"

Benjamin hobbled to the lotus blossom base and sat on a petal. "I'll wait here."

"You can't stay down here."

"I sure can't climb stairs. Go on."

Warren collected his gear, paused at the stairs. The goat bag hung from his shoulder. He stared hard at Benjamin. "Any objection?"

Benjamin didn't answer.

To Diana, Warren said, "Coming?"

She kept her eyes on Benjamin. "No."

Warren shrugged, started up with his arsenal.

Benjamin watched Diana as the sounds of Warren's heavy footsteps receded. "You're being ridiculous," he said. "There's no future down here—"

"I'm a lousy shot."

Benjamin looked at her. "An Australian?"

"I won't go, Ben. And you're in no position to make me."

Warren had made it up to the third gallery by now . . . "I can see them." There was a slight echo to his voice. "They're fanned out in the street, checking houses as they come." His footsteps became quicker.

At the fourth gallery he stopped again, checking through the wind vent. "It's windy as hell . . ." His voice sounded distant.

Looking up, Benjamin and Diana could just see Warren in a patch of moonlight.

"I'm on top of the world here, Ben. I can see half of China." He started up the last set of stairs, the echoing footsteps moving faster.

"Warren"—Benjamin caught a glimpse of him as he moved into another bar of light, weapons in both hands, the goat bag swinging from under his arm.

"I can see—"

A gust of wind caught him sideways, forcing him back a step, snagging the leather bag on the gnarl of a wooden beam. He turned, pulling on the thong, then gave it a yank. The strip of leather snapped, momentarily rocking him off balance. Then, with the embarrassed smile of an athlete caught in an awkward moment, Warren reached out to support himself, and stepped into space.

Diana screamed as Warren plunged fifty feet headfirst, eyes and mouth wide. Shelkagari struck the stone floor an instant ahead of his body, a muffled crack followed by a rebounding thud and the clatter of skittering weapons.

Benjamin hobbled to the broken body and knelt beside it. Warren hadn't screamed when he fell, too surprised to call out. His head lolled to one side, a drop of blood at his ear. Within grasp of his outstretched arm lay the Stone of Miracles, shattered inside the skin of a goat.

Behind Benjamin, Diana suddenly could not make a sound. She thought she was choking. Forcing back what she had seen. Benjamin looked up through a wind-vent and saw the silhouettes of figures along the wall above the causeway, standing against the glow of fire. He saw Angdu Pal, still wearing Warren's hat. The *khampa* leader just stood there, staring across space, surrounded by his men.

"Why don't they just come and finish it?" Benjamin got to his feet, wincing against the pain in his ankle. "Why don't they just come?"

"I think I confused them," Diana said, finally able to talk. She went to Benjamin, supporting him, looking away from Warren's body. She helped him to the steps. "Maybe I startled them when I screamed. I don't think they can see into the darkness." She wiped his face with the hem of her *chuba.*

"Confused?" Benjamin looked up at her. "You screamed and . . . you screamed . . ." He stood up, ignoring the pain, looking out at the *khampas* trying to look in. He took the lighter from his pocket. "God, please make this thing work."

Diana looked at him. "What good will that do?"

"Diana . . . can you climb up there? To the top?" He pointed to the highest gallery.

"What's the point?"

Benjamin took hold of her arms, turned her to face him. "Diana, listen to me. You have to climb up to the top gallery, to the highest wind-vent. When you get there I want you to take off your clothes—"

"Have you gone crazy?"

"Listen to me. *All* of your clothes, do you understand?"

"Benjamin, what—"

"This will be the greatest acting job you've ever had." He held up the lighter. "I'm going to light this place up until it glows. When I tell you, step into the wind vent."

"*Why?*"

He nodded toward the *khampas.* "Let them see you. All of you. Your white skin, your red hair . . ."

Her eyes widened. "Oh, God. A Churel. You want me to be a Churel."

"They heard you scream and it stopped them, for a while. They haven't seen us. They don't know who—or what—is in here."

Diana looked up. Benjamin saw her eyes find the spot Warren had fallen from.

"Don't think about it, just do it. And scream, Diana. Scream like you never did before."

He watched her go, watched as she climbed every step as if it were the way to the block. When she reached the fifth gallery, he snapped open the lighter, closed his eyes. Please make this work. Please. When he opened them again he was looking at the Buddha. He started lighting the butter lamps.

*   *   *

The God House came slowly to life now with a glow that built to a brightness Angdu Pal had never seen there before. The Most Revered One turned from shadowy outline to golden brown through the long windows. Pulling his hat tight against his head, he started across the causeway, one hand holding his *chuba* high so as not to trip, the other with his *khukuri* knife raised.

He heard the scream as he was halfway across, a sound like the one before, but stronger, nearer. He held his knife up against the light from inside, searching the lowest gallery for the source of the cry.

From the wall his men cried out, pointing in terror at the top of the God House. One by one, they turned and ran.

Angdu Pal looked up.

Her skin was the whitest of white, her red hair streaming back like flames from her head as in the most terrible of his dreams. She stood without clothes, chilled by winds of a thousand demons, and from her mouth came the songs of death.

Angdu Pal stepped on his *chuba* but his eyes remained fixed on the fading white vision, even as his new red hat drifted above him in the netherworld of stars, even as he hit the bottom of the Kali Gandaki gorge.

Benjamin held her tight, bundled and shivering inside the *chuba*. She had cried and stopped and cried again. But it was over. They were alive, safe in God's House, surrounded by bodies.

"What do we do now?" Her voice was calm. She held Benjamin's hand in both of hers. The cold from the wind on her bare skin was still in her bones.

"We wait."

"Wait?"

"For daylight," Benjamin said. He caressed her hair. "To finish it."

◆ SEVENTY-ONE

DIANA TOUCHED HIM, AND Benjamin came quickly awake. "It's time," she said.

Benjamin massaged his eyes. The air was still strong with the smell of smoke. His leg was stiff and numb.

"Help me up."

She got her shoulder under his arm, raising him to his feet, and helped him up the stairs. Hobbling along the railing at the top of the God House, he could see the top of the great, smooth Buddha head and, below, Warren's body, his broken, unfired weapons near him. Benjamin looked away, pushing himself out onto the parapet that encircled the crown of the God House. He held himself steady with an arm around a thick prayer-flag stanchion and motioned for Diana to move away.

"I'm okay."

Sunlight touched the uppermost crown of the God House. Benjamin waited, holding the goat bag pouch by its leather drawstrings. When it was time, he began swinging it round and round his head.

"For all the pain . . . for all the suffering . . ." His eyes stung, recalling three lifetimes of misery. He kept the momentum of his swing high and smooth. "Take it back, damn you. *Enough* . . ." And he let loose the leather bag.

The pouch sailed straight into sunlight, above the gorge, source of the Kali Gandaki River. Diamonds spewed out of the spinning bag as it rose toward the dawn. Exposed to light that had not touched them in a thousand years, the stones gleamed brilliant in the morning sun. Too many had searched, and died, to own these stones that for fifty generations had remained hidden in darkness. Now, for a frozen moment, at the apex of their trajectories, they were free. In that instant of time they hung in the clear, frigid sky as if Ushas herself held them there to admire, recalling a boy prince and his music beside a glimmering pool. And then they fell, the pouch drifting after them, and silently disappeared into the vast gorge below.

"Done." Benjamin turned to Diana. "It's done."

Her dirty face was streaked with tears. She took his arm, supporting his weight, and they began the long walk home.

◆ EPILOGUE

HOME

IT HAD RAINED IN Chicago until noon, but by two the sky had opened and let in the sun.

Laura met Benjamin at the airport. She wore a red suit, a bit out of fashion, and carried an umbrella just in case. She had known he was bringing a girl with him, but seemed pleasantly surprised, even relieved, when he introduced her to Diana.

Laura drove, talking like someone who had saved a thousand things to say, but none of it about diamonds or foreign places or former presidents. At the house Benjamin left the bags in the foyer and kissed Abby on the cheek.

"Where is he?"

Abby's glance touched Diana, then returned to Benjamin's blue eyes. "With your father."

Laura led Diana upstairs to the guest room. Abby pulled back the curtains from the French doors. Afternoon light glistened on the wet panes. Outside, two men strolled side by side in the rain-softened earth, fifty yards from the house.

Diana watched them, unable at this distance to distinguish which was Yurev, the one who had started it all. Then Benjamin appeared below her, walking out toward them, favoring his leg.

"Did Benjamin tell you about his father?" Laura was standing at the window. She spoke without averting her eyes from the figures outside.

"Yes . . . some. He told me about China . . . what it meant."

477

Laura nodded. Tears had come in her eyes.

"Mrs. Kane—"

"It's all right, my dear," Abby said from behind. She touched Diana's arm. "It's all right."

They watched as Benjamin caught up with the two men in the shadows of a stand of large elm trees. One of the men spoke to him, set his hand on his shoulder.

"I don't understand what's happening," Diana said. Benjamin was speaking to the man whose arms hung at his sides. She turned to Abby. "What's—"

"A reunion," Abby said with a quiet smile. "A reunion of sons."

After a moment, she saw Miller raise his hand too and place it on Benjamin's shoulder. He spoke to his son, a brief word and a nod. Then they walked together, the three of them, out of the shadows, back toward the house.